# DEADLY SWEET

## In Ann Arbor

**Jerry Prescott**

**Proctor Publications of Ann Arbor • Michigan • USA**

Library of Congress Catalog Number: 96-70303

**Cataloging In Publication Data**
*(Prepared by Quality Books, Inc.)*

**Prescott, Jerry J.**
**Deadly sweet in Ann Arbor / Jerry J. Prescott.**
**p. cm.**
**ISBN: 1-882792-33-5**

**1. Ann Arbor (Mich.)--Fiction. 2. Detective and mystery stories. I. Title**

**PS3566.R56D43 1996        813'.54**

This novel is a product of the imagination of the author. All the characters portrayed are fictitious. None of the events described occurred. Though many of the settings, buildings and businesses exist, liberties have been taken in several instances as to their actual locations and descriptions. The story has no purpose other than to entertain the reader.

**Printed in the United States of America**

This book is dedicated to the vast number of friends and family members who provided me with support and advice and encouraged me to publish *Deadly Sweet In Ann Arbor.* Special thanks and appreciation goes to Linda Flanery, who proofed and typed several drafts of the manuscript and offered sage counseling. Thanks also to Hazel Proctor, my publisher, for her kind and gracious guidance, suggestions and enthusiasm. And thanks to my wife, Lorna, for her patience, understanding and love and the enthusiasm and support of Sydney, Tom, Kristi, and Dorie, our four children; Joan and Kit, my sister and brother-in-law; and Leslie and my other business associates. They and others made this book possible and I truly hope you'll find it a pleasurable read.

Looking West along North University from Hill Auditorium

Drawings of Ann Arbor by Milt Kemnitz

# DEADLY SWEET

## In Ann Arbor

## Chapter 1

There was a slight mist with the first signs of daybreak as Mark Turner and Rob Sebastian jogged toward the entrance to the University's Arboretum. Third-year medical students and roommates, the times their schedules coincided to allow them to indulge in this pleasure together were not too frequent.

Passing the Ronald MacDonald House on their right, the two observed leftover signs of the previous day's Halloween activities. Jack 'O Lanterns, ghosts, cobwebs and witches could be seen in the windows with a cluster of pumpkins and haystacks at the front entrance. Mark side-stepped the remains of a smashed pumpkin on the pavement in front of him as they neared the pillars marking the entrance to the Arb.

The two men navigated through the turnstile which served to keep motor vehicles out and then picked up their pace, jogging along the wood chip-lined path through the Arb's famous peony gardens. A glorious sight each spring, it was a drab area now. The sky was growing a little brighter as Rob glanced to his right toward the hillside bordering the gardens.

"Take a look over there," Rob said, pointing up the hill to their right. "Looks as if someone was trying to turn the Arb into a spook house. It's a Halloween costume or scarecrow of some sort."

Mark squinted, staring in the direction Rob had pointed. "You're right, let's go over and take a closer look."

1

They veered off the path and headed up the hill. As they drew closer, the details of the object became clearer.

"Looks like a character out of Alice in Wonderland," Mark said with a grin.

Beneath a large, black top hat was a huge, colorfully made-up clown face with a relatively tiny body below in baggy pants. As they approached nearer they exchanged looks of concern as they saw the huge face was the torso of a woman. Her head and raised arms were concealed under the hat. Her breasts had been colorfully decorated to give the appearance of bulbous eyes. Lipstick had been applied to her navel, forming a mouth with nostril dots above the lips. From the hips down she was dressed in a tiny jacket, shirt and tie. Little arms hung from the protruding shoulder pads. Bright colored green pants covered her legs from the knees down. The illusion was a dwarf with a huge head. The memory of some of his fraternity brothers donning similar outfits a couple years ago in a campus variety show flashed through Mark's mind.

"Let's hope she's only sleeping off a hangover," Rob said, kneeling down and attempting to lift back the hat covering her face. Mark leaned down on the opposite side of the woman, assisting Rob. As her face became visible, the two realized she was dead. Her eyes and mouth were open with her head tilted to the side. As Rob placed his hand on her neck, feeling for a pulse, he nodded to Mark, indicating the abrasions there.

"One of us should call the police," Mark said. "Why don't you stay here while I find a phone."

Mark quickly rose to his feet and dashed down the hill. Reaching flat ground, he ran through the peony garden, towards the entrance Rob and he had come through only moments before. Two coeds in warm-ups were just approaching. Mark realized he should say something to them. Whoever strangled the girl might still be in the Arb. Holding up a hand to flag the girls down, Mark quickly explained how he and his roommate had just discovered a young woman's body. They listened wide-eyed as Mark explained he was on his way to call the police. They nodded in agreement at his suggestion they stay out of the Arb until after the police arrived, staring at Mark as he ran off, heading toward the Ronald MacDonald House.

Rob was continuing to kneel next to the body of the young woman. He thought about closing her eyes, but decided against it – remembering the admonition, "Don't touch anything at a crime scene."

The light mist had caused the make-up to run on the young woman's

2

torso. The eyes (her breasts) now gave the appearance of a sad clown's face with multi-colored tears dripping down over her stomach. Rob was reminded of the roars of laughter Mark's fraternity brothers had provoked with their similar costumes. Inhaling and exhaling while twisting their stomachs had given the impression their belly buttons were the mouths from which songs were flowing, as their heads were hidden under the top hats. What a hilarious, happy time compared to the sadness he now felt looking down at this young woman's body, shaking his head. Extremely attractive. Tall, maybe five-eight or five-nine. A slender body with an athletic look. Light brown hair, drawn back in a ponytail of sorts. Blue eyes. Delicate facial features.

Rob glanced down below her waist where the starched collar, polka dot tie and coat of the costume covered her, noticing something protruding from the pocket of the tiny jacket. He bent down for a closer look. It was a PayDay⁽ᵗᵐ⁾ candy bar.

Rob heard a sound and sensed someone was watching him. Glancing up, he thought he saw a movement in the shrubbery and trees off to his right and higher up the hill. Possibly a bird or a squirrel. He stood up, squinted his eyes, staring at the spot. The eerie thought that it might be the person or persons responsible for the girl's death momentarily crossed his mind. He strained to listen as he viewed the area. While contemplating over whether he should walk up for a closer look, he heard car doors slamming and voices in the direction of the Arb entrance.


## Chapter 2

Kelly Travis turned in bed and looked at the clock radio. Nearly seven-fifteen a.m. She stretched, yawned and shrugged her shoulders a couple times going through her wake-up process. Her thoughts turned to last night and a smile surfaced.

Kelly had been an employee of the Ann Arbor Police Department for nearly two years. Born and raised in Ann Arbor, she'd begun her college career at Miami of Ohio. As a youngster, she'd been enthralled with Nancy Drew and other childhood detective books. Her father introduced her to Sherlock Holmes, and some of her favorite memories were times spent with him discussing Holmes' thought process. At one time she thought she'd like to be a lawyer. In her junior year she decided to transfer to

3

Michigan State University to pursue a degree in its Law Enforcement Program. After obtaining her Masters, she'd spent nearly three years with the FBI in the Washington, DC area. When her mother became ill, she'd felt it necessary to return to the Ann Arbor area to be close by to assist her father in her mother's time-consuming care. She'd been fortunate to obtain a position with the Ann Arbor Police Department. Though her father may have pulled some strings, she knew her test scores, education and work experience ranked high above the other applicants. For the past ten months she'd held the title of Detective rather than Investigative Officer. She lived alone in a condominium a couple miles from the home she grew up in, and where her parents still lived.

The smile on her face was prompted by her recall of the two episodes last night she'd been involved in. While Devils' Night had been an unusually quiet one for Ann Arbor, Halloween night activities had resulted in a slew of 911 calls. One had been from a man who was livid, having fallen for one of the oldest tricks on record. His doorbell had rung and on opening the door, he discovered a brown paper bag engulfed in flames on his porch. As the initial flames began to subside, he raised his foot and began stomping out the fire. To his chagrin he discovered the glowing embers had masked the contents of the bag – a collection of dog droppings. When two officers arrived a short time after his call to console and appease him, he continued to cuss out those damn kids. He wanted to offer a $1,000 reward for information leading to the arrest of the culprits. The officers attempted to soothe him as he ranted on about the kids he'd heard laughing in a clump of bushes across the street from his house as he stamped out the fire. He wanted an all-points bulletin issued, programming interrupted on Cable TV and local radio stations to announce his reward offer. At the very least, a major story in Saturday morning's paper. When one officer suggested that all this publicity could backfire, just be a public recognition of the prank and result in the stunt being duplicated tenfold next Halloween in Ann Arbor and other areas, the man became even more belligerent. The officers had Kelly doubled over in laughter as they described the incident.

In a bit of an irony, a short time later that night Kelly found herself in the position of pleading with the *Ann Arbor News* to highlight a story in this morning's edition in regard to another prank. At approximately the same time the man called in about the dog doo trick, there were several calls from people attempting to verify a letter they'd found in their mail boxes concerning the city's action to temporarily suspend its ordinance prohibiting the burning of leaves. One caller had faxed a copy of the very official-looking letter, which carried the mayor's signature. The letter gave residents permission to burn their leaves between the hours of nine a.m. and three p.m. today and explained the reasoning behind this decision. City council members ranked among their favorite memories of childhood, the smell of smoke from bonfires on a fall weekend and the joys shared roasting marshmallows over the glowing ashes, and they wanted to give Ann Arbor's parents an opportunity to allow their children to experience these same nostalgic memories.

The initial calls were from individuals seeking to verify the accuracy of the letter. Most indicated they believed it was a prank and were simply calling to confirm that belief and to advise the police the forged letter was being circulated. Two irate people were critical of the "bone-headed action" council had taken. Although the mayor couldn't be reached, two city council members had assured the department that no action of this nature had been taken or even discussed. They both saw the humor in this prank letter and asked for copies. But as the calls continued to pour in, many failed to grasp the humor after being told the letter had no validity and wanted to know what the police were going to do about it.

One officer had mapped out the relatively small area east of Washtenaw from which the calls were originating. Two people had suggested that police circulate a letter explaining the other letter was a bogus one, warning the residents not to burn leaves. This possibility was ruled out as calls also came in from other sections of the city, miles from where the initial calls had originated. A decision was eventually made to contact the *Ann Arbor News* and the local radio stations to get the message out. Kelly recalled her conversation with the *Ann Arbor News*, whose Saturday morning edition had nearly been put to bed. Similar to the officers attempting to reason with the man who had stomped on the dog stools, the individual she'd reached at the *News* had suggested to Kelly that it would be a mistake to blow this story out of proportion. Rewarding the kids who had planned and executed the prank with front-page coverage of the stunt, he reasoned, would only serve to encourage them or others to pull a similar prank at some future date. Kelly explained the predicament the police found themselves in. Some very influential citizens were now demanding something be done to prevent the potential pollution which might occur. With a home football game on Saturday, the police were in no position to patrol even one neighborhood, let alone the city, advising residents seen raking their leaves of the situation and the fact that the prohibition against burning leaves hadn't been suspended. The conversation had its humorous side, and Kelly was eventually able to obtain an assurance the paper would highlight a brief article in this morning's edition.

She'd just started to open her door to get her paper to see how the paper had handled it when the phone rang. She glanced at the clock again – seven-thirty-five – wondering who was calling at such an early hour on a Saturday.

"Good morning," said Kelly cheerfully, after lifting the receiver to her ear.

"And top of the morning to you, too."

She immediately recognized the voice of her immediate supervisor, Mike Cummings.

"Hi, Mike. What's up?"

"It's not good. A young woman's body was discovered a few minutes ago in the Arb. I don't have any details except the fact she was dressed in some sort of costume. How about if I pick you up in ten minutes?"

"Fine. I'll be ready."

•

Four or five police cars and an ambulance were clustered on the street bordering the Arboretum's entrance as Kelly and Mike drove up. Quickly parking, they worked their way between the vehicles. There were thirty to forty people, most appearing to be students, gathered in small groups on the opposite side of the street. The officer stationed at the entrance recognized Kelly and Mike and pointed them to where the body had been found.

Larry Martino was the officer in charge and as they approached they spotted him among a group of officers standing on the hillside next to the body. The large top hat which Mike had described on the ride over now sat a few feet to the side of the body. The woman's arms were still extended over her head. Someone had closed her eyes.

Officer Martino gave them an opportunity for a closer look and then motioned them over to a spot a few yards away, where he quickly brought them up to date. Cause of death was still undetermined. What appeared to be rope burns were apparent on the woman's neck, wrists and ankles. The chief medical officer, Richard Newman, who was still in the process of examining the body, believed she'd been dead at least four hours, probably closer to eight. The neck abrasions in his opinion did not appear severe enough to indicate she'd been strangled.

"We're thinking a wound, bullet or knife, might show up hidden under the make-up," Martino continued. "Thus far, nothing of that nature has been discovered. He'll know more this evening after an autopsy."

One of the other officers approached and told them Dr. Newman had completed his preliminary examination and the body could be moved. Officer Martino exchanged looks with Kelly and Mike, checking to see if they wanted to take another look or have anything further done before the body was removed.

"I think we're set, thank you," Mike responded. Then addressing Officer Martino, he asked, "You've been able to get all your investigating done around the body?"

Martino nodded. "Nothing much there either. No signs the body had been dragged. As you can see, there was no attempt to hide the body. Whoever's responsible, wanted it to be spotted. One or more people must have carried her here. Nothing in the way of footprints. The leaves, of course, would mask those. We've checked a fifty foot radius around the body and come up with nothing. No litter, trash, objects of any kind. There's no identification on the body except for the name of that costume rental company down on Main Street on several pieces of the costume. We found a PayDay(tm) candy bar in the jacket pocket. We'll be checking it for prints as well as the hat and other pieces of the costume."

Kelly made notes as Martino continued. "I think you're aware that two medical students who were out jogging discovered the body. That's one of them over there," Martino said, pointing. "I asked them both to wait to talk with you – but one needed to be at work by eight-thirty and I told him he could go. I've got both their names, but neither has much to offer. The one over there stayed with the body while his friend went to notify us. He told us he thought or sensed someone was watching him from up there," continued Martino, nodding toward a location farther up the hill. "We checked out the area. There's an indentation in the ground behind a log where a person or animal could have been concealed. We did find what appeared to be cigarette ashes. No cigarette butts, just a couple tracings of ash. Frazier was the one who spotted them. They were nearly overlooked. Those tree limbs," Martino again pointed, "pretty much cover the area, but it's still surprising the ash droppings were fairly dry, appeared recent. With the light mist earlier this morning, the dryness could mean someone had been there smoking in the past hour or so. Maybe the motion," Martino checked his pad, "this boy, Rob Sebastian, noticed. Could have a bearing on this," he said, indicating the body, "or nothing to do with it. Could have been a street person who woke up to find he was in the midst of a potential problem and got the hell out of here in a hurry. You'd think we'd find some cigarette butts or litter if that were the case though, and we haven't." Martino paused, welcoming questions.

"Good work, Larry. How about introducing Kelly to the young man who found the body while I ask Dr. Newman a couple questions."

•

Kelly smiled and extended her hand to Rob Sebastian as Martino introduced them. She thanked him for waiting and assured him she'd only be taking a few added minutes of his time. She had Rob repeat his story. He explained once again having the feeling he was being watched as he studied the body and then believing he'd seen some movement in the woods. As he talked he began doubting himself more than ever over whether he'd actually seen anything, and he explained that to Kelly.

"Don't apologize. We want you to try and recall anything you or your friend saw or heard. Any people or vehicles you may have seen at the Arb gate when you entered, for example?"

Rob shook his head no.

"If anything comes up, please contact us. That goes for your friend as well," Kelly continued. She handed Rob two business cards, pointing out the fact she'd written her home phone on the reverse sides. "Anything. Don't hesitate. Please make that clear to Mr. Turner as well, and give him one of these cards.

"One note of caution, Mr. Sebastian. We'll only be releasing some of the overall details to the news media. We'd appreciate it if you and your friend kept quiet about specifics. You and he may have noticed some abrasions on the body – her neck, wrists and ankles. We won't be releasing those details just yet."

Rob nodded, remembering the marks he'd seen on her neck and wrists, they hadn't examined her ankles.

"We'd also like to keep the exact location of the body, how she was positioned, confidential for now."

Rob nodded again and assured Kelly he'd pass the word on to Mark, along with her card. He also promised they'd call if they remembered any other details they'd forgotten to mention, adding he didn't believe that would be the case.

"Going to the game today?" Kelly asked. Rob nodded yes. "I'd planned to also, but not now. Hope it's a good one. Thanks again and don't hesitate to call."

She saw Mike was still talking to Dr. Newman and headed toward them. Mike turned as she approached. "All set?" he asked. "Dick and I are just winding up. He hopes to have the autopsy completed later tonight. I think our first step should be a visit to the costume rental store," Mike suggested. "But first I need to speak with the news reporters I've been told are out by the entrance. It won't take long."

•

Mike was true to his word. Ten minutes later, Kelly and he were in his car on their way to the costume shop. He dropped her off in front of "Costumes Plus," saying he'd catch up after finding a place to park. The business was located on the second floor of a building on Main Street, housing one of Ann Arbor's more popular restaurants, The Big Apple, a New York-style, deli-type eating establishment. A line of mostly students stretched out onto the sidewalk from the stairwell leading up to the costume store. They'd speculated there would probably be a crowd at the store with people returning costumes. Kelly made her way up the downside of the stairwell, attracting several stern stares in the process from people wondering why she wasn't taking a spot at the end of the line.

There were three people working the main counter inside the store. Two, a girl and a boy, were fairly young. The third was a middle-aged woman who appeared to be keeping her eyes on the activities of the two younger workers in addition to handling customers herself. Kelly waited as the woman finished up with a boy returning a Dracula costume and then motioned to her, holding up her badge. The woman gave her a "what now?" look and glanced at the crowd of people waiting to be helped.

"You can see how busy we are. Will this take long?"

"Hopefully not," replied Kelly. "Is there a spot we could talk?" The woman ushered her into a small office a few feet behind the counter and while still looking over her shoulder, asked "So what's the problem?"

Kelly introduced herself and learned the lady's name was Patty

9

Sheehan. She quickly briefed her on the purpose of the visit, the discovery of the body in the Arb earlier that morning, and the fact the young woman had been dressed in a costume from the store. Kelly briefly described it.

Ms. Sheehan nodded. "I know exactly who you're talking about. A slender, attractive brunette, fairly tall? We always rent those particular costumes to men and I was surprised when she said she planned to wear it herself. She tried on the smallest size we had. I didn't actually see her in it, but she came out of the dressing room smiling, saying it would be perfect."

"Do you have her name and address?"

"Yes. I remember she paid cash. The deposit alone is a hundred dollars on that particular costume. She was hesitant about giving me her name and address and I told her unless she wanted to purchase the costume outright, she'd have to. Just a minute, I'll get it for you."

She went back to the counter and moved a file in front of her. Kelly noticed Mike making his way through the entrance door as the woman flipped through the file, and motioned to him to come back to the office. He was about to enter the office as Ms. Sheehan returned from the counter holding a billing copy. A hundred dollar bill was attached with a paper clip.

"Ms. Sheehan, this is Detective Michael Cummings. He's in charge of this case."

The two shook hands as the woman passed the billing copy to Kelly. Sure enough, at the bottom of the page was a signature. Katherine Edwards. Above the signature was the printed name Katherine Edwards, with an address and apartment number on Packard.

Kelly glanced at Mike with a smile. "We're all set. Name and address." Turning to Ms. Sheehan she continued, "We'll keep this and be back in touch with you."

"What about the hundred dollar bill?" she replied, starting to reach out for the paperwork Kelly was holding. "I'm sorry. That was uncalled for. I'm sorry she's dead. You still don't know how she died?"

As Kelly and Mike shook their heads, Mike answered. "Not yet. We'll know more soon."

Kelly continued the conversation, saying "We'll probably have a few more questions for you, too. Thanks for your help. I know it's one of your busiest days of the year, we'll get out of your way."

The woman nodded, still somewhat embarrassed at having raised a question about the deposit and costume in light of the young lady's death.

The address on Packard, a few blocks east of the State Street intersection, was only a five minute drive from where Mike had parked. Though still early, a quarter to ten, both car and pedestrian traffic was building with less than three hours to kick-off. Today's Michigan game was being televised in the early, twelve-thirty, time slot.

The address was easy to find, large numbers on one of the front porch pillars of a three-story, rambling, freshly painted older home. Mike turned into the driveway and drove to the rear of the house. There was outdoor parking for six or seven cars. All but one of the spots was occupied. After parking, Kelly and Mike walked back down the driveway to the front of the house. There were six mail boxes inside the front door. The name K. Edwards appeared under the one marked number six. Under the name card was a note reading "Rear Entrance." Two young men were coming up the steps as Kelly and Mike turned to leave.

"Excuse me," said Mike. "Do you live here?"

They nodded in unison as they sized Kelly and Mike up.

"We're looking for a Katherine Edwards. Do you know her?"

The two looked at one another before shaking their heads no.

"Is she supposed to live here?" the taller of the two asked.

Mike pointed down to the mail box with her name. "Yes, the name card shows she's in number six."

"We've just been here since August," said the other. "We still haven't met her. Her entrance is at the back. Do you think she's the one who drives the green Saab?" he said, turning to his friend.

As they were talking, a young lady came bouncing down the stairs. Mike addressed the same questions to her, with the same results. She and her roommate had never met Katherine Edwards. In fact, she'd thought K. Edwards was a man. After the three left, the young men heading up the stairs and the girl leaving down the front steps, Mike opened the mail box marked K. Edwards. There were several pieces of junk mail plus one letter addressed to Katherine Edwards. The return address was in New Jersey. Mike tucked the letter in his pocket as Kelly jotted down the name and phone number from a wall sign identifying the manager of the complex. Going around to the rear of the house, they found a flight of stairs leading up to apartment six. They rang the bell several times and could hear it ring.

There was no answer. The two went back to the car, where Mike called headquarters to start the process rolling to get a search warrant. On hanging up he explained to Kelly they were in luck. One of the judges was in and a patrol car would have a warrant out to them in less than an hour.

Mike next called the real estate management company. After talking to three people, he was told to call another number. This proved successful. The man he talked to, a Mr. Devlin, was very cooperative. He'd been the one who arranged Katherine Edwards' original lease. That had been over a year ago and he hadn't seen her since. She was never past due. He remembered her as a very vivacious, attractive girl. He thought she'd told him she was an English major, a transfer student from another Big Ten school. He couldn't remember which one. He assured Mike it would be no problem for him to bring a key over. He'd also check his records to see if he had any more information on the Edwards girl. "I can be there before eleven," he assured Mike.

The subpoena and the key arrived at the same time, with the police cruiser following Thomas Devlin into the drive at ten to eleven. Devlin introduced himself.

"Are you certain it's Katherine Edwards' body?" he asked.

"We're still investigating," Mike replied, "but yes, we're fairly certain it is. The descriptions we've been given by you and others supports that conclusion."

As Devlin gave them the key, he promised to help in any way he could. He'd brought a card with the home address Edwards had used when she filled out the rental contract. Kelly and Mike exchanged glances, both realizing the address matched the return address on the letter they'd found in Katherine Edwards' mail box.

"I just met her the one time," Devlin explained. "I sure wouldn't trust my memory to identify her body."

Kelly said they didn't think that would be necessary and thanked him for getting the key to them so soon. Devlin, somewhat sheepishly, told them he was headed for the game and asked them to be sure the door was locked after they'd finished up.

Mike unlocked the door to the apartment and stepped back to allow Kelly to enter first. Their initial reaction was how immaculate the apartment looked. The door to a bedroom was open at the end of the fairly small living room. Off to the left was a kitchenette and dining area. The living room walls were decorated with numerous frames of poster art for Museum Exhibitions, Art Fairs and Travel Destinations. A bookcase on one side of the living room was crammed with a combination of hard cover and pocket books. There were several text books. An avid reader herself, Kelly recognized at least a half-dozen titles published during the past few months. It was a colorful, light and airy room. Moving into the kitchen area, the two could smell the odor of Mr. Clean or some other type of disinfectant. The area was spotless. No dirty dishes. Nothing in the trash bag under the sink. Mike opened the door of the refrigerator. It contained only a handful of items. Everything neat. He checked the dates of the milk and a bottle of fresh orange juice. Still in date; recent purchases. The fruit and vegetables also appeared fresh.

"Doesn't it appear a little strange to you, Kelly, not to see at least one note or memo or photo on the refrigerator?"

She nodded her head in agreement, moving to the counter next to the sink where a phone sat. "No notes here, either."

She pulled open the drawer beneath the phone and found a phone book, scissors, scotch tape, a screwdriver and hammer. Paper clips and rubber bands were neatly organized. She flipped open the phone book and leafed to the back. The page for listing special numbers had been torn out. Remnants of the torn page were visible. Kelly held the book up closer to determine if by chance any imprints existed on the page that had backed it. There didn't appear to be. After checking the cupboards and a small closet, all of which were immaculate, Kelly and Mike walked back through the living room to the bedroom. Both the kitchen and living room had several plants, some hanging. Mike touched the dirt in several and found they'd been recently watered. Entering the bedroom, they saw a small dresser to their right which had not been visible through the open door. On top of the dresser was an eight-by-ten head and shoulders photograph of the young woman whose body they'd viewed in the Arb. Kelly and Mike experienced a similar reaction. The first sign of life, identification of the person who occupied the apartment, was a photo of someone now dead. Mike checked out the bed, which was covered by a white comforter with several colorful, decorative pillows. He pulled back a corner of the comforter and then the sheet underneath.

"The sheets are clean. Not a sign of a wrinkle, hair or stain. Strange."

Kelly had been checking out the closet and dresser drawers. Though not an abundance of clothes, everything was neatly organized. There was no sign of dirty laundry or clothing set aside for dry cleaning. Everything

13

appeared to be the type of clothes, shoes and undergarments you'd find in any college coed's room. The small bathroom off the bedroom also shone.

"No ring around the tub," joked Mike, picking up a comb and hairbrush. "Not even a hair."

A toilet article kit had been placed on the top of the toilet stool. Nothing out of the ordinary. Everything you'd expect. Kelly opened the medicine chest above the sink. Dental floss, toothpaste, Tylenol, Vaseline, lotion. Nothing unusual. In the lower right-hand corner there was a jewelry pouch. Kelly untied the draw-string and pulled the top apart. She walked back into the bedroom and dumped the contents onto the comforter. There were several bracelets, rings, a couple gold chains, a pearl necklace, a dress watch and numerous sets of earrings. She picked up a monogrammed pin with the initials KEM. The E was centered and in a larger size than the K and M.

Looking over her shoulder, Mike commented, "It's the same as the monogrammed needle-point pillow on the chair over there."

Kelly looked over at the pillow Mike referred to, having missed noticing it earlier. "Katherine M. Edwards," Kelly mouthed. Her eye was also drawn to a print on the wall behind the chair. She walked over for a closer look. The pastel drawing was of a young girl dancing through a field of flowers. Possibly a pre-teen. The print was signed, "To Kath with her dancing eyes. Love, Jeff."

Mike interrupted Kelly's train of thought, saying, "I think we're only seeing what someone has planned for us to see. It's too perfect, no one's this organized. There's nothing here that would tell us more about," he hesitated, "Katherine or Kath. A college coed's room with the only photo her own. Ridiculous! No party favors, souvenirs, group photos? Photos of her family? It doesn't make sense. This apartment's been sanitized. No names, phone numbers, notes, letters – impossible. And that clean smell. It wouldn't surprise me if the apartment was void of prints."

"I agree," said Kelly. "I've had an eerie sort of feeling ever since we arrived."

Mike went back into the kitchen and took a knife out of one of the drawers. Taking the letter they'd found in the mail box out of his sport coat pocket, he used the knife to carefully pry the envelope open. The enclosed one-page, two-sided letter was written on pink note paper. Mike unfolded it and after a glance, turned it over. "To 'Dear Kath' from 'Your Loving Mother'," he said. He flipped it back to the front side and held it so he and

Kelly could read it together.

The letter told of having tried to reach Kath by phone with no success. It thanked her for money she'd been sent. She'd been surprised and hoped Kath was all right. There were a couple paragraphs concerning Kath's brother. The brother must live near her, as she mentioned having him for dinner and commented on his new job. The next paragraph began with the statement, "Your sister seems to enjoy living in Chicago." Later on the sister was referred to as Beth. The letter concluded with the request, "Please call," with the please underlined several times.

Mike handed the envelope and letter to Kelly. "We'll take this with us. I'm going to call and get someone started getting phone records. I'll also get them started on a legal request for her student records. Devlin indicated she was an English major. Do you think there's anyone at the Registrar's office on a Saturday morning?"

"Possibly. Maybe just 'til noon," Kelly added, checking her watch. It was nearly twelve now. "I'll use the car phone while you're making your call."

•

When Mike came out of the apartment a few minutes later, he saw Kelly talking with a young man, both standing next to Mike's car. Kelly looked up as he approached them.

"This is Steve Kuzec. He and another student share the number three unit. This is Detective Cummings, Steve." Addressing Mike, she explained, "Steve and his roommate have never observed anyone entering or leaving this apartment. But earlier this morning, when Steve was getting into his car, he noticed lights were on in the apartment. It was shortly after seven a.m. He's seen a dark green Saab convertible parked behind the apartment house a few times, but always empty. No idea of who owns or drives it. He doesn't recall seeing it this morning or even during the past month. He remembers there had been a parking permit on the dashboard."

"Parking's so scarce around here we asked the landlord to furnish each of the apartments with one pass," Steve explained to Mike. "We check with everyone before we have a car towed," he added, smiling as he pointed at the "Violators Will Be Towed" sign. "I've been here over a year and can only remember it happening once."

Kelly and Mike questioned him in regard to the other tenants. Two of

15

his descriptions matched up with one of the two boys and the girl they'd seen earlier. Changing the conversation, Kelly explained to Mike they'd been in luck.

"I was able to reach someone at the Registrar's Office. They're checking records for us now and I'm to call back in fifteen minutes."

They thanked Steve for his time and Kelly gave him her card. "If you should notice any activity in this unit, lights on again or something, or see that green Saab, please give us a call." He nodded, indicating he would.

•

Kelly called the Registrar's office during their drive back to headquarters. She was surprised to learn the computer check showed no enrollment for a Katherine Edwards. The girl went on to explain that there were eight Edwards registered, but none with the first name of Katherine or anything close to that. Six of them were men. One woman was named Kimberly and the other Judith. Kelly thanked her for her efforts.

"You heard," she asked Mike. "Not registered. We can try Eastern, possibly Washtenaw."

Mike was shaking his head. "Devlin seemed to think she'd transferred from another Big Ten school. That doesn't sound like Washtenaw, even Eastern might be doubtful."

Eastern Michigan University was located in Ypsilanti, a neighboring community to Ann Arbor. It was one of the foremost schools in the country in terms of the number of teachers graduated. Washtenaw was the local community college, located between Ann Arbor and Ypsilanti.

"Just dawned on me," said Mike with a smile. "Maybe she was previously enrolled at the University. Last year or this past summer. Can you try again?"

"I bet you're right, I should have thought of that. They might have already checked that out. We'll see," she added, reaching for the phone again.

The girl Kelly had spoken to previously had left for the day. The one she was speaking to now was not nearly as cooperative. Checking historical records would take more time than the original request. In addition, without a formal, written, legal request, she didn't think she was authorized to give out student information. She did promise Kelly if she could get such a request over to them by two p.m., she'd do an immediate search.

Otherwise it would have to wait until Monday.

•

Twenty minutes after they'd arrived at headquarters, Kelly and Mike were on their way to the U of M Administration building with the legal request in hand. Within a few minutes, they were talking to the young lady Kelly had spoken to earlier. Her name was Mary Donelli. After handing her the formal request, Kelly and Mike were delighted to learn that, in anticipation of receiving it, she'd already gone into the computer files and found Katherine M. Edwards had been admitted as a transfer student from Indiana University in August of the previous year. She'd dropped out of school this fall after having successfully completed the summer term. After they'd both thanked her, Mike asked for additional information, firing off a barrage of questions.

"Do you have a photo of her? Her previous class schedules including her grades? The names of her professors? Can you do an inquiry to determine the names of current students who'd been in her classes? Would you have anything giving the reason she dropped out?"

Mary had thought she'd been the one in charge and now realized this was no longer the case. Kelly left them as Mary was nodding her head at Mike and making notes.

Mike had suggested that Kelly get over to the Student Activities building, which was only a short walk, while he waited for Mary to come up with additional answers. Even though it was Saturday and a home football game to boot, Kelly and Mike had been told most of the offices at S.A.B. would probably be open. Without class conflicts, Saturday was one of the busiest days for these volunteer student activities. Kelly took the copy of the legal request in case she'd need it. As she entered the Student Activities building, she heard students cheering. A radio was on full blast and the announcer was again describing Michigan's scoring play. The point after would put Michigan up by four points with less than a minute to half-time.

## Chapter 3

Rob Sebastian was in the stands, still savoring the thrill of the touchdown Michigan had just scored to put them ahead for the first time this afternoon. Football Saturdays were a special time for him. Even with the pressures of Med School, he'd only missed three or four home games since his freshman year at Michigan. Some of his friends teased him, suggesting he went on to Med School so he could continue attending games. Rob and his girlfriend, Betsy Harris, had successfully worked themselves up to some great seats during their stay at the University, sixty rows up, around the thirty-five yard line.

It had turned into a glorious day weather-wise. Following the gray, misty morning, there were now only a handful of clouds. Blue skies, bright sunshine, low sixties, Michigan ahead. What more could you want? Rob glanced up and viewed the procession of planes circling the stadium, towing advertising banners. This was as much a part of a Saturday afternoon's football activities in Ann Arbor as the U of M cheerleaders ganging up on the visiting team's mascot. Rob read some of the messages. Marie was celebrating a fiftieth birthday. The usual number of auto dealers and restaurants. Some political advertisements. A "Judy...Will You Marry Me?" banner from "Jeff." Rob's eyes widened as he read another banner. "Next PayDay$^{(tm)}$...Section 24 Row 63 Seat 17." The memory of having seen the PayDay$^{(tm)}$ candy bar earlier that morning crossed his mind. Just a coincidence?

Everyone was beginning to stand for the kick-off following the Michigan touchdown. As Rob stood, he took a pen out of his pocket and looking up once again, copied the seat location on the banner onto the cover of his complimentary pass-out program. He tore off the piece of the cover he'd written on and tucked it in his shirt pocket. Betsy noticed and asked him what he was doing. In between plays he briefed her. She smiled, without a word, suggesting his imagination was possibly in overdrive.

"Why don't you check out who's sitting there? It's just the next section over," Betsy suggested.

During the next time-out, Rob followed through on Betsy's suggestion, using the pocket binoculars he brought to most of the games and focusing them on that location, five rows up from their seats.

Counting in from the aisle, he saw an extremely attractive African-American woman in the seat. Next to her on her right was a man Rob immediately recognized from seeing his photo in the *Michigan Daily* and the *Ann Arbor News*. His name was John Jameson, the new dean of the LS&A school, also an African-American.

"It's Dean Jameson," he said to Betsy. "A woman, probably his wife, is in the actual seat, but he's sitting next to her."

"Really! Are you certain? Let me take a look." Betsy was a senior in the Lit school and very familiar with who Jameson was.

"You're right, it is him. They seem to be the center of attention, people probably asking about the banner. He seems to be shrugging his shoulders, indicating he doesn't know what it's about. Here, take another look," Betsy said, giving him back the binoculars.

Rob looked again. Was it just his imagination or did Jameson appear to be clearly angry and agitated as he glanced up at the plane? His look changed as he flashed a broad smile at a couple sitting two rows in front of him who'd turned around to say something to him.

"I hate to disappoint you Rob, but I think that message refers to the past controversy over his salary. Do you remember hearing or reading about it?" Betsy asked.

"Only vaguely, they referred to it in the *Ann Arbor News* article about him when he was named Dean this past summer. I don't recall the details."

"That's true, the appointment triggered a rehash of the episode last year shortly after Jameson joined the faculty. You might not have followed it. Getting him to come to Michigan was a real coup. He'd shined in previous positions on both coasts, Stanford and Yale or Harvard. When the salaries of the highest-paid University people were published, about a year ago now, an enterprising reporter discovered Jameson was drawing two salaries. The administration didn't help matters when their response was they had bigger plans for him than just being a professor in the English Department. The woman, who was then Dean of LS&A, had publicly clashed with President Robinson and speculation immediately began that Robinson was trying to force her out and Jameson would be her successor. I don't know the details, but she did in fact resign early this year. I think it was to accept a position at some southern university, I've forgotten which one. I think they waited a few months before naming Jameson as her replacement in hopes of avoiding unfavorable publicity."

"Too bad, I've heard he's doing a great job, admired by faculty and students," Rob said. "I think you sang his praises a couple weeks ago."

Betsy nodded. "I probably did. He's already initiated some changes that everyone appears to like. No one's questioning his credentials or abilities. Except for the pay flap, I haven't heard one negative about him. As you say, it's too bad that flared up again." Pointing up to the sky she added, "And I think it's about to again, I think that's what the message is all about, someone with an ax to grind who doesn't want to let the matter rest."

"You're probably right," Rob said. That would certainly explain Jameson's apparent look of anger and concern, he thought. As the game continued though, Rob couldn't shake the thought that there might be some association with the woman's body Mark and he had discovered in the Arb. If the message on the banner was a threat or warning of some kind and something was to happen to Jameson, he'd regret not having said anything. He recalled the conversation with Detective Travis. She mentioned they wanted to keep some of the details regarding the young woman's death confidential. She hadn't talked about the PayDay(tm) candy bar specifically, but it could be only a handful of people knew about it. There were certainly plenty of police around the stadium this afternoon, but how many knew about finding the PayDay(tm) bar? Detective Travis had said she wouldn't be coming to the game. That might also be true of any others who would make an association with the banner. The abrasions on the woman's neck and wrists – ankles, too, Detective Travis had said – point to foul play of some kind, if not murder.

"I can tell you're deep in thought," Betsy said. "You didn't hardly react to that fumble just now."

Rob smiled. "You're probably correct, it's someone still disgruntled over Jameson's inflated pay; wanting to embarrass him again. But even so, I'm still going to contact the police. The coincidence, the timing – it's too much to ignore."

"I know you too well to try to dissuade you once you've made up your mind," Betsy said. "Besides, even if there's only a remote chance there's some association with that girl's death, you should say something to someone. Maybe you should go over and say something to Dean Jameson."

"No," Rob answered shaking his head. "I'll just call the detective I talked to and let her handle it. Don't let me forget."

Betsy laughed, shaking her head.

"One other thing Betsy. Jameson's wife is the one who's actually in the seat. Of course we don't know if that's the case every game, but maybe she's the one being threatened, the one in danger."

Betsy laughed again.

•

It was nearly nine p.m. when Mike dropped Kelly off at her apartment. After splashing some cold water on her face and pouring herself a glass of wine, she played back the messages on her answering machine. There were three. One from her mother and father just touching base, wondering if they would be seeing her this weekend. One from Rick. She'd had to cancel out of the dinner/movie date they'd planned on. She'd left a message on his answering machine around three-thirty, after realizing she'd probably be working on this case well into the evening. Rick Forsythe was a good friend and they'd been dating for over a year. Not the love of her life, and she probably wasn't his either, although he always seemed to leave the door open for that to change. They did enjoy one another's company and he always seemed to be there when she needed him. The third message was from Rob Sebastian. He began the message by saying something had come up he'd like to discuss with her, and left his number. After a short pause he continued speaking, saying she might already know the reason for his call. He then described the banner he'd seen at the game.

"I've just got this gut feeling it might be related to the body Mark and I discovered this morning. Please give me a call."

Kelly's initial reaction was a grin. However, the more thought she gave to it, the more credence she gave to a possible connection. Rob hadn't mentioned if he knew whose seat had been referred to. She could get that information Monday morning from the U of M Ticket Office. Rob had left his message shortly before five. Kelly dialed Rob's number. She got his answering machine and had just started to leave a message when Rob picked up. She recognized his voice. He thanked her for getting back to him, apologizing for calling her at home. He asked if she'd known about the banner.

"I'm glad you called, and no, I hadn't known anything about it before hearing your message."

Rob repeated the message on the banner. "Next PayDay<sup>(tm)</sup> ...Section 24 Row 63 Seat 17. That seat is just a couple sections over from mine. I was able to determine who was sitting in the seat. It was Dean Jameson, the new LS&A dean."

Kelly knew John Jameson. He was a neighbor of her parents. Her parents had hosted a neighborhood gathering this past spring and Dean Jameson and his wife had attended. Kelly had spent several minutes chatting with them. They'd been very personable and she'd been impressed by both. They were in their early forties and had appeared to be delighted to be at the University and living in Ann Arbor. Kelly had assisted her parents in hosting the party. The Jamesons had been very interested in learning about Kelly and her work with the police department. She empathized with the two of them this past summer when she read the news coverage following his appointment as Dean. Kelly listened as Rob told of watching Dean Jameson's reaction to the message on the banner.

"He seemed to be putting on a good front for those seated around him. Laughing, smiling, shrugging his shoulders and shaking his head no in response to questions and teasing. But in between times, I sensed he was extremely angry and agitated. It could have been my imagination. My girlfriend, Betsy, thinks that may be the case. I don't know. But I was concerned if I didn't say anything and something was to happen to him, I'd have always regretted it."

"You're thinking that 'Next PayDay(tm)' might be a threat or warning to him?" asked Kelly. "Sounds crazy, doesn't it?" Rob replied. "Somebody trying to further embarrass him over the high salary he was paid before being named Dean is far more likely. Do what you think best, I'm certainly not going to second-guess you."

"I'm not worried about that. I think you might be on to something and I'll definitely contact Dean Jameson. I'm so glad you called. Thank you."

"You're welcome. A question. Have you determined whether she was murdered?"

Kelly was cautious with her answer. Less than an hour ago Mike had briefed her on some of Newman's initial findings. He'd found burn marks on her breasts and indications pliers or some similar instrument had been used on her nipples. There were also injuries to her genital area, signs of torture.

"We're treating it the same as a murder case. We think she was tortured. Her death may have been the result of an overdose of a drug or sedative, accidental or intentional, we still aren't certain. We're fairly sure of her identity and her mother's been notified. She and the deceased's brother will be flying in tomorrow afternoon and they should be able to verify the identification."

Changing subjects and leading toward an ending of the conversation, Kelly commented, "Great game, I heard. It's been a while since Michigan scored sixty points. You had a great day weather-wise, too."

"It was fun. I'm afraid my mind wandered too much though in that second half. I didn't savor the victory as much as I should have. One more question. Will you let me know what happens or should I just rely on the papers?"

Kelly laughed. "Probably the news media. I'd like to say it would be otherwise. We really do appreciate your help and maybe I'll surprise you with a call. And one more reminder, we'd appreciate it if you'd keep everything to yourself for now, what you saw, what you've told me and what I've shared with you."

•

Immediately after completing the phone call to Rob Sebastian, Kelly grabbed her briefcase. Opening it, she rifled through the papers. There it was; the copy of Katherine Edwards' transcript. She nodded her head as she traced a line on the copy. English 305. Last spring. An A. The professor's name was Jameson. She next found the phone book and looked up Jameson's number. She thought of various ways of approaching him, finally concluding the more direct the better. Jameson answered the phone. Kelly introduced herself and apologized for the late hour.

"Kelly. Nice to hear your voice. Haven't spoken with you since last spring at your parents' party. Hope they're okay."

"Yes. They're both doing well, thank you. Mother's cancer seems to still be in remission. I'm actually calling in a professional capacity. I have a couple of questions, if you have a minute?"

"Sure. Go right ahead." He chuckled. "This is a first for me. A police investigation?"

"Yes. We're touching all the bases. Would the name Katherine Edwards...possibly Kath Edwards, mean anything to you?"

"Sounds vaguely familiar. Should it? I have contact with a vast number of students."

"She was in your 305 English class last spring. You gave her an A."

"Sure, now I remember. Very smart. Beautiful, too. What about her?"

Kelly told him a body believed to be Katherine Edwards' had been discovered in the Arboretum early that morning. Suspected murder. It was a moment or two before Jameson responded to her statement.

"I heard about a body being found on the radio driving home from the game. No name was given, nor the fact she was a University coed. Nothing was mentioned about her having been murdered, either. That's horrible. Tragic. Do you have any suspects?"

"We thought you might be able to shed some light on that."

"How so?"

"The 'Next PayDay$^{(tm)}$' banner towed over the stadium today with your seat number. What did it mean to you?" Kelly was wishing she'd confronted him face-to-face to ask these questions.

Again, there was a moment or two of silence.

"Kelly, that's a very involved story. Maybe you could come to my office early Monday morning, say nine o'clock. I assure you I didn't murder Katherine Edwards. I wasn't totally honest with you earlier. I've had some recent contact with her. I'll tell you everything on Monday. I made a major mistake. But murdering that girl, no way."

"I really wasn't suggesting or implying that, Mr. Jameson."

"You just did. You called me John at your parents' house. Mr. Jameson sounds as if you're about to arrest me."

"No, no, John. Hear me out. You're not a suspect. Katherine or Kath was dressed in a Halloween costume when her body was found. A PayDay$^{(tm)}$ candy bar was tucked in a pocket of the outfit. We don't know its significance. Whether it was meant to convey a message. Learning about the banner made us wonder if you were being threatened by the same person or persons who'd possibly killed Katherine Edwards. That's the purpose of my call."

Once again, Jameson seemed to hesitate before responding.

"I understand. I suppose I should be thanking you for your call. And I should. My wife and I have a major family commitment tomorrow. A family reunion of sorts in Chicago. We're driving down early and back late. Would nine a.m. at my office on Monday work out for you?"

This time it was Kelly who hesitated. She wondered if she should press for an earlier time, still tonight. No.

"That would be fine. Refresh me on how best to get to your office."

•

Marian Jameson called down to her husband from the top of the stairs.

"You better come up soon if we're going to be on the road by six. Who was that on the phone?"

"Kelly Travis. Remember meeting her at her parents' home last spring?" answered John, coming to the foot of the stairs. "Could you come down for a few minutes? I need to talk with you."

"Is it about her parents? Are they all right?"

"No. And yes. They're fine. Remember this afternoon hearing on the radio about a young woman's body being found this morning in the Arb? She was a former student of mine."

From the top of the stairs Marian could see John's look of concern. "I'll just be a minute."

A few moments later she came into the family room, patted him on the shoulder and leaned over and gave him a kiss. She sat down across from him, sensing her husband's tension and worry.

"I should have confided in you sooner," John began. "I thought I was protecting you. Giving you one less worry. I was wrong."

For the next half an hour, John held Marian's attention as he poured out the details of events he'd kept to himself. They had begun a little over three weeks ago, on a Thursday.

"I finished up one meeting sooner than anticipated and learned my next meeting had been postponed for half an hour. It was that glorious autumn afternoon with the temperature near seventy degrees. I walked over to one of the coffee houses on State Street and found a vacant table on the sidewalk. Sipping coffee, reviewing some papers, basking in the sunshine . . . a perfect day. People-watching was fun as well. I remember hoping all the students passing by weren't cutting classes.

"I heard someone call out my name and I looked up and saw the smiling face of one of my former students, Katherine Edwards. One of my best and brightest, very vivacious and a delight to teach. She sat down at my table and started talking non-stop. She said I'd been her favorite professor and she'd learned so much. She had begun writing a novel and I'd been her inspiration. She was succeeding in inflating my ego and I couldn't hide my smile. She'd reached out and placed her hand over mine, squeezing it as she complimented me on being appointed Dean.

"I remember telling her that in exchange for all those compliments I should be buying her a coffee, but that I had a meeting to get back to. She'd said she was already late for an engagement herself, and continued to gush over how great it had been to have run into me. As we stood to leave, she appeared to get her feet tangled and toppled toward me. I reached out and grabbed her, breaking her fall. She laughed, throwing her arms around me, surprising me with a kiss on the lips. I was startled by her boldness and quickly pushed her back, wondering if I'd made a mistake and egged her on by being nice to her. She smiled, winked, thanked me for preventing her fall and was on her way.

"I remember picking up my papers off the table, chuckling to myself as I looked around to see if anyone had observed what had happened. Everyone seemed preoccupied with their own concerns.

"I planned to tell you about the incident, but it was one of those evenings when we both had dinner meetings and by the time we finally were together later that night, I'd truthfully forgotten all about it. That is, until a week later when I received a large, manila envelope marked "personal," to my attention only. I think you're aware that Virginia opens all my mail. She asked me about the one marked personal and I gave her the go-ahead to open it. More times than not, the mailings marked personal and confidential identify junk mail. A short time later when Virginia brought in my mail, she pointed out the large envelope on top, marked 'For Dean Jameson's eyes only.' She explained it had been inside the other envelope. I remember her having smiled, saying they'd taken a double precaution."

Marian moved forward to the edge of her chair, anticipating where her husband's lengthy explanation was headed as he continued.

"As I opened the envelope, I immediately saw it contained several eight-and-a-half by eleven photographs. The top photo pictured me having coffee that day with Katherine Edwards. I remember my anger building, realizing what a patsy I'd been. The photo showed us both smiling broadly, staring at one another with Katherine holding my hand. The second photo showed the two of us hugging as Katherine planted a kiss on my lips. If the photo had been taken a fraction of a second later, it would have shown my shocked expression. The third photo took my breath away. You could easily identify Katherine, coupled in intercourse with an African-American man. You just saw the man's nude back and muscular body, his head or face wasn't shown in the photo. It was pornographic, it had been staged. But associating it with the other photographs gave the implication it was me. Believe me, it wasn't."

Marian started to say something, but he waved her off. "That's not all, there was a fourth photo, similar to the third. Only this time she was on top of the man, with her head tilted back, eyes closed, an expression of ecstasy on her face. The man's head and face weren't shown in that photo either, just his hands grabbing Katherine's hips. Though I was shocked, it was the next photo, the last of them, that left me reeling in disbelief. It was an enlargement of the man's left hand, wearing the monogrammed ring

26

you surprised me with on our tenth anniversary. I'm not even sure I told you I'd misplaced it, I was so sure I'd eventually be finding it."

Marian was wide-eyed. "Oh, John! I'm having difficulty comprehending all of this. It's all so unbelievable. Why would – ?"

John held his hand up again as he answered. "Blackmail. A vicious scheme to scare me into paying her so no one else would see those photos. I'd been set up. She'd included clippings of the mastheads of the *Michigan Daily*, the *Ann Arbor News* and the *Detroit Free Press* and *News* in the envelope. The implication was clear – the photos I'd just seen could have been sent to one or all of those papers."

"Oh, John, why didn't you tell me about this sooner? Why didn't you confide – ?"

Once again he held up his hand. "I realize now I should have. It was a mistake not to. I panicked. My first thought was to go on the offensive, to go right to the police, to tell you and President Robinson. My mind was racing and I was confused. The embarrassment I'd caused the University over my compensation, which surfaced again when I was named Dean, had been traumatic. I'd thought it was all behind us and now I could see it all beginning again. I was fearful I might not even be believed, and where there's smoke there's a fire type of reaction. It was clearly me in the photographs someone had taken in front of the coffee shop. I kept looking for a demand for money in the envelope, but there wasn't any. That's when I thought of the possibility of just waiting to see what would happen next, maybe being presented with an opportunity to entrap Katherine and whoever else was involved. I reasoned she had to have had help, someone to take the photos, someone to have posed as me. I couldn't comprehend how they'd gotten hold of my ring."

Marian sat on the edge of the chair with her hands clenched, eyes watering, her look communicating her love and understanding as John continued.

"I had a luncheon meeting that day and could hardly focus on what was being said. When I returned to my office I found half a candy bar sitting on my desk, still in its wrapper. As I picked it up I discovered the half was cut into two pieces. As I placed them back together, I saw I was looking at half the wrapper of a Nestle 100 Grand<sup>(tm)</sup> bar. I buzzed Virginia on the intercom and asked if she'd seen anyone in my office over the noon hour. She explained she'd been away from her desk for several minutes and no, she hadn't seen anyone. She asked me if anything was wrong, saying I'd looked preoccupied with much on my mind earlier. I told her someone had left some candy on my desk and she laughed, saying it was probably you. As I was talking to Virginia, the significance of the candy dawned on me. I was being asked for fifty thousand dollars, split into two payments of twenty-five thousand dollars each. My immediate reaction was that wasn't going to happen, even if I were to pay her, there was no assurance the demands wouldn't continue. Besides, what would I be paying her for? I'd done nothing wrong, nothing to be ashamed about. I promised myself to contact the police after I'd discussed it with you and President Robinson. I tried to call you, but you were out and Jim was having a meeting. Besides, you were the first one I wanted to ask for advice.

"A few minutes later Virginia buzzed me to say there was a woman on the line. She wouldn't identify herself, but said it was very important that she talk to me. I had an ominous feeling as I lifted the handset. The woman said hello and asked if I recognized her voice. It was Katherine Edwards. I exploded, cussing her out with language I didn't realize I knew. I heard her crying as she mumbled something about how sorry she was, how wrong it was, how she wasn't going to let him do it. I was having trouble understanding what she was saying, and continued to lash out at her, threatening to do everything I could to see her behind bars. She interrupted me, saying she was going to give me all the prints and negatives, that this never should have happened and she was sorry it had. I asked her how she could have been a party to this and whether she was on drugs. She didn't answer, instead asking me if I was aware he wants fifty thousand dollars. 'Don't pay him,' she said, 'he'll never let you off the hook.' I asked her who 'he' was. She said I didn't have to know, that I would no longer need to worry about him. She then promised to meet me on the front steps of the library in the Law Quad at two o'clock on Monday, saying she'd hand over everything to me at that time. I remember feeling elated, wondering if it could possibly be true the matter could be put to rest so easily. That you could be spared the worry, potential grief and humiliation. Robinson and the University, too. Then came the zinger. She asked me if I could give her five thousand dollars to help her disappear, to start a new life.

"My immediate reaction was that I was being conned. Those photographs of her were etched in my mind. I was having a problem believing her, sympathizing with her. I felt she knew the sum of five thousand dollars would sound tempting compared to the fifty thousand, a relatively small amount in relation to the ton of trouble that could be avoided if I could believe her, trust her. My mind was also racing with the thought of notifying the police, bringing them with me on Monday, taking her into custody, seeing she was punished for what she'd done. She interpreted my delay in responding as a rejection. Sobbing, she said she understood my reluctance, apologizing for even asking. She said she'd still have all the prints and negatives for me on Monday.

"I asked her if we could make it sooner. She said no, saying she wouldn't be able to verify if she had everything until then. After hanging up, I sat in my chair for the next hour, considering my options. I pondered over whether I should confide in you, in Robinson; whether I should notify the police, whether I should give her any money?"

Marian looked down at her clenched hands and then up at her husband again. It was a look of understanding, but also a look of disappointment, of criticism. She stood and walked over behind him and began to massage his shoulders as he continued.

"Not telling you is what I regret most. I did think I would be sparing you some worry and anguish. Otherwise, for the good of all, I thought I'd made the right decision. If I was being tricked and there was a further request for money, I could always go to the police. I was awake most of the night wondering if I was doing the right thing, for everyone, not just for me. The next morning I contacted the branch manager at our bank. I made up a story about having some work being done to our house and the crew wanting to be paid in cash. We had nearly eight thousand dollars in our savings account and I explained I wanted to draw five thousand in cash from it. I told him I'd stop by at noon on Monday to pick it up, and he said that wouldn't be a problem and thanked me for briefing him in advance.

"I arrived at the Law Quad about ten minutes early on Monday, with the five thousand in an envelope in my coat pocket. I was just checking my watch again when she came out of the library and down the steps toward me. She was wearing dark glasses and a raincoat. She was carrying a rather heavy manila envelope and immediately handed it to me. I unfastened the clip and saw there were a couple dozen or so photographs and several negatives inside. She said she was certain she'd found everything. Saying she was sorry, she turned to leave. I reached out and grabbed her shoulder, handing her the envelope of money as she turned. She thanked me and re-entered the library. I went back to the office and borrowed a pair of scissors from Virginia. I spent the next ten minutes cutting the photos and negatives into tiny pieces – including the ones from my desk. On the way home from work, I deposited the envelope containing all the pieces in a trash container. I remember the sense of relief I felt as I said a silent prayer.

"As the week went on I began to relax, thinking I'd made the right decision. In fact I recall you making a comment on my change of mood, saying I'd been a bear. You can probably imagine how angry I was when I looked up and saw that banner. I was devastated. I'd been had. They were already asking for more money. I tried to conceal my true thoughts, from you and those around us, feigning ignorance and forcing a smile. I promised myself to tell you everything on the drive to Chicago tomorrow, hoping you'd understand why I'd acted the way I did. I knew I'd have to tell Robinson and the police on Monday, and wondered how critical they'd be about not having been briefed sooner. Kelly's call brought everything to a head quicker than I anticipated. I tried to stonewall her when she initially asked if I knew Katherine Edwards, not knowing how much the police already knew. I was embarrassed when Kelly said she was aware Katherine had been in one of my classes, second-guessing myself for not having gone to the police sooner. Then came the shocker when Kelly explained the woman's body they'd found in the Arb this morning was Katherine's.

"It didn't dawn on me at first that the police might be viewing me as a suspect. Kelly questioned me about the banner. I assumed they'd established the connection and tried to get her to agree to meet in my office Monday morning before answering additional questions. The thought of whether I should be getting an attorney involved flashed through my mind. Then, more because of my confusion and anxieties than anything she'd said, I became very defensive and lashed out at her. That was a mistake."

Marian's hands tensed on her husband's shoulders. She knew him. She knew the dilemma he'd found himself in. He hadn't even mentioned the racial implications, a high-profile black at the University carrying on an affair with a white student. He'd acted to protect the University as much as himself, as much as her. She'd never questioned his faithfulness.

John glanced over his shoulder, up at her. "I know it should have been sooner, but you're the first one to hear the whole story. I really don't believe the police are considering me as a suspect in Katherine's murder. Kelly was emphatic on that point. The reason she said she called was to tell me they'd found a PayDay$^{(tm)}$ candy bar in a pocket of the costume Katherine had been dressed in. The police don't know its significance, but they're concerned the 'Next PayDay$^{(tm)}$' message on the banner might imply I'm the next target for whoever killed her."

As Marian's eyes widened in alarm and she came around to stand in front of him, John quickly added, "I don't think that's the case. It's far more logical it was a message to me to get ready to make another payment. It had to have been planned before she was killed. I just don't know."

John stood up and embraced Marian, tears streaming down both their faces.

"I love you," whispered John. "I've never been unfaithful and never will be."

Marian hugged him harder. "I know. I know," she whispered in reply. "I love you so much. Do you think we should cancel on Chicago?" she asked, stepping back.

Shaking his head he replied, "No. Kelly agreed to come by my office on Monday morning. I'll tell her everything. One additional day shouldn't change anything."


**Chapter 4**


Kelly slept in Sunday morning. Her mind had been in overdrive last night and she'd had difficulty falling asleep. It was just past eight-thirty. She'd planned on attending the early church service before meeting Mike at the office at eleven. She realized she'd have to put a move on.

She opened the front door and reached for the newspapers on the porch. As she'd expected, the *Ann Arbor News* featured the story on its front page. "Woman's Body Discovered in Arb" was the headline. Only sketchy details were provided. The news media hadn't been supplied with many. The article stated the body of an unidentified woman had been discovered in the Arboretum early Saturday morning by two joggers. It gave their names. Cause of death and the results of an autopsy still weren't known. The article went on to say the woman was Caucasian, in her early twenties, and gave her approximate height, weight, hair and eye coloring. There was a sentence about the body being dressed in an unusual Halloween costume. The rest of the article was historical in nature, detailing other instances of bodies being found in the Arb – suicides as well as killings. There had only been a handful of incidents over the past thirty years.

The *News* had handled the article well, Kelly concluded. She was relieved the article hadn't attempted to cultivate the fear and near-hysteria that had surfaced in the recent past in regard to a serial rapist who had terrified the community for over two years. He'd also killed one of his victims.

The *Detroit Free Press* article contained much of the same information, somewhat shorter in length and appearing on the third page.

Kelly looked at the clock and headed for the shower. She had just enough time to get to church.

•

Mike was already there when Kelly arrived just before eleven. He was in the conference room, busy writing notes on the blackboard. He'd just added the words "Green Saab Convertible" to one of the columns.

He looked up and smiled at Kelly. "Good. I was just finishing up. Judy and Steve will be here at noon. It will give us a few minutes to talk."

Judy Wilson was one of the senior detectives in the division. She was good and a real asset to the department. Kelly had been a beneficiary of Judy's vast knowledge and many years of experience. Judy was in her late forties and single. She was truly married to her work and thrived on details. There had been speculation Judy would be appointed to head up the Investigative Division prior to Mike's appointment the previous year. Though with less seniority, Mike was a far more popular and welcomed choice by the vast majority of the staff. Kelly could sense Judy still felt bitter about being passed over. When leaks occurred, which were sometimes embarrassing to the department and therefore, personally to Mike, some were quick to point a finger at Judy. Nothing had ever been proven. Kelly herself enjoyed a good relationship with Judy, although she was certain Judy harbored some jealousy over the close relationship Kelly enjoyed with Mike.

Steve Renz was a ten-year veteran in the department. Gung-ho and personable, he was extremely popular with his peers. His forte was getting potential witnesses and suspects to confide in him. He did it through charm rather than coercion. In his mid-thirties, married with three or four children, he made very effective use of his time. Kelly was pleased she'd have a few minutes with Mike to update him on her conversations with Rob Sebastian and John Jameson before the others arrived. She wasted no time getting into the subject.

When she'd first begun she could tell from Mike's broad grin he was skeptical over any association between the murder of Katherine Edwards and the sign being towed over the stadium. As she went into more detail about Jameson being in the seat location appearing on the banner and her follow-up call to him, Mike leaned forward in his chair with great interest. Kelly sensed his disappointment when she said she wouldn't be following up with Jameson until tomorrow morning. She could tell that wouldn't have been his decision.

"You're welcome to attend," Kelly said.

Mike smiled and shook his head. "You'll do fine on your own. But depending on what he has to say, I might get involved later."

As Mike went to the blackboard and began writing "Airplane Banner/ Dean Jameson," he praised Kelly for having followed through with Jameson at once following the conversation with Rob Sebastian.

Judy entered the room and was warmly greeted by Kelly and Mike. She was early; it was only eleven-thirty. Kelly was pleased she'd been able to complete her discussion with Mike.

Mike asked Judy if she'd be available to participate in the media briefing scheduled for six o'clock.

"David will be with you," Mike said, referring to the Chief of Police, David Benton. "He'll be here shortly after one o'clock to hear our suggestions about what should be said."

Mike also informed them that Katherine Edwards' mother and brother would be arriving around two o'clock. He asked Judy if she'd be willing to meet with them and also be present when they identified the body.

"Am I late?" asked Steve, entering the room. "I thought you'd said one o'clock", he said, checking his watch.

"No. You're actually early," Mike replied. "Means we can get started that much sooner. Does anyone want coffee?"

All declined and Mike went right into his briefing, beginning with the autopsy results. He described the injuries to the breasts and genital area, explaining there was no doubt the Edwards girl had been tortured. Newman believed all the mutilations had occurred prior to her death. The abrasions on her neck, wrists and ankles were caused by a coarse rope. Partial strands had been found. Whoever had bound her was clearly not concerned about her comfort, Mike remarked. In addition to restraining her, the rope may have been used to drag or carry the body.

"The implication is she was hog-tied at some point. It may have been

33

part of the torturing."

There were half a dozen needle marks on the body, indicating she'd been injected with some substance.

"The problem, thus far, is the blood tests haven't shown what the substance was. Newman has several theories, some suggesting she'd been injected with more than one type of drug. One scenario, he suggests, would be a mixture of sedatives and stimulants over an extended period of time. Another possible explanation is the injection of one of the so-called truth serums. A third scenario, of course, is a lethal drug with the clear intent to kill her.

"As you've probably already concluded yourselves, it could be a combination of all three theories. The multiple needle marks, all recent, would support that. As I mentioned before, the problem is these type of drugs should have showed up in the blood tests. Newman's having some further tests run. In the meantime, he says that without the evidence of torture and the body having been bound, his autopsy would point to a normal death – whatever that is.

"I questioned Newman on whether the trauma of being bound and tortured could have precipitated a heart attack or panic seizure of some kind which resulted in her death. Possible, he says, but there's nothing to suggest that. The autopsy showed her to be in excellent health. The identity of the drugs is the key.

"Now comes the scary part. Newman suggests the possibility drugs were used which would counteract or mask one another. Eliminate any trace of the substances in the blood stream. It's a complex subject. It would have to involve an individual with a thorough knowledge of the science of testing blood, and how various drugs react with one another. It's high-tech."

"So you're saying even if we're able to track down her killer, currently we can't prove how she was killed or even if she was murdered?" asked Steve. "It would be an assault and battery charge?"

"That's about right," Mike replied. "Her death could have been an accident," he said, raising his eyebrows. "An accidental overdose. Or the use of two or more drugs in a combination which proved lethal. The person would still have had to have injected one or more non-detectable drugs to remove traces of the original drug or drugs. Her death could have been planned. Use of a poison or a deliberate overdose."

The four sat quietly for several minutes, mulling over all the implications of what they'd learned. Steve finally broke the silence.

"The additional blood tests Newman ordered could end up with something, couldn't they? Let's hope that's the case."

The others nodded in agreement. Mike then asked Kelly to brief the other two on her news. She quickly did so. They were fascinated as she related the conversations she'd had the previous night. Steve asked her to speculate in regard to Jameson.

"Do you think he'd had or was having an affair with Edwards?"

Kelly replied she wanted to have the talk with Jameson first before engaging in any conjectures. She also reminded them the airplane banner might just be someone trying to embarrass Jameson over the previous compensation controversy.

Mike stood and moved to the blackboard. They worked down the list of other items which required discussion. As they proceeded, they also decided which of them would be responsible for specific areas of the investigation. Steve was delegated to check out who'd made arrangements for the airplane and banner. He was also assigned to trace down the ownership of the Green Saab convertible. The residents at Edwards' apartment complex had been of little help. One had volunteered he was sure he would have noticed if the car had an out-of-state license plate. No one knew the model year or recalled any numbers or letters on the plate. Nor could they recall whether or not the car had any unique decals. They had determined none of the current apartment residents owned the car.

Following discussion of the final item on his list, Mike announced they next had to decide what information would be shared with the media at the six o'clock briefing.

Judy presented a strong case for sharing almost everything except for the problem with the blood tests and the possible Jameson tie-in.

"We can explain we're still awaiting the final results of the blood tests. If we don't mention the cause of death, I think the media will assume we're holding back some key information for a good reason. We should definitely leave them with the implication she was murdered. Everything points to the fact it wasn't just a random death. We owe the community the responsibility to get that message out. Otherwise there will just be rumors. A rapist and killer on the loose."

"She wasn't raped, was she?" asked Steve.

"I didn't say she was," Judy snapped back at him. "That's the point I'm making. Rumors will get started. It's just a matter of time before details of the costume are known. Besides, I think releasing all the details will prompt people to provide us with some additional information. We know next to nothing about Katherine Edwards. Who were her friends?"

Kelly interrupted. "What about the PayDay$^{(tm)}$ candy bar?"

"Good point," said Mike. "We should keep that piece of the puzzle among ourselves for now. I agree with Judy for the most part. But things such as the Green Saab convertible shouldn't be talked about until we do some preliminary work. Otherwise everyone in town who owns one will be looked at as a potential suspect."

Within a few minutes they were completely in sync over what should be held back. When Benton arrived and was told of their recommendations, he complimented them for reaching such a quick agreement.

Mike brought the Chief up to date on other developments in the case, including the possible tie to John Jameson. Benton commented they needed to be very careful in dealing with Jameson. "We don't want to embarrass the man, his family or the University without a damn good reason."

One of the officers on duty came to the door and informed them Mrs. Edwards and her son had arrived. The Chief and Judy excused themselves.

Kelly was relieved that Mike had asked Judy to meet with the Edwards. Kelly knew of no one who enjoyed being present when relatives or friends identified a body. Simply informing people of a relative's or friend's death or murder was tough enough.

Mike had discussed with Judy some of the questions she should ask Mrs. Edwards and her son. The names of present and former roommates, boyfriends, friends in general, present and former organizations she'd belonged to and jobs she'd held were among the items he suggested she cover with them. Specifically, he asked Judy to see if they knew the identity of the Jeff whose signature appeared on the painting in her daughter's, his sister's, bedroom, and if Katherine had owned a car. The latter question could lead to whether they knew of anyone who drove a Green Saab convertible, Mike suggested.

•

Mike spent another ten minutes or so with Kelly and Steve before telling them while they were welcome to stay and attend the six p.m. briefing, they were free to go.

"We can meet tomorrow, let's say eleven a.m. That seems better than trying to squeeze it in before Kelly's appointment with Jameson at nine. If Judy comes up with anything special, I'll give you both a call."

"I promised my parents I'd try to stop by sometime today," Kelly said. "Eleven should give me more than enough time for Jameson. I'll see you both tomorrow then."

Steve said he'd also be leaving, spending some time with the family. Kelly and he walked out to their cars together. On the way, Steve commented on how little they had to work with at this juncture.

"Maybe getting out the additional details at the briefing will prompt some leads. Let's hope so, I'd love to nail that son-of-a-bitch."

•

Kelly's parents were delighted to see her. They asked how the investigation was progressing. Kelly had called earlier and told them she was working on the case. She provided them with a basic overview and explained the mother and brother from New Jersey were currently identifying the body.

"How sad," her mother commented. Over the years, her mother had given her several lectures, questioning Kelly's decision to pursue a career in law enforcement. Kelly knew both parents worried about her and she tried to play down the potential dangers. Her mother had been horrified when she first learned Kelly had a gun, and had later been relieved she did. "Take care," was always the admonishment from her mother when they parted.

Kelly helped her father rustle up an early, light Sunday supper. After the meal and clean-up, they watched "60 Minutes." Explaining she had a full day scheduled for tomorrow, Kelly excused herself, smiling as her mother said, "Take care."

•

On arriving at her apartment she found a message on the answering machine from Mike. He asked her to call him, saying he'd be up late. Mike answered following just one ring. Kelly laughed and teased him about sitting next to the phone, waiting for her call.

"Not quite," he replied. "I have been busy on the phone, though." He asked how her parents were and then began by saying, "We've had a surprise. Katherine Edwards has an identical twin sister."

He then explained the confusion which occurred when Katherine's mother and brother had attempted to identify the body.

"Mrs. Edwards believes the body is the sister's. Sam, the brother, is convinced it's Katherine's. In between tears, Judy tried to get Mrs. Edwards to explain why she thinks the body is Beth's, the sister. Just a feeling, just a mother's knowing was really her only explanation. On the other hand, the brother pointed out a birthmark, a scar on her head and signs of a previously broken finger as reasons for believing the body is Katherine's. The mother claims he's mistaken. She says all those things prove it's Katherine's sister's body. It really turned into a mess, according to Judy."

"I can imagine," said Kelly, still shocked over the revelation.

"Judy and David and I had separate conversations with Mrs. Edwards and her son, Sam, a little later. The brother suggested his mother was extremely upset over not having been able to contact Beth in Chicago. He said she's terrified both daughters might be dead, that his mother is in shock. He seemed very confident the body is Katherine's.

"The mother was very emotional. She said she can't fathom why Sam is so confused. She described in the minutest details the accidents Beth had as a little girl which resulted in the head scar and the broken finger. She's as certain the body is Beth's as the brother is that it's Katherine's."

"What happens now?" asked Kelly.

"Mrs. Edwards thinks she has birth records and some medical reports that may help in an identification. The problem is, Mrs. Edwards isn't sure where she's stored them. If she remembers, she could probably get a friend or relative, possibly a neighbor, to go over to her house and locate the records and get them to us. Otherwise we'll have to wait until she gets home.

"We've already contacted the Chicago police and they've placed a high priority on locating Beth."

"How did you handle the media briefing?"

"We had some intense discussions over that subject. We involved Mrs. Edwards and Sam, the brother. We agreed we all wanted to do everything possible to track down whoever was responsible as quickly as possible regardless of which sister had been murdered. We reasoned the best way to do that would be to identify the body as Katherine Edwards' and at the same time, advise the media she had a twin sister.

"Hopefully the Chicago police will be able to quickly locate Elizabeth Edwards. She might even see or hear the news and contact us or her mother. If it is Elizabeth's body, hopefully Katherine will learn the news and make contact. We debated over just waiting, but decided this was the best course of action. I called to get your input but you weren't home and I decided not to bother your parents."

"I think you made the right decision. Sorry I wasn't there to help," said Kelly.

Mike then reviewed some of the information Judy had been able to gather from Mrs. Edwards and her son, Sam. Katherine had had a roommate to share the cost of the apartment when she'd initially signed the lease. The roommate dropped out of school after the fall term and Katherine found another girl to share the apartment. She graduated this past spring. Judy has both their names. Neither was believed to still be in the Ann Arbor area. Neither the mother or brother knew if she'd had anyone living with her since the second roommate.

"Except for the living room couch, it didn't appear the apartment was set up to accommodate two people," Kelly commented.

"I agree. As a matter of fact, Judy said the mother remembers Beth complaining about how uncomfortable the couch was for sleeping. Both indicated Beth had visited Katherine several times. They also thought Beth had a key to the apartment. And no, neither Beth nor Katherine own a Green Saab convertible," Mike said with a chuckle. Kelly smiled in response.

Mike continued, saying although the two knew Katherine was dating, they couldn't provide any names. The Jeff who'd signed the print in Katherine's bedroom had been a friend in Bloomington. They didn't think he'd been a true boyfriend.

Katherine had obtained a job at Borders Bookstore shortly after coming to Ann Arbor. After a few months, she left Borders and took a waitressing job at Gratzi, where she could make far more money.

"We've already checked with Gratzi and learned Katherine's final day of work was a week ago today. She'd provided them with only a three day notice and no explanation. They'd enjoyed having her, but were disappointed over the circumstances under which she'd left. She had requested her final paycheck be sent to her mother's New Jersey address."

Katherine had also worked while attending Indiana University. She'd initially been employed in one of the University's libraries and then had been excited over obtaining a position at the Post Office for considerably more money. She'd supported herself for the most part, including her schooling. She and her brother and sister had each received several thousand dollars four years ago when their grandmother died.

"By the way, the money Katherine sent her mother was a payback of sorts. She mailed her $1,000 in cash last week. This past summer Katherine asked for $300 to have some wisdom teeth pulled, and a month or so later for $200 to get contact lenses."

"I didn't notice any contact lens solution or containers in her medicine chest or toilet case – nothing to suggest she used contacts," said Kelly.

"I didn't either," replied Mike. "And this will also be of interest to you. We've already checked the body for wisdom teeth. They're all there."

"Doesn't that support Mrs. Edwards' belief the body isn't Katherine's, Mike?"

"That was my initial thought too. But there's another possibility, Kelly. Katherine may have just made up a couple reasons for need of money her mother would buy into."

"You could be right. I hadn't thought of that. It would be nice to know where she got the money to pay her mother back. With hefty interest," Kelly added, mulling over this information.

"Tomorrow, Steve will be talking with some of her co-workers at Gratzi. We may learn something from them," Mike said.

"Judy also learned Katherine's sister dropped out of college after her first year. She'd attended Miami of Ohio."

"That's where I went," Kelly interjected. "I was long gone before she arrived."

Mike laughed. "I thought that was the case. Not long gone, but I heard you attended Miami a couple years before transferring to State."

Kelly acknowledged he was right, and listened as he continued.

Mrs. Edwards and her son hadn't known where Beth was currently employed. They hadn't known much about the job she had when she first moved to Chicago. Various waitressing jobs, they thought. Judy had commented to him they'd seemed reluctant to answer questions on that subject. She sensed there was a strained family relationship of some sort with Beth. They'd both acknowledged Katherine had a closer relationship with Beth than either of them had been able to maintain.

Kelly asked if Judy had learned where the brother, Sam, had gone to college.

"Yes," Mike answered. "He attended Rutgers. Judy didn't mention if he'd graduated from there. She did mention he'd just been recently employed by M&M/Mars in Hackettstown, New Jersey."

"In the candy business?" asked Kelly. "Is PayDay$^{(tm)}$ one of their brands?"

Mike smiled again. "I had the same thought. No, PayDay$^{(tm)}$ is made by a company called Leaf. I think they're located somewhere in Illinois."

"A thought just occurred to me, Mike. You mentioned Katherine had worked at the Post Office when she'd been in Bloomington attending I.U. I seem to recollect a person needs to be fingerprinted before being hired for any federal job."

"I think you're right, Kelly. I'll get on it right away tomorrow. That could get the identity question settled in short order. Great idea!"

"Unless," said Kelly.

"Unless what?" asked Mike.

"Unless Beth and Katherine swapped identities prior to Bloomington."

"Why would you even think that?" Mike angrily asked.

"I guess because of all the surprises we've already had. I'm sorry I even suggested that possibility."

The conversation ended with Mike saying he'd see her at eleven tomorrow, and wishing her well with her interview with Jameson in the morning.


# Chapter 5

Kelly was a few minutes early for the meeting with Jameson. It was the first time she'd been in Angell Hall since the recent major refurbishing. She was amazed over what had been done. She'd had no difficulty finding Dean Jameson's office.

A woman who Kelly presumed was his secretary was on the phone when Kelly entered the office. She'd acknowledged Kelly's arrival with a smile and gestured, indicating she'd be with her in a moment. The name plate on the desk read Virginia Dooley.

Kelly could overhear an appointment was being rescheduled. The secretary was explaining to whoever she was talking with that Dean Jameson would be back in the office by Thursday or Friday. Kelly's initial reaction had been Jameson might be rescheduling his appointments to make room for her's. But as she overheard more of the conversation, she realized

Jameson wasn't there.

The woman hung up, flashed Kelly a smile and stood up, offering her hand.

"You must be Kelly Travis? I'm Virginia Dooley, Dean Jameson's secretary." Her smile turned to a look of concern as she explained the Dean had been involved in an accident on his way in to work. Seeing the look of alarm on Kelly's face, she quickly assured her he was going to be fine. She explained she'd just spoken with him on the phone.

"He's at University Hospital. He was struck by a car. He managed to avoid serious injury by leaping out of its path. He just joked now how fortunate he'd been to have been hit where he had the most padding. It struck him," Virginia smiled and blushed, "in the fanny. X-Rays show no broken bones, but he did get scraped up pretty badly on his hands and face. He says he was very lucky, only having some massive bruises."

In answer to Kelly's question, Virginia explained the accident had happened on North University, close to the Michigan League. She'd then described the Dean's daily routine. Parking in the structure to the west of Hill Auditorium and then walking to his office.

"He's an early bird. Always here by six-fifteen a.m., give or take a minute or two. He said he was half-way across the street, possibly day-dreaming, when he heard a screech of tires. He looked up and saw a car headed directly for him. Just the headlights really. He thinks he froze for a second or two and then lunged for the sidewalk. The car clipped him and accelerated his sprawl."

"That's terrible," Kelly commented as her mind whirled, wondering if the accident had anything to do with the "Next PayDay$^{(tm)}$" message. "Do you know if he was able to determine the make or model of the car? Get a license number?"

"No. I mean yes. He told me he wasn't able to. The car's taillights were over a block away when he'd lifted his head. There doesn't appear to have been any witnesses either. Not much activity in that area at that early hour. He was fortunate one of the campus police cars came by a few minutes later. The officer was able to help him and drove him over to emergency at University Hospital.

"He still wants to meet with you. Here's his room number." Virginia handed Kelly a card. She asked Kelly to assure the Dean everything was under control at the office, and she'd already been able to reschedule most of the day's appointments.

"He thinks the driver must have been high on drugs," Virginia said. Kelly had other thoughts and believed Jameson did, too.

Kelly had parked in the lot behind the Michigan Union. She called Mike from her car and told him what had happened to Jameson. He said he'd try to learn more about it, take a look at the police report and talk to the investigating officer. Kelly told him she might be a little late for the eleven o'clock meeting.

•

Even though Virginia had explained Jameson had sustained various injuries in the accident, as she entered his room Kelly was startled by the number of bandages covering his body. His eyes and lips were the only visible parts of his face. Jameson's eyes lit up as he spotted her.

"It's not nearly as bad as it looks. Most of these," he explained, holding up his bandaged hands and referring to the gauze dressings, "will be gone by tomorrow. They're guarding against infection."

Kelly smiled and told Jameson how alarmed she'd been when Virginia had told her about the accident.

"I'm so happy your injuries aren't serious. By the way, Virginia wants you to know she has everything under control."

Jameson's smile was barely detectable. "I'm sure of that. Thank you for coming."

Kelly lowered her voice as she asked him directly whether or not he believed someone had intentionally tried to injure or kill him. He also lowered his voice, replying he'd like to think it was just a freak accident with weird timing.

"But it wasn't an accident. The driver clearly veered, even over the curb a little, trying to hit me."

"I thought as much," said Kelly.

Jameson began shaking his head. "I can't believe this is happening. It's been a nightmare."

Just then a nurse came through the door. "Who's having a nightmare? How we doing in here?"

The middle-aged, somewhat chunky woman flashed a smile in Kelly's direction. "How do you like our creation? He's a work of art, isn't he? We've thought about hanging a sign around his neck – 'White on Black.'"

They all laughed. Sometimes humor was the best means of therapy,

Kelly thought. The good nurses seemed to realize that.

As the nurse continued to chat with Jameson, the thought passed through Kelly's mind that possibly security precautions should be made for Jameson. She'd discuss it with Mike. As the nurse turned to leave, she asked if they wanted the door closed. Kelly nodded and Jameson replied, "Yes, please."

They turned to one another. Jameson began the conversation with an apology for his behavior during their phone call Saturday night.

"I was evasive. I shouldn't have taken my anger out on you. I'm sorry."

Kelly acknowledged his apology with a nod. She smiled. "John, I assume you didn't have an opportunity to see this morning's paper. I've brought a copy," she said, handing him the front section of the *Detroit Free Press*.

He returned her smile. "At least you're calling me John. That's a good sign."

Kelly recalled their previous conversation, when he'd become defensive, saying the fact she was calling him 'Mr. Jameson' indicated he was a prime suspect. Kelly watched his reactions as he read the front page article.

Through the bandages Kelly could see his eyes widen and begin to water. Jameson began shaking his head. "She was tortured. She'd been tied up. Damn."

The article was continued on the back page and with his bandaged hands, he was awkwardly trying to reposition the newspaper. Kelly leaned over and assisted him.

He let the paper fall onto his lap when he finished. Kelly could see what an emotional impact the article had had on him. He was teary-eyed as he looked up at her.

"In a way, I could be responsible. Not directly of course. But if I hadn't allowed my fear to override my better judgment, this might not have ended this way. I didn't see any mention of the PayDay$^{(tm)}$ candy bar being found on her body."

Kelly nodded. "That's one of the details we decided to hold back. There're some others I'll tell you about after we've talked."

Kelly asked if she could tape their conversation.

"Certainly." She noticed he'd hesitated for a second or two.

"When we talked Saturday night," Jameson continued, "the thought crossed my mind I might need a lawyer. Kelly, what I did was wrong. But hopefully you'll understand, even if you don't agree, why I behaved the way I did. I had the motive, but I didn't hurt Katherine in any way. Yes, you can tape everything.

"It all started about three weeks ago," began Jameson.

Kelly held up her hand to interrupt him. "Sorry, John, if we could, let's start with when you first met Katherine Edwards. Okay?"

He nodded. He spoke of Katherine in glowing terms. He recalled his contacts with her from the first day in class to several individual conferences they'd had. Very intelligent, conscientious, enthusiastic, self-confident, were all terms he used to describe her.

"She was a lovely girl. We enjoyed a warm relationship. Strictly professional – student and professor." She'd never overstepped her bounds with him. Never attempted to flirt with him. There'd been nothing to hide in the relationship.

Jameson had then digressed for a moment or two, explaining the fear or danger of a sexual harassment claim being filed had caused all educators to be extra cautious in their dealings with students. In addition to having a wonderful marriage with Marian and not being tempted, it would be career-suicide for him to have an affair with one of his students.

"I've done some dumb things over the years, but I'm not stupid," he said, summing it up.

Jameson then described meeting Katherine in front of the coffee shop three weeks ago. As Marian had become engrossed the night before last, Kelly found herself becoming fully immersed in the flow of John's narrative.

He'd been somewhat embarrassed as he described the photographs. In addition to relating the events, John also described his emotions and thoughts at the time. As he'd indicated she might, Kelly found herself empathizing with him and could understand his motivations for not having discussed his predicament with his wife, Marian, his boss, President Robinson or the police. She'd been fascinated when he'd told of finding the pieces of candy bar on his desk and how he'd interpreted them to mean Katherine and her accomplice wanted $50,000 in two installments. She thought of the PayDay(tm) candy bar and how it had led her to meeting with Jameson this morning.

She glanced at her watch. It was already eleven-fifteen. John had noticed.

"I'm just about finished."

Kelly assured him she'd only been checking the time because of a later appointment. "I've plenty of time. You're doing a beautiful job. Please continue."

He'd been explaining the ruse he'd used to get the $5,000 in cash. He continued, describing the meeting with Katherine in front of the library entrance at the Law Quad.

Kelly's mind was whirling. Katherine had wanted to disappear, get away from a man who she'd claimed forced her into the blackmail scheme. Perhaps he'd discovered Katherine had taken the photographs and negatives. Perhaps he was the one who tortured her. Maybe he'd been trying to get her to tell him what she'd done with them, to tell him where the money she'd obtained from Jameson was hidden. Maybe he'd just gone crazy and cruelly murdered her. Was he the one seeking revenge against Jameson, trying to injure or kill him because of the role he'd played in the collapse of the elaborate blackmail scheme? Who was he? Where was he now? All these thoughts and others flooded Kelly's mind as Jameson continued.

He described how with each passing day his anxieties had lessened. He'd grown more confident that he'd made the right decision to protect Marian, his job and reputation, and the reputation of the University. And then came Saturday afternoon. When he'd seen the banner he'd realized his mistake. Katherine and her accomplice had never had any intention to let him off the hook, he'd reasoned. He was still in a turmoil when Kelly had called later that evening. Jameson appeared exhausted as he finished his story.

"I forgot to ask you, Kelly. Where do you stand in the investigation? Do you have a suspect? Did anything I had to say help you?"

Kelly nodded. "Yes. And thank you for being so straightforward with me."

"I hope you understand now Kelly why I wasn't overly concerned about the PayDay(tm) association. I assumed the banner was a threat. But only warning me I'd have to come up with more money. Maybe this," Jameson continued, referring to his injuries, "could have been avoided if I'd leveled with you sooner – postponed the trip to Chicago."

"You asked if your information helps the investigation. Yes, it does. We knew Katherine had obtained some money. Now we know the source. A question for you, John. Did you know Katherine had a twin sister, Beth?"

"No. She never mentioned that to me."

Kelly then explained the confusion over the identification of the body.

"Katherine's mother firmly believes it's Beth's. Her brother is certain it's Katherine's. We're hopeful we've found a way to determine whose body it actually is in the next day or two."

There was a knock at the door. Kelly called out, "Come in."

The same nurse who'd been in earlier came in. "Sorry to bother you, but your wife's on the phone, Mr. Jameson."

"Thank you." Addressing both Kelly and the nurse, he explained he hadn't spoken to his wife since the accident. He'd left a message on their answering machine and had assured her he was fine.

"Can I take it here?" Jameson asked, reaching for his phone.

"Yes. We'll transfer it. It'll just be a second," said the nurse as she left the room.

Jameson confirmed to Marian once again he was in good shape with no major injuries. He played down the accident. All of a sudden he lunged forward into an upright position. He grimaced in pain, having agitated his bruised hip.

"Marian, that's the ring that was in the photographs," he shouted into the phone. "Where's Barney?" After hearing her answer, with a look of growing concern he spoke again. "Marian, listen carefully. I want you to get out of the house immediately. Use the back door. Don't take time to lock up the house. Head down to the corner of Arlington, a police car will be there in a few minutes. They'll bring you up here to the hospital. Now move! Fast!"

As Jameson attempted to hang up, he turned to Kelly.

"Can we do that? Get a police car there right away? She just found the monogrammed ring on my bureau in our bedroom. The one the man having intercourse with Katherine was wearing in the photograph!"

He handed the phone to Kelly. She called 911, introduced herself and explained what needed to be done.

"It's an emergency. Tell the officer to bring her to University Hospital. Drop her off at the main entrance. That's right. Picking her up immediately is the main concern."

Kelly hung up. "I'll go down and meet her. Could the ring in the photograph have been a duplicate of yours?"

"Possibly, I guess. But mine was missing. They wouldn't need a copy." Jameson regretted now he'd destroyed all the photos. The police may have learned something from them. "One photo was a blow-up of the

47

man's hand, showing the ring."

"I remember," said Kelly. "I think I'll go back to your house with the officer and take a look around. You think someone came in and placed the ring on your bureau?"

Jameson nodded yes.

"By the way. Who is Barney?"

In spite of his tenseness and concern, Jameson was able to smile. "Our dog. A black Lab. Marian dropped her off at the vet earlier this morning."

## Chapter 6

Standing inside the main entrance to the hospital, Kelly saw a police cruiser turn into the driveway. She went out to the curbside to await its arrival. Marian spotted her from the passenger seat and flashed her a smile. Kelly opened the cruiser door for her.

"Are you okay?" Kelly asked, embracing Marian as she exited from the car.

Marian hugged Kelly tightly in return, replying, "I'm fine, but how's John?"

"He's doing well. His biggest concern is you. He's anxious to see you. Considering how serious he could have been injured, he's in excellent shape. Don't be shocked by all the bandages. He says most of them will be removed by tomorrow."

Kelly recognized the officer, Jeff Miller, who had walked around the car and was now standing beside them. She nodded her head in recognition as she explained to Marian.

"Jeff and I are going back to your house to have a look. Did you happen to notice anything else out of the ordinary – in addition to finding your husband's ring?"

Marian shook her head, saying "No, not really. I'd only been home for a few minutes and then after talking with John I immediately left."

Knowing Marian was anxious to see her husband, Kelly apologized for delaying her. "I'll be in touch with you shortly."

•

Kelly used Jeff's car phone to call Mike at headquarters. She quickly provided him with an overview of her conversation with Jameson, the call from his wife, and explained Jeff Miller and she were on their way to the Jameson's home to take a look around.

"I recorded his complete story and will bring it in with me. Could you give some thought in the meantime to whether we should be considering any security for the Jamesons? Unless we run into some surprise, I should see you in an hour or so."

Mike told her there had been some added developments that he'd discuss with her then.

As they continued east on Geddes on their way to the Jamesons', Jeff briefed Kelly on his conversation with Mrs. Jameson. He explained she'd come home shortly before noon after running several errands, including dropping the dog off at the vet for shots and grooming. She'd carried a couple bags of groceries into the house and taken a few minutes to put them away. She'd stopped by the bank to make a deposit and had gotten some cash for herself and her husband. Just normal spending money. She'd taken the envelope containing money for him upstairs to their bedroom to leave on her husband's dresser top. She'd noticed the ring then.

"She told me just a little about the ring being used in a blackmail scheme. She said she hadn't made that association when she first spotted it. Rather, she said, she was pleased that the woman who comes in to clean each week had probably come across it and put it on the dresser. She went back downstairs to check the answering machine for calls and that was the first she knew about her husband's accident. She immediately called the hospital, and . . . "

"Just a minute, Jeff. Pull over." They were now on Arlington, less than a block away from the Jamesons'. "Did you notice that parked car we passed? Was it a Saab?"

Jeff glanced in his rearview mirror. "Could be. It's a convertible." He had put the cruiser into reverse gear, backing up towards the car they'd just passed. Kelly explained why she'd asked, telling him about the green Saab convertible witnesses had seen at the murdered girl's apartment complex.

"We still haven't determined who owns it or if it has any bearing on the case," Kelly said.

Jeff waited for another car to pass and then backed around the parked car so the license plate could be seen.

"You're right, Kelly. It's a Saab and dark green. Illinois plates."

Kelly noticed the Illinois plates as well. Just a coincidence, she pondered. Katherine Edwards' sister lived in Chicago. Could this car be connected to the person who'd entered the Jamesons' house with the ring? The individual who might still be there?

"Jeff, take down the number. We'll run a check on it."

"I might be able to do better than that," Jeff said, climbing out of the car. He went to the door of the Saab and winked back at Kelly as he found it unlocked. He entered the car and leaned over to the glove compartment. A moment later he exited the Saab and returned to the police car.

"Sorry, Kelly. The glove compartment's locked. I thought we'd be able to save time; find the registration."

Kelly smiled. "It was worth the try. Let's get over to the Jamesons'. Park a few doors away. Don't use the driveway," Kelly suggested.

As Jeff turned the corner and pulled over to park, he commented. "There was nothing in the car, just some candy on the front seat."

"Candy!" Kelly exclaimed, with the thought of the PayDay$^{(tm)}$ bar immediately coming to mind. "What kind?"

Jeff looked at Kelly, surprised by her reaction. "Just a small bag of Hershey's Kisses$^{(tm)}$ and a Kit Kat$^{(tm)}$ bar."

"That's all? Did you notice a PayDay$^{(tm)}$ bar?"

Jeff smiled over her curious question. "No, just the two items."

Kelly debated over whether she should explain the significance of her question to Jeff. She decided not to. She directed their conversation to how they should go about checking out the Jamesons' home. Mrs. Jameson had explained to Jeff a key was hidden under a flower pot on the back door steps.

"They have an alarm system but Mrs. Jameson said they frequently didn't turn it on during the day. It wasn't armed this morning," Jeff informed Kelly.

•

Kelly's and Jeff's search of the house came up with nothing new. Everything looked as if it was in its proper place with no open drawers or closet doors. Their extensive exploration convinced them no one was still in the house. They'd worked as a team and had their guns out covering for one another during the search. They found no signs of a forced entry. There were a couple wet leaves on the kitchen floor near the back entrance and also on the front stair. They could have as easily come from Mrs. Jameson's shoes as the intruder's. The Jamesons would have to determine if anything had been taken or if anything appeared out of the ordinary.

They returned to their car. Kelly asked if she could be dropped off at her car in the University Hospital parking structure. Jeff made a U-turn and they turned onto Arlington.

"The car's gone," said Jeff.

Kelly nodded. "We'll try to get the owner identified. We've no reason to put an alert out just yet. Maybe we'll have to interview nearby residents. See if they know who it belongs to or saw who was driving it. Possibly Jameson's neighbors as well. See if they saw any strangers this morning," Kelly said.

•

Following Kelly's arrival, Mike had invited Judy Wilson and Steve Renz to join them in the conference room. As she took a seat, Kelly could see Mike had been busy. Further information on the case was apparent on the wall panels – notes, statements and questions.

Mike began by asking Kelly to brief them on her interview with Jameson. Everyone seemed to be aware of the events of the morning and how Jameson had ended up at University Hospital. After a few comments, Kelly turned on the tape and played the entire conversation for them. As they heard Jameson describe the photographs and the blow-up showing a man's hand wearing his ring, Mike showed particular interest as he made notes. The three exchanged looks as they heard Jameson say he'd given five thousand in cash to Katherine Edwards. As Kelly had done, during Jameson's story the others appeared to identify with his plight and motivations for having acted in the way he did. When Jameson described his reaction to seeing the plane over the stadium towing the banner with the "Next PayDay$^{(tm)}$" message followed by his seat location, Kelly could sense the others identifying with Jameson's read of the message as a notice he'd be asked to pay additional money and his angry reaction.

When the tape ended, Kelly reviewed the phone conversation Jameson had with his wife, and his concerned and fearful reaction on learning she'd found the ring on his bureau. Kelly concluded by telling them of her search of the Jameson home with Jeff Miller. Reaching into her pocket for the card on which Jeff had written the license plate number, Kelly told them about the dark green Saab convertible they'd seen parked a block away from the Jamesons' home.

"It had Illinois plates. This is the number," Kelly said, handing the card to Steve. Kelly explained that Jeff had found the car door unlocked and had tried the glove compartment. "It was locked. There was some candy on the passenger seat, a bag of Hershey's Kisses[tm] and a Kit Kat[tm] bar. When Jeff told me he'd seen some candy in the car, I got excited thinking it might be some PayDay[tm] bars," Kelly said with a smile.

"By the way – the car was gone when we returned from searching the house. Can you follow through on this?" she asked Steve.

"Right away. I was able to get a listing of owners of green convertibles from the Saab dealer this morning. Individuals they've either sold or serviced. There are over thirty; six from out of state. Two from New York, three Ohio and one Indiana. None from Illinois."

"Thanks Steve," Mike said. "There's been a new development that I haven't shared with any of you yet."

"Before you do, can I ask Kelly a question?" asked Judy, interrupting Mike.

"Go ahead."

Turning to Kelly, Judy asked, "Are you convinced Jameson has been completely truthful? Earlier this morning we were discussing his accident. It certainly throws off suspicion, but there weren't any witnesses. Really just his word. All his injuries could have been self-inflicted. No sign of a break-in at their home. Do we know where he was Friday night?"

"Yes and no," Kelly answered. "Jameson raised the same questions you have. He saw with his clear motive how someone might have those questions. I gave him the *Free Press* article to read at the hospital this morning. I believe he was truly shocked to learn Katherine had been tortured. As to Friday evening, he was home with his wife. She went up to bed early, even before all the trick or treaters had come. She was sound asleep when he came up, he says.

"My gut feeling is Jameson had nothing to do with Katherine's death. It wasn't an act of momentary rage or temporary insanity. Someone took time to inflict those injuries. Whether whoever it was really intended to kill her, I guess we still don't know. Yes, Jameson's story is the only thing leading us to believe there was a man – accomplice, boyfriend – forcing her into the blackmail scheme. A person she had to get away from. Whether that's true or not, I'm inclined to believe that's what Jameson was told.

Mike and I saw how sanitized the apartment looked.

"Yes, I think he's leveled with us. I think whoever killed Katherine Edwards holds Jameson responsible for foiling the elaborate blackmail scheme and giving Katherine the means – cash – to attempt to flee. There are still a multitude of unanswered questions. I don't think we'll find Jameson has any more answers for us than he's already provided. I feel sorry for him and his wife. His career may be in jeopardy and they may be in danger of further injury."

Judy nodded. "I share your thoughts. You've dealt with him personally, I just thought the question needed to be asked."

"You're right," said Mike. "I think we've all asked the question ourselves. Kelly, I've already talked with the hospital administrator regarding security for Jameson. His wife will be spending the night at the hotel facility in the hospital. She'll be escorted by hospital security personnel who'll also be keeping an eye on Jameson. I talked with both the Jamesons. They're comfortable with those arrangements. He'll probably be discharged tomorrow. We'll play it by ear as to whether or not or what kind of security we can provide for them at home."

Judy had slipped a note in front of Kelly. On the paper Judy had written the names of the candies Jeff had seen on the front seat of the Saab. She had circled the "she" in Hershey, the "is" in Kisses$^{(tm)}$ and the "KAT" in Kit Kat$^{(tm)}$. She'd also circled the "H" in Hershey and drawn an arrow to move it to the end of the word KAT.

Kelly saw what Judy had done and looked up. "She is KATH. You're either a genius or really grasping for straws," Kelly said, passing Judy's note over for Mike and Steve to see.

"Do we have anything more on the identification of the body?"

Mike and Steve were smiling as they saw what Judy had done. "We sent fingerprints from the body to the FBI in Washington this morning. They have Katherine Edwards' prints on file there and will make a comparison. You were right Kelly, about her being fingerprinted for employment with the Post Office. We should have an answer by tomorrow morning."

"Judy, you're suggesting whoever was driving the Saab might have purchased the candy with plans to communicate to someone the same message you have. Seems we're stretching credibility a bit, but guess we can't rule it out. Steve, any idea how long it will take to get information back on the Illinois plate number? I don't think we can ask the chief to put out an alert on the car on Judy's theory alone."

"I'll get someone working on it immediately. High priority. Hopefully, we can have something within the hour," Steve said.

"Get it started and then get back here. I still have the other new development I want you all to hear," Mike said.

•

While Steve was gone, Judy and Mike brought Kelly up to date on some of the other areas of the investigation. The Chicago police had still not located Elizabeth Edwards. Her apartment was unoccupied. A neighbor indicated it wasn't unusual for Beth to be gone for a few days or even a week. The neighbor knew of a sister in Ann Arbor, Michigan, who Beth would visit from time to time. She also said Beth had a boyfriend and believed she would spend a night or two with him every few weeks. She didn't know the name of the boyfriend, although she'd seen him several times. She thought she remembered him being introduced to her as Joe. Beth had also once mentioned to her he was a free lance photographer. The other neighbors knew even less about Elizabeth Edwards. None knew where she was employed. Two thought she was a model or actress.

"One surprise," said Judy, "was learning the apartment building she's in is fairly upscale, with rent in the $2,000 per month range. The Chicago police also concluded she hadn't been in the apartment for several days, on the basis of unclaimed mail and finding items in her refrigerator with expired freshness dates – late October."

"They left a note for her to contact them," said Mike. "Even though her name's on file as a missing person and they've promised to keep checking the apartment, I'm not optimistic."

"Nor am I," Judy commented. "Records don't show a vehicle registration under her name. Some of her neighbors think she has a car, but have no clue as to its make or model."

The conversation then moved onto what had been learned from the pilot of the plane which towed the sign on Saturday.

"Steve says it's a one-man operation. Brad Oberdahl is his name. He books the orders, collects the money in advance, assembles the banners and flies the plane," Judy said. "Last Thursday morning he had a call from a woman wanting a message flown on Saturday. He told her she was too late and that he needed a minimum of one week's notice. She asked him his price and he explained the charges to her. The cost varies based on the number of letters in the message and the number of passes over the stadium."

Judy continued, saying Mr. Oberdahl then told Steve the woman had become very emotional, saying she'd been told a week ago to make arrangements and she'd probably lose her job if she couldn't convince him to make an exception. A winner of a lottery of some kind was being announced, and chances had been sold on the basis of the winner being announced in this fashion at the football game on Saturday. She tearfully told him she'd pay double his normal charge and pay cash. Steve said Mr. Oberdahl explained he'd felt sorry for her and agreed to do it.

"Steve thinks the amount she was willing to pay, in cash, prompted his change of heart," said Judy with a grin.

"Two hours later the money was dropped off in a plain white envelope by a man driving a motorbike," Mike said. "Oberdahl said he was probably in his twenties. He was wearing sunglasses and a baseball cap. Oberdahl couldn't provide much of a description. He didn't remember how he was dressed or any design on the cap. The fellow simply handed him the envelope, saying he'd been told to deliver it to him."

Steve entered the conference room just as Mike was finishing up. "We won't have anything until tomorrow," he said.

"How come so long? Why the delay?" asked Mike.

"I talked to them myself. It's the best they'll do. They've tightened procedures since being hit by some kind of scam. People were using the info to create counterfeit titles to sell stolen vehicles. We'll have it tomorrow."

Steve then turned to Kelly and asked, "Did you or Jeff notice if the car had any damage to the passenger side front end?"

Kelly shook her head. "I didn't notice any. I'm sorry I didn't look. Maybe Jeff noticed something."

Explaining why he'd asked the question, Steve said, "I thought if there was, we could send out an alert on the basis of the car possibly being involved in a hit-and-run accident. I'll ask Jeff. I'll contact him after Mike's gone over the new development he wanted to brief us on."

"I hadn't planned to delay sharing this information with you," Mike began. "But in hindsight, it works out for the best with all of us now having been appraised of Jameson's story and other facts. Benton had a call from Ty this morning."

That statement alone piqued everyone's interest, as Mike knew it would. Ty was the near-legendary head football coach at the University of Michigan. One of those rare individuals who could be identified by a first name and all would know who was being discussed. Ty Partinelli was regarded as one of the best – if not the best – football coaches in the country.

"He was calling on behalf of one of his assistants and asked David if he and the assistant coach, Tim Masterson, could meet with him on a confidential basis this morning. He met with them at eleven o'clock in Ty's office."

Mike then paused and cautioned all of them that the Chief wanted this matter to remain very confidential.

"David will be amazed when I brief him on Jameson. I think he'll have the same opinion there."

Mike then proceeded to tell them what David Benton had learned that morning. Tim Masterson had been blackmailed by Katherine Edwards in almost the identical way in which Jameson had. Masterson had been in a speech class with Edwards this past summer. He said a friendship developed, but there was absolutely nothing of a romantic nature involved. He described her as a lovely girl with a delightful personality and they'd simply joked and chatted in the classroom. He said he'd never met with her privately.

"A month ago, Katherine called Masterson and explained her father was coming to visit and she'd like to take him to a football game. She hadn't been able to obtain tickets and wondered if he could help her. It was tickets for this past Saturday's game, incidentally," Mike continued.

"He told her he was sure he could and they discussed how he'd go about getting them to her. Masterson had a meeting scheduled at the Michigan Union the next day and suggested she meet him prior to the meeting. She was waiting on the front steps when he arrived. She was very appreciative. They chatted for only a couple of minutes. At one point she'd taken his hands in hers, joking about whether he'd been able to control his habit of overly gesturing with his hands as he spoke. He'd been teased in their speech class over it. As she was excusing herself, she nearly tripped on the steps. He grabbed her to prevent her fall. She thanked him again for the tickets and for breaking her fall, and with her arms clinging to him gave him a brush kiss on the lips. Sound familiar?" Mike asked.

"Masterson's reaction was similar to how Jameson described his. He was flustered and shocked, had glanced around to see if anyone had noticed in the hub of activity – with hordes of students and others going up and down the steps. Edwards was gone in seconds.

"Then came the envelope with the photos. One of the staged ones showed Katherine dressed in a cheerleading outfit, nude from the waist down, engaged in sex with a muscular man whose face was hidden from view.

"Now you'll be thinking I'm making this up. One photo showed an enlargement of the man's hand and the Rose Bowl ring he was wearing. Masterson received one in the early seventies when he played for Michigan. He says he doesn't wear it much except for athletic and University functions. He didn't know it was missing until he checked after he received the photos.

"The clippings of the mastheads of the *Michigan Daily*, *Ann Arbor News*, *Detroit Free Press* and *News* were sent with the photos, similar to what Jameson received. And get this. There was a Now & Later(tm) candy bar enclosed as well. Taped above the words Now and Later(tm) were circles with the number ten, probably taken from the wrappers of ten-cent pre-priced candies.

"The next day he had a telephone call. A whispering voice, he couldn't tell if it was a man's or a woman's, said with two payments the photos and negatives would be his. When he'd tried to talk with the person, the whispered talk just continued and he realized it was a recording. The essence of the message was he would have to pay $10,000 now, prior to Halloween, and $10,000 later, or prior to Christmas. Cash in $50 denominations or less was specified. The voice said he'd be given payment instructions the following Monday.

"On Monday morning, a week ago today, he was told to bring an envelope containing the money to the side door of the Michigan Union at eight a.m. the next day. He was to hold the envelope in front of his chest. Someone would approach him and say, "Thanks, Coach" and take it from him. This was a recorded message also. He was warned if there were any tricks, he wouldn't get a second chance. The message ended with the statement the money requested was small potatoes compared to the contract he'd soon be signing.

"Masterson explained and Ty confirmed that four major universities were interested in him as a head coach, and the University had given them its permission to talk with Masterson. Similar to Jameson, you can sympathize with the predicament Masterson was in. He knew he should be confiding in Ty, informing the police, while at the same time seeing the possibility his life-long dream to be a head coach was in jeopardy.

"He obtained the money, a story in itself, and was at the Union's side door a little before eight a.m. A man on a motorbike suddenly appeared on the sidewalk in front of him, said, "Thanks, Coach" and grabbed the envelope. He drove the bike down the sidewalk towards State Street, crossed over and then quickly disappeared along the walkways leading to the Diag – the middle of campus. If Masterson would have had someone, even us, watching – it would have been nearly impossible to have tailed him."

Steve was shaking his head. "Gives more credibility to Jameson's story. Makes you wonder how many others she or they may have entrapped. How did he get the money?"

"He had just over ten thousand dollars in a savings account and he transferred it over to his checking account. He has a neighbor who manages one of the Kroger stores. He told him he was surprising his wife with a used car and needed $7,500 cash. His friend cashed the check for him. The manager of one of the local sporting goods stores was also given a similar story and was glad to accommodate him."

"Has Masterson been contacted in any way since he made that first payment?" Kelly asked.

"No. The story in this morning's paper made him realize his mistake and the jeopardy he could be placing himself in. He went to Ty immediately and Ty called David."

"Was Masterson able to provide a description of the man who picked up the money?"

"No, not much of one. Masterson said he was wearing a helmet and sunglasses. He was dressed in a brown leather jacket, blue jeans and athletic shoes. The description was similar to the one the pilot gave. Perhaps the same person, in his mid-twenties, he'd guessed."

Kelly knew of Tim Masterson's reputation as the all-American boy. He'd been a star fullback and All Big Ten selection during his playing days at Michigan. He'd also had a high grade point average and been a co-captain. He'd returned to his alma mater eight or nine years ago and had been the offensive coordinator for the past four years. During that period, Michigan had been among the top two or three teams in the country every year in points scored and total yardage. He enjoyed nearly as high a profile on campus as Ty Partinelli. Over the past year there had been much speculation over Masterson leaving to become the head coach elsewhere. Notre Dame was said to be very interested.

In last year's Rose Bowl, with time running out, Michigan had kicked for a tie rather than go for the two-point conversion. The decision had not been popular with some fans. Michigan had finished third in the national polls and fans thought a victory would have given them a strong chance for number one. As a result, bumper stickers had surfaced with the name "Tie Partinelli." His career would probably always be tainted by that decision. There were even some letters to the editor, suggesting it was time for Ty to move on and Masterson should be the new head coach.

"I'd like to tell Jameson about Masterson being blackmailed," Kelly said. "I think it would put his mind at ease somewhat to know he wasn't the only one to be suckered – the only one to have allowed himself to be blackmailed. Masterson should be told about Jameson, too. Perhaps it could be done without revealing identities. Misery loves company and both have to be second-guessing their decisions at this point."

"I think you're right, Kelly," Mike responded. "There should be some type of communication. When we're done here, you and I can update David and get his opinion on how best to proceed."

"I wonder if Elizabeth Edwards has a photograph of her boyfriend in the apartment," Judy commented. "If so, perhaps we could have them send us a copy. I'd like to show it to Overdahl and Masterson."

"You're thinking he's involved?" asked Steve. "Makes some sense. One of the neighbors suggested he was into photography. He could have been the one who took the photographs – the staged photos as well – with the access and ability to get them developed and make prints."

"Just a thought," said Judy, "but I mentioned Elizabeth's mother and brother were reluctant, seemingly embarrassed to talk about her employment. The cost of the apartment would suggest she must have a substantial income. One of her neighbors also indicated she was into modeling or acting. Might be stretching things a bit, but what if she were involved in being photographed for the adult magazines or videos? It could explain the staged photos and access to other models. It could be Elizabeth in those posed photos. I guess all the photos, when you think about it. Maybe impersonating her sister."

"You might be onto something, Judy," Mike said, "especially with the seeming disappearance of the sister. I've had an uncomfortable feeling about Katherine's involvement in the blackmail. Both Jameson and

Masterson described a girl who would be highly unlikely to conceive and be involved in the extortion scheme. Bright, beautiful, enthusiastic – still strange things happen. I suppose her sister and the boyfriend could have concocted the whole thing without her knowledge. Katherine finds out and attempts to reverse the damage – even blow the whistle."

"She would have had to be aware, wouldn't she?" asked Steve. "I think it's more likely she may have been roped into it and then got cold feet. Maybe her conscience got to her. Innocent girl being conned by her sister seems far-fetched to me."

"We'll know more tomorrow when the fingerprint analysis comes back, and maybe something on the car," Mike said. "If the plot blew up in the sister's and boyfriend's face and they either intentionally or unintentionally killed Katherine, why would they continue to stay in Ann Arbor? That is, if things happened the way Jameson says."

"And we don't have any reason to believe he's lying," said Kelly. "But you're right. If one of the blackmail targets was responsible for Kath's death, it might explain why someone is still hanging around. And how does that absurd costume fit in? I think Steve raises a good point with his suggestion there may be a number of others who were being similarly blackmailed. Maybe without revealing details or identities we can tell the media about the blackmail element in the case. See if it prompts others to come forward. They might have better information about the man involved or also have some written messages or other photographs which could help us. Were Masterson's photographs tested for prints?"

"Yes," Mike answered. "And the only prints we found were his. Not surprising. We're dealing with someone or more than one who gave considerable thought to this extortion plan. Because of unusual circumstances, Jameson and Masterson were particularly vulnerable. Someone was clever enough to put that together. We should try to determine who else on campus the Edwards girl may have had contact with that may have also been vulnerable to being blackmailed."

## Chapter 7

When Kelly and Mike arrived at Benton's office a few minutes later, his secretary explained he was on the phone. "It's the President of the University," she confided to them in a hushed tone. "This morning the

Chief had a meeting with Ty."

Kelly and Mike both smiled. She was definitely excited and taking pride in the fact her boss was communicating with two of the highest pro-filed individuals in town. As they chatted with her it was evident she felt her status had just risen a notch or two.

It was another ten minutes before David opened his door and ushered Kelly and Mike inside. Motioning them to chairs, he said, "This Hallow-een murder gets spookier by the minute. Let me brief you on that conver-sation. First, though, give me an update on Dean Jameson. Was he being blackmailed?"

Mike gestured to Kelly, who quickly related to Benton the essence of her conversation with Jameson. As she talked she made comparisons to some of the details Benton had learned from Masterson earlier in the day. He clapped his hands and smiled when Kelly mentioned Jameson's ring. An enlarged photograph showing just a hand wearing the ring was also used, Kelly explained. Benton's smile was replaced by a look of alarm and concern when Kelly told of the ring's mysterious appearance on the dresser in Jameson's bedroom.

Kelly also told Benton about seeing the green Saab with Illinois plates parked within a block of the Jameson's. He chuckled when Kelly told of the candy on the front seat and Judy's interpretation. As she finished, Kelly stated her reasons for believing both Jameson and Masterson should be told someone else had been blackmailed in an almost identical fashion. Mike intervened, saying he agreed with Kelly and went on to suggest some-thing should be said at the media briefing in regard to the extortion element in the case, in hopes others who'd been targeted would come forward. David smiled. "I will. Good point. And someone already has."

Kelly and Mike glanced at one another. Could President Robinson have been a target? The case continued to grow in magnitude and com-plexity.

"I was on the phone with President Robinson. Just prior to the call, he'd been meeting with Clare Singleton."

Clare Singleton was the assistant athletic director at Michigan and responsible for the majority of the women's teams. She'd been highly successful and as a result enjoyed an excellent reputation on campus. The women's teams were now beginning to match the traditional winning ways of the men's teams. The volleyball and basketball teams were close to paying their own way. The turnaround since Clare Singleton's arrival had

61

been dramatic.

Controversy had flared in the past few months, however, when news surfaced of a screening policy to reduce and/or eliminate the number of lesbians participating in various sports. This had been a painful and embarrassing episode for the University and Clare. It tarnished the success which had just begun to materialize for women's sports at Michigan. The controversy had generated national as well as local attention and still simmered.

"Clare told Robinson she'd been the target of a blackmail attempt by Katherine Edwards. The circumstances are very similar to those of the other two, Masterson and Jameson. Compromising photographs, a request for money – the difference being that according to Clare, she'd told Katherine to get lost."

Benton then proceeded to summarize the details. At some of the women's sports events there were frequently only a handful of spectators. When the Michigan team was victorious it seemed everyone in their enthusiasm hugged, and sometimes kissed, one another in joy – teammates, coaches and fans. Clare only remembered Katherine Edwards vaguely as a spectator at one or two events this past fall. The batch of photographs Clare received showed two of her and the Edwards girl embracing one another. The photos didn't show the setting, giving the impression the two were carrying on in private. Other photographs showed two women engaged in oral sex. One was clearly Edwards. The face or identity of the other couldn't be determined due to their positions and the camera angle.

"Clare frequently wears a unique, braided hairdo. The unidentified woman's hair was done in a similar fashion. In addition, the unidentified woman in the photo was wearing a charm bracelet. Clare has a bracelet containing charms, some custom made, of all the sports programs with which she's been associated. Similar to the photos sent to the men, one was an enlargement of the woman's arm and hand, clearly showing the bracelet – Clare's bracelet.

"Clare told Robinson she was unaware the bracelet had been missing. After receiving the photographs she went to her condo over the lunch hour and the bracelet was there, in the same dresser drawer where she always kept it.

"One possibility I thought of, in addition to someone having removed it and replaced it, is a doctored photo. A photo could have been taken of Clare when she was wearing the bracelet and used in a way to show Clare's arm wearing the bracelet on the woman resembling her in the staged photos."

Benton glanced at his watch. "The press conference is scheduled in twenty minutes. I'll give you the other details later." He grinned. "Just one more thing, however. Clare's a spunky lady. She'd been instructed to bring an envelope containing $5,000 in cash to the West Quadrangle Dormitory at ten a.m. a week ago today – the west entrance. She prepared an envelope containing a stack of bill-sized slips of paper and a note saying she wouldn't ever pay a cent and she'd do everything she could to see her tormentors in prison. In addition," he said, smiling, "she gave them a taste of their own doing by including a Zero candy bar in the envelope."

Kelly and Mike also smiled as Benton continued. "That's not all. She dressed in a warm-up suit to make the delivery and concealed a softball bat in one pant leg. As she was waiting on the steps, one of the top players from the women's basketball team came out of the door, recognized Clare, and started to talk. A minute or two later a young man grabbed the envelope and ran into the dormitory. In attempting to retrieve the bat from her pant leg, Clare stumbled down the steps and twisted her ankle. Robinson said Clare laughed as she'd described the incident, joking she hoped the player wouldn't transfer. Clare didn't provide her with much of an explanation and said she'd left her wide-eyed, wondering what was going on.

"We'd better get to the briefing. I think I can handle it, but why don't the two of you join me. We'll make it short, and then get back together. Singleton knows we'll be contacting her."

•

The Chief was handling the briefing well, Kelly thought, giving the illusion considerable information was being disseminated while sharing very little. Kelly was surprised by the turnout, nearly forty people plus at least three television crews with their equipment.

Benton explained the ongoing investigation had unearthed evidence showing Katherine Edwards had recently been involved in attempts to blackmail several individuals in the University community.

"We still don't have a complete picture of how this relates to her murder or the number of other people who may have been involved. We're seeking your help to ask persons who may have been a target of an extortion attempt or know of someone who was victimized to come forward. As in the cases which we are aware of, we promise complete confidentiality. They can call me directly or Detective Cummings, whom you have previously met, who's heading up our investigation. People are invited to use our 800 Hot Line as well."

Mike had raised his hand as Benton referred to him, to introduce himself to those who had not been present at the earlier briefings. Benton continued by explaining the department had still not been able to locate Katherine Edwards' twin sister, Elizabeth, who lived in Chicago.

"We're very anxious to talk with her. The Chicago police are cooperating with us. You can also be of help by spreading the word we wish she would contact us."

Following his introductory comments, David opened up for questions. They were fairly basic and Benton had no difficulty addressing them. Most called for a re-telling of facts shared at the Sunday briefing. Then came the zinger. Kelly's mind had been wandering and she hadn't seen who had asked the question.

"Is it possible the body is the twin sister's, Elizabeth Edwards, rather than Katherine Edwards'?"

Kelly could picture tomorrow morning's headlines – "Police Unsure of Body Identification," "Body Could Be Twin's." Her concern and fear proved unwarranted, however, as David immediately and directly answered the question.

"As we told you yesterday, the body has been identified by members of the immediate family. We have also been fortunate to have Katherine Edwards' fingerprints. She'd been employed by the federal government – the post office department – when she attended Indiana University in Bloomington. The FBI is assisting us in making the comparison. Ms. Edwards' mother and brother were also able to provide us with some added details, scars from childhood injuries for example, to assist us in the identification. Further questions?"

Benton appeared to have successfully addressed the subject without revealing a question still remained. If it turned out the body was in fact not Katherine's, but the sister's, Benton hadn't said anything which could later be used to accuse him and the department of intentionally deceiving the media or lying to them. Let's hope, Kelly thought, Mrs. Edwards doesn't go to the media with her belief that the body is actually Elizabeth's until we have the FBI comparison tomorrow. Winding down, Benton explained the next briefing would be held at the same time tomorrow, Tuesday.

"If anything major occurs, we'll inform you of plans for a special briefing. Thanks for your help. I repeat – the investigation is proceeding smoothly and we hope to have further significant details for you soon."

•

Back in Benton's office, David provided Kelly and Mike additional details in regard to Clare Singleton. They also informed him of other aspects of the investigation. They concluded with a discussion over whether special security or protection should be arranged for the Jamesons following his discharge tomorrow. David said he'd make arrangements.

"We don't want to embarrass the Jamesons or alarm the neighbors with a cruiser in their driveway. We'll do it as inconspicuously as possible. Tell Jameson we'll be contacting him with the pertinent details when you brief him on the fact he wasn't the only one being blackmailed."

"What about Singleton and Masterson too?" asked Mike. "Should we be considering protection for them? At the least, informing them they could be in danger."

"Let's do the latter. When you speak with Clare and Tim, Kelly, advise them one of the others being blackmailed was involved in a suspicious hit and run accident. Maybe even take it a step further. Explain a home was possibly broken into by someone tied in with the blackmailing. Also, caution them on the car, the green Saab, which may be involved. You'll probably want to talk to Clare face to face. Tim and Jameson can probably be handled by phone. Advise them to take some precautions, to keep their doors locked. To be on the alert for anything or anyone that seems suspicious. And most important, tell them to let us know immediately if something occurs."

David smiled. "One other point. Remind them not to take matters into their own hands, the way Clare was planning to do."

As Kelly approached her office a few minutes later, she could hear Judy lashing out at Steve. Kelly poked her head through the door to Judy's office and said, "Whoa! What's going on? The tension getting to everyone?"

Judy looked up, still with a glare on her face. Steve looked sheepish. Judy tossed a package of Doublemint Gum in Kelly's direction.

"We have a murderer on the loose and Steve's treating it as a joke," she said in a loud, angry tone.

65

"The joke backfired. I said I'm sorry," Steve responded.

Kelly had the gum in her hand, reading the typed message taped to the pack. It read, "Call me," with a telephone number followed by the initials "K.M.E."

"What's the phone number, Steve? The morgue, probably." Judy was still angry.

"Let's just forget it happened," pleaded Steve. "The gum was sitting in my desk drawer. I thought you'd appreciate the humor, I'm sorry."

The least said the better, Kelly thought, finding it difficult not to smile. She'd grown up with the Doublemint twins. Though the wrong time and wrong target, she could still appreciate Steve's humor. She briefed the two of them about Clare Singleton, explaining she was going to meet with her and also contact Masterson and Jameson to advise them they hadn't been the sole targets of the blackmail attempts by Katherine Edwards.

"I'll also be advising them to take some precautions. Steve, were you able to ask Jeff if he noticed any damage to the Saab?"

"I was, but no, he doesn't recall one way or another. We'll have to wait until we hear from Illinois tomorrow."

Turning to Judy, Kelly asked, "Did we ever learn what name Katherine's middle initial represents?"

Judy had simmered down. "I thought I'd told you." She smiled as she explained she had learned from Katherine's mother that Katherine had chosen it herself. Her parents hadn't given her a middle name. With the three syllables in Katherine, her parents hadn't believed it was necessary. Katherine thought otherwise. The "M" stands for "missing" – the missing middle name.

## Chapter 8

Jameson had been pleased to receive Kelly's call and learn he hadn't been the only one who'd been targeted in the blackmail scheme. Kelly didn't go into all the details, but did tell him enough so he could see the elements in the other instances they were aware of were nearly identical to his. She explained that she'd be keeping his identity confidential in conversations with the other two individuals who'd been victimized and any others who surfaced. He thanked her, saying he appreciated this consideration. He'd been intrigued by the fact an article of unique jewelry had been used to give credence to the staged photos in both other cases and had said, "I'm sad for the others, but at the same time pleased their stories give mine more credibility. Can I share the information with Marian?"

"Certainly. I forgot to mention candy played a role in the other cases, too. Not a PayDay<sup>(tm)</sup> bar, but other brands and items."

Kelly told him someone would be contacting him in regard to arranging some form of security following his discharge. To reinforce the need for it, she told him of seeing the green Saab parked near his home and finding candy on the front seat. She also told him that information on the ownership of the car would probably be obtained before his discharge and she'd keep him informed. As they ended the conversation, Jameson told her the name of another professor whose name had come up during conversations with Katherine Edwards. "She said he was her other favorite instructor. Lying here, I've tried to think of anything that could help you."

Kelly thanked him and made a note to pass the name on to Judy.

•

Kelly next called Clare Singleton, introduced herself and asked if she would be available to meet with her this evening. Clare said she had been expecting to be contacted and to just name the time and place.

"How about your place, maybe nine?" asked Kelly, checking her watch. It was already past seven-thirty.

"That's fine for me, I'll be expecting you."

Kelly then called Tim Masterson. His wife answered and explained her husband had just left to drive the kids to a basketball game. She explained he was planning to just drop them off and should be back in fifteen or twenty minutes. Kelly told her the nature of her call, and Masterson's wife suggested Kelly could stop by their house. "Unless you want him to come to your office or just return your call."

Kelly recognized the Masterson's address and knew it was on the way to Clare Singleton's. "No, I'd prefer to stop by now if that isn't too inconvenient for you. Maybe closer to eight-fifteen. It should only take a few minutes."

•

Masterson greeted Kelly at the door. He towered over her. He was a handsome man, but his face showed a look of concern as he ushered Kelly into the living room. Kelly recalled seeing photos of him, always with a broad grin or smile.

"Ginny knows everything," he said, referring to his wife. "I'd like her to stay and hear what you have to say, if that's okay with you?"

"It certainly is," Kelly answered with a smile. "I think you'll both find what I have to say extremely interesting."

Kelly went on to explain the investigation had revealed two other individuals had been blackmailed by Katherine Edwards, and the facts in those cases were almost identical to Masterson's. She could sense the level of tension in the Mastersons lowering as she continued, especially when she explained one of the main objectives of the department was to keep the identities of the individuals who'd been targeted confidential.

Tim and Ginny each thanked Kelly for sharing the information with them. Both asked some very intelligent questions concerning the status of the investigation. Tim asked if any of the individuals who'd been black-mailed were suspects in Katherine Edwards' murder. He volunteered that he had gone to his office on Halloween night and had stayed late. He'd been the only one there. Kelly explained that the current thrust of the in-vestigation pointed to the person or persons who'd been accomplices of Katherine Edwards as the likely assailant.

"She couldn't have done this on her own. Someone had to take the photos. Others posed in the photographs. As you know, a young man was used to collect payments. Whether there was a falling out which led to her death, we still don't know. That's our suspicion. Your reputation and the reputations of the other known victims make it hard to believe any of you were parties to the murder . . . and torture. We may find that others were also being blackmailed. All I can say is, currently neither you nor the others are being viewed as suspects. Hopefully, none of you will ever be. Actually, one or all of you may be in some danger from the person or per-sons responsible for her death."

Kelly went on to tell them that one of the people being blackmailed had been recently injured under very suspicious circumstances.

"We think it's related." Kelly also told them about the ring which appeared in the photos sent to that same person mysteriously showing up on his bedroom dresser. "We suspect someone broke into the home and placed it there, to convey a message or threat of some nature."

Kelly glanced at her watch. She was due at Clare Singleton's in ten minutes. Perhaps she should call and explain that she'd be delayed. Better to wrap this up, she decided.

"One other bit of information I'd like to share with you, and then I'll have to excuse myself, is that in one instance Katherine Edwards told one of the individuals she was trying to stop the blackmail. She returned sets of the photos and negatives. In this particular instance, she was given some money to supposedly be used to distance herself from the man – she said – who was behind the blackmail plot. Locating that man is our highest priority. Meanwhile, please take some precautions. Contact us immediately about anything that appears suspicious. We'll try to keep you appraised."

•

On the drive to Clare Singleton's house, Kelly questioned whether she'd shared too much with the Mastersons. No, she concluded. Sometimes she believed the department went overboard in maintaining confidentiality.

Clare Singleton was waiting and greeted her warmly at the door. She was tall, perhaps five-feet-nine or -ten, in excellent physical shape with a somewhat masculine appearance. She was extremely attractive, but would perhaps never be referred to as beautiful. She had a warm smile and her eyes sparkled as she extended her hand, giving Kelly a firm handshake. Kelly began the conversation by suggesting it might be best if she began by briefing Clare on the status of the investigation.

"To begin with, you weren't, or aren't, the only one Katherine Edwards attempted to blackmail. We're aware of at least two other individuals who were set up and confronted in nearly the identical fashion that I've been told you were. Photographs, the implied threat they would be circulated to various newspapers, the use of a unique piece of jewelry – in both other cases it was a ring – and a request for a large sum of cash in low denominations. Rather public, high-traffic campus locations were chosen for the pick-up of the money. Candy was involved in some fashion in all three instances."

Clare's eyebrows raised as Kelly shared these facts with her. She grinned when Kelly told her cash was delivered in the other two incidents. As she'd done with Jameson and Masterson, Kelly explained that the department would be making every effort to conceal the identities of those individuals targeted by the blackmailers. She then told Clare why she might be in some danger. As Kelly continued, Clare smiled and pointed to the vestibule, where a softball bat leaned in the corner. Though she also smiled, Kelly told Clare that under no circumstances should she take any action on her own.

"If anything, anything unusual occurs, you should immediately contact us. The 911 operators have already been briefed and will quickly pass any information on to us."

After a few questions from Clare, Kelly directed questions to her concerning the attempted blackmail. These questions eventually led to a discussion of the photographs. Clare walked to a bookcase, removed a couple of books, reached in and retrieved an envelope. As she handed it to Kelly, she asked if she would like a cup of coffee. Kelly said she actually would; black would be fine.

While Clare was in the kitchen, Kelly studied the photos. Recalling Mike's comment over the possibility of the photos being doctored, Kelly paid particular attention to the arm of the woman wearing the charm bracelet. Kelly realized she certainly wasn't an expert on the subject, but she saw no sign that the pictures had been altered in any way. Clare's present hairstyle didn't match the braided style of the woman in the photograph. The athletic-looking body could possibly resemble Clare's, but the easily-identifiable bracelet was, in Kelly's mind, the only significant feature in the photo which suggested the woman was Clare.

Clare returned with a steaming cup of coffee. As she handed it to Kelly she said, "Yes, I've changed my hairstyle. And no, I'm not sexually attracted to women."

There were tears in her eyes. Her lips trembled as she said, "I've fought the lesbian tag some people have wanted to saddle me with for years. Not being married is not my choice. I'm still searching for Mr. Wonderful." She smiled through her tears. "It's just that he hasn't been searching for me."

Kelly's eyes teared as Clare spoke. This woman, who projected an image of extreme self-confidence and toughness, had been very vulnerable to the blackmail attempt. She'd been injured by the implications the photos suggested. The pain and concern were very evident on her face. Kelly reached out and took her hand. Clare initially jumped back, withdrawing her hand. Then, sobbing, she extended her arms as Kelly stood and embraced her. They stood in that position for several minutes. Finally Clare stepped back.

70

"Thank you," she said.

Kelly asked if she could have the photographs. She assured Clare only a handful of people would see them as she suggested they could be of value in tracking down the people responsible. As she departed, Kelly invited Clare to call her at any time for any reason. She handed her a card with her home number as well as the office number.

"Remember. For any reason at all."

•

As Kelly started her car and headed back across town to her apartment, she noticed it was already twenty minutes to eleven. She took a deep breath. It had been a long day. She hadn't noticed the car which had been parked around the corner from Clare's condo. She didn't notice it was now following her.

## Chapter 9

On arriving at her apartment, Kelly tossed her briefcase and coat onto a chair, kicked her shoes off and headed to the answering machine. The first message was from her mother, just touching base and asking for Kelly to call when she could. The next message was from her boyfriend, Rick Forsythe. She could hear the anger in his voice as he asked whether she'd dropped off the face of the earth or was just sending him a message. Shaking her head, aware that he'd left two previous messages, Kelly vowed that even with the late hour, she'd call him now. Rick was a good friend and didn't deserve to be treated so shabbily. As the next message – from Mike – began, she was trying to think when it would work out best for getting together with Rick.

The doorbell rang and a voice called out "Domino's." She smiled, thinking a slice of pizza would taste good about now. Maybe she shouldn't tell him he had the wrong condo. Still smiling as she opened the door, she thought it was odd the man was holding the Domino's carton in an upright position, blocking her view of him.

"Sorry, you have the wrong . . . "

The man lunged forward, charging into her, using the Domino's container as a shield. She back-pedaled as she was being shoved into the room, faster than she could react. Her feet became tangled and she fell backwards, her head bouncing off the corner of an end table as she tumbled to the floor. As he lowered the carton and tossed it off to the side, she saw he was wearing a ski mask. He leaped into the air, bending his knees in the process, and came hurtling down onto Kelly's abdomen and chest. She was momentarily incapacitated, gasping for air and unable to scream. The man jumped to his feet and began to viciously kick her in the ribs. Grimacing in pain, she tried to twist her body to avoid his kicks. She noticed as he reached under the dark colored sweatshirt he was wearing and removed what appeared to be a large duffel bag. Leaning down, he began to slip it over her head. Kelly raised her hands, trying to fight him off and reached out to grab the mask. He removed his right hand from the duffel bag and balled his fist. Lunging back, he rammed it into Kelly's stomach. The pain was excruciating and she fought for air. The duffel bag was being slipped over her head and pulled down over her body. Summoning all her willpower and strength, she began to kick. She was elated for a moment as she felt one foot strike him, hopefully in the face. She heard him swear as he yanked the bag over her feet and grunted as he hoisted her legs into the air. The last patch of light vanished and Kelly sensed he was tying the drawstrings. She was being dragged across the floor, her legs still elevated, her head throbbing. She reached up and felt the blood on her forehead.

He'd stopped dragging her and her legs were now being lowered to the floor. A second or two later she felt herself being lifted and then being balanced on a hard surface of some type for a moment before being shoved. As she felt herself falling, her body turned so she was now facing down. Her face and chest immediately smashed onto a hard surface, a fall of only a couple feet. It suddenly dawned on her she'd been dumped into her bathtub.

With the suddenness of being attacked, there had been no time for fear. Now as she continued to struggle to get her breath, she began to panic. She feared she'd hear the sound of running water any second. He was going to drown her and there was nothing she could do to prevent it from happening.

Engulfed by the darkness, seeing only a glimmer of light at the small opening in the bag near her feet, Kelly flailed out with hands and arms, feet and legs fighting her confinement and her feeling of claustrophobia. The flicker of light suddenly vanished and she was now in total darkness, as she continued to gasp for air in the confines of the bag. She reached up to her head and felt the wound. She was relieved to discover it was only a small gash and the blood was already beginning to coagulate. She stopped moving and strained to hear. There was only silence.

She surmised he'd left her and switched off the bathroom light. Still dazed, she tried to analyze her plight. Perhaps she could maneuver around and try to open the bag. The bag was bulky and she did have some freedom of movement. She struggled to pull her legs up and move her head and shoulders towards the other end of the bag. Her chest ached and her head continued to throb as she twisted about. It was several minutes before she had successfully reversed her position in the bag and was able to claw at the opening. There was only room to insert two or three fingers. She could feel the rope used to tie the bag and imprison her. Though her level of adrenaline was still high and her heart was beating rapidly, she sensed her exhaustion as her feeling of panic and fear subsided.

She concentrated on how she could escape. The heavy canvas prevented her from trying to tear the bag open or possibly chewing a hole which she could rip open with her hands or feet. The opening wasn't large enough to work a hand out to attempt to untie the knot. Had any of her neighbors heard the commotion? Her feeble attempts to yell and shout? Doubtful. Would her assailant be returning? Where was he now? Would anyone know of her plight? Rick had already called and the chances of him calling again tonight were remote. Mike had left a message; she was just starting to hear it when the doorbell rang and a voice called out, "Domino's." Would he call again? She reasoned that the best she could probably hope for, was that Mike or someone else at the department would become concerned when she didn't show up tomorrow morning and attempt to contact her.

She thought she heard her phone ringing and strained to listen. She heard her answering machine come on, but she couldn't distinguish what was being said. There was silence once again. She wondered if the man who assaulted her was still in her condo. Had he heard the message? She grimaced in pain as she attempted to enlarge the opening in the bag to allow for more air. She eventually became frustrated and tried to stretch out into a more comfortable position. I could be here for several hours, she thought as she mulled over the situation. Could this have been a mere robbery, unrelated to Katherine's death? Highly unlikely, she reasoned. Perhaps she should be counting her blessings in still being alive.

She placed her hand on her rib cage beneath her left breast, tensing as the pain shot through her body. Maybe some ribs are broken, she thought. She remembered having heard a cracked rib was sometimes more painful than a broken one. I have to try to relax, let the healing process begin, she thought. I could be here a long time. Her mind was still racing. The best thing that could happen now would be to fall asleep, she reasoned, trying to clear her mind. Think about something else, she told herself.

She thought of the pain and fear she'd experienced as a little girl when she'd fallen off her bike and broken her arm. She'd been about seven or eight. She remembered having run home in tears and her mother taking her to the hospital. She'd really had quite an injury-free childhood, she thought, far fewer traumas than most kids experienced. She smiled to herself though, as she thought about when she'd broken her leg. She'd been seventeen, her senior year in high school.

She'd been sitting for the Arnold boys, two real hellions, six and eight years of age. Their mother had told Kelly she was the only sitter who could really control them and still be their friend. They'd been out in Kelly's back yard, playing, when the phone rang. She was expecting a call from her boyfriend and had run in to answer it. It had been him and they talked over plans for the following week's Homecoming Dance. When she came back out into the yard, she saw the youngest of the Arnold boys high up in one of the apple trees. The older brother was picking apples up off the ground and throwing them at his little brother, calling him a sissy.

She soon sorted out what had happened. The younger boy had become frightened after climbing so high, crying and scared to come down. After standing under the tree, trying to soothe him and give him confidence to climb down without success, Kelly climbed up the tree to get him. It wasn't easy, he'd climbed to a point where the branches were fairly small and she remembered hoping they'd be able to handle her weight without breaking. But she was successful, reaching him and carrying him down a ways, to a point where he could scamper down the rest of the tree on his own. She must have relaxed and become a little careless as she followed him down. Her foot slipped and she tumbled out of the tree onto the ground, breaking her leg.

She smiled to herself again as she recalled seeing the doctor a week after he'd put on her cast. He'd said that in all his years, he'd never seen such a highly decorated cast, so many drawings and signatures. He'd teased her, saying after he removed it the University Art Museum might want to put it on display.

Kelly had been elected to the Homecoming Court prior to the accident. While the names of the young women on the Court were publicized before the Homecoming Game, the identity of which one was Queen was kept as a surprise until that night. She recalled her excitement and happiness on hearing her name announced, as she stood at mid-field on her crutches. She also recalled how devastated she felt the next night at the Homecoming Dance, when as she entered the ladies room she overheard a comment. One of her classmates was telling another girl that she hoped the entire Court wouldn't pull a Kelly next year, break a leg in hopes of being elected Queen, getting the sympathy vote. The two girls had looked up and seen Kelly. Flustered, the one who'd made the statement tried to apologize, saying she'd just been joking. Kelly remembered turning on her crutches, trying to fight back her tears, as she exited the restroom.

Two days later she found a large card taped to her locker, congratulating her on being elected Homecoming Queen with nearly two hundred signatures. She was certain her best friend, an Asian-American girl, had orchestrated it. In addition to their signatures, each person had written a message. Some short, such as "You're the Greatest!" and "Your Dimple Did It!" and others more lengthy, such as "The nicest, smartest, most attractive, most talented, most admired girl won!"

Kelly remembered bringing the card home and sharing it with her parents and her father's compliment. "Over thirty of your classmates, boys and girls, refer to you as their best friend. That's the ultimate tribute, Kelly. We're not surprised, just proud to be your parents."

•

Kelly must have dozed off. She woke to the sound of a voice calling her name. "I'm here," she yelled. "In the bathroom!"

In a moment she heard the door open and a voice – Rick's – shouting, "Is that you Kelly? Good Lord!"

As tears of relief came, Kelly shouted out. "Yes! Thank you!" She was crying. "Can you get me out?"

Rick was asking if she was hurt as he struggled to untie the rope. "Just a minute, I'll get a knife."

Thank heaven Rick had come, thought Kelly. He was one of the few who knew where she hid a key. A few minutes later, the bag was being opened. She saw the look of alarm on Rick's face as he saw her. He'd reached down and helped her up and out of the bag, oblivious to the blood now dried and caked on her hands and face. She smiled through her tears as he hugged her, and she hugged him in return. He noticed her wince.

As she began to tell him what had happened, Rick held up his hands. "We need to get you to a doctor."

She was amazed over how quickly Rick had reacted, helping her to a chair in the living room and then calling 911. Following a brief explanation, he said he'd have Kelly at University Hospital's Emergency Room in ten minutes, asking the operator to call the hospital so Kelly could be met at the door. As he was making the call, Kelly was surveying the room – the broken lamp, the pizza carton, blood stains. Her briefcase was missing from the chair she'd tossed it on.

True to his word, Rick had Kelly in his car and at University Hospital in just over ten minutes. During the drive he'd explained how he'd come for a midnight visit. He'd seen her on the eleven o'clock newscast during a segment on Benton's briefing session. It was a five-minute segment and he'd succeeded in taping all but a minute of it. Kelly had been standing next to Benton and could be seen during most of the interview. Rick had called and gotten her answering machine. He realized she'd had a long day and thought he'd surprise her by going to her condo and loading the tape in her player with a note. When she did come home, she'd be able to watch herself on television. Rick turned to her with a smile. "Seemed like a dumb idea as I was driving over, but it must have been ESP. Feel any better?"

Kelly nodded as Rick pulled in front of the Emergency entrance. Two people were there with a stretcher and a wheel chair. They opened the car door and had Kelly out and through the entrance door in seconds.

•

During the drive to the hospital, Rick had promised Kelly he would call Mike Cummings. After the initial briefing from the doctor, he placed the call. The lengthy delay in having his call answered and the tone of Mike's voice made it obvious that he'd been asleep. Rick had some difficulty getting Mike to understand who he was. They'd been introduced a couple of times, but had never had occasion for much of a conversation.

"That's right, Kelly's friend," Rick said. "Yes, she was assaulted in her apartment a couple of hours ago. I'm at University Hospital with her now."

With that news, Mike was fully awake. He fired questions as Rick explained what had happened and why he'd swung by Kelly's apartment. No, Rick answered, he hadn't seen anyone and no, he didn't recall seeing a dark green Saab convertible. He explained what he'd been told by the doctors.

"Kelly may have one or two cracked ribs. The scalp wound will require several stitches and she may have experienced a mild concussion. It appears they want to check her in for the night. They've just taken her down for X-Rays. Otherwise they say she's in good shape considering what happened, and that there shouldn't be any permanent injuries. She'll be sore for a while; the bruises are extensive. Is there anything you want me to tell her?"

"No, I guess not. It actually may have been fortunate she struck her head when she fell. It might have saved her from being even more seriously injured. You might not want to tell her that just now, but I think it's probably true. I'll be checking in during the night to see how she's doing. You can tell her I'll be in to see her early tomorrow – I mean today. I'm sure glad you arrived on the scene when you did, though. Thanks for all you've done, Rick."

•

Mike hung up and mulled over what he'd just been told. According to Rick, there hadn't been time to see her assailant. His face had been concealed by the ski mask. Maybe she'd remember some additional details by later this morning. Her briefcase had been taken. It contained all her notes and reports on the case – including the photographs she'd just been given by Clare Singleton. Were they the main motivation for the attack? They already had similar photos from Tim Masterson. Maybe her assailant hadn't been aware of that. He would be by now, in addition to being privy to other information. He'd now know they'd have a fix later today on the owner of the green Saab that Kelly and Jeff had seen on Arlington yesterday. Maybe they should accelerate the schedule and put out an alert on the car now, in hopes that whoever he is believes he's safe to drive it until later today.

That could prove to be embarrassing, however. There was a possibility the car might not be connected to the case. Nothing ventured, nothing gained, Mike thought as he picked up the phone and dialed the Hot-Line.

## Chapter 10

Kelly eased herself out of bed. Rick had driven her back to her apartment about three-thirty a.m. After learning the X-Rays showed no broken bones, she had convinced the doctor she would be more comfortable at home rather than being assigned a bed at the hospital. The doctor believed she'd experienced a mild concussion, but there was no sign of internal bleeding and he'd suggested she just take it easy for a day or two. Eight stitches had been required for her head wound and the doctor told her to expect a mild headache for a day or two. Kelly could see the bald spot where she'd been shaved by tilting her head in front of the bathroom mirror.

Rick had been very supportive, spending the night on Kelly's couch and checking on her throughout the morning. He'd just left after having prepared her breakfast. It was ten-thirty, and Mike would be coming by at eleven. She glanced around the condo. Except for the missing lamp, there were no signs of the assault. Rick had cleaned up and straightened the furniture. An officer had found her empty briefcase in the dumpster behind the building. They'd reasoned her assailant didn't want to risk being stopped and having to explain Kelly's briefcase. She thought of getting dressed and then decided against it. She did feel a little light-headed, but no head-ache. However, the slightest movement caused the level of soreness and pain in her rib-cage and stomach muscles to escalate.

•

When Mike arrived, he complimented her on making sure it was him before opening the door. "Keep the chain on, too," he cautioned.

During the next few minutes they discussed her injuries and reviewed the details of the assault. She could sense how relieved Mike was that she hadn't been more seriously injured. Mike reached into his pocket and handed her a fax showing a head and shoulders photo of a man. "The Chicago police faxed this to us this morning. It's a copy of the photo in Elizabeth Edwards' apartment that we'd requested. We think it's the boyfriend. They're going to try to verify that with some of Beth's neighbors."

Kelly studied the photograph. She shook her head. "Can I keep this copy?" Mike nodded.

"I have no idea what the man who attacked me looks like. I'm not even sure of his size. I think he was under six feet and probably less than two hundred pounds. But that's really a guess. It all happened so fast."

"I understand. Don't blame yourself."

"I'm not, but I'd have loved to have ripped the ski mask off."

"Seriously Kelly, it's probably best you didn't. If he's the one who killed Katherine Edwards, he might have reasoned he'd have to get rid of you, too."

A chill swept through Kelly as she recalled her terror when she thought he might drown her.

"As you know, I tried to reach you last night," Mike said. "You said you'd just been listening to my message when the doorbell rang. What I had wanted to share with you was some information Judy obtained.

"I think you're aware that several individuals contacted us who'd seen a girl dressed in a costume similar to the one Katherine Edwards was found in. They'd all seen her at a party at East Quad, a fairly wild affair which

79

we're told has become an annual event. Around seven o'clock last night, Judy received a call from the young man who was with Katherine Edwards at the party. His name's Frank Zupo, a U of M student who was in a class with her this past summer. Judy set up a meeting to hear his story. It provides some added pieces to the puzzle."

Mike explained that Frank Zupo had seen Katherine Edwards in one of the hallways at University Hospital about three weeks ago. She was engaged in an animated discussion with Dr. Broadstead. Zupo recognized him because of the many times he'd seen Broadstead's photo in news articles and University literature.

Kelly was also familiar with Dr. William Broadstead, or "Dr. Bill" as he was frequently referred to. Still in his forties, he was a well-known and popular personality on campus and in the local Ann Arbor community. While giving the air of a caring country doctor, he was regarded as one of the major players in turning University Hospital into a world-renowned medical research center. There had been recent rumors that he might be asked to serve as the U.S. Surgeon General. One article had commented that accepting the appointment would be a major step down for him, considering the fast track he was on.

Zupo told of watching Edwards grab Broadstead's hands during the conversation. As this was being done, from the corner of his eye he noticed a man with what appeared to be a small camera taking a photo. Zupo glanced back toward Edwards and Broadstead and saw she was planting a kiss on his lips. Broadstead had immediately recoiled, his smile replaced by a look of anger. He'd verbally lashed out at Edwards, reprimanding her for taking such uncalled-for liberties. Zupo glanced back again over his shoulder and saw the man he'd noticed a second ago hurriedly retreating down the hallway. Though there were a number of people in the corridor, Zupo thought he was the only one to notice what had occurred between Edwards and Broadstead. The entire sequence of events had taken only a minute or two. Katherine Edwards had mumbled an apology, turned, and was rapidly walking away. Still angered, Dr. Broadstead had looked up and seen Zupo staring at him. He wheeled around and quickly started down the corridor in the opposite direction from the one Edwards had taken.

Kelly interrupted Mike to comment. "They certainly did their homework in selecting the ones to target."

"That's for sure," Mike responded as he continued with the story.

Frank Zupo had hurried down the corridor to catch up with Edwards and called out her name as he approached within a few feet of her. Zupo said the two of them had developed a fairly close friendship over the summer. Several times after class, they'd shared coffee together. He was surprised and hurt when she'd glanced over her shoulder and failed to recognize him. She had continued on until Zupo caught up with her and grabbed her arm. He asked her what was going on. She'd given him a blank stare and had shaken her arm loose. She told him to get lost. Zupo said this infuriated him and he'd said, "Hey! This is me, Frank. What are you trying to pull?" She'd then smiled and apologized for not recognizing him. He was still angry and told her he had seen what had happened. She'd played innocent, saying she didn't know what he was talking about.

He told her he'd seen her with Broadstead along with the man taking pictures. She smiled and according to Zupo, tried to sweet-talk him and minimize what he had observed. She told him a story about putting together a calendar with casual shots of her and some of the leading personalities on campus. Once it was complete, she said, she'd be showing the finished piece to all involved and getting their permission to use the photos. They might not go along with prior permission, she explained, but she was sure they'd go along once they saw how the photos would be used.

He wasn't buying into it and said he thought he'd have a talk with "Dr. Bill." She begged him not to spoil things for her, asking what she could do to convince him not to. He was still aggravated over the way she'd initially turned him off and wanted to get back at her. Just that morning he'd been talking with his roommates about the Halloween costume party at East Quad. In discussing what they were going to wear, the type of costume Katherine had been found in had come up and been ruled out. The end result was Zupo persuaded Edwards to come to the party with him dressed in that costume.

He said he'd actually been surprised she agreed to wear such an embarrassing outfit, and had some second thoughts. He reasoned if it was that important to her that he not say anything to Broadstead, he probably should be contacting him. However, he was carried away by the excitement of believing he'd pulled a real coup. Katherine and her costume would be the highlight of the party. They'd probably still be talking about her years from now.

Even though he'd said he thought he'd be able to borrow a car to pick her up, Katherine said she'd just meet him at the party. She didn't want to be walking the streets in that outfit. He told her he'd be wearing a Mr.

Peanut[(tm)] costume – the famous character associated with the promotion of the Planters nut brand. Their top hats would be similar. The Mr. Peanut[(tm)] costume had been in his family for years and he was sure his parents would UPS it to him in time for the party.

Until she actually appeared at the party, Zupo had doubts as to whether she would really follow through on her promise. As he'd predicted, Katherine was the highlight of the party. The revealing harem outfits and bikinis some of the other girls wore didn't command nearly the attention. Katherine was a good sport and Zupo said he'd felt some regret over what he'd orchestrated.

He was able to borrow a car and drive her back to her apartment on Packard. That was shortly after eleven p.m. he says. The last thing she said to him was to remember she'd kept her end of the bargain, reminding him in exchange he'd promised not to tell anyone about the incident he'd witnessed with Dr. Broadstead.

Zupo's grandmother died last week and the funeral was on Monday. He'd taken an early flight home on Saturday morning and hadn't gotten back to Ann Arbor until yesterday evening.

"That was the reason he hadn't contacted us earlier," Mike explained as he finished the story. "So what do you think, Kelly?"

"It certainly explains the costume. Did we hear from Washington yet? Has the body definitely been identified as Katherine's?"

"We heard, but the identification is still in doubt. On the basis of the fingerprints alone, they can't be certain. It could still be the sister's body. Mrs. Edwards did find some birth records which may be of help. They should be arriving today."

"When you explained Katherine didn't appear to recognize Zupo when she first saw him, I wondered if the girl was really Katherine's twin sister. I'm sure you've asked yourself the same question."

"I have. Everyone we've spoken with about Katherine – her classmates, her fellow workers at Gratzi, even some of those targeted for blackmail – have all described a person you'd never expect to be involved in something like this. If it was actually the sister and orchestrated by the boyfriend, it might make more sense. As we theorized the other day, maybe Katherine had no knowledge of what was going on. Maybe she stumbled onto what was taking place."

"I tend to agree, Mike. It's concerned me that Mrs. Edwards was so convinced the body wasn't Katherine's. Maybe the brother, Sam, knows more than he's shared with us. Maybe in some way he thinks he's helping Katherine, who might still be alive, by trying to convince us she was the one who was killed. Katherine might have fled Ann Arbor, with or without the help of her sister. She might still not be aware of what's happened. I would assume that, whichever one it was who went to the party was the same one who was murdered. It doesn't make sense for someone – maybe more than one person – to have taken the time and gone to the elaborate effort to switch the costume and make-up from one sister to the other. I realize we're just making conjectures, but I think it's Elizabeth who was killed. Hopefully, Katherine's still alive."

Mike nodded. "We still don't have anything further from Chicago. No word on Elizabeth; she hasn't been back . . ."

The phone rang. Kelly started to get up from the chair she was sitting in and grimaced in pain.

"Stay where you are," Mike said. "I'll get it."

The call was for Mike. It was Steve Renz. Kelly could just hear Mike's side of the conversation and observe his reactions to what he was being told.

"Joseph P. McConnell." Mike repeated the name which Steve must have given him. "Do we have a photo, a copy of his driver's license?" Kelly observed Mike was frustrated by the answer Steve had given him.

"How soon will they have it to us?" Mike was shaking his head and glanced up at Kelly. "They've found the car," he told her with a smile, covering the mouthpiece with his hand. "Oh, no," he said in response to something Steve had said. As he listened, Kelly saw Mike's face flush in anger. As he finished the conversation, he told Steve he'd be back at head-quarters in half an hour.

"As I said, they found the green Saab," Mike explained to Kelly. "At the Glen-Ann lot." She was familiar with the service station Mike was referring to, one used by the department for storing impounded cars until fines were paid.

Mike shook his head in frustration. "Guess where it had been picked up? Right in front of the police station. I put out the alert last night after I heard you'd been attacked. Sometime during the night someone parked it in front of our main entrance. Talk about the right hand not knowing what the left hand is doing. About ten o'clock this morning it was ticketed and towed over to Glen Street. And this is the clincher. The car was empty – nothing in the glove compartment or the trunk, just some candy on the front seat. Three boxes of Nerds$^{(tm)}$."

Kelly couldn't help but smile. In spite of his anger, Mike grinned too. "He's right, he is making nerds out of us. The choice of three packages was probably intentional, too, the three stooges." Mike took a deep breath. "I really want to nail this bastard. He's sick, playing a game. His attack on you was vicious. There was no need to be so violent. You should take a day or two off to recover. We can handle things. You need some time to heal. Don't force yourself, I promise I'll keep you informed."

"I'm just a little sore," Kelly replied. "I'm feeling much better, I'm sure I'll be rarin' to go by morning."

## Chapter 11

Kelly hadn't realized how exhausted she was. She returned to bed right after Mike left, and after spending a few minutes mulling over the case, she drifted off to sleep. She didn't wake up until nearly five-thirty in the afternoon, when she heard a key in the door. It was Rick coming back to check on her. He gave her a kiss on the forehead and inquired about how she felt. Asking if she was hungry, Rick explained he'd picked up some Chinese take-out on the way over. Kelly wasn't at all hungry, particularly not for Hot Sour soup and an egg roll. But she concealed her reactions and thanked Rick for his thoughtfulness.

"Why don't you help yourself to a drink," Kelly said. "I'm going to take a shower, I'll join you in a few minutes."

•

The shower was very soothing and Kelly was surprised at how good she felt. Though still sore, the instances of severe pain were not nearly as frequent as they had been. The wine tasted good as she discussed some of the highlights of the investigation with Rick. After downing the egg roll, she excused herself, saying she wanted to call the office and see if there had been any new developments. No one was there. Mike, Judy, Steve, even David Benton, were all out. Mary Tucker was on the switchboard. Kelly asked her if she could have someone check her desk for messages. Mary said she would and then call her back.

"Here's something else you may be interested in," Mary said. "I just had a phone call a few minutes ago, from a woman wanting to talk with whoever was in charge of the murder investigation. No one's here, so I tried to persuade her to leave her number. She refused and said she'd call back at around seven p.m."

Kelly glanced at the clock. It was six-thirty. "I can be there," she said. "Forget about checking my desk, I'll do it then." Mary asked if she should also be contacting Mike about the call. "Sure, go ahead. But let him know I'll be there and can handle it. Thanks, Mary."

Rick questioned her judgment after she'd briefed him on the call, but Kelly convinced him it was what she wanted to do and that she was almost back to normal. She did agree to let him chauffeur her.

Kelly and Rick arrived at the station a few minutes before seven. Kelly informed Mary that she would be in her office, and if the woman who'd called earlier called back, to forward the call in to her.

One of the items on Kelly's desk was a memo from Judy Wilson. Kelly had been copied in along with Mike, Steve and David Benton. The memo stated that Judy had tried to contact Dr. Broadstead earlier that morning to follow up on the information obtained from Frank Zupo. It went on to say Broadstead had been difficult to track down and it was three o'clock before she finally spoke to him. At the start of the conversation he'd been very cordial, anxious to help in any way. He denied having any contact with Katherine Edwards and said there hadn't been any attempt to blackmail him. As she pressed him, Broadstead's mood and behavior changed. In addition to raising his voice in anger, there was a meanness in his answers, Judy wrote. He'd abruptly said that any further conversation would be through his attorney. He'd given her the lawyer's name and phone number and hung up on her.

A short time later she called the attorney. It was apparent that Dr. Broadstead had just spoken with him. The attorney first started to stonewall her, but "that just worked up my ire," Judy wrote. Broadstead hadn't given her the opportunity earlier to fully explain the instances of other prominent personalities on campus being set up for an extortion attempt. She stressed to the attorney the fact the department was treating all of the information, and the identities of the parties involved, in a strictly confidential manner. The investigation wasn't designed to embarrass anyone. Nothing would be released to the media. Broadstead's attorney said that while what she'd said was interesting, his client wouldn't have anything further to say.

The memo went on to say she'd then delivered the zinger. She explained to him the murdered woman had been given injections of some unknown substance – which would point to the involvement of a person with considerable medical knowledge. His client, she explained, was the only one unearthed at this stage of the investigation who possessed such knowledge. The attorney immediately changed his attitude and promised to speak with Broadstead and get back to her. He called back fifteen minutes later and a six p.m. meeting at the attorney's office with Broadstead had been arranged.

There was a post-script on Kelly's copy of the memo, saying Mike would be joining her at the meeting.

While Kelly was reading the memo, Rick had been studying some of the photos on her bulletin board. There was a photograph of Katherine Edwards, a copy of the photo of the body as it had been found at the scene.

The intercom buzzed and Mary announced the call they were expecting had come through – the woman was holding on line two.

Kelly picked up her phone and gave her name by way of introduction. She thanked the woman for calling back. There was a nervousness in the woman's voice as she asked Kelly what her role was in the investigation. The woman said she had some information regarding the Edwards murder and she wanted to pass it on face-to-face to someone rather than just communicating it over the phone. Kelly asked her where she was calling from, saying she was in her office and could meet with the caller now. The woman said she'd prefer meeting elsewhere and suggested the west end of the Nickels Arcade in about ten minutes. Fearfully, the woman asked Kelly not to tell anyone she'd be meeting her, and to come alone.

"I'm scared," she volunteered.

Kelly agreed to the timing, seven-twenty, and the place and said that she'd be there. She filled Rick in on the details of the call. His immediate reaction was concern for Kelly.

"This could be a set-up. After last night, you need to be careful. Maybe they want to finish . . ." He stopped mid-way through his statement. "I'm sorry, but I think you should let someone else handle it."

Kelly answered that she believed the woman was frightened about the possibility someone would learn she was providing information to the police.

"The woman had no idea I'd be the one who'd be taking the call. I can't picture this as an attempt to get to me; that there's any danger in that regard. It could be Elizabeth Edwards."

Rick agreed to drop Kelly off at the Arcade, but said he'd try to park so he could watch her from the car.

"If you're too obvious we might frighten her off. Why don't you drop me at the State Street end of the Arcade. I'll walk down to the Maynard Street end. If you can find a place to park on Maynard, fine. If not, I'll meet you back at the State Street entrance about seven-forty-five."

•

The temperature had dropped to the low forties. Kelly stood just inside the Nickels Arcade entrance. She glanced in the window of the gift shop next to her. As a little girl and many times since, Kelly had studied some of the drawings in the store window. One particular print had been in the same position ever since she could remember. Titled "Vanity," it pictured a young woman holding a hand mirror and studying her reflection. From one angle you saw a beautiful young woman. From another angle you saw an ugly, old hag of a woman. Kelly smiled, remembering dreaming about the eerie print as a youngster.

The Arcade was fairly deserted, with only a few people sporadically entering and exiting the skylight passage way. She smiled as she saw a young coed with a blond ponytail enter the doorway. She was wearing a baseball cap with a picture of Grumpy, one of the Seven Dwarfs. When the Snow White video had been released, Rick had given her an identical cap for her birthday. The girl, dressed in a dark blue warm-up suit, was browsing along the Arcade, studying the window displays. She turned and walked back in Kelly's direction. As she drew closer, Kelly realized with a start, the face she was staring into was Katherine Edwards'.

"Kelly Travis?" she asked as she drew closer. Kelly, still startled, nodded, extending her hand. "Yes, I'm Katherine Edwards. I know I should have contacted you earlier. Is it too cold outside for you? I'd prefer we talk as we walk outside."

"That's fine," Kelly answered. "I'm dressed warmer than you are."

"I've been on the west coast," Katherine began. "I didn't hear about my sister until yesterday. I should have called. I flew back this afternoon."

As they started south down Maynard, Kelly spotted Rick's car on the opposite side of the street. She explained to Katherine that her boyfriend had a car and could drive them to Kelly's apartment, where they could continue their conversation in private. With each step, Kelly experienced a slight pain. She knew she wasn't up to a long hike.

A look of fear and suspicion passed over Katherine's face. But nodding, she agreed. "That's probably best, isn't it. Where is he?" Katherine was surprised and again showed a look of fear when Kelly had simply pointed across the street. Kelly saw Rick's look of surprise as Katherine and she entered the car. He'd been studying the photos in Kelly's office just minutes ago. Kelly hadn't fully briefed Rick on their suspicions that the murdered girl might actually be Katherine's twin sister. Kelly introduced them and told Rick they wanted to go to her apartment. As Rick turned on the ignition and drove off, Kelly turned to Katherine. "How do I know you're not Beth?"

"You don't. After I've told you everything, I hope you'll be convinced who I am. Can we talk in front of – is it Rick?"

Kelly nodded. "Yes, that's right. And yes, you can speak freely. Rick's aware of several aspects of the investigation. He's been virtually at my side for the past day."

Rick filled in. "Kelly was assaulted last night. I drove her to the hospital."

Katherine's eyebrows raised. "Related to my sister's murder?"

Kelly nodded yes. "A man forced himself into my apartment last night. I didn't have a chance to really see him. He was wearing a ski mask."

"The same apartment you're taking me to?" Katherine asked in surprise.

Kelly nodded again. "I think he got what he wanted, all my files on the case, some photographs. There's no reason he should be coming back."

"The man involved is Joe McConnell, Beth's boyfriend. He's weird, dangerous. I'm certain he's the one who murdered my sister."

Kelly reached into her handbag and removed the faxed photo Mike had given her. "Is this Joe?" Kelly asked, handing the photo copy to Katherine.

"No. Doesn't even resemble him. I don't know who this is," Katherine answered, returning the copy to Kelly.

"There was a photograph of this man in your sister's apartment in Chicago. We had assumed he was her boyfriend. One of the neighbors had thought Beth's boyfriend was named Joe. But this isn't him?"

"No. Joe has dark, bushy hair. Piercing eyes. He's good sized, muscular and stocky, considerably older than Beth. Mid to late thirties, I'd guess."

Rick interrupted. "We could go to my apartment. Phil's out studying tonight. I don't expect him home until midnight."

Phil Gardener had been Rick's roommate for the past year and a half. After a couple of years working for Ford, he'd returned to get his Masters.

"Would you prefer that?" Kelly asked Katherine.

"You decide. Either's fine," Katherine answered. "The reason I didn't come to the police station was I thought Joe might see me. I'm sure he wants to get rid of me, too." There was a tremble in her voice.

"Rick, let's go to my apartment. I think I need one of those pain pills and we can brew some coffee, too." Rick nodded.

•

As they drove, Katherine began to relate her story. Kelly asked if she could tape her comments. After a moment of hesitation, Katherine nodded yes.

"I was keeping quiet to protect Beth. I shouldn't have. It all has to come out now."

Katherine explained that her sister had been a frequent visitor to Ann Arbor, at least a weekend once a month. Beth and she were good friends and enjoyed an open relationship, sharing each other's thoughts, aspirations and experiences. She defended Beth as basically a good person who'd been corrupted by Joe McConnell. Beth and Joe had been together for nearly two years and over that period of time, she'd gradually severed ties with her mother and brother. Katherine was the exception.

Kelly interrupted. "Do your mother and brother know you're alive?"

Tears formed in Katherine's eyes as she answered. "I'm not sure about my mother. I did call my brother after I left Ann Arbor. I told him why I'd left and that I didn't want anyone to know where I was. I told him not to say anything to Mother. I was afraid she'd accidentally say something to Beth. Remember – I didn't know Beth was dead until yesterday."

"Your mother told us the body was Beth's rather than yours. What confused us was your brother saying he was equally convinced the body was yours. In hopes of quickly tracking down the killer, we elected to proceed on the basis you were the one who'd been murdered. We have your prints from when you worked in the post office down in Bloomington. We'll need to get a set of your prints."

Katherine nodded. "I'm sure Sam thought he was helping me. We can't alter the fact Beth's dead, but we can keep him from . . ." Katherine was shaking and began to cry. Kelly placed an arm around her shoulders in an attempt to comfort her. "You're going to be fine. With your help, we'll be able to lock him up so he won't be able to hurt anyone else."

Between sobs, Katherine blurted out, "He wants to hurt the University. He's paranoid. He's out to make Michigan pay for what was done to him. He . . ."

Kelly patted Katherine on the back and gave her a squeeze.

"We're almost there. We'll get you a cup of coffee or a drink. Then you can tell us everything."

•

After using the bathroom and taking a couple of sips from the glass of wine Rick had poured for her, Katherine regained her composure. With the tape recorder turned on, she picked up with her story.

Towards the end of the summer, her sister had visited for the weekend. It was the first time Beth had brought her boyfriend with her. Katherine commented she had negative vibes from the moment they met. Joe appeared insecure and kept trying to impress Katherine over how bright he was, how skilled a photographer he was, and how much money he made. When they learned Katherine was planning to drop out of school for a semester for financial reasons, her sister suggested they could loan her money. Rather than a loan, Joe indicated she could earn some substantial money the same way Beth was – modeling for him. Not only could Katherine make some decent money, she'd also help her sister and him increase their income. Being twins, their photographs would command a higher price. Katherine said she'd initially been excited over the idea and was disappointed that her sister wasn't more enthused. In hindsight, she said, it shouldn't have surprised her. As close as the two were, Beth had never wanted to discuss her modeling work. One time, she'd remembered bringing up the subject and Beth had replied, "You don't want to know."

As Joe continued to pursue the modeling idea, Beth had become angry and told him to drop the subject. Sensing Katherine's confusion, the two of them had explained the photos Beth posed for were no longer mainstream. Beginning with nude photos, they had now progressed a step further.

90

"They were into pornography," Katherine said. "Not Playboy or Penthouse stuff – worse than that."

When Beth was out running an errand the next afternoon, Joe had approached Katherine again, saying posing for a few pictures could solve her money problems in a hurry, and no one would be the wiser. She could always stop, he'd said. She'd told him in no uncertain terms that she wasn't interested. She insinuated that he should be ashamed of what he was doing; what he was asking her sister to do. She told him she was going to try her best to get her sister to stop and to terminate her relationship with him in the process.

Joe had become angry, arguing that it wasn't like drugs – no one was being hurt. He was just supplying others' perverted tastes and was making damn good money in the process. "Forget I gave you the opportunity. You're the loser," he'd screamed. "But also forget about any loan from us."

She'd screamed she didn't want his dirty money anyway. Then she'd stormed out of her apartment. When she returned a few hours later, neither Joe nor her sister were there, and they'd taken all of their things. She assumed they'd returned to Chicago. She tried to call Beth a few times this fall and had left messages, but she hadn't spoken to her or seen her until about two weeks ago. She'd been walking through the Farmer's Market near Kerrytown when she'd nearly collided into Beth. Surprised, she asked her what she was doing in Ann Arbor. Beth was embarrassed. Saying it was a long story, she asked her sister if she could buy her a cup of coffee.

•

Over coffee, Beth told her that she and Joe had stayed on in Ann Arbor after they'd moved out of Katherine's apartment. She explained that Joe had attended the University in the late seventies, for nearly three years. Beth said he'd loved it here, loved Ann Arbor, loved the University.

All that changed in the second semester of his junior year. Joe had his heart set on going on to medical school. He'd had close to a four-point and thought he had an excellent chance of being accepted. But then, that spring, his world fell apart, Beth had said.

"He was involved in what he'd described to her as a campus prank," Katherine continued. "He and two of his classmates had broken into one of their professor's office and stolen an exam. It all came to light when one of

91

the others had a perfect score on the professor's exam, even correctly answering two questions which had typo errors. During the investigation, the University determined Joe had been the ring leader and he was expelled, asked to leave the University while the other two were only put on temporary probation.

"Beth said that Joe told her he had the lead in one of the University's upcoming drama productions. The opening performance was less than a week away. He tried to appeal his expulsion, to no avail. He tried to at least get a temporary waiver so he could perform in the show. Again, the University turned him down. He was infuriated, he vowed he'd have his revenge someday. His hatred toward the University grew over the course of the years."

Katherine paused for a moment, taking another sip of wine before she continued. "She then told me that Joe had devised an elaborate scheme to get back at the University, to obtain his revenge. She said she'd been trying to get him to stop, but it was a vendetta for him. The problem, she said, was that it indirectly involved me. She said she'd promised herself that when it became apparent Joe couldn't be dissuaded, wouldn't back off, she was going to inform me."

Katherine bowed her head for a moment before saying, "I'm not sure that would have been the case. It had been a coincidence, an accident running into her, confronting her. She was embarrassed to look me in the eye. She said Joe would probably kill her if he found out she'd confided in me. She said it had probably gone too far, that he was in too deep, to be able to pull out at this stage. That he was so immersed in his insane idea to blackmail a number of prominent people on campus that it had become a game for him. She said he wasn't doing it for the money, that his sole objective was to tarnish and trash the reputation and image of the University."

Katherine continued by telling them the details of Joe's plans which Beth had divulged. Kelly had the benefit of already being privy to many of those details. Rick didn't. He stared at Katherine in wide-eyed amazement, flabbergasted over what he was hearing.

"Did she give you the names, any of the names, of the people they were setting up?" Kelly asked.

"Yes and no," Katherine answered. "She told me how they were being set up with her impersonating me, taking advantage of the association I'd had with some of the individuals they'd targeted. I asked her point blank if one of them was Dean Jameson. Reluctantly, she told me he was. She refused to give me any other names, saying she'd be putting themselves, her and Joe, and me in too much danger if I knew everything. Their danger, she implied, was in being exposed in case I decided to contact any of the people, the University or the police. My potential danger she implied was from Joe. She said she didn't know what he might do if he found out we'd talked. She warned me, saying if I blew the whistle we might both be history. He's totally consumed by this madness, she said, with his dream of revenge for over the past fifteen years finally coming to fruition. She said she thought he loved her in his way, but thought he might go totally berserk if his plans were to go haywire.

"Though I feared for Beth, I became very angry, shouting the question of how she could possibly have gotten involved and compromised in this idiotic nightmare. Didn't she realize that if Joe carried through on this, my reputation would be totally destroyed?

"I told her that Joe and she would eventually be caught and exposed. I remember shouting at her, Don't you understand that! How could you have dragged me into this?"

Though Beth agreed they'd probably be caught, Katherine said she was sad to see that in some ways her sister was relishing in the excitement and danger of Joe's plan. "Although Beth kept assuring me that she was still hopeful she could persuade Joe to terminate his plans, I'm sorry to say I wasn't convinced she wanted them canceled.

"She kept apologizing for getting me involved and suggested she could help by providing me with a substantial amount of money to disappear until, one way or another, this was all over.

"We must have talked for another hour or so. Finally we left it that we would meet the next day at the south entrance to Jacobson's in the Briarwood Mall. She promised to call me if there was a change in plans. "As you might imagine, I had a very restless night, digesting all I'd learned from Beth and mulling over what options I had. Beth might still be alive if I'd followed through on my first inclination – going to you, the police. But I didn't," Katherine added, shaking her head.

"We met the following day and I persuaded Beth to give me all the photographs and negatives they had of Dean Jameson. Along with them, she'd give me $10,000 and I would disappear from Ann Arbor. It was a stupid decision. I guess it makes me an accomplice of some kind, but in exchange for the photos and negatives, I promised not to tell anyone what

I knew."

Katherine then explained how she'd obtained the photos and negatives from Beth, contacted Jameson and given them to him. She hesitated a minute before mentioning Jameson had also given her $5,000 of his own money.

"So you were the one who spoke with Jameson, the one who met him at the Law Quad?" Kelly asked.

Katherine's face showed a look of surprise. "You already know much of what I've been telling you, don't you?"

"Not really, but what you're telling us all fits in with what we do know."

"Beth was the one who actually called Dean Jameson," Katherine went on to explain. "From my apartment, I was with her. She was frightened that Joe might walk in on us. She didn't want me talking to him directly, she was afraid I might volunteer too much information. That was fine with me, I wanted her committed to give him all the photos and negatives. Asking him for money was her idea. I remember shaking my head and waving my hands to get her to back off on that.

"Beth was the one who handed the photos and negatives to Dean Jameson, too. I was standing just inside the door of the library though, so I could verify she actually gave them to him.

"I was confused, frightened for my sister, frightened for myself; I didn't know where to turn. As I told you earlier, I did call my brother."

For the next hour or so Kelly continued to question her. No, she hadn't been told the identities of any of the others, who was or would be blackmailed. No, she had no idea where her sister and boyfriend had been staying in Ann Arbor. She said she'd tried numerous times to find out the answers to those questions, but hadn't been successful.

One of the questions Kelly had asked was when was the last time she had seen her sister and Joe. Katherine said she hadn't seen Joe since she'd stormed out of her apartment at the end of August. She'd seen Beth a week ago Monday, when she'd met Jameson. An added piece of information to come out was Katherine's mention of seeing bruises on her sister's neck and wrists, and in concern inquiring about them. Her sister explained that Joe had photographed her in some kinky bondage poses. In his desire for realism, he'd bound her too tightly with a heavy rope. Beth said she'd nearly strangled herself and had been terrified. Joe, she said, had just laughed it off, saying the look of fear added to the value of the photographs.

94

Katherine also said Beth had made the comment that Joe was thinking up weirder and wilder ideas for his photo sessions.

Kelly asked Katherine if she had any photos of Joe. She nodded yes and said there was an eight-by-ten framed photograph of him with Beth in her apartment.

"I think I have several; maybe one of just him, in my photo album. That's at my apartment, too. It'll be easy to get them. I was scared to go there on my own, but if you'd come with me it would only take a minute or two to get them."

Kelly told Katherine of being in her apartment and the fact it had appeared someone had removed all of her photos, correspondence and personal items. "Except for a picture of you, your apartment had the look of a hotel suite."

"I guess I'm not surprised," Katherine nervously responded. "Did you go through my dresser and nightstand? I think I might have some snapshots tucked away in the bookcase, too."

"Were you planning on spending the night there?"

"I really hadn't decided. I guess I was hoping you'd be able to take Joe into custody right away."

"If we can find him, we will. Do you know the names of anyone else involved in this, with Joe and your sister? The other people in the photographs? From the way you described Joe, I think they had someone else collecting the blackmail payments."

Katherine shook her had no. "Beth said they'd be using some of the people she worked with in Chicago in those staged photographs. According to her, they would just assume it to be a normal photo shoot – the same type of thing they'd posed for in the past. Do you have any idea how many were being blackmailed? Who some of the others were?"

"For the time being we're keeping the identities of the others we're aware of limited to only a handful of people. They're innocent victims and we don't want to compromise them in any way. We are aware of three others in addition to Jameson, though."

"I'm sorry. I thought if I knew, I might be of help. I really don't see how, though. Do you?"

"Perhaps. Let's hold on that for now. Can you tell us anything about your sister and Joe's use of candy in their plans?"

Katherine had a blank stare. "Oh, yes, I forgot to mention the 100 Grand$^{(tm)}$ candy bar they sent to Jameson. Is that what you're referring to?"

Kelly nodded. "Yes, that was one example. Candy was also used in other ways."

Katherine's face lit up. "Yes, I recall now. Beth told me Joe's family was in the candy distribution business in Chicago. When she came to visit she often had one of the newest bars on the market – some I'd never seen or heard of before. His family's company didn't manufacture any of them themselves. They just sold a variety to retailers – Hershey bars, M&M's(tm), Goo Goo Clusters(tm), all kinds." Katherine smiled. It was the first time since they'd begun talking that she'd shown an expression other than fear, concern or sadness.

"Do you recall what kind of car Joe has?" Kelly asked.

"He had at least two. He let Beth borrow a nifty green Saab convertible when she drove up from Chicago to visit. They were driving it when they came up together this fall. I don't remember what make his other car was; I don't think I ever saw it. Just the Saab."

The phone rang. As Kelly started to rise from her chair, she grimaced in pain. Rick asked, "Do you want me to get it?"

"Why don't you," she answered.

Kelly could tell from the conversation that it was Mike Cummings. She signaled to Rick that she would take the call on her bedroom phone. As she slowly stood and moved toward the bedroom, she told Katherine that Rick would be glad to get her something more to drink. "The bathroom's just down the hall in case you need it. I'll just be a few minutes."

## Chapter 12

Mike asked how she was feeling. "I heard you were in for a few minutes. I told you, that's not necessary. Rick said I didn't wake you. I was worried I might."

Kelly giggled. "No, I wasn't sleeping, and I think you'll be surprised to hear what I've been doing for the past two or three hours."

"What are you up to? I know Rick's there, but I don't think you're in shape for much snuggling," Mike said laughing.

"You're right about that." Kelly then explained that Katherine Edwards was there with them. She told of Katherine's phone call, meeting her and some of the highlights of what she'd learned over the past few hours. Mike's comments and questions reflected his excitement and surprise over Kelly's news.

"The faxed photo we received from Chicago isn't Joe McConnell's," Kelly explained. "There's no resemblance to the man Katherine describes. She says she has photographs of him at her apartment, but I told her the apartment was pretty much cleaned out and that they're probably no longer there. She still wants to take a look."

"We did get a copy of McConnell's driver's license late today," Mike said. "It's a poor photo, but good enough to learn the earlier photo we received wasn't his. I'll come over right away if that's all right with you. I also have some information to share with you. Not nearly as startling but I just hung up from talking with Dean Jameson. When he pulled down their bedspread tonight he found half a PayDay(tm) candy bar, unwrapped, on his pillow. At first glance, he said it looked similar to . . . one of those dog stools you were telling me about Saturday morning. We both agree it was probably placed there at the same time the ring was put on his bureau. As you can imagine, it did shake him and his wife up, though."

"Are you interpreting the message the same as I am, Mike? That trying to run him down was half a payback and the half a bar's a warning for him to be on guard for another attempt to harm or kill him?"

"I'm afraid so, Kelly. That's also the way the Jamesons are reading it. David's working on intensified protection for them right now. There's also some other news.

"I think you're aware Judy and I met with Dr. Broadstead and his attorney this evening. Turns out he is being blackmailed. He even made a payment – ten thousand dollars, to be exact. The most interesting thing we learned, however, was in regard to identifying the substance injected into the body. We're saying Elizabeth's now, right? Do you think it's safe to make that assumption?"

"I think so. I told Katherine we'd need to take her prints. Unless she's one heck of an actress, I'm confident she's who she says she is. You can judge for yourself. I want to check with her first before having you come over. I promised I'd see her alone, but I'm sure there's not going to be a problem. Let me call you back."

"But first tell me what you were about to say. You were right in the midst of telling me something about the injections."

"Yes, I'll try to be quick. Broadstead says that with the added drug testing in athletics, there have been rumors of a couple serums that have the effect of masking out most other drugs in the system. He also said there have been a couple of new so-called truth serums used in the recent civil war conflicts in Eastern Europe and Africa that can be very lethal. He believes one of them might be responsible for . . . Elizabeth's death, a possible accident scenario. Broadstead has volunteered the U of M facilities for further testing and is optimistic he can determine what was administered. I found your statement that McConnell was a pre-med student very interesting. You're going to call me back right away?"

"In just a minute or two," Kelly answered.

•

As Kelly came down the hallway, she saw Rick going through Katherine's handbag. He'd just unsnapped her billfold. He flashed Kelly a sheepish grin and motioned that Katherine was in the bathroom.

He whispered to Kelly. "You probably can't do this, but I thought I could." He glanced inside the billfold, raising his eyebrows as he glanced up at Kelly. He whispered again. "She has the name Bethany Winters on her driver's license; also a credit card with that name."

They heard the bathroom door being opened and Rick quickly slipped the billfold back inside the purse.

"Refill?" he asked Katherine, holding up her glass. She shook her head no and then said, "Maybe just some water. A little ice, too, if that's not too much trouble."

"You've got it," Rick answered, moving towards the kitchen area.

Kelly told Katherine that Mike Cummings was also anxious to talk with her. "It's actually his case. You'll like him. He'll probably have some questions to ask that I didn't think of. I told him I had to clear it with you."

After considering for a moment, Katherine nodded her head. "Sure, if you think it'll help."

"Great! I'll call him back."

Mike suggested it might save a little time if he were to meet them at Katherine's apartment. "Then I can follow you back to yours. The sooner we can come up with a decent photo of McConnell, the better. Let's say in twenty minutes, at ten-thirty."

•

Rick said he could drive Katherine over to her apartment on his own and suggested Kelly could use the time for a bath or shower and a little rest. "You shouldn't push yourself. You'll just aggravate your injuries."

Initially reluctant, Kelly finally did agree that made sense. "Is that all right with you?" she asked Katherine.

"Yes, as long as I have someone with me."

Rick cautioned Kelly. "Now be sure to lock this door. Do you want us to pick up anything? A pizza?" he said, smiling.

•

Katherine directed Rick to her apartment. The timing with Mike was perfect. He pulled into the drive ahead of them, and was just getting out of his car as they pulled up next to him. Mike opened the door for Katherine and introduced himself.

"Where's Kelly?" he asked. Rick explained and Mike nodded his approval. He pointed up towards Katherine's apartment and asked, "Did you notice all the lights on in your apartment?"

"I see," Katherine answered. "I don't know what that means."

Rick and Katherine noticed Mike pull out a gun as he headed up the stairs. He took the key from Katherine and cautioned them to stand back while he went in and determined whether anyone was there.

Mike was back in a minute or two. "No one's here now, but someone was clearly here earlier. I'm sorry," he said, turning to Katherine, "it's a mess."

Even though Mike had prepared them, Katherine and Rick were startled as they went through the door. Books were scattered everywhere. Drawers turned upside down with their contents strewn on the floor. The scene was similar in the bedroom. The linens had been pulled from the bed. All the dresser drawers had been pulled out and dumped. The closet was also in a state of disarray. They proceeded into the kitchen. The small dining table was bare except for two Chuckles[(tm)] bars.

Mike struck his forehead with the palm of his hand as he exclaimed, "Hell, I should have thought of that. He's bugged Kelly's phones. Maybe the entire apartment. Call her – warn her – tell her we're on our way. I'll go on ahead," he yelled over his shoulder as he raced out the apartment door.

•

Kelly was enjoying a leisurely soak in her bathtub. She'd treated herself to a bubble bath and was savoring every minute of it. She smiled to herself as she recalled being in the same tub less than twenty-four hours ago, tied up in the canvas bag. Hard to believe it was just last night. She heard her phone ring, thought about answering it, and then decided to slip back in the suds for another moment or two. She heard the answering machine click on, but couldn't decipher who it was or what was being said. She'd check it out in a minute or two.

•

Mike swerved to avoid a near collision at the East U intersection as he sped down Hill Street. He'd placed a flashing dome light on the roof of the car above his door. It was providing help as he navigated through the intersections. He'd forgotten how many stop signs there were on Hill. Even at this late hour, there were scores of pedestrians, mainly students, to watch out for in addition to other cars. The flasher was doing its job in gaining the attention of the usually blasè students who assumed they had the right-of-way when crossing a street at any point. They jumped out of the way as Mike accelerated ahead.

Mike questioned whether he'd made the right decision in not calling for a patrol car to meet him at Kelly's apartment. He should be there in ten minutes. Perhaps his fear and concern for Kelly were unwarranted. But if McConnell was aware she was there alone . . . Mike pressed his foot down on the accelerator a little more. There was no way to predict McConnell's behavior. He blamed himself again for not having considered Kelly's phones or apartment were bugged. Had McConnell stolen a key so Kelly's locked door was meaningless? Kelly hadn't mentioned it, but maybe she hadn't checked. Hopefully, she'd attached the chain lock.

•

Still traveling at a fast clip, the tires squealed as Mike turned into the parking area of Kelly's complex. He braked in front of Kelly's building and his heart sank as he noticed the door of her apartment was partially open, with the light from inside casting a glow on the entryway. He experienced a shortness of breath as he exited the car and ran towards the door. He clicked the safety off the gun now in his hand and pushed the door to a fully open position. He couldn't see anyone inside and he strained to listen as he cautiously proceeded forward. Nothing appeared to be out of the ordinary. He moved down the hallway towards Kelly's bedroom. The door to the bathroom was closed. He first checked out the bedroom and closets and then returned to a position outside the bathroom door.

"Kelly, is that you in there? Are you all right?" Mike shouted. He heard her voice and breathed a sigh of relief.

"Is that you, Mike?"

He turned the knob and pushed the door open, in a crouch with his arm extended, holding the gun. He saw Kelly sitting in the tub, wide-eyed, attempting to adjust a wash cloth over her chest.

"What's wrong?"

Mike's face flushed and he tried to suppress a grin as he answered. "Nothing, I guess. We were worried about you."

He turned his back to her as he continued. "I think your phones are bugged. Someone was at Katherine's apartment, just ahead of us, it appeared. It was a mess. Someone, probably McConnell, completely trashed it in the process of looking for something; I think the photographs Katherine told you about. I'll be out in the living room."

"I'll only be a minute or two. Are Rick and Katherine with you?"

"They should be here any minute. When I left them Rick was trying to call you."

"I heard the phone ring, but . . . I'll just be a minute. Let me get some clothes on. Help yourself to a drink."

"Your front door was partially open when I arrived, Kelly."

"But I locked it."

"I think someone was here. I'll have a look around."

•

Mike unscrewed the handset of Kelly's telephone. Sure enough, it had been bugged. He started to remove it and then had second thoughts and hung up the receiver. Kelly had already gone into her bedroom. Mike was sure he'd find a similar bug in the bedroom phone. As he moved to close the front door, he saw Katherine and Rick hurrying up the walkway.

"Is she all right?" they both asked in unison. Mike explained that

Kelly was fine and had been taking a bath.

"She's just getting dressed. Someone was here, though. The door was partially open when I arrived. I'll just attend to my car; be back in a minute."

"Good, 'cause we've got some good news," Rick said, handing Mike a small photograph. "Katherine remembered she had this in her billfold."

It was a photograph, he assumed of Beth, with a man, probably Joe McConnell. They were arm in arm. Beth had a broad smile; Joe just a trace of a smile.

"Fantastic! This is wonderful. I'm sure we can get this enlarged; a blow-up of him to circulate. It is McConnell, isn't it?" Mike asked Katherine.

She nodded. "I wish it were a better shot. His hair was fuller, for one thing, when I last saw him."

"We'll have to make do with what we have," Mike said with a smile, tucking the photo in his pocket. "I'll get the car now."

•

The flasher was still on and several people were standing in the vicinity of Mike's car. He assured them everything was fine, but that Kelly's apartment had been broken into. He asked if any of them had seen anything unusual, an unfamiliar car or person in the area. None had.

He thanked them for their concern and then switched off his flasher and placed it in the car. He climbed inside and pulled his car into a nearby empty parking space.

Kelly was standing in the doorway of her apartment as he returned, waving to her departing neighbors and assuring them all was okay.

"My tape recorder's gone," Kelly whispered to Mike. "I left it on the coffee table, next to where Katherine had been sitting. It probably means we'll have to have her go over everything again. I'm sorry."

"Could be far worse," Mike assured her as they moved into her apartment. "Does anything else appear to be touched or missing?"

"Yes, my spare house key is also missing. It could have been taken last night, rather than tonight, though. That would explain how he entered so easily tonight."

Mike and Kelly explained to Katherine that the recorder was missing, and that they were sorry, but they'd have to put her through the entire process of telling her story once again. Katherine replied that was no problem, but she was concerned that McConnell would now know not only the fact she was back in Ann Arbor, but also everything she'd told them.

"You don't know him. I'm more frightened now than ever."

Kelly sympathized with Katherine's concern and could see Mike did, too. She was currently the key witness to tie McConnell into everything. She realized it as well and had a right to be nervous.

Kelly, going to the refrigerator, asked if anyone wanted something to drink before they resumed. As she opened the door she gave a gasp. She reached inside and removed a Nestle Crunch$^{(tm)}$ bar and a cello package containing a candy watch. She held them up for the others to see.

"I hadn't mentioned to you, Kelly, he left a calling card at Katherine's apartment too – two bars of Chuckles$^{(tm)}$. Now he's saying it's crunch time."

"What does that mean?" Katherine asked.

"It refers to the last few minutes in an athletic contest," Mike replied. "Or a point in a game or match when the winner might be decided. A goal line stand in football. The last of the ninth in baseball. That sort of thing."

"He's indicating he's either going to succeed or be caught within a very short time frame," Kelly suggested.

"Or," said Mike, "slamming our efforts thus far, saying we'll have to raise them another notch if we're to succeed in stopping him."

"He's treating this as a game, isn't he?" said Katherine. "No remorse at all over having murdered my sister."

"That appears to be the case," said Mike, glancing at his watch. "I want to give David a call and bring him up to date. I'm going to use my car phone. Also, I think we should give some thought to going back to headquarters to continue our conversations. I'll just be a minute."

After Mike had left, Kelly suggested to Rick he should call it a night. "You didn't have much of a sleep last night. You must be exhausted."

"Possibly, but not at all tired," Rick replied. "This has been quite a day. If I'm in the way, I'll be glad to leave. If not, I'd prefer to keep you company. I'm thinking I should spend the night again."

"We'll need a place for you, too," Kelly said, addressing Katherine. "Maybe we should check into a hotel, share a room. I'll discuss it with Mike. I appreciate everything you've done, Rick. I don't know how long we're going to be tonight. Why don't you use my bed? Remember to put on the chain lock, though."

Rick smiled and nodded. He hadn't been able to get Kelly aside to discuss the identification he'd found in Katherine's billfold. Maybe they could excuse themselves now and go back to the bedroom and discuss it. Maybe that wasn't necessary, Rick thought, coming up with an idea.

"Katherine, I have a question I've been meaning to ask you. When you left Ann Arbor, did you take any special precautions so McConnell wouldn't be able to locate you?"

Katherine shrugged her shoulders. "Not really. I didn't even tell Beth where I was headed. One risk I did take was using some I.D. Beth offered me, a driver's license and some fake credit cards. Beth was the one to suggest it. She said I should pay cash so I wouldn't leave a paper trail. She thought I could use the false I.D. to book flights and for room registrations. It worked, too. My only worry was Beth telling, or being forced to tell, Joe the I.D. I was using."

"You used a set of false I.D.'s she had?"

Katherine nodded. "Beth had several sets. I guess that's common-place in the porno industry. No one uses their real names. I used a set with the name Bethany Winters. It was an easy name to remember. Beth said Joe would have no idea of the name I was using. She told me there wasn't a record of the names under which she had fake I.D."

Rick had glanced up at Kelly during Katherine's explanation. It all made sense and she didn't appear to be hiding anything from them. Kelly nodded and Rick thought she probably was in tune with his thinking.

"I just had a thought," Kelly said. "If your sister had all these sets of fake I.D.'s, it probably means Joe does, too. He could be passing himself off under a variety of names here in Ann Arbor."


**Chapter 13**


There was a knock at the door. "It's me," Mike called out. Rick went to the door and let him in.

"David's delighted you found the photo," Mike explained. "He's going to meet us at his office in thirty minutes. He wants to get copies out on the street right away. He's also going to schedule a press conference for ten a.m. tomorrow, in time to make the afternoon edition of the *Ann Arbor News*.

"There's been an added development. McConnell mailed sets of his photos to various newspapers. One twist is he's only sent one set to each paper. The *Michigan Daily* received Singleton's. The *Free Press* received the ones of Masterson. 'Dr. Bill's' went to the *Ann Arbor News*. The *Detroit News* received some, but they won't tell him whose. Maybe they don't know, but he doesn't think that's the case. David's spent the past four hours trying to persuade the papers not to publish anything. He's delighted he can get back to them now in regard to tomorrow morning's briefing. It'll give him the opportunity to have another crack at convincing them to hold on any mention of the photos.

"The fact he sent only a single set of photos to each paper works in our favor. The editors' and publishers' main concern is not to get out-scooped by their competition. David has told them they all have different sets of photos; arguing that while they each have an exclusive, they'd be solely responsible for the injury and damage publication would result in for a totally innocent person. He's explained to them the way in which the victims were set up and the similar circumstances in all the cases. David is trying to get them to agree to hold off any story for now and to run similar stories which conceal the identities of the parties following the briefing."

"How confident is he over getting them to agree?" Kelly asked.

"He thinks our added information will help in that respect," Mike answered. "He's optimistic. He's had President Robinson contact the papers, too. Both David and he have played up the point that in addition to the individuals involved having their reputations destroyed, the image of the University would also be hurt."

"After you've had a chance to hear Katherine," Kelly said, "you'll see that's McConnell's whole motivation – to hurt the University. According to her, he doesn't care about the money. He's oblivious to the havoc he'll cause in the lives of the individuals he's targeted."

"I hope the photos the *Detroit News* received weren't Dean Jameson's," Katherine said. "Beth assured me she'd given me all the prints and negatives. He's the one for whom I feel most responsible."

It suddenly dawned on Kelly that Katherine had just learned the identities of others who'd been blackmailed.

"It could be they received photos of someone we don't even know about yet," Kelly said. "I'm sure David's going to keep pressing them to find out, accusing them of holding back possible evidence. Did any of the other names mean anything to you, Katherine? Did you have contact with any of them?"

She shook her head. "Not really. I know their names, of course. I was actually in a class with Masterson. A small class; we referred to him as

"Coach." Nothing like my relationship with Dean Jameson."

Mike motioned to the three of them to join him on the front steps. In a lowered voice he told them he was almost positive Kelly's condo wasn't bugged, just the phones.

"I have the gut feeling McConnell didn't realize you were in the bathroom, Kelly. You're not as major a threat to him as Katherine is, that's for certain. But I still can't imagine him not taking advantage of the opportunity to get you out of the way – possibly just severely injure you. I would think he's surprised you've recovered so quickly from your first encounter with him. I think you're lucky you were taking a bath – he probably would have heard the shower. If the entire apartment was bugged, he'd have known you stayed behind when Katherine and Rick left to go to her apartment. I think I'm making a safe assumption, but Benton will have someone here in the next hour to make sure. It's good you'll be here, Rick. I probably would have asked you to stay."

Kelly had briefed Mike on the fact Rick would be staying at the condo until it was determined where Kelly would be spending the night.

"Knowing the phones are bugged, David and I think we may be able to turn that to our advantage. I'm going to be calling him now and pretend to brief him on the recent developments. I'm going to suggest we need to make arrangements for the two of you," Mike said, indicating Katherine and Kelly, "to spend the night somewhere other than this condo. I'm going to say you're both exhausted and we should hold off further questioning of Katherine until early tomorrow morning. Benton is going to agree to that suggestion and volunteer to make the necessary arrangements. The plan is for him to call back a few minutes later and provide the details. He's working on that now. Tentatively, we're trying to set it up for the Bell Tower Hotel across from Hill Auditorium. It's fairly isolated and we think we'll be able to set up good surveillance there. What we hope is McConnell will see the opportunity to . . . get to Katherine and you too, Kelly, before you've had the chance to fully communicate with David and me and others, since he has the tape. Maybe it will prompt him to expose himself and with luck, we'll nail him."

"Won't we be exposing Katherine to some added risk?" Kelly asked.

"Sorry," Mike answered, apologizing. "I wasn't making myself clear, I guess. Katherine and you won't be anywhere near the Bell Tower. David's making plans for adjoining rooms elsewhere, maybe the Campus Inn, not far from headquarters. No, we don't want to expose either of you to any added risk."

"What about Rick?" Kelly asked. "He heard Katherine too, and could also be in danger."

"You're right," Mike said, breaking into a smile. "You're a step ahead of us. Maybe I can arrange for an officer to stay here with him tonight. I'll work on that."

Mike smiled again. "And in suggesting that you and Katherine are exhausted, I know I'm speaking the truth. However, Benton and I would like to talk to you now, Katherine. We'll try to make it short. Though I'll say on the phone I'm dropping the two of you off at the Bell Tower, we'll actually be going right to headquarters, Benton's office. Do you have any further ideas or suggestions – or questions?"

"It's a great idea Mike, let's hope we're successful," Kelly replied. "How about you, Katherine. Any questions?"

She shook her head no.

"By the way, Katherine, do you have a bag, luggage stashed any-where?" Mike asked.

Katherine nodded. "I do. I took a shuttle in from the airport this afternoon to the Marriott in Ypsilanti. I didn't actually register. I checked my suitcase at the bellstand and immediately took a cab into Ann Arbor."

"Do you have a claim check? It's better if you're staying here in Ann Arbor. I'll have your bag picked up and brought to the station while we're meeting with David."

Katherine reached into her purse and removed the claim check. Hand-ing it to Mike, she said, "The luggage tag reads Bethany Winters, with an L.A. address."

Mike nodded. Kelly had told him about Katherine's fake I.D. and the fact McConnell was probably also using an alias.

"I'll call David now. You might want to pack a few things for tonight, Kelly."

•

The calls went as planned and within twenty minutes, Mike, Kelly and Katherine were on their way to the station.

"I thought of the possibility of going through the charade of having you check in at the Bell Tower and leaving by a rear entrance," Mike said. "But I think our timing makes that unnecessary. The registration clerk and night manager already have you checked in, in case there's an inquiry. Hopefully, McConnell will be taking some time to plan out his course of action. Even if we did take the time to check in now, I don't think he'd have time to be there to observe you, and we'd only be doing it for his benefit."

During the drive to headquarters the three of them mapped out a game plan which would expedite Katherine's briefing of David and Mike.

"David also promised to have a new tape recorder for you too, Kelly," Mike said with a smile.

She smiled in acknowledgment. "A deduction in next week's paycheck?"

Their combined laughter helped to break the tension. Throughout the drive, Katherine in particular had been nervously staring out the car window as if she was expecting to see Joe McConnell in the shadows. It was past one a.m. when they arrived at police headquarters.

## Chapter 14

David greeted them warmly in his office. He expressed his concerns to Katherine over the death of her sister and assured her they'd be doing everything possible to apprehend and convict her killer.

Benton told them the surveillance team was already in place at the Bell Tower, and now it was just a waiting game to see if they'd be successful. Mike had given David the snapshot of Beth and Joe. David excused himself for a moment to get someone started preparing flyers picturing McConnell.

•

Immediately after David returned, Katherine began a repeat of her story for his and Mike's benefit. Kelly assisted her, asking questions to highlight points Katherine had communicated to her earlier. Katherine was nearly finished when David's phone rang.

Steve Renz was on the line, reporting there had been a phone call to the Bell Tower to inquire whether Katherine Edwards and Kelly Travis were registered. The desk clerk had told the caller they were, but in answer to the man's second question, asking for their room numbers, told him it was the hotel's policy not to release room numbers. The desk clerk had asked the caller if he wanted the call directed to one of the women's rooms, but he'd hung up as the question was being asked.

"We'd already made arrangements in case someone placed a call to either of you, to have your lines busy," David said. "With this call, it wasn't necessary.

"I think we have his attention," David continued with a smile. "Now with your help, Kelly, I'd like to sink the hook in a little deeper. I want you to call your boyfriend. Tell him you're fine and give him your room number, room 104. Explain you have a connecting room with Katherine's. Tell him you have the front corner room on the first floor, a lovely, spacious room with windowed doors facing the street. Gush a little over the small porch or balcony outside your window."

Kelly nodded. She recalled the room David referred to. She'd noticed it this past summer when she'd had dinner with Rick at the gourmet restaurant inside the hotel.

"I think I can handle that. Why don't I use the phone in my office while Katherine continues on with you."

The scene was quiet at the Bell Tower. Steve was confident that the preparations he'd helped coordinate were adequate. One officer was hidden behind the registration desk, sitting on the floor with his back against the wall. There were four officers stationed outside the hotel. All were equipped with infra-red binoculars for night-time viewing. Steve and another officer were in the room Kelly had described to Rick. On opposite sides of the window overlooking the street, they had an excellent view of the sidewalk and street fronting the hotel.

All of the officers were armed with ready access to their weapons. Included with the information the Chicago Police had supplied on McConnell was the fact a .38 caliber pistol was registered in his name.

Steve yawned. It might be a long night and he hoped all their efforts weren't in vain. He smiled, thinking of a candy bar he remembered from years ago. He hadn't seen one in a long time; it probably was no longer being made. It was called "Gotcha." The implication was once you tasted one of these bars, you'd want more; they'd have you hooked. He'd love to have one of those bars now to ram down McConnell's throat once they caught him. While he'd joined in the laughter over the packages of Nerds[tm] candies, McConnell had left in the Saab. It was angry laughter.

109

•

The conversation was just winding up in David's office. They had been interrupted twice. Once with the news there were no signs of Kelly's apartment being bugged, just the phones. Mike had smiled, relieved that he'd made an accurate assumption. The second interruption was the news that Katherine's suitcase had arrived. There had been no word from Steve.

"Why don't I take Kelly and Katherine over to the Campus Inn," Mike suggested. "It's nearly three a.m. You might not sleep much, but I'm sure you can use the rest. We'll let you know immediately if anything happens."

David nodded, asking Kelly if she had her gun with her. Kelly replied she did. David explained to them that McConnell had a gun registered in his name.

"So be sure to keep yours handy, and don't hesitate to use it. I've made arrangements for adjoining rooms for you."

Kelly asked if there was any way she could reach Rick without going through her phones. David explained they could call the officer who was staying with Rick.

"He has a portable phone. I see no reason for having Rick stay any longer now. They could both go home. I'll get you the number."

•

Mike escorted Kelly and Katherine to their rooms. "Remember, I don't want either of you leaving these rooms on your own. If you don't hear from me sooner, I'll call you at nine a.m. You have my number Kelly, if you need me for any reason before then. Don't hesitate to call. Now try and get some sleep."

They both thanked him for his care and concern. "Now be sure to let us know if Joe shows up," Katherine said.

## Chapter 15

Steve had just checked his watch about five minutes earlier, making the time four-fifty a.m. when the hotel's alarm system sounded. Steve tensed.

"It may have something to do with our friend," he called across the room to his partner for the evening, Eric Smith, who nodded.

Steve went to the phone, dialed the front desk and received a busy signal. Going to the front window he saw the shape of a person just starting to stand across the street, alongside the wall of Hill Auditorium. He raised his binoculars and saw it was one of the members of the surveillance team.

"See anything?" asked Eric, raising his voice so Steve could hear him above the noise of the alarm.

Steve shook his head and tried to get through to the front desk again. Still busy.

"You wait here," he said to Eric. "I'll check in the lobby to see what's happening."

As he stepped into the hallway, Steve saw half a dozen people coming down the hall towards him. A couple were still in their nightclothes, pajamas and a nightgown. A young boy, looking confused, was in his underwear. Others had hurriedly dressed and were still adjusting their clothing. More people were opening their doors and coming into the hallway as Steve turned toward the lobby. There was a din of voices in addition to the ringing alarm. All were questions. "Fire?" "False alarm?" "What should we do?"

The desk clerk was standing in the middle of the lobby. He was explaining the fire department and police had been called. No, he didn't know what was wrong. There were reports of smoke on the third floor. No sign of fire had been reported, just smoke coming from the ventilating system.

The hotel was small, less than sixty rooms, Steve recalled. That was one of the reasons they'd chosen it. The number of people in the lobby had continued to increase. Some had ventured outside, chilled by the night air. Steve walked out the door and crossed the street. It was cold, but not cold enough to see his breath. The officer he'd spotted earlier came out from the shadows as Steve approached.

"Seen anyone?" Steve asked.

Shaking his head no, he asked, "Is it a false alarm?"

"We don't know yet. There have been reports of smoke on the third floor. Stay on the alert; I think our man may be involved."

Steve saw a fire truck with its lights flashing, just turning the corner at Washington Street and driving towards the hotel. He spotted four people coming towards him down the alley bordering the Bell Tower, across the street from where he was standing. Two were elderly men and the other two, a middle-aged couple in bathrobes. They must have used an exit at the rear of the hotel.

"Bring the other officers in closer to the entrance," Steve said, motioning to the officer's walkie talkie. "Have them be on the lookout for anyone approaching the hotel trying to blend in with the other guests. I'll check on those four," he said, pointing to the people who were nearing the entrance to the alley across the street.

"Have someone stake out the rear of the hotel to make sure he doesn't gain access there."

Steve darted across the street and confronted the four in the alley. He flashed his badge and attempted to verify they were guests. They gave their names and showed him their room keys. The fire engine was just pulling up in front of the hotel. Another, with its siren blaring and lights flashing, was just coming around the same corner the first one had. Steve thought McConnell might be nearby, enjoying all the confusion which would play into his hands. He asked the four if they'd seen anyone else when they were exiting the hotel.

"Was there anyone trying to get in?"

The two elderly men shook their heads, but the woman looked at her husband and said, "You tell him, John."

"No, why don't you," the man replied.

Someone tell me, Steve thought, frustrated knowing time might be of the essence.

"All right, I will," the woman said to her husband. "When we came out of the fire door exit, there was a man standing there outside next to the door in his bathrobe. He asked us if everyone was out and we told him no, we thought we were probably among the first to get out. He grabbed the open door and started inside. I said, 'You aren't going back in, are you?' He replied, 'Yeah, it was a false alarm.' We assumed we might as well go back inside too, but he pulled the door closed. Right in our faces. He nearly caught John's fingers in the door. We were standing there, surprised by his rudeness, when these two gentlemen came out. They told us about smelling smoke and we came up the alley with them."

Steve pressed the couple for a description of the man. As they began to tell him, behind them he recognized one of the other members of the surveillance team running past, heading to the rear of the hotel.

"Just a minute, Bill," Mike called out.

"What color was the robe?" he asked, turning back to the couple.

"The one that rude man was wearing?" the woman asked.

In frustration, Steve nodded.

"Plaid, a bright red plaid," she said.

"How old would you say he was?" Steve asked.

The woman glanced at her husband before replying, "Young, in his mid-thirties."

"Hear that, Bill? A young man in a bright red plaid robe. Detain him if you see him. Guard that door! Don't let anyone else in."

Bill nodded and jogged off towards the rear of the hotel as Steve obtained a more complete description of the man the couple had seen. They described a man about six feet tall and well built.

"Stocky, but not fat," the man said.

"He glared at us," the woman said. "His eyes made me shiver. Did you notice them, John? I think they were blue."

The husband shook his head. "I don't recall, but you're right, he wasn't very friendly."

Steve thanked them and suggested they wait outside, in front of the hotel, until the seriousness of the fire was determined. It had been nearly ten minutes since he'd left Eric. He's probably wondering what happened to me, Steve thought as he quickly walked to the hotel entrance. Holding out his badge as he went through the doorway, he had to step over a couple of fire hoses. He went up the short flight of steps to the first floor corridor and knocked on the door of the room he and Eric had been in.

"Eric, it's me, Steve." There was no answer. He knocked louder and called out again. There was still no response. He was hoping Eric hadn't left the room as he reached into his pocket, fishing for his room key. As he opened the door he saw the flashing lights from the fire engines reflecting through the front window and off the walls of the room.

In the glow he saw Eric, sprawled on his back in the middle of the room. Steve knelt down next to him. Eric groaned and as his eyes fluttered open, he raised a hand towards the back of his neck. He was still in a daze as Steve asked, "What happened?"

Eric blinked a couple of times and Steve helped him up to a sitting position.

"I'm not sure," he said, holding his neck and turning his head from side to side. "There was a knock at the door and I heard a man's voice saying there was a fire and everyone should vacate their rooms immediately. I had my gun out when I opened the door. There was a young man in a bathrobe outside the door. He excitedly explained that he'd been drafted to make sure everyone was out of their rooms. He asked if I was the only one in this room. I nodded and remember putting my gun back in my holster. He noticed and I explained I was a police officer. He asked if I knew if there was anyone in the room next door. I told him there wasn't. As he turned to leave he mumbled something. I think he said, 'That's what I expected.' Then he whirled around and caught me in the neck with a karate-type motion. He caught me off guard. I staggered back and he kneed me, pushing me at the same time he was landing another blow or chop to my neck."

Rubbing his neck again, Eric said, "I must have blacked out for a few minutes."

"Do you remember the color of the robe?" Steve asked.

Eric nodded. "Yes. It was red, a bright red plaid."

Steve jumped up. "I'll get you some help. I'll be back in a minute or two."

"I'm sorry, Steve. It was him, wasn't it?"

Steve nodded and raced out the door, down the few stairs to the lobby area and went outside. Holding up his hands, he motioned to the officers he could see on the fringe of the small crowd of people in front of the hotel to join him. He led them inside and briefed them about Eric.

"Try to stay out of their way," he said, referring to the firemen, "but let's check the hotel out the best we can. Richard, get that EMS unit in to look after Eric, and then guard the front entrance. Bill's in back; I'll brief him. Grab some master keys and check every room. Remember – be careful," Steve cautioned over his shoulder, as he ran up the few steps to the first floor corridor and raced down the hallway. He opened the emergency fire exit door and saw Bill standing outside with his gun drawn.

"Seen anything?" Steve asked.

"No, how about you?"

Steve briefed him in regard to Eric, explaining that the man who'd assaulted him had been wearing a red plaid robe, probably the same man the couple had seen earlier entering this door.

"There were two people who did come out a minute or two ago," Bill said. "One was a very elderly woman, extremely confused over what was happening. The other was a visiting professor who's been staying at the hotel this semester."

Bill checked his notepad. "Name of Jeffrey Potter, he's an Englishman, quite an accent. He's been staying in room 312. The woman's name is . . ."

"Tell me more about the man," Steve asked. "Describe him."

Steve cringed as Bill gave the description. Physically he matched the profile of the man the couple had described earlier. The difference was the personality, the man Bill described, projected.

"Very personable, a broad smile. He volunteered to assist the woman out to the front of the hotel. As I said, she was very confused and needed the help. I mentioned he had a marvelous accent. He was very gracious and gentle with the woman."

"Bill, I'll wait here inside while you go out front and see if you can find the two of them. If you can, try to verify if, you said the name was Potter? Check to see if he's a registered guest. Room 312, I think you said. Get back to me as soon as you can. By the way, did he show you any identification?"

Bill shook his head no. "He patted his back pocket and said he'd left it in his room. He asked me if I wanted him to go back and get it. With the possibility of a fire and all, it didn't make sense. If the woman hadn't been here, I might have done things differently. But with that accent, I can't believe he's our man."

"Did he show you a room key?"

Again Bill shook his head. "Let's hope I can find him. Damn – I hope I haven't goofed things up."

•

Ten minutes later one of the other officers on the surveillance team came down the stairs. He had a red plaid robe over his arm.

"We found this at the end of the corridor, just above you, on the second floor." Opening his hand he said, "We found these in one of the pockets."

Resting in the palm of his hand were four small rolls of Smarties candy. "Sorta cinches it, doesn't it?"

Steve nodded. The mumbled comment Eric had mentioned made by the man who attacked him about having expected to find the rooms empty, along with the candy, spelled out to Steve that McConnell had been suspicious he was being set up. As Steve mulled this over, he saw Bill coming down the corridor, a glum look on his face.

"I did find the woman," he said as he approached Steve. Then with a touch of sarcasm he added, "That nice Englishman left her as soon as they'd started down the alley. She didn't see the direction he headed and hasn't seen him since. There's no Jeffrey Potter registered."

Steve's face showed his disappointment. "Let's get everyone together and brief them. I don't think there's anymore we can do here."

As they were leaving the hotel, Steve learned they'd determined the fire had been caused by some flammable materials being ignited in one of the roof vents. There had been very little damage. That was the only good news.


**Chapter 16**

Steve dialed Mike as soon as he returned to headquarters. He dreaded the call. He was aware of his own disappointment and frustration. It had been Mike's idea to use Kelly's tapped phone to convey the erroneous information to McConnell in hopes of getting him to expose himself. The idea had worked. Steve knew Mike had thought about handling the surveillance himself, but Steve had assured him he could handle it and Mike was best getting a few hours of sleep. At the time, Steve thought he'd been doing Mike a favor in the belief it might be just a long night, with McConnell not falling for the bait, not making an appearance. Steve wondered if things would have gone differently if Mike had been there.

Mike was very supportive, telling Steve not to blame himself. Steve could tell, however, how angry Mike was over their failure to apprehend McConnell.

"Sorry it didn't work out," Mike said. "Let's hope Eric's injuries aren't serious. Advise me when they have the X-ray results. I'll give Benton a call and brief him. I don't know how he'll want to handle this at the media briefing tomorrow morning. I guess it's this morning, isn't it?"

"I know you've had a long night, Steve. Don't second guess yourself. McConnell suspected he might be being set up. We're going to get him eventually. The copies of the photo of McConnell that Katherine provided us with are already being circulated. I better call David now. Get some sleep, Steve, and I'm not being sarcastic when I say thanks. You did a great job! We've probably underestimated McConnell."

•

It was nearly six-thirty when Mike hung up from his call to David. Tired and dejected, he knew he should be calling Kelly and Katherine as well. Kelly picked up the phone after just one ring and he surmised she hadn't had much sleep either. He asked if Katherine was also awake and Kelly said yes. As a matter of fact, she said, they were just having coffee together, hoping they'd hear from him. She asked if she could put him on speaker.

"I hope I can figure this out," she said as she pushed a button.

Mike related the details of the fiasco at the Bell Tower. After he'd finished, Katherine commented she'd forgotten to mention that Joe considered himself a master at mimicking various dialects. He'd used them in telling some very gross jokes to her and her sister, she said. "Remember, he was into acting when he was here in school," Katherine reminded them.

The thought of what else she'd forgotten to tell them passed through Mike's mind. He held his tongue, however; Katherine had enough to worry about without him taking his frustrations out on her.

"David is wondering if we should have Katherine at the press briefing this morning. He has mixed feelings. What do the two of you think?"

They discussed the pros and cons and finally agreed it would be a good idea. Mike explained he was going to have a shower, possibly catch an hour or so of shut-eye and pick them up around nine o'clock.

"It will give us time to go over the format for the briefing with David. I'll let him know you've agreed, Katherine.

"How about breakfast? Are you hungry?" he asked them.

"We both decided we can skip breakfast," Kelly answered. "Perhaps we can have an early lunch together after the news conference. Should we meet you at the front door about nine?"

"Definitely not," Mike retorted. "I want you to stay in your rooms. Have the bell captain send up a newspaper if you want one, but be careful – keep the chain on."

•

Mike checked his watch. It was a few minutes before nine as he

117

knocked on the door to Kelly's room.

"Is that you, Mike? Do you have the password?"

"Yes, it's me," he said and laughed. "A password is probably not too bad an idea, come to think of it."

Kelly opened the door and greeted Mike with a smile. "I was joking, but you're right, Mike. McConnell might be able to impersonate people's voices with his gift for dialects. Let's remember that."

Katherine came through the door from the adjoining room. She'd been dressed in a warm up suit with the blonde wig yesterday. He was taken aback to see her now, without the wig, in a skirt and blouse with a blazer. She was a beautiful girl. She looked almost identical to the photographs of her sister, which were pinned to the walls in Mike's office. She also smiled at Mike.

"I'm sorry things didn't work out better at the hotel," she said. "We could tell how disappointed you were. It was a good try, though. How's the officer who was injured?"

"He'll be fine. His throat is the worst part. It'll take a while to heal."

"All set?" Mike asked. Kelly and Katherine nodded.

"Should we be taking our things, Mike? Are we checking out?" Kelly asked.

"No, why don't you just leave them here for now. I don't want you back at your condo until we have McConnell in custody."

"That might be a while. Katherine and I could stay there together and we'd promise to keep the door chained."

"What about when you're not there? Remember, he has a key. We'd have to constantly check the apartment and your phones for listening devices. Even after we change the locks, I'm just not comfortable. Maybe we can get you something you'd prefer more than this."

"No. These rooms are fine," Kelly replied. "But," she smiled, "there's no place like home."

•

David was pleased to see them. He briefed them on the subjects he was going to cover at the press conference, what he was going to say as well as what he wasn't going to say.

"I plan to bring you in at the end, Katherine. Maybe a little dramatic, but it will take their minds off what they haven't been told."

"Just a minor point," Katherine said. "I really don't go by the name of Katherine. All my friends call me Kath. My sister was Beth and I was Kath for as long as I can remember. I'd feel more comfortable if all of you would refer to me as Kath, too."

David smiled in understanding as Kelly nodded. "I think we can arrange for that, don't you, Mike? As you said, Kath, it's a minor point. But I identify with it. In the reverse actually. I've always been a David, but you'd be amazed over how many people try to turn me into a Dave.

"Did you see the *Free Press* this morning?" The three of them had and nodded. "Let's hope the other papers handle it in a similar fashion, mentioning the blackmail perspective to the case while only mentioning prominent University personnel had been targeted, with no mention of who they were or the details.

"We do have a minor problem," David continued. "Bill Averill, the member of the surveillance team who was duped by McConnell's impersonation of a visiting professor from England, contacted me after he'd seen the photo of McConnell we planned to hand out this morning. He says it's not a very good likeness of the man he saw. He goes so far as to say that even if he'd had access to the photo, he might have let McConnell get past him.

"Bill's a good officer. Still, I thought he might be trying to take himself off the hook after what happened this morning. It would be the normal thing to do, almost expected. But he assured me that wasn't the case and suggested Eric Miller be given a look at the photo. We did, and his reaction was similar to Bill's. They fear use of a photo bearing only a slight resemblance to McConnell will work in his favor. They wanted to work with our artist and come up with a composite drawing which would be more indicative of McConnell's current appearance. We took it one step further. We're also working with the couple who saw him at the emergency exit. They're all together working on it now, making good progress. The next step is to get you involved, Kath."

"Fine, tell me when. I'm sorry I don't have a better photo of Joe. I mentioned to Kelly and Mike that he looks a little different now. My photo is at least a year old. Beth gave it to me when she first started to become serious about him. I agree, a good drawing might be better."

"It's probably something we should have done anyway," Mike said. "I'm glad Bill spoke up. With the computer software we have now, you'll see how accurate we can get. It's quick, too. You still want to have something for the briefing?" Mike asked, turning to David.

David replied, "Yes, if at all possible."

"We'll do our best. I'll take Kath up to the lab now," Mike answered. Glancing at his watch he added, "Not much time, but it's possible."

·

Upstairs, Kath and Mike found a series of computer-generated sketches of McConnell spread out on a table. Bill Averill and Eric Smith were there, working with two of the computer technicians. Mike introduced them to Kath and also introduced himself and her to the middle-aged couple who'd been brought over from the Bell Tower. They were seated at a smaller desk in the corner, holding up various drawings and discussing them among themselves.

"These are amazing," Kath commented, picking up one of the sketches. "It's him, all right."

She whispered to Mike, "I was concerned that Joe might have someone else working with him. I'm sure you had the same thought. But this is Joe. That's a relief."

Kath made several suggestions, a slight change to the nose, a little higher forehead, and enlarging and lowering the ears. The new drawing came off the printer and everyone gathered around.

"We're coming closer," Eric commented. Looking at Kath he asked, "Shouldn't the eyebrows be a little fuller?"

She nodded. "Just a little, you're right. Can you do anything about the neck?" she asked, looking at one of the technicians. "Make it a little fatter, maybe shorten it up, too."

The man nodded. "I can give it a try. Any other suggestions?"

The next pass had everyone enthused. "That's it, perfect!" Bill exclaimed.

Kath and Eric were also pleased and even the couple from the Bell Tower was enthused. They had wanted to give the eyes a more piercing appearance and to picture McConnell with a sneer. But they now both raved over how realistic the computer drawing looked.

Mike asked the technicians how soon before he could have thirty or forty copies. For internal use, he asked if it was possible to get a few copies with McConnell wearing eyeglasses.

"Maybe a couple with him wearing a baseball cap too, one with glasses and one without. He may try to alter his appearance, especially after he sees this drawing in the papers and on TV."

•

As soon as the copies were completed, Mike headed downstairs with Kath. Kelly was standing outside the door to the room where David was conducting the briefing.

"Good, perfect timing," Kelly said. "He's just about ready for you," she told Kath. Mike handed her a copy of the sketch of McConnell.

Kelly nodded. "It's better than the photo," she said as she studied it. "What do you think?" she asked Kath.

"I'm pleased. The other officers who saw him are too," she answered, also telling Kelly of Mike's suggestions to get copies with Joe wearing glasses and a cap.

"The rumors are already out that you're here," Kelly explained to Kath. "Don't let all the cameras and lights make you nervous. Just relax. One bit of advice – avoid smiling too much. The public could misinterpret a photo of you with a grin on your face. But there's no need to be on the defensive. We need the media's cooperation in tracking down McConnell. Don't hesitate to ask for their help."

"Should I mention talking to my mother and brother this morning?"

"Fine, if it comes up. I don't think you should volunteer it. Don't worry about saying something wrong. David will be right there with you and he's planning on keeping the questions to a minimum. You'll be fine."

Mike slipped his arm over Kath's shoulders and gave her a squeeze as he nodded in agreement. "I'll take these in to David," he said, referring to the stack of sketches in his hand. "I'll be back to get you in a minute or two."

•

The door to the briefing room was ajar and Kelly and Kath could hear David Benton. He was just explaining "the investigation has unearthed an added, sinister element. The suspected killer has conceived a devious plan. His objective is to mar the reputation of the University of Michigan. He targeted a handful of high-profile campus leaders in a vicious blackmail scheme."

121

David went on to point out that many of those present at the briefing were aware of the plot. "In a time when the media is frequently and heavily criticized for its insensitivity and irresponsibility in trashing the reputations of many public figures, rather than publishing innuendoes and half-truths, I want all of you and the public to know that in this instance, you and your associates in the media can stand tall. You realized you were being manipulated, being provided with photographs which cast aspersions on the reputations of innocent persons, photographs which had been staged and altered to give the impression these people were involved in illicit behavior. All these people are guilty of is being successful and in the limelight among the University family.

"Their persecutor's motive is to destroy their reputations and, in so doing, blacken the image of the University. He was once a student here. He was involved in a cheating scandal and was asked to leave. This is his act of revenge. His motivation isn't the money he's attempted to collect. It isn't the havoc he's created in innocent people's lives. His motivation is hatred of the University of Michigan.

"Your collective decision not to be manipulated, not to be instruments of destruction to the reputations of good people, is going to thwart his plans. On behalf of the targeted victims, on behalf of the University – thank you."

Bravo for the chief, thought Kelly. If one of the newspapers was now to alter its decision not to publish the names and details associated with the blackmail scheme, it would risk a backlash of public opinion. None, Kelly thought, wanted to be classified with the supermarket tabloids such as the National Enquirer or Star Magazine.

Benton, with Mike Cummings' help, was now in the process of distributing the computer sketches of McConnell. Kelly and Kath could overhear David saying, "Remember, he's dangerous. Not only is he the major suspect in the murder of Elizabeth Edwards, he's also believed to be the perpetrator of the vicious attacks that I described earlier, on two members of this department. No one should try to apprehend or detain him on their own. People should call our Hot Line."

David went on to explain that one of the vehicles registered in Joseph McConnell's name, a dark green Saab convertible, had been impounded. "Authorities in Illinois have informed us McConnell is also the owner of a dark blue, 1994 Mercury Cougar. We just put out an alert earlier this morning. We have no idea if the second vehicle ever entered the state."

There was considerable stirring and an undercurrent of conversation as Mike escorted Kath into the room while David introduced her. He was praising her for voluntarily returning to Michigan and her invaluable help to the investigative team. The implication was clear. Kath had exposed herself to considerable risk in returning and assisting in the apprehension of her sister's murderer.

She nervously approached the podium and with visible emotion, expressed her appreciation for the media coverage which she was confident would eventually lead to the arrest and conviction of her sister's killer. She made a plea to those in the audience for their continued cooperation and assistance. As Kath spoke, cameras flashed and the television lens zoomed in.

At the open door, Kelly was nodding her head. The decision to involve her in the briefing had been a wise one. She was doing an excellent job of fielding the questions which followed her opening remarks.

Then, out of the blue, one questioner asked, "Miss Edwards, what do you believe the chances are of the public believing you knew nothing until two weeks ago, about what your sister and her boyfriend were up to?"

Slightly startled, Kath had replied, "Well, it's the truth and I hope people will believe me. I . . ."

The same person interrupted with another question. "Do you have any regrets about not coming forward sooner? When you first learned of the blackmail scheme? If you had, isn't there the strong possibility your sister would be alive today?"

David quickly moved to the podium and eased Kath to the side. "I think everyone realizes Kath has to have asked herself that same question more times than we can ever imagine. That was a low blow," David said, glaring at the man. "Our next scheduled briefing will be tomorrow afternoon, Friday, at four. Thank you."

"Thank you," a voice called from the rear of the room. Others were also nodding their heads in approval of the forthright manner in which the police were dealing with the media. The reporter who'd asked the last question was making a hurried exit, attempting to avoid the critical stares of his colleagues.

•

Kelly, Kath, Judy and Steve were gathered around the conference room table, munching on sandwiches which had been picked up from

Zingerman's, Ann Arbor's favorite deli, located only a few blocks from headquarters.

Mike and Kelly had discussed the possibility of driving out to Chelsea for lunch at the Common Grill with Kath. The break and change of scenery, they reasoned, might be good for everyone. Kath, sensing she was now a celebrity of sorts and still somewhat shaken over the way the press conference had ended, opted for just bringing in sandwiches. With considerable work to catch up on, Kelly and Mike were happy to acquiesce to her wishes.

The mood was upbeat compared to earlier in the morning. All believed the media briefing had gone extremely well, except for the minor glitch at the end. No one in the department had recognized the reporter who had asked the final questions. A number of his colleagues volunteered that he was also a stranger to them. However, as Judy had commented, there was a positive slant to the incident in that it gave David a perfect opportunity to cut off further questions.

"And I hadn't given us a ghost of a chance of keeping the names of those being blackmailed out of the press," Judy said. "I now believe there's a strong probability that their identities can be kept confidential."

Mike told them he'd just heard the *Ann Arbor News* was holding up the presses so the latest information could be highlighted in a front page spread. Everyone in the department was primed for the avalanche of calls that the extensive media coverage was expected to precipitate.

Mary's voice came over the intercom, informing them there was a phone call for Kelly. Kelly quickly excused herself and went down the hall to her office to take the call.

"How are things going?" It was Rick. Kelly enthusiastically told him about the press conference and the computer drawing of McConnell.

"How about lunch?" Rick asked.

She told him they were having sandwiches from Zingerman's. "Maybe we could get together with Kath for dinner, though," Kelly said.

She explained that Kath would probably be heading back to the Campus Inn by three o'clock.

"I have some paperwork to attend to on other cases and don't see myself getting away until at least five. Why don't you come to my room about six o'clock? We can have a drink and decide what we'll do about dinner. Any suggestions?"

"I'll bring a bottle of wine. We could have pizza brought in, or at the

Cottage Inn," Rick replied. "There's always the Red Hawk."

Kelly smiled. Rick was a good sport. He hated cheese and as a result didn't eat pizza. She recalled when he'd placed an order last year for a pizza without cheese. Domino's thought it was a crank call, even after his explanation and a call back to verify the order. When the delivery man arrived at her apartment, he said they'd made bets at the store whether it was going to be a legitimate order or just a joke someone was playing on them or someone else.

Kelly responded, "It's Thursday and we shouldn't have a problem getting in either of those places. We can let Kath decide. My room number is 610. We'll see you around six. And thanks for calling, Rick, and for being so supportive these past couple of days."

"See you around six then," Rick replied.

As Kelly hung up she had the thought it was kind of surprising Rick hadn't questioned her referring to Katherine as Kath now. She'd intended to mention something to him about Kath's preference for the nickname.

•

Mike was there when she returned to the conference room. He handed Kelly her car keys and three door keys.

"The locks on your condo have been changed," he said with a smile. "I also had them pick up your car while they were there. It's parked downstairs."

Kelly expressed her thanks. She had tried again earlier to convince Mike that she should go back to her condo in hopes of prompting McConnell's return, or to convey some information to him again on her tapped phone line to prod him to make an appearance again. In addition to wanting her to be with Kath, Mike said they didn't have the manpower to keep the round-the-clock surveillance in place which would be required to minimize her risks at her condo.

"As to the phones, we blew our chance there," Mike said. "He's wise to us. The possibility of it working a second time is remote at best."

Around two o'clock one of the other officers brought them several copies of the *Ann Arbor News*. The computer drawing was centered on the front page. There was also a photo of Kath which had been taken at the briefing. All was quiet for several minutes as they each read the article.

"It's about all we could hope for," Judy said, and the others agreed.

125

After further conversation among the five of them, most of it pertaining to the investigation, Steve offered to escort Kath back to the hotel. Kelly had briefed her on Rick's call and that he'd be coming to their rooms around six o'clock. Kath understood Kelly's need to devote some time to her other cases and as she left with Steve, told Kelly she'd see her in a couple hours or so.

"Remember, keep our doors locked and chained," Kelly cautioned her. "Both doors, not just yours."

Steve nodded, aware they had connecting rooms. "I'll check out both rooms before I leave her," Steve said to Kelly.


### Chapter 17

Kelly was making good progress in cleaning up odds and ends when Mike entered her office.

"There's been a new development, Kelly. We just had a phone call from the manager of the copy center located in the basement of the Michigan Union. This afternoon a boy had three hundred copies made of a flyer that the manager believes might have something to do with the blackmail aspect of our case. The clerk who handled the order told him she'd made copies of a flyer with a heading criticizing the University for muzzling the press. There were bullet items hinting at scandals involving top University figures. The flyer alleges President Robinson is attempting to keep the sordid details under wraps. The clerk remembers three of the people named – Dr. Broadstead, Dean Jameson and Liz Hernandes."

Kelly whistled. "Just when we thought our chances were good for keeping their identities out of the press."

"I know. The manager had been reading the *Ann Arbor News* article this afternoon and saw the possible tie-in to the conversation he'd just had with his employee."

"Was there any mention of how many people were named?" Kelly asked.

"Five or six was her best recollection. I've sent Judy over to the Union. We'll possibly know more after she's had a chance to question them. We do know they don't have a copy of the flyer."

"One new name," Kelly commented. Mike nodded as he went on to explain, "Judy is going to call me from the copy center. She'll be attempt-

126

ing to contact Liz Hernandes right away."

Kelly and Mike both knew who Liz Hernandes was. She fit the profile of the others who had been targeted. An assistant to the President, she was in charge of the University's Cultural Diversification Program for students, faculty and administrators. There were many who sang her praises. She'd held the position, Kelly thought, for less than two years. She also had her share of critics. A vast number of University people thought she was trying to move too quickly and was being overly aggressive in upsetting the status quo.

"Was the clerk able to provide a description of the boy?" Kelly asked. "Do you think it was McConnell?"

"We'll have to wait to see what Judy learns. I'm sure you share the thought that he's toying with us. Why would he choose the copy center at the Union? The heart of the campus? With a drawing of him on the front page of the paper, he has to think his disguise is so good he won't be recognized. Of course, he could have hired someone, maybe the same young man he involved in collecting the blackmail payoffs, to have copies of the flyer made."

The intercom on Kelly's phone beeped and Mary Tucker informed her she had a call on line three.

Kelly picked up her receiver and said, "Kelly Travis speaking, how may I help you?"

"Hi Kelly, how's it going?" It was Rick again.

"Fine, I'm just about through here. I should be leaving in another ten minutes or so. We're still on for six o'clock?"

"That's all right with me. What are the plans?" Rick asked.

Confused, Kelly answered, "The same as we discussed earlier. You're coming to our rooms around six."

"Okay. The Campus Inn? Give me your room number."

"Rick, didn't I talk with you around noon today?"

"No, not since last night," he answered.

Mike noticed the look of alarm spreading over Kelly's face.

"Rick, I think I've been conned. I think McConnell called earlier, impersonating you. I'll have to call you back."

Kelly hung up, staring at Mike with a look of fear and panic on her face.

"Did you hear that?" Kelly blurted out. "We have to warn Kath."

Mike reached inside his coat pocket and took out a small address book.

"I have the hotel's number right here. You think you spoke with McConnell earlier?"

"I'm sure of it. I thought of the possibility he might try to imitate people's voices. I think I mentioned it to you. And here I'm the one to fall for it."

Mike had reached over and was punching in the number to the Campus Inn on Kelly's phone.

"Keep your fingers crossed," Kelly said, holding the receiver to her ear. The hotel operator answered and Kelly asked to be connected to room 611. She held up her crossed fingers as she mumbled to Mike. "He must have learned about Rick on my answering machine tape, heard his voice, worked on imitating it."

The phone kept ringing as Kelly's anxiety increased. The thought of being too late passed through her mind. She remembered telling McConnell, thinking he was Rick, that Kath would be going back to the hotel ahead of her. But I warned her about keeping the doors locked with the chain on, Kelly thought. He must have convinced her with his voice that he was Rick. She must have unfastened . . .

The phone was picked up on about the twentieth ring and there was silence.

"Kath, is that you? It's me, Kelly."

"Hi Kelly." It was Rick's voice. "She must be in the shower. I was able to break away a little earlier and thought I'd come over and keep her company while we were waiting for you."

Mike saw Kelly's eyes widen and the fear in her expression as she mouthed to Mike, "It's him."

Mike bounded out of the chair and raced out the door.

Control your voice, Kelly said to herself as she replied. "You caught me by surprise, Rick. I was just calling Kath to see if she needed to have me pick up anything for her. I should be leaving here in about twenty minutes."

Don't panic him, Kelly thought. Keep him on the line. Mike's on his way, hopefully others as well.

"Could you call in to her and ask?"

"Sure, just a minute."

As Kelly waited, she prayed that Kath was all right, still alive.

How can I keep him on the line? she asked herself.

"She says no, but thanks you for checking. We'll see you in about half an hour then."

"Fine. Did you happen to see the article in the *Ann Arbor News*?" Kelly asked, hoping he wouldn't hang up on her.

"Yes. As a matter of fact, I was just reading Kath's copy when you called."

"What do you think of it?"

"We can discuss it when you get here," he replied.

"Oh, there's been another development, too. Someone had copies of a flyer made in the basement of the Michigan Union earlier this afternoon. I haven't seen one yet, but it appears related to the blackmail plot."

Mike was re-entering Kelly's office. He gestured with his hands, mouthing the message, "Keep him on as long as you can."

"The names of several of the individuals we know were among those being blackmailed appear in the flyer," Kelly continued.

"Interesting," he said. "We can discuss that, too, when you get here. See you soon." He hung up.

Mike sensed that he'd hung up, as Kelly, stunned, sat with the receiver still in her hand.

"Come on," he said. "Three or four teams of officers, in addition to Steve, should be converging on the Campus Inn in a couple of minutes."

The hotel was only a few blocks from the police station. As Kelly and Mike moved out of the office, he explained that a cruiser was waiting for them out front, waiting to drive them to the Campus Inn.

•

During the course of the short drive, Kelly discussed with Mike how easily she'd been duped.

"I did all the talking when I thought I was speaking with Rick this afternoon. He only spoke a couple of sentences. But his suggestion of pizza for dinner should have alerted me. It should have tipped me off, especially after I realized he was serious and not trying to be funny. Then my next thought was what a nice guy he is."

Mike, Kelly realized, was only understanding about half of what she was talking about. The car wheeled into the driveway of the hotel and the officer slammed on his brakes in front of the main entrance. Kelly and Mike bounded out of the car.

•

On the sixth floor, Kelly and Mike saw three or four officers outside of the open doors to Kath's and Kelly's rooms.

"No one's here, both rooms are empty," one of the officers volunteered as they approached.

Kelly felt her heart skip a beat. A feeling of disappointment, mixed with fear, engulfed her.

"Split up," Mike directed the officers. "Cover every exit. Question anyone you see as to whether they've seen a man with a young woman leaving the hotel."

Kelly and Mike entered Kath's room. Steve was bending over the coffee table, trying to piece a few tattered bits of paper together. He looked up and motioned to the opposite end of the coffee table. There were five or six small lollipops on the table where he pointed. Kelly picked one up and read the label: Spangler Dum Dums[(tm)].

"I think I have something here," Steve said. "It's a note to Kelly. It was torn up in the wastebasket."

Kelly and Mike noticed there were a couple cigarette butts in the ashtray on the coffee table. The aroma of smoke was still present in the room.

"Yes, there – I think I've got it," Steve said.

Kelly looked over his shoulder as Steve read, "Dear Kelly. I'm shopping for another wig and some . . ."

He shook his head. "Can't make that out. But I can this next part. I'll be back before five p.m. I'll be careful! Signed Kath."

Kelly and Mike both quickly glanced at their watches. It was about ten to five.

"Let's hope she's still not back," Steve said. "More likely than not, though, he might have confronted her in the past few minutes as she was returning."

The phone rang and Mike grabbed the receiver. As he listened, a broad smile swept over his face.

"Just a minute," he said to the caller. "Kath just came in the front door. She's on her way up."

Kelly and Steve both breathed sighs of relief, and Steve exchanged a high five with Mike.

Mike was still on the phone. "Keep watching the exits, just for a man now. Check with the desk clerk. That's right, get the names and room numbers of any single man who checked in this afternoon."

Mike then listened and as he did so, he looked up in Kelly's and Steve's direction, nodding his head. He briefed them after hanging up.

"One of their bellmen is missing. The last time he was seen, over an hour ago, he'd been assisting a man with his bag who was checking into room 605. He had requested the sixth floor. The desk clerk remembers thinking it was unusual. The officer on his way up with Kath is bringing a key to that room."

Kelly heard Kath's voice in the hallway and hurried out to greet her with tears in her eyes. She was wearing the same blonde wig and warm up suit she'd been wearing when Kelly first met her. Kath dropped the two packages she was holding onto the floor as Kelly reached out to embrace her.

"You two wait here," Mike advised after greeting Kath with the understated comment, "We're glad you're safe."

Together, Mike and Steve moved toward the door to room 605, their guns drawn. Steve knocked a couple of times. There was no answer. Mike used the key he'd been given and slowly unlocked the door. Kicking the door open, the two stood with their backs to the hallway wall on opposite sides of the door, their guns raised.

"Cover me," Steve said as he lunged into the room. It appeared empty. The closet door stood open, but the bathroom door was shut. Using the same procedure they had at the entrance door, they opened it. A young man was stretched out in the tub, bound and gagged. He stared wide-eyed at Mike and Steve, seeing their guns, trying to talk through the tape over his mouth.

Mike and Steve replaced their guns and leaned down to remove the tape and untie the knots in the ropes which bound the young man's hands and feet.

•

As they stood in the hallway as Mike and Steve entered the nearby room, Kelly was whispering to Kath, trying to fill her in on the details of what had occurred. Kath alternated between nodding and shaking her head. Kelly could tell she'd quickly grasped the implications of how lucky she'd been not to have stayed in her room.

Moments later Mike stuck his head out of the doorway of the room he'd just entered with Steve. "We've found the bellman, bound and gagged in the bathtub. He's just beginning to tell us what happened. There's no sign of McConnell. Why don't you take Kath into your room, Kelly. You can finish telling her about what's happened. I'll be with you in a few minutes. Be sure to keep your door locked, with the chain on, too."

•

Kelly was nearly finished telling Kath everything that had transpired since Steve had escorted her back to her room. They'd taken a couple cans of Pepsi from the room's refrigerator bar and had just started to drink them when they heard a knock at the door and Mike call out it was him. Kelly opened the door, keeping the chain attached to first verify it was really him. Seeing it was, she closed the door again and unfastened the chain. She then opened it again so he could come in.

Kelly asked him if he wanted something to drink. Mike shook his head and said, "We've learned how he was able to get in your rooms. Sorry I took so long, but we're hoping he's still here in the hotel. I was just briefing everyone. The bellman was very helpful and he doesn't appear to be seriously injured."

"That's a relief," Kelly said. "Was McConnell wearing a disguise of some kind?"

Mike nodded. "A turban, actually. A dark complexion. He checked in about an hour and a half ago, asking for a room on the sixth floor. He also asked for assistance with his single piece of luggage and the bellman led him up to his room. You saw it was only a few doors down from yours. Outside the door, McConnell had fumbled around, seemingly trying to locate the pocket he'd placed his room key in. He apologized for holding the young man up, saying the key had to be somewhere, he'd just had it in his hand. He spoke with a heavy accent.

"The bellhop says he told him that was no problem, and that he could use his master key to open the door. He told McConnell to just call the front desk if he still couldn't locate his key later and he'd bring him another. After they were in the room, McConnell asked him to check under the bed to make certain no one was hiding there. The young man said he remembers smiling to himself as he knelt by the bed, it was the first request of this nature he'd ever had. McConnell then struck him on the head from behind, a tremendous wallop. He thinks a blackjack of some kind was used rather than just a hand or fist. The next thing he remembers is waking up to find himself bound and gagged in the bathtub."

"It explains how McConnell was able to obtain a key to get into your rooms. He must have read your note, Kath, torn it up and waited for you. Did you know he was a smoker?" Mike asked.

"Yes and no," Kath answered. "Beth and he both mentioned that they were trying to kick the habit. I never saw him with a cigarette though."

"Well, it appears he's started up again. Maybe he's a little nervous after all. We'll try to get a print off this one," Mike said, referring to one of the butts in the ashtray, from which only a puff or two had been taken.

"It appears he'd just lit this one up when something interrupted him. Probably your phone call, Kelly. Maybe he spotted our people driving up from your window. I spoke with David and he doesn't see much point in continuing to check out every room. He suggests we keep people posted at the main door and the other two exits for the next few hours. We're going to get the two of you moved to another hotel. I think it'll be the Crowne Plaza, out by the Briarwood Mall, the former Hilton."

Kelly nodded, knowing the hotel Mike was referring to.

"David's making arrangements now. He'll be calling back.

"By the way, President Robinson called David to commend him on the efforts we're taking to keep the names of the individuals being blackmailed out of the press. David was disappointed when I told him about the latest development, the copies of the flyer being made."

The phone rang and Mike said, "That may be Judy now, or David with the hotel arrangements." He picked up the phone. After a brief conversation he covered the mouthpiece and told Kelly, "Rick Forsythe is downstairs. They're wondering whether to send him up."

Kelly hadn't called Rick back. She was glad he'd taken the initiative to come to the hotel.

"Of course," Kelly said to Mike and then smiled. "Tell them to ask him where he first met me. If he doesn't say it was a football game, tell them to apprehend him."

Mike laughed. "McConnell's pulled some bold moves, but I have to believe it's really Rick downstairs." Mike relayed Kelly's thoughts to the party on the other end of the line, and after hanging up told Kelly, "They'll be sending him up right away."

•

133

Rick drove Kath over to the Crowne Plaza and Kelly followed in her car. Kath was wearing the new wig she'd purchased. It was strawberry blonde in color and had a short, fluffy cut. It was amazing how this one thing could do so much to change her appearance. However, it also made all of them realize how easily McConnell could alter his appearance.

As Kelly followed Rick and Kath, she pondered over the further conversation she'd had with Mike. He'd suggested Kelly should attempt to contact the five people they knew of who'd been blackmailed, possibly later this evening from her room. Kelly and Mike agreed they all would appreciate being kept informed and being forewarned of the possible circulation of the flyer. Mike had promised to notify Kelly after he'd spoken to Judy. Judy could, possibly, contact Liz Hernandes and Kelly would just have to notify the other four.

The good news about this afternoon was the fact that McConnell hadn't left Ann Arbor. There was concern he might flee the area as the publicity intensified. As she drove, Kelly thought of the suckers McConnell had left in the room. There was no need for Benton or Mike to prod the department to bring this case to a head. McConnell's "sweet messages" were providing all the incentive needed.


## Chapter 18

After checking in, Kelly and Kath freshened up, taking showers and changing clothes, before heading to the Briarwood Mall with Rick for a leisurely bite to eat at Ruby Tuesday's. Though it would have been only a short walk, Kelly made the decision to drive. Walking across the roadways which circled the mall might attract unneeded attention.

During dinner, the conversation kept coming back to the subject of how fortunate it was that Kath had ventured out of the Campus Inn to shop for the wig.

Kath shook her head as she said, "The sales clerk was taking so long to write up my purchase. I was trying to hurry her. Thank heavens she was so slow. Otherwise, I might have walked in on Joe."

She shivered as she envisioned what the possible consequences of that could have been.

"You shouldn't have left your room, but as you said, thank heavens you did," Kelly said. "From now on, though, we're going to be like Siamese twins. Right?"

Kath smiled and nodded. After savoring coffee, the three of them headed back to the Crowne Plaza. Rick escorted them to their rooms before bidding them goodnight.

"Just give me a call if I can be of help," he said. "Do you want me to meet you for breakfast? How about chauffeuring?"

Kelly thanked him, but said she thought they could manage on their own. "I'll call you," she said. "Maybe we can have dinner again tomorrow night."

Thanking him once again, she gave him a kiss on his cheek.

•

The message light was blinking on Kelly's phone. Mike had phoned with the message to call him at the office. She immediately called, explaining they'd just returned from having dinner.

"I just wanted to bring you up to date," Mike said, "before you start making your calls. First, I'm sorry to say, he eluded us again. He left the Campus Inn about fifteen minutes after you did."

Mike then proceeded to give her the details. A man with a beard, dressed in a warm up suit and running shoes, had come down the elevator to the lobby shortly before seven o'clock. His build was similar to the description they had of McConnell and the two officers charged with watching the main entrance stopped him. The man became a little huffy with them, complaining that they were delaying his run and telling them he had another commitment and was already having to cut it short. His attitude only served to reinforce the officers' decision to thoroughly check him out.

The man seemed to sense that and immediately became extremely cooperative. He wasn't carrying any identification and volunteered to go back upstairs to his room to get it. He gave his name and said he was a frequent guest. He led the officers over to the front desk and asked the desk clerk to verify that he was registered. He'd given the name of Dr. Robert Cunningham, registered in a room on the third floor. While the desk clerk couldn't vouch for his identity, he was able to verify a Dr. R. Cunningham and his wife were registered in room 307.

The officers asked him to show them his room key and he explained he hadn't needed it because his wife was still upstairs in the room. He

135

suggested they call her. They attempted to reach her and received a busy signal. He commented that she'd been on the phone talking to her mother when he'd left the room, and added she was liable to be a while.

The desk clerk then interrupted to tell the man who he assumed was Dr. Cunningham that he had a note in his box. The message was from a local physician one of the officer's knew by name, saying he'd be by around seven-thirty to pick "Sally and you" up for dinner. The man checked his watch and asked the officers to try his wife again. Meanwhile, another man who warranted some attention was also wanting to exit the hotel. The Cunningham's phone was still busy.

The man claiming to be Cunningham had now become very cooperative. He told the officers it wouldn't be the end of the world if he didn't get his run in. He'd done a complete about-face from his earlier, antagonistic behavior. The other man was the one now in a rage over being detained. Cunningham told the officers he'd just skip his run and asked if they wanted him to bring down his identification now or when he and his wife went out to dinner. The officers conferred, and with the other man demanding their attention, agreed to let Cunningham leave for his run. They said Cunningham wasn't at all nervous and neither believed he could be McConnell.

Ten minutes later the same clerk motioned the two officers over to the registration desk. A couple who had just come in were standing at the counter. The desk clerk introduced them as Dr. and Mrs. Cunningham.

"As you can imagine, the two officers involved are devastated and very apologetic. They later determined the phone was off the hook in the Cunningham's room. McConnell must have seen Cunningham's name on their luggage in the room. The suitcase McConnell had with him when he checked in still hasn't been found.

"Of course, an immediate alert went out and the two officers plus the ones who'd been watching the Campus Inn's other exits scoured the area in proximity to the Campus Inn without success. McConnell is clever, but he's also been lucky. If your departure had been delayed a few minutes, Kath might have recognized him. If the Cunningham's had arrived fifteen minutes sooner, it would have been a far different scenario. As it is, we're back to square one."

"We've been so close twice now," Kelly said. "By this time, he may have an entirely different look. His appearance, clothes and I.D. could have all been changed."

"They did find his other car," Mike said. "The Mercury Cougar. It was on the top deck of the Maynard Street parking structure with stolen Michigan plates. It's already been impounded. If I'd known a little sooner, we might have left it there. Planted a homing device of some kind and kept it under observation in hopes he'd use it again. He might have planned to. If he was abandoning it, he would probably have left us a message. Perhaps another handful of Dum Dums(tm)."

Kelly could sense Mike's anger and frustration as he continued.

"Hopefully, his lack of wheels could be a break for us. We've already circulated his description to the local cab drivers and the campus security personnel. Ann Arbor Transit will be posting a notice for its drivers and we'll be keeping a close eye on stolen vehicle reports.

"Can't say I'm overly optimistic. Especially after seeing how that wig completely altered Kath's appearance."

"That's true," said Kelly. "But as you said, McConnell's been lucky. Not only with his timing, but also with the circumstances. If those officers hadn't had someone else demanding to leave the hotel at the same time McConnell was, the end result might have been far different. His luck's bound to change and the good news is, last we knew he was still here in Ann Arbor. Changing the subject a little, has Judy let you know how she made out at the Michigan Union?"

"Yes, and she just had a call that I'll tell you about too. First, McConnell wasn't the one who had the copies made. It was a young man with a slender build. From the employee's description, Judy and I surmise it's the same boy McConnell used to pick up the blackmail payoffs and to take money out to the airport. While the copies were being made, he mentioned something about his motor bike being on the blink. We don't have a copy of the flyer. The clerk tried to retain one, explaining the company kept a copy of every run for their records. He didn't buy into that and made sure he had all the copies in addition to the original. He became angry when the girl was cello wrapping the copies, accusing her of dawdling and reading something she shouldn't. As a result, the girl Judy interviewed could only provide an overall picture of the contents of the flyer. Not much more than we were told when the manager first called.

"The girl did say the boy appeared nervous and kept rushing her. One thing she noticed was the fact he was wearing a Louisville Cardinal baseball cap. Judy picked up on that.

"She went to the West Quad dormitory, which as you know adjoins

137

the Union, and was able to get a listing of the students living there, including their hometowns. Her thought was the boy might have chosen the Union to have the copies made because it was close to where he lived. And I know what you're thinking. The mere fact he wore a Louisville Cardinal cap, especially in this day and age, didn't necessarily mean he came from the Louisville area, or had any association with Louisville. The many shirts and other articles of clothing with the Slippery Rock College name you see students wearing are testimony to that. The more off-the-beaten-track the school is, the better. But Judy reasoned even though there was only a remote chance the boy was from the Louisville area, students who were from that area might have noticed him wearing the cap and be able to tell us his name.

"There were only two students from Louisville living in West Quad. One was a girl and the boy was an African-American. Judy was able to make contact with both, probably because of the dinner hour timing. But they weren't of any help except to say there were at least a couple of students across the way at South Quad who were from the Louisville area. The ones they knew of, however, didn't match the boy's description.

"Nonetheless, Judy went across the street to South Quad. She met a lady, just as she was locking up the office, who could furnish her the names and addresses of all the residents. She was helpful and gave Judy three names. One was a girl. The first boy she spoke with was of no help and the other wasn't in his room. Judy did reach the girl and she knew exactly who the boy was Judy described. The problem was, although she'd often seen him, she didn't know his name or on which floor he lived, or even if he lived in South Quad. She believed one of her roommates knew his name, but she wouldn't be seeing her until later this evening. Judy left her card and phone number and the girl promised to call if she came up with a name.

"Now the good news! Judy received a call thirty minutes ago from the actual boy. The girl had spoken to him and told him Judy wanted to talk to him. Judy says he's very confused and scared, more so after talking with her, over what he's gotten himself involved in. He refused to give her his name. After she finished talking with him, Judy tried to reach the girl she'd spoken to earlier, but she hasn't been able to reach her or her roommate. There was no answer.

"The boy admits he had copies of the flyer made. He's already given them to McConnell, who came to his room to get them. He says McConnell wasn't disguised in any way, similar in appearance and dress as to how he'd looked when the boy had had previous contacts with him. Judy pressed him for a description and he described a man with a beard and horn-rimmed glasses. His build was similar to McConnell's and the boy knows him as Joe McConnell. It appears that although he's used his own name in contacts with the boy, he disguised himself from the start.

"The boy professed not to have seen today's *Ann Arbor News* article. He pictured McConnell as a loyal alumnus of the University, doing the school a favor by calling attention to and forcing out a handful of individuals whose behavior could embarrass the University. As a result, the boy thinks he's done nothing wrong in helping McConnell get rid of the bad apples. He emphasized with Judy the fact those people wouldn't have paid any money, if they weren't guilty. He says he never saw any photographs and seemed genuinely shocked and surprised to learn the Edwards girl was in all the compromising photos. Judy suggested he get a copy of today's paper as she explained the people targeted were all innocent victims of a vicious blackmail scheme to discredit them and the University. She told him he could be charged as an accomplice in the scheme and also as an accomplice in Beth Edwards' murder.

"In regard to Beth, he told Judy that McConnell couldn't possibly be involved in her murder. He'd loved her. McConnell had told him he suspected one of the individuals they'd gotten the goods on and were blackmailing had killed her. He believes McConnell's now trying to determine which one. The flyers were going to be used in some way to zero in on who was responsible.

"Another thing Judy learned runs counter to our belief that McConnell had intentionally picked the Michigan Union to have copies of the flyer made to send a message to us that he wasn't worried about being identified and maybe wanted us to know about the flyer. When McConnell picked up the flyers, he asked to borrow the boy's motor bike. On being told it was out of commission, he commented, 'So that's why you had the copies made at the Union.' The young man asked him how he knew that and McConnell had just smiled. The original plan had been to get the copies made at a local business south of town where a classmate of the young man's was employed part time. The classmate was willing to arrange to let him make copies on his own in private for ten bucks."

As Mike related these facts, Kelly recalled telling McConnell, who was pretending to be Rick, about learning copies of a flyer had been made at the Michigan Union.

"Was McConnell angry over the fact the boy had the copies made at the Union?" she asked.

"Judy didn't comment on that, just the fact the boy was surprised that McConnell knew he'd had the copies made there."

Kelly volunteered, "McConnell learned that from me, while I was trying to stall him on the phone."

"I remember. No harm done. I think that about covers what Judy had to say."

"Was the call being traced?" Kelly asked.

"Yes, but it proved to be a pay phone outside the Blue Front." Kelly knew the popular convenience store on Packard and State Street, a few blocks from South Quad.

"We're hoping Judy's able to get the boy's name in the next couple of hours from the girl she spoke with earlier. The way it stands currently is the boy will be coming to headquarters to see Judy about eleven o'clock tomorrow. He says he has a major exam he's studying for, early tomorrow. He's scared and promises to fully cooperate. Even so, he still refused to give his name. He also says he doesn't have a copy of the flyer, that McConnell took everything."

"Did he have any idea as to how McConnell was going to use the flyers, how they'd be circulated?"

"Not really. He thinks McConnell is holding them in reserve to be used in the event something else doesn't pan out. He thought it was all about getting these people to resign and leave the University. He still holds the belief McConnell is the good guy with a noble purpose. I think what Judy had to say causes him to doubt himself now, though. She questioned him as to how he could be so naive to think anything constructive could be accomplished by the circulation of that slanderous flyer. He did tell Judy that there are only five individuals identified in the flyer. Hopefully, that means we know all the people now who were targeted by McConnell."

"What's your reaction to his statement about one of the individuals who was being blackmailed being responsible for Beth's death?" Kelly asked.

"I guess anything is possible. In my own mind, I think it would be incredible to think anyone other than McConnell is responsible for Beth Edwards' death. What's yours?"

"I agree. Any suggestions for me? I plan to make those calls now."

"Yes. I'd stress the point they should contact us immediately if

McConnell attempts to contact them in any way. Warn them about the potential danger of trying to entrap or capture McConnell on their own. I guess that scares me more than anything. They're all very bright people and sometimes that leads to doing something very stupid. I think as much as they'll be alarmed about the flyer, they'll be happy we're keeping them in the loop and hopefully getting closer to apprehending McConnell."

Kelly and Mike concluded their conversation by assuring one another they'd be in touch if anything important surfaced, otherwise they'd see each other at headquarters in the morning.

•

Kelly debated over whether to go next door and brief Kath before beginning her calls. It'll only take a few minutes, Kelly reasoned as she dialed her room.

"Still awake? I just hung up from speaking to Mike and thought I'd come over and update you."

"Fine," Kath answered. "Do you want me to come to your room? I'm still dressed."

"No, I'll come to your room. It'll be about five minutes."

Kelly was in the bathroom when she heard a knock at the door to her room.

"Just a minute," she called out, wondering if Kath had misunderstood her. Approaching the door she asked, "Who is it?" only to be met by silence. The door chain was attached and Kelly left it on as she slowly opened the door, peering out as she did so.

There was a manila envelope on the floor, propped against the door, which immediately caught her eye. There didn't appear to be anyone in the hall. She closed the door, unhooked the chain and quickly opened the door again. Leaning over, she retrieved the envelope off the floor. There was no one in the corridor. She closed the door and re-attached the chain.

The envelope was addressed to "Detective Travis" with the word "Confidential" in large caps, handwritten. Kelly quickly opened it and looking in, saw a white, business-size envelope and a candy bar. She reached in and removed a Dove(tm) candy bar. She also removed the white envelope and opened it. Inside were three pages. A copy of the flyer she'd heard described, a short, typed letter addressed to her, and another letter addressed to the five people whose names appeared in the flyer.

Kelly glanced at the flyer. The format and content fit the general description the clerk had given Judy. Under a bold header, "What the University of Michigan Doesn't Want You To Know," appeared a paragraph chastising President Robinson and the University for attempting to muzzle the news media into suppressing evidence of morally reprehensible behavior by several prominent individuals associated with the University.

This was followed by the statement, "You Have A Right To Know!" with a brief paragraph about each of the individuals McConnell was blackmailing. Their names were highlighted in bold print. Kelly grimaced as she skimmed the paragraphs. Liz Hernandes, described as the architect and implementer of the University's ambitious Diversity Program, was said to be promoting the theme of diversity in her private life by orchestrating and participating in sex orgies involving men and women of various races. "All-American" Tim Masterson was accused of "scoring" with a number of U of M cheerleaders. Dean Jameson was said to have used his "extra paycheck" to finance an affair with one of his students.

A paragraph at the bottom of the flyer stated evidence of this scandalous behavior included photographs and witnesses. In addition to the outrageous accusations, McConnell raised questions in regard to each of the individuals to further inflame the charges.

"How many abortions have resulted from Masterson's conquests?" "Have women athletes been sexually harassed by Singleton?" "Has Hernandes added a new criteria for the U of M Diversity Program, showing favoritism based on the willingness of individuals to participate in her extra-curricular activities?"

Shaking her head, Kelly began to read the letter addressed to her. McConnell was asking her to serve as the intermediary in collecting a "final payment" from the five victims. Kelly was amazed at his audacity in detailing his predicament and need for the money to "begin a new life." He'd lost his cars, apartment, personal possessions, his identity and the most crushing loss of all – the woman he loved. The letter went on to say that while most of the assumptions Kelly and her associates had made about him were true, the assumption that he killed Beth Edwards was not. He wanted to work with Kelly to unearth the real killer. Mutual trust would be necessary.

Unbelievable, thought Kelly as she continued to read. The final paragraph stated he would call her for an answer tonight at ten o'clock. She was asked to go to the hotel lobby at that time and he'd have her paged.

Kelly glanced at her watch. It was already nine-thirty-five. If her answer was yes, he'd mail the enclosed letter with a copy of the flyer to the five identified individuals, so they would have it by tomorrow.

Kelly had begun to read the letter addressed to the five as the phone rang. Kelly had been sitting on the bed and she leaned over to pick up the receiver.

"Hello."

"Hi Kelly, it's me," said Kath. "I thought you said you were coming over. Is everything okay?"

"I was and I still am. But I just had an envelope left outside my door. It's from McConnell. In addition to a letter to me, he enclosed a copy of the flyer we heard about, and also a copy of a letter he's planning to send to the blackmail victims. He wants me to act as an intermediary in collecting a final payment from them. I'll come over now. Keep your chain on until you're sure it's me."

Kelly grabbed the letters, the flyer and her purse, and cautiously opened her door, leaving the chain on. The corridor appeared to be deserted. She closed the door and unhooked the chain. Opening it again, she glanced in both directions and saw no one. Quickly she walked next door and knocked on Kath's door. She was pleased to see she was also being cautious and following her instructions, as the door opened and Kath peeked out to verify it was her.

Once Inside, Kelly handed her the copy of the flyer and the letter directed to her. Kath read those as Kelly scanned the other letter. McConnell was asking for $100,000. Similar to the letter to her, this one also outlined the reasons McConnell needed the money to make a fresh start. There was also a paragraph citing the reasons why this was a good "investment" for the University and the five blackmail victims. If the flyer ended up being circulated, the letter stated Masterson alone could lose much more than $100,000 in a coaching contract. The letter also claimed the University could lose millions of dollars in research grants. As long as he ended up with $100,000, he didn't care how the parties agreed to share the "investment." The final paragraph told them to coordinate their efforts through Detective Travis. The closing sentence was a threat to widely circulate copies of the enclosed flyer if he didn't receive the payment by noon on Tuesday.

Kath was still reading as Kelly picked up the phone and dialed the front desk. How had McConnell known where they were? The rooms were registered under the names Nancy White and Ann Hess.

"Hello. This is Nancy White in room 214. I just had an envelope dropped off outside my door. Do you know anything about it?"

As she listened she handed Kath the other letter. The desk clerk, a young man, was explaining yes, he was the one who dropped it off. A man had come in nearly half an hour ago and said he had an important packet of information which had to be delivered immediately to one of the hotel's guests.

"I told him we didn't have a Kelly Travis registered as a guest and he became very angry, saying he didn't have time to play games," the clerk said. "He seemed to know all about the police booking two rooms and said I'd be in trouble for impeding a criminal investigation if I didn't cooperate. I agreed to call your room, and I did several times, but your line was busy. He kept demanding your room number, but I wouldn't give it to him. It's a slow night and there's just two of us here. He kept threatening me and I finally agreed to deliver the envelope myself. He wanted to accompany me, but I told him he couldn't.

"I took the elevator to the third floor and then used the stairs to go down to your floor. I was concerned he might try to follow me. Brenda, who's on the switchboard tonight, was covering the desk for me. After I knocked I heard someone, I think it was you, say "just a minute." I probably should have waited, but I just left it propped against your door. I was worried Mr. Maloney might see me standing outside your door. I hurried back downstairs and he was gone. I just checked a guest in. I was planning on calling you to explain what happened and make sure you got the envelope. I hope I didn't do anything wrong."

Kelly assured him he hadn't and praised him for not having given her room number to the man.

"He used the name Maloney?" she asked.

"Yes. Michael Maloney. He said he was a private investigator working with you on a case."

Kelly glanced at her watch; nearly nine-fifty.

"I'm going to be coming down to use your fax and phone in a few minutes. You say Maloney's gone?"

"Yes. I haven't seen him since I left to deliver the envelope. He did leave a note for you. I was about to call you about that, too."

"Can you read it to me?"

"Just a minute, I'll get it."

Kelly was still trying to digest the correspondence and what she'd just learned as the desk clerk came back on the line.

"All it says is, 'Sorry about the time crunch. I'll call you at ten-fifteen p.m.' with his initials."

"Thank you. I'll be right down."

## Chapter 19

Kelly explained to Kath that although McConnell was aware they were both staying at the hotel, she didn't think he knew their room numbers. She told Kath she wanted her to stay in her room with the chain on while she went down to the lobby and faxed copies of the letters and flyer to Mike.

Kath argued that she wanted to go with Kelly.

"This might just be a trap, a trick of McConnell's to get you out of your room. You aren't being taken in by his claim he didn't kill my sister, are you?"

Kelly shook her head. "I don't think I'm in danger, though. McConnell is trying to use me to further his plans. His claim he didn't kill your sister wasn't totally new to us. It's the same story he told the boy who had the flyer copies made for him. I was coming to tell you what else we learned when the envelope appeared."

"Are you going to tell Joe you'll help him? I can't believe you would."

"I'm not sure. I want to discuss it with Mike. Maybe by playing along, we'll get another opportunity to catch him. I'm well aware if the police are involved in arranging a payment to him, we'll be wide open for being blackmailed ourselves. At the same time, I don't know if we can or should prevent the ones who will truly be hurt by that flyer from dealing directly with him. It's a tough call. And he's smart, he's not going to be easily tricked."

Kath continued to beg Kelly to be allowed to accompany her to the lobby.

"I'll be safer with you, with your gun and all, than staying here. I know he still considers me a threat, a key witness if he ever comes to trial. But please, give me the opportunity to help. I promise to stay out of your way."

Even though Kelly continued to argue that Kath would be better off remaining in the room, she finally conceded.

"You'll have to stay by my side. I don't want to have to worry about where you are."

•

Kelly and Kath arrived at the reception desk in the lobby a few minutes later. Kelly introduced herself to the desk clerk, James Patterson, who she'd spoken to earlier. Kath was wearing the new wig. Kelly introduced her by the Ann Hess name that had been used in registering for the room. As Patterson directed the two of them into the office and pointed out the fax machine and phone, he handed Kelly the note he'd read to her earlier over the phone.

"I already briefed Brenda that you're expecting a call at ten-fifteen. She'll buzz you here in the office."

As he'd talked, Kelly had studied the note. Her name was printed on the outside of the folded piece of note paper. She opened it and couldn't contain her smile. She handed it over to Kath. The word crunch in the line,

"Sorry about the time CRUNCH," was in capital letters and underlined. The signed initials had an ampersand between them. "M&M. Michael Maloney."

Kath also picked up on the note's reference to the Nestle Crunch[tm] bar and M&M's[tm].

"He's sick," she said. "Still playing his silly games after murdering my sister and putting those people through hell."

As Kelly faxed the copies of the flyer and letters to Mike, she reached out for the note that was still in Kath's hand.

"I couldn't agree more. I'm going to make a copy of this, too, and fax it over to Mike. One thing McConnell is succeeding in doing, is motivating us even more to nail him. I forgot to mention the Dove[tm] bar he included in the envelope with the flyer and letters. Trying to make peace."

As Kath watched the fax go through, Kelly dialed Mike's direct number. Luckily he was still at his desk. She quickly explained the recent developments and told him about the material being faxed.

"He's going to be calling you in ten minutes?"

"That's right. And I need your input on what I should tell him."

Mike left the phone for a minute to retrieve the faxes and then continued the conversation with the flyer, letters and note spread out before him on his desk.

"He continues to be lucky and a step ahead of us," Mike said. "I bet he's planted some type of sensing device on your car, Kelly. How else would he know you were there at the Crowne Plaza?"

"That could be, but the big question now is what do I say when he calls. I don't want to sound too eager, but it might be one of the last opportunities we'll have to trap him."

"You're right, but I certainly don't want you endangered in any way. I wish we had more time so I could discuss this with David, format a plan. Maybe you could stall him."

"Whether I did for an hour or a day, I hate to risk the possibility of blowing this opportunity," Kelly replied. "I'll just listen and play it by ear. If he gets suspicious, he might change his plans. He wants to get those letters in the mail tonight. If we delay him, he might seek to involve someone else as the intermediary, maybe one of those being blackmailed. We might be shut out from knowing what he's doing."

"I agree, we can't pass up this opportunity. But you have to promise me you won't agree to meet with him on your own. He might try to arrange a meeting with you tonight. Don't be tempted. He's a killer, mentally deranged. Be careful about what you say; I'm going to get Kath and you moved tonight. I'll be there in about twenty minutes and . . . "

Kath was pointing to the blinking light on Kelly's phone, mouthing the words, "It's him."

"His call's coming in now, Mike. I'll see you soon."

•

Kelly hung up and took a deep breath before picking up the receiver again and pushing the blinking button.

"Hello," she said.

"Hello to you too. I don't think introductions are necessary." He was speaking in a pronounced English accent. Kelly recalled he'd impersonated a visiting professor from England at the Bell Tower.

"No, I guess not."

"You received the envelope? Hope you enjoyed the Dove$^{(tm)}$ bar and appreciated my note." He was chuckling as he spoke. "Do you have an answer for me?"

"What exactly do you want me to do?" Kelly replied with her own question.

"I think you already know. Meet with the five of them, one on one or collectively, I don't care. Collect one hundred thousand in cash, nothing higher than a fifty dollar bill. Accomplish it by Monday evening. I'll contact you regarding delivery. Very simple."

He continued on. "You might want to know why I chose you. In addition to probably already being well acquainted with those five people, I believe you're extremely sensitive to the havoc it would cause them if the flyer is circulated. I also want you to call off the hounds. Give me a breather to track down Beth's real killer. Were you surprised to learn I didn't murder Beth?"

"Not surprised to have you make that assertion," Kelly answered. "We'd already learned, from the boy you had make copies of the flyer, that you claimed you weren't responsible for her death."

"You've talked to him?"

Kelly noticed his change of tone, a note of anger and concern.

"Yes. He's cooperating with us."

There was silence for several seconds, except for McConnell's heavy breathing.

"Whether you believe me or not, Kelly, this is a way to wrap up the case with no further injury to anyone. I'll destroy all the photographs and flyers after I have the money. I'll help you identify the guilty person. But if I learn of any plans to continue to pursue me or to try to entrap me when you deliver the money, the three hundred flyers and more will be distributed. You've been warned. Pass the message on."

"I can't stop the investigation. There's too much media pressure now."

"You orchestrated it, you can stop it. You're smart. You can circulate the story that I've been spotted in California; maybe even apprehended. Be creative. I'm serious about tracking down Beth's killer. I'd like to meet with you, perhaps tonight, to exchange information. Is that possible?"

Kelly's heart was racing. She remembered Mike's warning. Kath saw the look of alarm on Kelly's face as she answered. "Do you think Jameson killed her? Is that why you attempted to run him down?"

"You'd like to have me admit to that, wouldn't you? We'll discuss it. Give me your room number. I'll call you back in half an hour to set up a time and place to meet."

Kelly's mind was racing. Should she divulge her room number? He'd know Kath probably had an adjoining room. Mike would be here soon. They could stay in the office until he arrived. Mike said he'd get them moved tonight.

"I didn't hear you. What's your room number? We'll have to learn, as I said in my letter, to trust one another," McConnell chuckled.

"Two-fourteen," Kelly answered.

"Thatta girl! I'll call you at eleven. Cheerio!"

•

Kath's eyes had widened when she heard Kelly give him her room number. She was eager to hear everything he'd said. Kelly also explained that Mike was on his way and should be arriving any minute.

"We'll wait here for him. He's trying to get us into a different hotel tonight. That's one reason I gave McConnell my room number."

There was a knock on the door and James Patterson leaned his head in.

"Mike Cummings just called to let you know he's on his way. He said to also tell you that Steve and David were with him. He said you'd know

149

who he was referring to."

Kelly thanked Patterson and explained that the two of them would be staying in the office until Mike and the others arrived, if that was all right with him.

They discussed Kelly's conversation with McConnell in further detail as they waited, including his demand to have the investigation stopped and his request to meet with Kelly later tonight.

## Chapter 20

It was nearly twenty minutes to eleven when Mike arrived, accompanied by David Benton and Steve Renz. Kelly briefed them on the call from McConnell and the fact he'd be phoning Kelly's room at eleven o'clock to advise her on the time and location of the meeting he wanted to have with her later tonight. She also explained her reasoning for having given her room number to McConnell.

Before heading to Kelly's room, there had been a brief discussion with James Patterson. He'd provided a description of the man who called himself Mike Maloney. The height and build matched McConnell's. Bushy gray hair, eyebrows and a mustache were part of his latest disguise. He hadn't been wearing eyeglasses.

After they were seated in Kelly's room, David steered the conversation. Their first concern should be to determine how best to address McConnell's request for a meeting with Kelly. The question of how to handle his demand for a suspension of the investigation could be dealt with later.

"One thought I have," David said, "is for you to suggest to him that Mike be included in your meeting, on the basis he's in charge of the case and is more familiar with the homicide aspect of the investigation than you would be. You could say you've been focused on the blackmail side."

Steve had raised his eyebrows and was shaking his head no. "He's not going to fall for that. It would be nice if he did, but no way. I'm not saying it shouldn't be attempted, just that he's apt to laugh Kelly off. I'd opt for trying to get the meeting postponed to . . . possibly tomorrow afternoon."

"That would be nice, too," Mike said. "It would give us time to map out what Kelly should and shouldn't say. Not only about the whereabouts on Halloween night of the individuals he's blackmailing, but details about the body. We've also kept the discovery of the PayDay^(tm) bar confidential to this point. A delay would also give us more time to get Kelly fully rigged up. Show her what you came up with, Steve."

Steve removed a small plastic container from his pocket as he explained it was something brand new that the Federal Drug Enforcement Agency had just made available to local police agencies. He opened the container and showed Kelly a flat disk, slightly larger than a quarter.

"It has an adhesive backing, designed to be worn in the toe of a shoe, affixed to the upper portion. It's a combination listening and sensing device, to record a conversation and at the same time, pinpoint the location where the conversation is taking place. I saw a demo last week, truly amazing. The major negative is that the range is limited to approximately one thousand yards. But it's able to work from a vehicle, an office building or apartment complex, and in a crowded location."

Steve smiled. "You could sit on one side of the U of M stadium and pinpoint the seat location of someone wearing it on the opposite side. You could easily hear all the comments the wearer and his or her seat companions were making about the referees' or coaches' decisions."

"By tomorrow," Mike interrupted, "we could also get you set up with something for your purse or that you could wear with a far greater range. By the way, we'll get your car checked out tomorrow morning, Kelly. I'm sure McConnell planted something to enable him to trace you to this hotel. I'm having a slight problem getting the two of you rooms elsewhere. Tonight's no problem. Tomorrow night, with the Indiana home game, is the problem. Seems every room in town, except for these, has been booked."

"We don't want to have you moving every day," David said with a smile. "And we don't want you isolated somewhere. Going back to the Campus Inn is out because we know McConnell has a master key. Judy was still working on finding rooms when we left."

"Getting back to the major question, I guess the best bet is just to continue to sort it out as we go along," Mike said. "Involving me or getting the meeting postponed until tomorrow are certainly both worth a try. We'll try to give you a thumbs up or thumbs down sign, depending on how the conversation goes."

Kelly nodded. It was nearly eleven. "Speaking of signals, one thing I think we need to discuss is some way to determine it's really you, for example Mike, when I'm talking to you on the phone. McConnell did a

151

clever impersonation of Rick. Your voice was also on my tape. I don't want him to trick any of us again in that same way. Kath, possibly. Hopefully, he can't duplicate or imitate a woman's voice."

"How about if I just subtract my age from any number you give me," Mike suggested. "I'm forty-one, by the way. For example, you'd work the number forty-eight into our conversation and I'd respond with the number seven, weaving it into the conversation so it's not obvious. Of course, you can use any number, providing it's over forty-one. That way McConnell, if he's managing to hear the conversation, won't be aware we're using a code."

Turning to David and Steve, Mike smiled and asked, "Are the two of you willing to tell us your ages?"

David and Steve grinned and nodded.

"An even fifty for me," David said.

"I'm thirty-nine, and hope I can continue to use that number for a few more years," chuckled Steve.

"Satisfied, Kelly?" Mike asked.

"Sure, that's simple enough. How about for you, Kath?"

She nodded and also smiled. "I think I can handle it, but math never was my strong suit."

David checked his watch again. "It's five past. While we're waiting, why don't we discuss McConnell's demand to temporarily terminate our efforts to apprehend him."

David's suggestion led to a lively discussion with everyone, including Kath, making suggestions. It was just after eleven-fifteen when the phone rang.

•

"Sorry to be a little late; I was tied up with a few chores."

Kelly held the receiver away from her ear so that if the others strained, they could all hear. McConnell had now switched his accent to a Texas twang.

"I hope you weren't bedded down for the night."

"No," replied Kelly. "I've been sitting here waiting for your call."

"Are we still on to meet?" he asked.

"Quite frankly, I'm exhausted," Kelly answered, delighted that he'd asked the question. "Is there a chance we could schedule a meeting for, let's say . . . tomorrow afternoon? I'd prefer that."

152

"I'm sure you would. Let me tell you what I have in mind. I'd prefer a more neutral site than your office or hotel room. I'm thinking of Detroit Metro Airport."

David and Mike glanced at one another, both thinking of the problems involved when they were operating outside their area of jurisdiction.

"There's a red-eye flight to Chicago at one this morning on Southwest. I'll have a ticket waiting for you at their counter."

"You want to meet in Chicago?" Kelly asked in amazement. Trying to think of something to say to dissuade him from that idea, a thought came to her.

"Why on earth would you want to meet in Chicago when you're pretty certain the guilty party is here in Ann Arbor?"

"Let's just say my level of trust isn't too high just yet. I'm anxious to have a safe venue for me. By the way, do you think it would be wise to have your boss, what's his name, Cummings, involved? Would he be more familiar with the murder investigation portion of the case than you are?"

Everyone was grinning over their good fortune. Kelly quickly wiped the smile from her face and in a serious tone, answered.

"That's a good suggestion. It would make sense. You're right in assuming he's much more knowledgeable about that part of the case. He can tell you where people have said they were that night."

"I guess I could arrange for two tickets. Could you contact him to see if he'd also be available?"

"I can try. You have the right name. It is Cummings, Mike Cummings. I'll try to reach him now. But couldn't we schedule this for tomorrow rather than tonight?"

"Well now, possibly we could, on one condition."

All were curious as to what that might be, exchanging glances as Kelly asked, "And what's that?"

"That you come barefoot," he answered, chuckling. "Better yet, topless, so I'll know you're not concealing anything from me."

Kelly glanced up at the others. Was McConnell on to them? She could tell the others were also perplexed by his statement.

"No comment, Kelly?" he asked. "Maybe if I play a tape for you, you'll better understand my condition."

As the tape began, Kelly mouthed the words, "Oh no" and held out the receiver so all could hear. She covered the mouthpiece with her hand as a recording of their earlier conversation in Kelly's room was played back to them. Steve had already begun a search of the room, looking for a hidden mike.

David was shaking his head as he said, "Looks as if in the time between when you gave him your room number and our arrival, he came in and installed some type of listening device. I bet he was here at the hotel when he called you earlier. I doubt if he is now."

Mike's fists were clenched. "He's just been setting us up. Asking if it would be smart to include me. I . . ."

The recording stopped and McConnell started talking again, this time in an angry, no-nonsense voice, with no hint of a western drawl.

"I warned you Kelly, and I told you to warn your associates. Now I'll tell them, too. Keep this shit up and the flyers get circulated. Those five people will be history in terms of their reputations, and it will be on your consciences. I'm giving you one more chance. I'll call you at the office in the morning, Kelly. You can tell me then of your plans to call off the hunt. We can also discuss how best to pursue the one actually responsible for Beth's death.

"You tried to fudge it with me. It didn't and it won't work." They heard him laugh. "You might enjoy the treat outside your door. Remember, I'm giving you one more opportunity. Pardon my language, Kelly," he said, resuming the western drawl, "but don't fuck up!"

Steve was red-faced as he angrily reached for the knob on Kelly's door. Opening the door he leaned down and picked up a small carton of Murdick's Famous Mackinac Island Fudge off the floor in the hallway. He turned, tossing it to Kelly as he said, "Damn it! We're going to get that S.O.B."

David was smiling as he glanced at the others, who sat stunned, frustrated and angry.

"Excuse me, I can't help it. I've been a candy junkie all my life, a real chocoholic. And this creep is making it so I can't even stand the sight of candy."

"Don't blame yourselves. He had this all mapped out ahead of time, including the fudge. He's manipulating us, convinced he's calling all the shots. We need to figure him out and try to get one step ahead of him. That's easier said than done, I know, but that's our challenge."

Mike nodded. "I'll call Judy and see if she's come up with some rooms. Tomorrow is another day and we could all use some sleep. It's too late to make those calls tonight, Kelly, but maybe some of us could help you with them in the morning. I think it's important that we warn them before they get blindsided by the flyer and letter."

"What are we going to tell them, Mike? How are we going to advise them?" Kelly asked.

"I hear you," he answered. "Let's sleep on it."

## Chapter 21

Kelly, accompanied by Kath, arrived at her office shortly after eight. They'd spent the night at the Ann Arbor Sheraton Inn on Boardwalk, a few blocks from the Crowne Plaza. A cancellation had enabled Judy to obtain a room with twin beds through Sunday night. Kelly's car had been left in the Crowne Plaza parking lot. Mike was having someone check it out this morning to determine if McConnell had planted some type of sensing device on it. Steve had driven them over to the Sheraton around midnight, and had picked them up this morning a little before eight.

There was a note on Kelly's desk from David Benton, asking her to let him know as soon as she arrived. She dialed his extension and David informed her he'd spoken with Robinson, the University's President, late last night.

"I want to brief you on our conversation before you begin your calls. If you're free now, could you come up to my office?"

•

David began by explaining to Kelly he was aware President Robinson's normal schedule involved working until one or two a.m., sending out a raft of e-mail and other correspondence. David had been in luck last night and had caught Robinson at his office. He'd faxed him copies of the flyer and letters and later, they'd had a lengthy conversation.

"Robinson is very sensitive to the harm the circulation of the flyer and photos would cause to the reputations of five innocent people, for their families, and also to the University. But he's violently opposed to any idea, any thought, of paying McConnell dollar number one, for many reasons. His thinking meshes with ours for the most part.

"He believes that any payment of money would just lend credence to McConnell's allegations. He goes a step further, actually. He believes any payment of money could be used by McConnell to demand additional monies. Not only would he have the threat of circulation of the flyer and photos to use, he'd also have the added threat of disclosing the fact they'd already sought to buy him off.

"Robinson volunteered to be involved in discussions with any or all of the five being blackmailed, to convince them of the risks associated with any blackmail payment. He'd tell them a better use for their money would be to go on the offensive. Take out full-page ads detailing the blackmail scheme. Raise the questions that make it apparent the evidence has all been fabricated. Why, for example, does the same person, the dead girl, appear in most of the photographs? Why are five unrelated individuals all being blackmailed at the same time? Questions of that nature.

"At the same time Robinson wants to cooperate with us, he wants to see McConnell arrested and punished. He knows the risks involved, but would support us in putting together a plan to entrap McConnell."

"You mean he'll work with us in getting the five of them to agree to a plan to pay McConnell the $100,000, providing it's only a ruse to catch McConnell?" Kelly asked.

"That's about it," David answered. "In fact, he's volunteered to loan the $100,000 to the five. Not personally; the University would make the loans. Either $20,000 each, or split up in any way the five decide. He realizes the problems the five would have, we would have, in getting that much cash together on such short notice. He would need a letter from us acknowledging he's given the five of them, given us, the money only to be used to entrap McConnell. He wants to be protected in case our plans go haywire. Something to show that the University wasn't involved in any payment of blackmail money. He realizes the need to involve the five, that it be their money, in order to make McConnell believe they're acquiescing to his demand. We have to be very careful that we don't tip our hand, scare McConnell off. He seems to have an uncanny knowledge of what we're doing, what we're planning to do. This all has to be orchestrated as if we've bought McConnell's line, that we're all anxious to get this behind us in the interests of all. Robinson's pledged to help us in any way he can."

"I don't think we could ask for more," Kelly said. "You have to be delighted with his reaction."

"Definitely," David answered. "I want to caution you though, Kelly. I think at least one of the five, maybe more, will try to convince us to go along with McConnell's demand, to pay him in hopes he can be trusted.

That payment would put an end to their misery. Robinson and I really didn't discuss the question of whether or not McConnell could be believed, trusted. But I think that's an important point when we're talking to the five who are personally involved, the ones who have the most to lose if we fail to apprehend McConnell."

"I understand what you're saying," Kelly said. "They're probably going to also raise questions as to how confident we are we'll be successful in apprehending him."

"I'm aware of that," David said. "When McConnell suggested on the phone last night that he meet you in Chicago, I had the hunch it was his way of telling us in advance he'll expect the money to be delivered someplace other than Ann Arbor. Another city, maybe even another country. And of course, that increases the odds against our success. McConnell has outwitted us a couple times already. I can see why they'd have concerns, questions. We just have to convince them that we'll be using every resource available to put as foolproof a plan as possible in place to virtually guarantee success. We're committed to that. That's all we can promise."

"And the odds of us doing that, being successful in apprehending him, are far better than the odds he can be trusted," Kelly said. "I think we're in sync with our thinking."

"That's good," David said, smiling. "I'd hate to be the one to tell McConnell he'd have to use someone else as an intermediary."

"I hope you're teasing, David," Kelly said. "I would have never proposed that we be a party to anything other than the arrest and conviction of McConnell. We couldn't be involved in paying him off."

"I'm sorry, Kelly. We've been under such a strain, I was just trying to say something to break the tension. I would never – "

There was a knock at the door. Kelly had heard David tell his secretary he hadn't wanted to be disturbed. Must be something important, Kelly thought.

"Come in," David called out.

The door opened and Mike poked his head into the room. Kelly spotted Judy over his shoulder.

"Sorry to interrupt, but we've just learned some tragic news. The young man that McConnell had make copies of the flyer, is dead. Suspected suicide. A fall from the window of his sixth floor room."

157

## Chapter 22

David invited Judy and Mike into his office and offered them chairs as the two provided Kelly and him with additional details. The boy's name was Tony McGuire. Judy had finally made contact with the girl at South Quad she'd been trying to reach last night. Just a few minutes ago. That's when Judy first learned about what had happened. She'd remembered seeing the report on the possible suicide earlier this morning and immediately made the association.

The girl had been in tears, concerned that in some way she'd been responsible for the boy's death. She'd only learned about it minutes before Judy's call. Judy had explained to her that the young man had called her last night, but hadn't been willing to give his name. Judy told her that was the reason why she'd been trying to contact her. Judy told her McGuire had planned to come to the police station later this morning and sadly, yes, his suicide could be related to the reason she'd wanted to speak with him.

"I'm going over to see her as soon as we're through here," Judy said. "In addition to seeing her, I'll also try to talk to Tony's roommate. He's already been interviewed. The police report quotes him on statements McGuire made to him earlier last night. The nature of them was, how could he have been so stupid; how sad his parents were going to be when the news came out. He hadn't gone into any details, according to the roommate, but he'd been in tears. The roommate slept over at his girlfriend's apartment last night. He didn't know about McGuire's death until early this morning when he came back to his room for his books and to change clothes. He blames himself for not having been there and not realizing the seriousness of Tony's depression."

"It may have been suicide, but we know who's responsible," Mike said. "Judy's going to see if she can find anyone who may have seen someone resembling McConnell visiting or talking with McGuire last night – or early this morning. As near as they've been able to determine, he jumped out, or was pushed out, the window around five a.m. His room faced south. He landed on the sidewalk bordering the parking lot."

"The body was found about five-fifteen," Judy added. "He was probably dead then, but there were definitely no life signs when the EMS unit arrived a few minutes later. It's a setback for us. I was optimistic we'd learn a lot from him."

The others nodded. Changing subjects, David explained he wanted to briefly review with them the conversation he'd been having with Kelly. Kelly was delighted as the conversation progressed to find Judy and Mike clearly in sync with David's and her thoughts. News of Tony McGuire's death had probably reinforced everyone's resolve to track down McConnell and put him behind bars.

"I'll give Robinson a call now," David said. "I said I'd get back to him as soon as I ran the loan arrangement idea past you people. He can get started on it right away, set the wheels in motion. I think we're all in agreement it's a break for us. Avoids a delay or snag in getting that much cash together so quickly.

"At some stage, I think McConnell will be asking who's putting what into the pot. You can be truthful with him, Kelly. Robinson would just as soon not have McConnell aware of the University's involvement – in terms of the loans. And I don't think we have to divulge that. It's actually their money, the five signing for loans, that's involved."

•

David hadn't been able to reach Robinson, but had been assured by the President's secretary she'd have him return his call within the next half hour.

"I'll let you know as soon as I've spoken with him, Kelly. It's only nine-thirty. You should be able to begin your calls by ten. Hopefully, you'll still be ahead of the mail. If not, you'll probably be getting some calls."

Kelly walked back to her office deep in thought. McConnell would probably be calling her soon. They really hadn't spent much time on that subject, except to conclude they were confident Kelly would come up with the right answers and decisions, depending on what McConnell had to say.

Back in her office, Kelly briefed Kath about Tony McGuire's death. The phone rang in the midst of their conversation. It was David.

"I just hung up from talking with President Robinson. Everything's set. He'll have the necessary paperwork prepared. You'll be the contact, coordinating with him and the five individuals.

"He's really getting into this, he's come up with another idea. He proposes we tell McConnell the University is willing to spend up to ten times the money – a million dollars – to ensure his arrest and conviction if he defaults on his promise, if he goes ahead with the circulation of the flyer and photographs after he's been paid the money. Robinson believes it may serve to further convince McConnell everyone's buying into his proposal. I'm inclined to agree. What do you think?"

"I think it's a great idea," Kelly said, breaking into a smile. "I sort of like the idea of a reverse threat, too. It might also be an insurance policy of sorts, in case something goes wrong and we aren't able to apprehend him when the money's delivered."

David nodded. "We don't have to decide right away. We'll bounce it off Mike, too. Guess you can begin making those calls now. Let me know if you run into any problems, if I can be of help. I'd just as soon not have Robinson involved. Those five have enough to be concerned about without being also pressured by their boss. Judy spoke with Liz Hernandes last night. That was before you received the actual copy of the flyer and McConnell's letter. So you need to follow up with her, too."

"I should be here in my office all morning. Let me know as soon as you hear from McConnell. Thanks, Kelly."

## Chapter 23

Kelly was elated. Her initial conversation had been with Tim Masterson. After being briefed by Kelly, he shared with her the status of his negotiations for a head coaching position. Kelly empathized with him as he explained his concern over making a commitment which could blow up with dire consequences for him and the athletic director and University recruiting him.

He'd advised them it would be a few more days before he could give them an answer. In response they sweetened up the offer to prompt an immediate decision. He told them he'd let them know by Wednesday.

"I sure hope you can nail him by then. Financially, I probably have the most to gain or lose, depending on how this all shakes out. I'd be willing to commit to half – $50,000. That should make it somewhat easier for you."

Kelly agreed and promised to get back to him on the final details. As she talked, she realized obtaining the money would be the easy part.

The following call to Dean Jameson also lifted Kelly's spirits. He'd already received the letter and copy of the flyer from McConnell. He'd found it in his mailbox when he went out to get the morning paper. He explained to Kelly he'd called her condo and left a message. He said he and his wife, Marion, would be happy to host a breakfast meeting tomorrow for everyone involved – the other four being blackmailed along with Kelly and any others working with her.

"Anyone who wants to bring their spouse is invited to do so. Would eight-thirty be a good time?" he'd asked.

Kelly had assured him it was a great idea to get them all together, one she should have considered. She told him of her conversation with Tim Masterson, and Jameson had reacted by saying he'd be willing to assume responsibility for up to $25,000.

She'd buzzed Mike and told him about these initial calls and Jameson's offer to host a breakfast meeting tomorrow, Saturday morning at eight-thirty. He'd also been enthused and said he'd bounce it off David while she was continuing with her calls. Mike also explained her car was now in the parking area adjacent to the station, with the monitoring device removed, and he'd drop her keys off to her by noon.

•

Sitting across the office from Kelly, Kath had listened in on the conversations. Her smile conveyed the enthusiasm she also felt over Kelly's initial calls.

"It all seems to be falling into place. While you're contacting the others, I could dial up your answering machine and see if anyone else besides Dean Jameson has left a message," Kath volunteered.

"Good idea," Kelly answered. "The office next door is vacant. Here's my number."

Kelly handed her a card as she thought how frustrating it must be for Kath to not be involved hands-on. Checking on Kelly's messages would give her something to do, if only for a few minutes. As Kath left the office, Kelly was already placing a call to Clare Singleton.

Clare was in a foul mood. She, too, had already received copies of the flyer and letter. McConnell must have dropped them off in the mailboxes of the five late last night or early this morning. Tim probably hadn't checked his mailbox yet. In answer to Kelly's question, Singleton said the envelope they'd come in just had her name printed on it, with no address or postage. It appeared Clare had been fuming since she'd opened it, working herself into a frenzy. She was now proceeding to take out all her anger and frustration on Kelly. She seemed well informed over the fact the police had let McConnell slip out of their grasp a couple of times already.

"How can you even be contemplating humoring him, being a party to buying him off? That's ridiculous! All your efforts should be concentrated on catching and convicting him. If he's roughed up in the process, so much the better. He's a low-life, a murderer. Don't give him respect by treating this as a business arrangement. You're empowering him, giving him confidence. You should be trying to scare him into turning himself in. Better a prison sentence than being gunned down in the street. That's the approach you should be taking."

Kelly held the receiver away from her ear as Singleton continued to rant and rave in a loud voice.

"I hear you. I understand what you're saying, but just hear me out," Kelly said, interrupting her. "Our goal is to apprehend him, not send him on his way with a bundle of money. We don't want to chase him out of the area. He could disappear and we'd never find him. To catch a rat you need bait. We think this is our best option for eventually capturing him, flushing him out."

It took another twenty minutes before Clare finally simmered down and reached a point where she was at least professing to understand Kelly's position, even though not willing to be a party to it.

"You'll have to do it without me. I'm not going to put in a cent. Do you still want me at the Jamesons' tomorrow morning? I might screw things up for you if the others are willing to play along, and you already said that Tim and Dean Jameson are."

"Yes, please come. I'm not worried about that. I think it would be good for you to see and hear the others. They're every bit as angry as you are," Kelly added.

That was exhausting, Kelly thought as she hung up the phone. She needed to collect herself for a minute or two before making the final calls. Kath had returned while Kelly had been on the phone.

"There were only two calls other than the one from Dean Jameson. One from your father, just checking to see how you were, and the other from Michigan's Citizen Lobby. The girl who left the message said they'd be back in touch."

"I'm sure of that," Kelly said with a smile. "I think I'm on their easy touch list, a person to call every time a special issue comes up which requires extra funding."

"There's a problem with your answering machine," Kath continued. "It clicked off just as Jameson was beginning his message. I tried a couple of times and it kept doing the same thing."

Kelly glanced at her watch. It was nearly noon.

"Maybe we could stop by my place when we go for lunch. I need to pick up a couple of things and I should change the message. Direct calls here. Hopefully, we'll be able to correct whatever's wrong."

•

The calls to Dr. Broadstead and Liz Hernandes took only a short time. Broadstead still hadn't received the flyer and letter. He had guests from out of town for tomorrow's Indiana game. He explained he'd just as soon miss the breakfast meeting at the Jamesons' and said he'd agree to put in the final $25,000, which might make the meeting unnecessary.

"You can probably better spend the time in determining how you're going to apprehend him anyway. And besides, I don't especially want to sit and sulk with the others. Commiserating with them doesn't get us any closer to nailing the bastard. By the way, I'm sorry we still haven't been able to determine the substance injected into the Edwards girl. One of my associates thinks an air bubble in her bloodstream, whether intentional or accidental, could have been the cause of death. We're continuing to work on it."

Kelly thanked him for the information and verified that he'd be available Monday morning to sign for the $25,000 loan from the University.

The call to Liz Hernandes was an even shorter one. She'd received the flyer and letter. It was the first time Kelly had had an opportunity to speak directly to her. The conversation was very stilted. Kelly sensed Liz was holding back something. She had no desire to attend the breakfast and was nonchalant in her reaction to Kelly's explanation that three of the others had agreed to pay the $100,000.

Kelly promised to keep her informed and Hernandes concluded the conversation by wishing Kelly and the police good luck. Even this comment was made with scant enthusiasm. As she hung up the phone Kelly wondered if perhaps she was reading too much into Hernandes' air of aloofness. Perhaps she's still in a state of shock, Kelly thought.

Glancing over at Kath, who was trying to read her thoughts, Kelly said, "Hungry? We'll just take a minute to brief Mike and David and then we'll be on our way. I'll see what they have to say about following through on the breakfast meeting. Being game day, I'm sure Masterson would just as soon not be asked to come. Sounded like a good idea, but I think I'll let Jameson know we won't be going ahead with it with at least two, possibly three, no shows. Clare will probably think we're canceling out because of her. We'll see what David and Mike have to say."

## Chapter 24

Getting away for lunch took much longer than Kelly had anticipated. Following her conversation with David and Mike, who agreed the breakfast meeting should be postponed, Kelly wanted to notify the Jamesons before they'd made any special preparations. She also placed a call to Clare Singleton, leaving a message on her answering machine. Mike and David had shared Kelly's concern over still not having received a call from McConnell. Mike said he'd make arrangements to take Kelly's calls while she was at lunch. Kelly considered changing plans and just bringing in sandwiches, but thought Kath needed a bit of fresh air after just sitting around the office all morning.

They'd had an enjoyable lunch at Cookers on Plymouth Road, which was on the way to Kelly's condo. Though they'd eaten quickly, it was nearly two o'clock when Kelly pulled her car into the deserted parking area in front of her complex.

"Want to come in with me? I'll just be a minute if you'd rather just soak up some of this sunshine," Kelly said as she opened the door of her car. Though chilly, it was a gorgeous day with a clear sky. Hopefully, this will continue for the football game tomorrow afternoon, Kelly thought as she exited the vehicle.

"I'll keep you company," Kath said. "Want me to lock the doors?"

"No, that shouldn't be necessary. We'll just be a minute or two and I've left my window down to air out the car.

"Seems ages since I was here," Kelly said as they proceeded up the walk towards her condo. Smiling, she winked at Kath as she added, "No place like home."

Kelly unlocked the door and stepped inside, switching on the lights. The drapes were closed, covering the sliding glass doors which led to her back patio. Kath followed her inside, hunching her shoulders, shivering.

"It's colder inside than it is outside," she observed.

"I noticed that too," Kelly answered as she walked over to the wall thermostat. "It's set for sixty-eight degrees. I can hear the fan."

Kath still hadn't closed the door behind her. The drapes were billowing and Kelly could feel a draft.

"I think the sliding door may be open," Kelly said as she walked toward it. She reached for the pull cords in the corner and opened the drapes. She was startled to see a portion of the glass door had been cut out, beginning near the lock and continuing to floor level, leaving an eight- to ten-inch wide opening through which the cold air was entering the room. Kelly also noticed the stick of wood, used for added security to prevent the sliding door from being opened, had been removed and was resting on the floor.

"Looks as if I've had a break-in," Kelly said, turning toward Kath. "A professional job. Whoever it was had a glass cutter."

With a look of concern, Kelly held a finger to her lips, signaling for Kath to remain quiet. Kelly walked a few steps towards the hallway leading to her bedroom and bathroom. Both doors were closed.

Kelly motioned towards the front door, again placing a finger to her lips. She opened the door and gestured for Kath to get out. Kelly followed, quietly shutting the door behind her.

"Whoever broke in may still be inside. Maybe it's McConnell. He could have tinkered with my answering machine in hopes we'd do exactly what we have done. I'll call Mike from the car."

The two quickly walked to Kelly's car and climbed inside. Kelly immediately picked up the car phone and used the speed dial feature.

"Just hang up."

Kelly's head whirled around in the direction of the sound of the man's voice, and her cheek slammed into the barrel of a revolver. Kath began screaming as a hand grabbed her hair, yanking the wig from her head.

"Shut up!" the man whispered. "Unless you want Kelly's head blown off." His one hand was now gripping Kath's actual hair as his other forced the gun barrel deeper into Kelly's cheek.

"I'm not here to hurt either of you, just for ten minutes of conversation. Now shut up!"

Kelly trembled in fear. She could see McConnell's face in the rearview mirror. Kath had stopped screaming, grimacing in pain as her hair was being pulled, trying to twist her head to get a look at her attacker.

"Just relax and no one's going to get hurt," McConnell said as he released his grip on Kath's hair. Kelly felt the pressure easing from the gun barrel, still jammed against her cheek.

"Face to face is much better than a phone call," he said with an ominous chuckle. He was enjoying this, thought Kelly, taking satisfaction from their shock and initial panicked reaction.

"I don't want anyone trying to be a hero. I guess I should say heroine, shouldn't I? Believe me when I say I won't hesitate to use this gun. Understood?"

Kelly and Kath were nodding as they both were able to turn their heads to get a clearer view of McConnell.

"That's better," he said as he leaned back, the gun still in his hand, pointing back and forth, first towards Kelly and then towards Kath. He was smiling, dressed in a black warm-up suit.

"I don't think anyone has heard or seen us, but just in case, it's probably best if we have our little chat elsewhere. Turn on your motor, Kelly; remember, no tricks or surprises."

As she started the engine, Kelly glanced in the rear-view mirror, observing McConnell. He looked very similar to the computer sketch they'd made. He'd made no attempt to disguise his facial features.

"Why did you kill her?" Kath blurted out.

"We'll get to that," McConnell answered. "To begin with, I didn't. I want to catch the person who did as badly as you do. First though, let's get squared away on where we're headed."

He asked Kelly if she knew of the parking area at Gallup Park, off Geddes and just east of Huron Parkway. Kelly was very familiar with it. She'd often parked there for a walk or jog through the park which bordered the Huron River, adjacent to the University Arboretum. It was less than two miles from her condo.

"I brought a tape for you, Kelly, for you to play during breakfast at the Jamesons' tomorrow. If anyone is being hesitant over paying me the $100,000, I thought hearing directly from me might persuade them. Let them know the consequences of not complying and the risk involved in trying to use the payoff as a ruse to capture me. It's for you and your bosses to hear as well as them. I assume you can locate a tape player."

As Kelly listened, she wondered if she should volunteer the fact the breakfast had been cancelled. But how was he even aware of the breakfast? Jameson's message on her answering machine.

"Well?" he said, waiting for a response.

"We'll have the $100,000 by Monday afternoon. They've agreed to pay. They . . . we . . . need time to get the cash assembled."

"I thought so, that's why I suggested Tuesday for delivery. But they've agreed, that's good!"

Kelly's fear for her own safety had subsided. He needed her to complete the payment transaction. But what about Kath?

"I gave some thought to kidnapping the two of you, or at least Kath, to provide an additional incentive to pay the money. I still haven't ruled it out. After I'd been given the money and was out of harm's way, I'd call and let you know where to find her. But it may be best to have you both free to root out the person responsible for Beth's death."

As McConnell continued to talk, to himself as much as to them, Kelly thought of how stupid she'd been not to have checked out her back seat before entering the car. It was second nature for her to do that, even before becoming involved in police work. On the other hand, that may have led to Kath or her being injured, even killed, as he tried to get them in the car. Funny how things worked out. Maybe, Kelly thought, I can humor him, encourage him so he concludes holding Kath or both of us hostage would just cause more trouble than it was worth. Lead him to think he's raised some doubts over whether Beth was killed by someone else.

"When are you planning to take delivery of the money?" Kelly asked as he paused for a moment.

He laughed. "You'd like to know that ahead of time, wouldn't you? I'll be calling you at your office Tuesday afternoon at two-thirty. I'll give you directions. You should be there, too," he said, turning to Kath. "I might want the two of you involved in a joint delivery."

"We'll both plan to be there then," Kelly replied, growing more optimistic over the possibility he'd eventually be releasing them. "I'm supposed to communicate a message to you from the University's President, his name's – "

"I know who the hell he is," McConnell interrupted. "So I have his attention, too. Good! What's the message?"

"He wants you to be aware if you go back on your word and circulate the flyer or any photographs of the five people you've been blackmailing, the University is ready to spend up to ten times the $100,000 you're being paid to assure your apprehension and conviction."

"Is that so?" he said. Kelly and Kath would later describe the look on his face as evil personified. "Maybe I should have asked for more. Tell him I don't appreciate threats. I want this whole episode behind me, as much as the rest of you should want to bring this to a quick end. Tell him I intend to honor my promise. You'll all hear it when you play the tape."

•

Kelly turned into the Gallup Park parking area. There were two cars in the lot, both empty. Their drivers, and possibly passengers, were probably in the park . . . walking dogs, jogging, or just taking a casual stroll in the sunshine.

"Drive down towards that end," McConnell said, pointing to the westerly portion of the parking area.

After parking, he continued the charade of trying to convince them someone other than he had murdered Beth. He questioned Kelly on the whereabouts on Halloween night of those individuals he'd been blackmailing. Kelly saw no reason to hold anything back. She played along with him. His lack of questions regarding Beth's cause of death just reinforced Kelly's belief that McConnell was responsible. She'd already made the decision not to share the information Dr. Broadstead had discussed with her earlier that morning. Throughout the conversation, Kath had glared at McConnell. He realized he wasn't convincing her of his innocence. At one point he'd raised his voice in anger, saying Beth hadn't been a wide-eyed innocent in the blackmail scheme. Kath had shouted back, "She wanted out and that's why you killed her. Why did you have to torture her, too?"

The gun had trembled in McConnell's hand and his face flushed in anger as he pointed the weapon at Kath. Kelly wondered if the glaze in his eyes was an indication he was on drugs. He gained control of himself in a few moments and grinned. Kelly was relieved, sensing the immediate danger had passed. McConnell changed subjects and spent the next few minutes apologizing to Kelly over having roughed her up at her condo. Kelly attempted to hide her emotions as he spoke. She didn't believe him for a moment. Even as he attempted to sweet-talk her, she sensed the evil in him. She suspected he'd relish the opportunity to injure and terrify her again.

He finally finished, again emphasizing the consequences of trying to entrap him, now or when the money was being delivered or after he'd been paid off. He spoke quietly in a menacing tone. The look in his eyes sent a chill down Kelly's spine. His promise that the onetime payment would end the matter didn't ring true. Rather than scaring her off from using the payoff to trap him, she was more convinced than ever it was the only realistic option.

He'd become maudlin and teary-eyed as the conversation ended, almost pleading with Kelly and Kath to sympathize with him. Kelly glanced at Kath and thought she was probably having similar thoughts, that he was deranged, mentally ill. Kelly hoped Kath could restrain herself and not say or do anything to further provoke him. He wiped his eyes and reached into the carry-all bag he had with him on the back seat. He pulled out two pairs of handcuffs. Smiling, he swung into a W.C. Fields voice imitation.

"Tell you what I'm gonna do, ladies. Just handcuff you to one of those little trees over there. I'll make a call in about ten minutes to let what's-his-name, Cummings, know where you are. I'll leave your purses next to you. Out of your reach, of course. I assume you're both carrying," he said with a chuckle.

He's so damn sure of himself, Kelly thought. Even assuming she and Kath had weapons in their handbags, he'd made no attempt to remove them from the front seat. Maybe his over-confidence can work to our favor, she reasoned.

"Why do you have to handcuff us?" Kath asked angrily. "What if some crazy should find us like that?"

He laughed. "Some crazy besides me, you mean?"

Cool it, thought Kelly, glancing at Kath. Let's not prompt him to change his mind about letting us go.

"You've got a point, I suppose," he answered with a grin. "I can probably get the time window I need if you just walk out over that path a couple hundred yards or so. Let's say to that third bridge," he said, pointing. "Wave when you get there.

"And, oh yes. I have a couple of hugs for you before you go." He reached down again into his carry-all and took out a handful of Hershey's Hugs(tm). With a smirk on his face, he handed several to each of them.

"Leave the keys in the ignition, Kelly. Wave when you get to the third bridge out there. And please leave your handbags where they are. I'll hide them under that red-leafed bush," he said, pointing to a cluster of shrubbery a few yards from Kelly's car. "Expect my call at two-thirty on Tuesday. Now remember, no tricks. I'll get out first," he said as he opened the rear door on the driver's side. He then gestured to the two of them to exit the vehicle, pointing his gun in their direction as they did so.

"Now just pretend you're having a casual stroll through the park. Have a nice weekend," he added with a wave, a grin on his face.

Kelly and Kath walked through an opening in the bushes and turned to their left on the path which would take them over a series of bridges. They'd only gone a few feet when they heard and saw a pick-up truck drive into the parking area. Glancing back they saw McConnell had noticed it and had already slipped his gun into the pocket of his warm-up. The sky-blue pick-up pulled in to park about twenty-five yards east of Kelly's car, directly in front of Kelly and Kath. They could see a young man behind the steering wheel with what appeared to be a golden retriever or lab sitting next to him on the front seat. They were surprised as the driver beeped his horn.

Opening the truck door, the man leaned out and called, "Kelly, is that you? Wait up."

Kelly recognized Greg Collier, the reporter from the *Ann Arbor News* who had been writing the articles on the murder investigation from day one. She glanced back again at McConnell, wondering how she should react. They were too close to Greg to ignore him. He climbed out of the truck with the dog following him.

"I thought I'd give Taffy an airing before this afternoon's four o'clock briefing. It's such a great day!"

Greg was glancing toward McConnell as he attached a leash to his dog. The dog pulled him in the women's direction. Kelly forced a smile as he approached.

"We thought we'd take a break too," she said. She reached out to pat the head of Greg's dog.

Greg was continuing to smile as he commented, "Those shoes aren't ideal for much hiking."

He'd turned again to look in McConnell's direction as he spoke. Kelly and Kath glanced down at their dress shoes. Greg's dog had begun to bark at McConnell and tug on its leash. Greg looked back over his shoulder at Kelly and Kath. "Something's wrong, isn't it? Is that who I . ."

The next few moments were a blur. Greg's dog was suddenly bounding toward McConnell. They couldn't tell if Greg had detached the leash or if his dog had just snapped it loose. Its barking had changed to a growl. McConnell was back-pedaling, bumping into Kelly's car, as the dog bounded toward him. The dog sprang at his chest as a shot sounded. Whether luck or skill, the dog's head exploded with a burst of blood, flesh and fur. The dog's momentum carried its body into McConnell, who would probably have been knocked down if he hadn't been propped against Kelly's car.

Greg started to lunge towards McConnell. Halfway there he stopped, glancing back at Kelly and Kath. They could read his mind. But for them, he would be ignoring the gun now pointed in his direction and charging into McConnell, who was righting himself, the dog's body sprawled at his feet.

"You crazy son of a bitch," Greg shouted. "Taffy never hurt a soul. You didn't have to shoot her."

"I didn't plan to," McConnell replied, a quiver in his voice. He'd been visibly shaken by the incident. "But it shows you I won't hesitate to use this if I have to," he added, waving the gun.

"I want you to go with the ladies; they know what they're supposed to do. Now, get moving."

Greg stood with his fists clenched. Tears had begun to well up in his eyes and his body trembled. He started to take another step forward and then turned and walked back towards Kelly and Kath, who were still standing in shock and disbelief. McConnell motioned with his hand for them to start heading down the pathway.

"I'll hide your handbags and the dog's body under that bush," McConnell said as he pointed. "I'll . . ."

Greg whirled around as he shouted, "Don't you dare touch my dog!"

McConnell held up his hands. "Okay, okay, I won't. Just get moving."

•

They'd gone nearly a hundred yards and were just crossing the first, short bridge before any words were exchanged between them. Greg was having difficulty getting his emotions under control. He finally turned to them and asked, "Tell me what's going on?"

Kelly briefly outlined what had happened as they continued to walk. As she talked she had some reservations about how much detail she should be supplying Greg. Rather than seeking his pledge of confidentiality to begin with, she'd waited until she'd provided him with most of the facts.

"I'm going to have to ask you to clear this with Chief Benton or Mike

Cummings before you publish any of it."

Greg nodded and glanced back over his shoulder to see if he could tell if Kelly's car was still in the lot.

"I think he's just leaving. I have a car phone. Do you think he'll head back to your condo?" Collier asked.

"I think so," Kelly answered. "He probably has a car of his own there, nearby. We have to be careful, though. If we set the wheels in motion to try to apprehend him there, we have to be fairly certain we'll succeed, that he won't elude us again. If we try and fail, it just may be the factor which triggers him off to forget about the payment on Tuesday and to start circulating those flyers and no telling what else."

Collier nodded, acknowledging he understood. Kath had been silent throughout their walk and spoke up now, telling Greg how sorry she was about his dog being killed.

"But you've lost a sister," he replied, adding that even though he'd interviewed her twice, he'd never had an opportunity to tell her how sorry he was about her sister's death. Kelly wondered if she should tell Greg about McConnell's contention someone else was responsible for Beth's death. That could wait, she decided.

"I think he's gone," Greg observed, again staring back toward the parking lot. Looking down at their shoes he said, "I'll run back ahead of you and try to get Benton or Cummings on the phone. I'll begin to brief them and then you can take it from there, Kelly. I'll tell them of your concerns."

.

Kelly and Kath had slipped off their shoes and followed Greg back over the pathway as quickly as possible. They arrived at the parking lot a few minutes behind him. They saw he'd already retrieved their handbags, which were sitting on the hood of the pick-up. He'd climbed into the driver's seat of the truck with his door open. As Kelly and Kath approached, they could see the tears in his eyes as he looked up.

"He ripped out my phone. He also drove over Taffy." His voice rose in anger as he added, "Not just once, two or three times." Kelly and Kath winced, not knowing what to say. "I've put her in back. I'll get you to a phone or down to police headquarters. Hop in."

172

## Chapter 25

Kelly had called Mike from a pay phone. After her quick briefing, he had rounded up Steve and the two of them had driven to Kelly's apartment complex in hopes they might be lucky enough to intercept McConnell. To send the nearest cruiser was too risky. They'd found Kelly's car parked in front of her condo, the keys on her seat. There were splatters of blood on the door panel. Mike and Steve were relieved to have known about Collier's dog. Otherwise, finding the blood on Kelly's car would have precipitated all sorts of worries and concerns. They'd checked out Kelly's apartment. The rumpled bed suggested McConnell may have been living there for the past day or two. They exchanged glances as Steve removed a paper clip from Kelly's answering machine, cleverly placed to allow for only limited playback of messages. Though they'd spent several minutes driving around the area, they'd seen no sign of McConnell. On returning to headquarters, they'd immediately come to Benton's office.

It was nearly three-thirty. Kelly, Judy and Kath were already there.

"The first item of concern is to make sure we're all on the same wavelength in respect to the four o'clock briefing," Benton said. "I've spoken to Greg Collier. He's assured me he'll clear anything the *News* is going to publish with us. More than ever," Benton grimaced, "Collier wants to assist us in apprehending McConnell. I told him we were planning on saying very little at the briefing. Perhaps suggesting we had reason to believe McConnell had left the area. That we were getting full cooperation from the Chicago police department, which has a high priority alert out for him. There will be no mention of the flyer. No associating the suspected suicide at South Quad with our case. Any comments or questions?"

"We're all going to have an opportunity to hear McConnell's tape?" Judy asked.

Benton nodded yes. "We'll do it immediately after the briefing and also review our plans for Tuesday then," he answered.

"Are we certain there were no witnesses to what happened at Gallup Park?" Judy asked.

"We haven't had any calls. Kelly and Kath believe there weren't. Right?" Benton asked, turning towards them. They nodded.

"Should anything be mentioned about spotting McConnell in the vicinity of Kelly's condo?" Steve asked. "Ask for help in notifying anyone who may have seen him to contact us. Possibly we could get a line on the car he's currently driving."

"Can I voice an opinion on that?" Mike said. Benton nodded. "While normally I'd agree that would be a good idea and we could be lucky, I think we shouldn't take the risk of scaring McConnell off or prompting him to change his plans for collecting the $100,000 on Tuesday. He's asked us to suspend all efforts to apprehend him. While I don't suggest that, chances are he may have changed cars already, or driven into Detroit for the weekend. I hate to put all our eggs into one basket, but I opt for trying to come up with a foolproof plan for Tuesday. With the killing of the dog, he may already be re-considering his options. Let's not do anything further to prompt him to alter the current schedule of events. The deliberate act of driving over Collier's dog concerns me."

"Amen," said Judy. "We're dealing with a very volatile situation. I agree with Mike." The others, including Steve, nodded in agreement.

"Anything else?" asked Benton. "If not, we'll meet at five o'clock in the conference room. I'd like you," he said, referring to Mike, "and Kelly to join me at the briefing. I'll try to limit questions, but I may require your help."

•

Kelly was standing to the right of David as he began the briefing. There were close to thirty people present in the room. Kelly recognized many of the faces from past briefings. True to pattern, there were a handful of individuals who were new to her. David had just completed his opening comments and was inviting questions.

The first question came from a woman who Kelly recognized as being from Channel Seven. She was asking if McConnell had made any direct contact with the individuals he'd been attempting to blackmail in the past twenty-four hours. Without reference to the flyer, Benton acknowledged there had been some communications from McConnell. David explained he couldn't go into details except for the fact he believed everyone was cooperating with the investigation.

"We believe the department has been kept informed of all contacts or attempts to contact them."

As David spoke, Kelly had focused on a man sitting in the rear of the room on the opposite side from where she was standing. Unlike most of his colleagues, he didn't appear to be making notes. He had bushy gray hair and was wearing thick glasses. He still wore his raincoat and was constantly bending over and raising his arm to check the time on his wristwatch.

The next question had come from a young man who Kelly remembered as a reporter for the *Michigan Daily*, the University student newspaper. He made the statement there were rumors that candy was associated in some way with the case, and asked Benton if this were true and if he could comment.

David had smiled and nodded his head before addressing the question. He began by saying he'd only be able to answer the question in general terms, as some details essential to the investigation were being kept confidential.

Kelly's eyes again focused on the man she'd noticed earlier. He appeared to sense her gaze and smiled. More of a smirk than a smile, Kelly thought. Was it her imagination or could it possibly be she was staring at McConnell in disguise? Would he actually have the audacity to make an appearance here? Risk being detected and apprehended? Kelly had quickly shifted her eyes away from him.

The audience was laughing as Benton completed the story of finding packages of Nerds[(tm)] candy on the seat of McConnell's car. Trying to be as casual and unobtrusive as possible, Kelly had begun walking up the aisle on her right. Benton was describing finding the handful of suckers, Dum Dums[(tm)], in the room at the Campus Inn.

Out of the corner of her eye, she noticed the man she'd been observing rise and quickly move toward the rear of the room and the exit. As she'd looked in his direction, he'd also glanced at her. I think I'm on to something, she reasoned as she quickened her pace.

Kelly called out to the officer standing next to the door. "Detain that man! Don't let him out!"

The man had shoved the officer off to the side and was already bolting out through the door. Heads had turned as Kelly had shouted, first towards her and then towards the commotion at the back of the room. Kelly was now running and had already reached the door, following the officer who had righted himself and who was now in close pursuit of the man who'd shoved him aside.

The briefing room was on the second floor of City Hall and Kelly and the officer were navigating the staircase. She was pleased to see the officer

175

was so agile and was distancing himself ahead of her. At the bottom of the stairs, shoving the door to the lobby open as it was closing, they knew they were only moments behind the man. Entering the lobby, they could see the man just exiting the building and turning to his right, towards the north side of City Hall.

Perhaps their luck had changed, Kelly thought as she saw Larry Martino outside the building's entrance. He'd been one of the officers involved the morning Beth's body had been discovered. The man had raced past Martino, who had briefly glanced at him and then spotted the other officer and Kelly running towards the door. Quickly perceiving they were pursuing the man who'd just barged past him, Martino turned and raced after him. Glancing over her shoulder, Kelly saw Mike just behind her. As they raced across the parking lot, they saw Martino had tackled the man and was now wrestling with him on the front lawn of a house fronting the north side of City Hall. The other officer was several yards ahead of Kelly and Mike and had immediately entered the fray with Martino to subdue the man whose wig, Kelly had been right in assuming he'd been in disguise, was now on the ground off to the side of the fracas. The man's glasses had also come off as he'd struggled with the officers.

"It's not him!" Kelly exclaimed as she and Mike crossed the street. "I had a hunch it was McConnell," she said, turning to Mike.

Martino and the other officer had now been able to secure the man's hands behind his back with a set of handcuffs. The man was still squirming and shouting, "I didn't do anything wrong. This is police brutality."

The officers were now helping the man stand.

"Who are you? What were you doing at the briefing?" Mike asked in a brusque voice.

The man was shaking his head from side to side. "I wasn't causing any trouble," he said. "Get these cuffs off me and I'll show you some identification. My name's Gary Tippel."

"Are you with a news service?" Mike asked.

The man shook his head no. "It was just a lark. I didn't intend any harm."

"Bring him in to my office," Mike said to the officers. Martino had removed a small tape recorder from the man's raincoat pocket and showed it to Mike and Kelly.

"He's not armed," Martino said. "Should we keep the cuffs on?"

Glancing back over his shoulder, Mike could see several of the people who'd been in attendance at the briefing were now mingling about in front of City Hall, staring over in their direction. One held a video camera which was focused on them.

"Take them off, but watch him closely," Mike replied.

Directing his next statement at the man they'd apprehended, Mike said, "We want to question you. I'll be reading your rights to you. We'd appreciate it if you didn't say anything to the news media just yet. Any problem with that?"

The man shook his head no. His cuffs had now been removed and he was massaging his wrists.

"Honest, I haven't done anything wrong. I really don't have a thing to tell you."

"We'll be the judge of that," Mike responded, motioning to Martino and the other officer to bring the man along behind him and Kelly. Reporters were calling out a number of questions as they preceded the others across the street.

"Who is he?" "Why are you arresting him?" "Is it McConnell?" "Does this have anything to do with this case?"

Mike shrugged off their questions. "We don't know anything more at this point than you do. It's not McConnell. We just want to question this man. He's not connected to any news service. We'll let you know as soon as we learn anything else," he said as the reporters cleared a path for them to make their way back into the building.

•

After about twenty minutes of questioning in Mike's office, Kelly was resigning herself to the fact she'd probably overreacted. The man professed not to know McConnell or be involved in the case in any way. It had been more of a stunt to impress his friends that he'd been able to crash the news conference. He had no previous criminal record. He lived in Ypsilanti, a small town just east of Ann Arbor, and was employed by Home Depot, one of the large building supply retailers in the area. Mike had therefore surprised her when he told Tippel he should contact an attorney.

"We're going to be holding you for a while," Mike said. "Being implicated in a murder and blackmail case is no minor matter. As an accomplice, you can be charged yourself. It doesn't matter how minor your role might be. Knowing that, you might want to come clean with us now – save

177

yourself a ton of grief."

Turning to Martino and the other officers, Mike said, "Lock him up."

The man's face had paled. He nervously looked from one person to the other, conveying the impression he was having difficulty comprehending what was happening. As the officers were leading him out the door, he turned back towards Mike.

"I didn't know what I was getting into," he blurted out. "I didn't have anything to do with the murder, the blackmail. I just had the chance to make a quick hundred dollars by recording the briefing. That's all!"

Kelly and Mike exchanged glances, having difficulty hiding the feeling of elation they both felt. Maintaining a somber expression, Mike said, "Okay. Sit down. We'll start again."

•

Over the course of the next ten minutes, an entirely different scenario emerged. The young man had been approached on Main Street less than an hour ago by another man, who they were quite certain now had been McConnell in disguise. The man had an English accent and best remembered by Tippel was his small, trimmed mustache. He didn't look at all like the sketches of the man he'd seen in the newspapers and over television, Tippel claimed.

With the enticement of making a fast hundred dollars for less than an hour of his involvement, the man persuaded Tippel to record the press conference in its entirety. He'd given Tippel the recorder. His explanation as to why he couldn't do it himself was simple. As a foreign news correspondent, he'd previously been ejected and refused entry at the previous briefings. An orchestrated attempt by the State Department, the man had explained, to discourage reporting of crime in the United States, which was hurting the tourist industry. Tippel admitted it sounded farfetched, but the man had handed him a fifty dollar bill and told him he'd get another one when he returned the recorder.

Mike had excitedly asked him where and when that was supposed to be and Tippel had answered, "In front of Sweet Lorraine's at five-fifteen this afternoon."

Mike checked his watch. It was already five-twenty. Kelly could read his mind. Would McConnell still be there waiting? Could they set a trap? Had McConnell witnessed Tippel's apprehension? Had he already been scared off?

Tippel was saying, "I didn't think I was doing anything wrong. I wasn't intending to commit any crime."

Mike interrupted him, asking if he'd be willing to try to help them apprehend the man by going ahead with the delivery.

"If that gets me off the hook, sure," Tippel replied. Mike nodded, indicating it would, and turned to the others with a rapid-fire series of instructions.

"We'll have to involve people McConnell doesn't know, hasn't seen," Mike said. "That eliminates you," he said, addressing Kelly, "me, Steve . . . Judy could probably be involved, you too," he added, turning to Martino. "Who else is available? No uniforms."

Over the course of the next five minutes, a plan was in place. In addition to Tippel, six others would be involved, carrying out roles from a bag lady to a delivery man.

"We don't want to do anything to prompt McConnell to change his plans about Tuesday. We're better off letting him escape now than alerting him of our attempt to apprehend him. We have to be very cautious. But if we succeed now in catching him . . ."

Mike let the statement hang. They were all well aware of the benefits of apprehending McConnell now – the elimination of the need for an elaborate plan for Tuesday.

Benton had been briefed. His reaction had been, "It's a risk, but one well worth taking."

●

Two of the detectives participating in the hastily planned attempt to nail McConnell were wired as well as Tippel. Judy was one, dressed as a bag lady, heavily padded and pushing a shopping cart.

Over half a dozen people were in Benton's office listening in, including Mike, Steve and Kelly. The police station was only a couple of blocks from the Farmers Market/Kerrytown area where Sweet Lorraine's restaurant was located.

"I don't see any sign of him yet," Judy's whispered voice came over the speaker. "Tippel's in front of the restaurant now, just wandering back and forth a few steps, with his hands in his pockets. He's doing a good job, not taking note of me or any of the others."

Martino's voice was next to be heard. He was making a delivery to Argiero's Italian restaurant, across the street from Sweet Lorraine's. The restaurant had been notified and its employees were playing along with the orchestrated plan.

"No sign of him. I'm just going back in with a second load of product. Judy and her cart are getting quite close to Tippel now. She looks the part."

For the next few minutes there was only silence. Then Judy's voice was heard.

"Damn it. I think he's on to us. There's a candy bar in front of me on the sidewalk."

As Judy spoke, Martino's voice came over another speaker. "Judy's doing a heck of a job. Bumbling along, appearing to be talking to herself, a great acting job. She just stopped to pick up something on the sidewalk. She's carefully studying it and just tossed it in her cart. If I didn't know differently, I'd think she was – "

Judy was speaking again. "I was right, it's a Zero$^{(tm)}$ bar. On the underside of the wrapper is a smiley face sticker along with the message, "Long Gone!" It's typed on an adhesive label next to the smiley-face. He's one step ahead of us again. He'd of had to plan for this in advance. I'll wind this up as we discussed. See you in a few."

A look of disappointment was on everyone's face as they exchanged glances. In an angry tone, Mike said, "Just shows more than ever how well prepared we'll have to be for Tuesday. To be one step ahead of him for a change. He's right, we've batted zero up to this point."

"It was worth a try," Steve said. "We're still going ahead with the surveillance on Tippel, aren't we?" Mike nodded.

The game plan called for Tippel to proceed back home to Ypsilanti if McConnell didn't show after twenty minutes or so. A team was in place over the next twenty-four hours to watch for any attempt to contact him.

"I think we need a break," Benton said. "Get your thoughts and suggestions together and we'll meet at seven-thirty in the morning to plan for Tuesday. That'll give you time now," he added, referring to Mike, "to finalize details on having the money by Tuesday afternoon. Set it up like we discussed."

Mike nodded. "I'll attend to it. My suggestion is for all of us to pretend we're in McConnell's shoes. What would we be planning to do? Where, when and how would we plan to take delivery of the $100,000?"

Heads nodded in agreement as David added, "Amen to that. Thanks Mike. Let's really stretch our imaginations on this. Any thoughts you have, no matter how far-fetched they might seem, should be aired during our discussions tomorrow."

David glanced down at his wristwatch as he asked if anyone had any additional questions or comments. "If not, we'll see you in the morning. I'll check now and see how we stand with the news media."

## Chapter 26

Kelly lingered as the others drifted out the door. Turning to Kath, she said, "There's one other point I want to discuss briefly with David and Mike. I'll be back in my office in a few minutes."

Kath nodded and followed the others through the door.

"This will only take a couple of minutes. I need direction. You're both aware of McConnell's assertion someone else was responsible for Beth's death. My question is, what do we do with that? How much time, if any, do you want me to devote to exploring that possibility? McConnell contends it was one of the blackmail victims."

David responded first. "My personal opinion, Kelly? Let's not waste any time on it at this juncture. Our initial priority is apprehending McConnell. There will be plenty of time afterwards for checking out his allegation, determining if there's any validity to it."

"I agree," said Mike. "While we can't truly block it out of our minds, let's not burden ourselves with that issue now, taking time would distract from our immediate objective. I sense that's your thinking, too. Am I right, Kelly?"

She nodded and was just starting to respond to Mike's question when there was a knock at the door.

"Yes, what is it?" David asked.

"It's me, Kath. I have an envelope I found sitting on Kelly's desk. It's marked urgent. I thought it might be important."

Mike opened the door and motioned Kath in. She handed the bulky white business envelope to Kelly. Kelly's name was hand-printed on the front with the message, "Urgent – Deliver At Once" in even larger letters.

She tore open the envelope and dumped the contents on David's desk. There were three bars of Airheads(tm), a chewy candy manufactured by van

Melle, along with a note. Kelly unfolded it and began to read it so all could hear.

"Dear Kelly. You Airheads<sup>(tm)</sup> are trying my patience! The deal was for you to call off the hunt and to deliver the $100,000. I'm giving you one more opportunity. Anymore tricks and you'll be responsible for the consequences. It's signed 'True to His Word' with a PS – 'Sorry about the dog.'"

"So sorry he drove back and forth across its body at least twice," Kath said angrily, her face flushed. "That's his deal! You never agreed to it. He's the airhead! He's sick!"

Mike gestured in an attempt to calm her down. Her outburst served as a warning they all had to keep their emotions in check.

"He also needs a lesson in how to win friends and influence people," Mike said. "Calling us Airheads<sup>(tm)</sup>, Nerds<sup>(tm)</sup>, Dum Dums<sup>(tm)</sup> and such doesn't really encourage us to play his game."

"I know you're just trying to help me get my emotions under control. But hearing that tape really worked me up. My sister's dead and he's asking for sympathy, like he's been victimized rather than being responsible for everything. The death of two people and a dog, the anguish he's caused for those people he's blackmailing – "

"Excuse me, Kath," Kelly said, interrupting. "With everything that's happened, I completely forgot about the tape. You too?" Kelly asked, looking toward David and Mike.

"Not totally," David answered. "Kath and the others heard the tape while you and Mike and I were involved with the briefing. I guess it was sometime after we questioned Gary Tippel and set the plan in motion to try to apprehend McConnell that Mike and I discussed the contents of the tape with those who'd heard it. Sorry, I'd thought you were there, Kelly. I was intending to give everyone an opportunity to hear the tape again tomorrow morning. It's right here. Why don't we play it. Mike and I haven't heard it yet, either. From what Judy and Steve told us, there's nothing said which would surprise us. They both advise against sharing the tape with those being blackmailed, getting them together to hear it. Of course, I'm aware that's what McConnell asked for. They reasoned it would only serve to alarm them even more. Possibly prod them to put more pressure on us not to try to apprehend him. Why don't we all hear the tape. Do you want to sit through it again, Kath?"

She nodded and then smiled as she said, "You'll see for yourselves why I'm so worked up."

"Just a minute, David," Mike said. "I'd like to know when and how that envelope reached Kelly's desk."

He reached for the phone and dialed Steve Rentz's extension. He explained to Steve what had occurred and briefed him on the contents of the envelope.

"I'd like you to see if you can discover how the envelope made it to her desk. Who put it there? Who dropped it off, possibly at the reception desk, and when? Let me know as soon as you have any answers. I'm in David's office."

"Everybody set now?" David asked. Receiving nods, he pushed the button to start the tape.

"Ten, nine, eight," McConnell's voice came over the tape. "The countdown has begun. In a few days your anguish will be over. I will have vanished from the scene and the nightmare I subjected you to ended. With the $100,000, I will begin a new life. You'll never hear from me again."

"Don't count on it," Kath mouthed as McConnell's voice continued.

"In my attempt to punish the University for the wrongs inflicted on me, you were targeted because of your high profiles. I apologize for the misery I've caused you. While I don't deserve your sympathy, understand I have lost nearly everything. My identity, my possessions, my home and most tragic of all, my beautiful Beth. The police would have you believe I was responsible for her death. Perhaps, indirectly I was. But I believe it was one of you who actually murdered her. The only one of you who needs to fear me in the future is that person.

"Seven, six, five . . . I said at the beginning of this tape we're in a countdown. A countdown to bring an end to your fears and apprehensions. Or a countdown to disaster. It's your decision!"

McConnell's voice had increased in volume and the previously friendly tone and manner had now turned mean-spirited.

"The deal on the table is for me to be given $100,000. I don't care how much each of you contribute, just so it totals $100,000. In exchange, I promise to disappear and never bother you again. The Ann Arbor police have been asked to call off their efforts to apprehend me. I've offered to help them track down Beth's killer. Thus far, only minimum harm has been done. Everyone is better off if I just get paid and vanish.

"The alternative is for the police to continue their efforts to arrest me, perhaps try to apprehend me as the money is being delivered. If this happens, I will be forced to publicize all the demeaning photographs and innuendoes about each of you. I've made arrangements for their circulation if I should be arrested or killed. The police would love to catch me in a hail of bullets. But that would only result in destroying your careers and upsetting your personal lives."

As McConnell continued, his voice became even louder, with a more threatening tone. He detailed the dire consequences to each of the five. In addition to tarnished reputations, McConnell emphasized the financial consequences.

"The $100,000 is a bargain. I'm letting you off easy as a way of making amends."

"Making amends my ass," Kath mouthed silently, as the others noticed her becoming worked up and angered once again.

"Which direction the countdown takes is in your hands. Tell the police not to act in a way which will virtually destroy your lives and careers. You could probably use this tape to show you've been threatened, blackmailed. But I'm sure you all know – the retraction, the correction seldom gets the same coverage as the initial charges. Page ten compared to page one.

"You might think the prior news coverage saying innocent people had been set up for blackmail will minimize the damage the release of the photographs and allegations would cause. Don't believe it! Don't take the risk!

"Persuade the police, Chief Benton, Detective Cummings and Detective Travis, and the dozens of others assigned to this case, to back off. Persuade Beth's twin sister, Kath, too. If she had half the brains and class of her sister, she'd be trying to solve this dilemma rather than prodding the investigators on. She can't seem to accept the fact I didn't kill her sister.

"Maybe four of you can't either. But the other one of you knows I'm innocent. But innocent or not, you have much to gain by getting the police to step back. Much to lose if they don't. It's not worth the gamble!

"Quite frankly, I've reached a point where I don't give a damn what happens. Plead your case to the police. Which countdown occurs is up to you. Four, three, two . . ."

The tape ended with McConnell chuckling. His last words were, "You've been warned!"

David pushed the stop button and arched his eyebrows as he glanced around at the others.

"Tell me the truth," Kath exclaimed. "Doesn't he make you want to just haul off and hit him? Or shoot him down in a hail of bullets, as he suspects you want to?"

"Definitely the former," David answered, and then with a slight smile, he added, "Maybe not the latter."

"Can we really keep this tape under wraps?" Kelly asked. "I mean, don't we have some obligation to pass it on to the individuals it's directed to? What are the repercussions if – "

David held up his hand. "Kelly, I didn't mean to suggest earlier that a final decision had been made. There are a multitude of questions and factors involved. I think we have to consider them all. When we were all together in the morning, I had intended to play the tape and thoroughly discuss our options."

"I understand," Kelly answered. "It's just that these people have a big stake in what's happening. They suffer the most if we botch things up on Tuesday. Even if we're successful, if we're to believe McConnell, his arrest could lead to the disclosure, the making public of the photographs and allegations."

"You just hit on the heart of it, Kelly, with your statement 'if we're to believe McConnell,'" Mike said. "I'm of the belief we can't and shouldn't. I think regardless of what happens, he's going to try to get his slander out to the media. He's just setting us up as a scapegoat."

"I tend to agree," said Kelly. "But also remember, we're dealing with some intelligent, knowledgeable people here. They're perceptive. I don't think they're going to be taken in by his assurances. We're not concerned about protecting a bunch of juveniles from some knowledge which would cause them trauma or nightmares. These are adults. They can deal with it."

"You're right of course, Kelly," said Mike. "But our main charge is to apprehend McConnell. If not a murderer, perhaps a double murderer, we know he's responsible for the blackmail, the assaults. We need to spend all our time and attention on catching him, not being distracted and occupied with convincing people we're doing the right thing. I . . . "

David smiled. "You've both outlined some of the issues. I'm sure we'll be having a lively discussion in the morning. We can all sleep on it." Looking at his watch, he continued. "What time did I suggest for tomorrow? Let's delay the meeting until nine-thirty. We all could use a few hours extra sleep, and we want to be . . . "

Steve knocked and poked his head in the door. "Sorry to interrupt.

185

Just wanted to let you know we haven't been able to find anyone who knows anything about the envelope that ended up on Kelly's desk. Of course, that was around the time of a shift change. We're making some calls now."

David advised Steve the meeting for tomorrow morning had been re-scheduled for nine-thirty and asked if Judy and the others were back yet. "They're just filtering in now. I'll tell Judy about the time change. Do we want Larry Martino there too?"

"That's probably a good idea," David answered. "I'll be out to see them in a minute or two. Guess that wraps it up for us," he added, turning to Kelly and Mike. "Kath, it's up to you whether or not you want to sit in on our discussions tomorrow. You're welcome, but it's really not neces-sary. Kelly told me McConnell wants you here on Tuesday when he calls."

"I'd like to sit in, if you're sure I won't be in the way," she answered. "I'll try to keep my cool and not sidetrack you."

"Fine, we'll see you in the morning then."

"I'll drop you off at the Sheraton when you're ready," Mike volun-teered as they left David's office.

"I think my car was brought back from my condo and parked in the garage," Kelly said.

"I know, but I'd just as soon not have it parked in the Sheraton lot. We know he'd recognize it. Whether he knows where Kath and you are stay-ing now is another question. I can drive you there and pick you up in the morning."

Kelly seemed hesitant. "Does that present a problem?" Mike asked. "Did you have plans to go out to a restaurant tonight?"

"Not that, but I thought I'd swing by and check on my parents. On the way to the Sheraton."

"No problem. If you won't be long, I'll just wait for you."

"Maybe I can reach Rick and he could pick us up at my parents'. I'll try to call him now."

"Any way you want to work it out is fine with me," Mike replied. "I'm just suggesting you keep your car here until Tuesday and let someone else chauffeur you."

•

Rick had been delighted to hear from Kelly, and was more than willing to pick up them up at her parents and drive them to the Sheraton. Rick offered to take them out to dinner, but Kelly declined, saying she just wanted a quick bite to eat at the hotel and then to get her thoughts down on paper before tomorrow's meeting. Maybe, she said, if Rick was willing, she could talk Kath into joining him for a movie.

•

Kelly's parents were delighted to see her. They were very kind to Kath, expressing their sympathies over the death of her sister and complimenting her on the wig, commenting on how much it altered her appearance compared to the photographs they'd seen of her in the newspaper.

Rick arrived approximately twenty minutes after Mike had dropped them off. He joined in the conversation for the next ten minutes, before Kelly explained they'd have to be on their way. No, she told them, she still wasn't staying at her condo; that Kath and she were sharing a room elsewhere for the next couple of days. She hesitated before telling them they were at the Sheraton. Her dad wrote down the Sheraton's phone number and their room number in case the need arose to contact her.

"I'm not registered under my own name, so don't lose this," Kelly explained. She could tell the explanation caused them concern. True to pattern, her mother advised her to be careful as they said their good-byes.

## Chapter 27

The Sheraton was a hub of activity as they entered the lobby. Nearly everyone appeared to be dressed in red and white or maize and blue. The Indiana-Michigan pre-game festivities were well underway.

The three were fortunate to obtain a table in the hotel's restaurant. They all opted for the buffet, more out of concern to reduce the time spent having dinner than to satisfy their appetites. On the drive over, Kelly had persuaded Kath to join Rick at a movie in the nearby Briarwood Theater Complex. Kath had hesitated but then agreed, sensing Kelly perhaps had a need to have her out of her hair for a few hours. Rick purchased a newspaper and found the movie the two of them wanted to see began at nine-twenty-five. With little time for conversation, they finished their dinners shortly after nine o'clock. Kelly decided to linger a few minutes with a cup of coffee after Kath and Rick excused themselves. Rick had good-naturedly asked Kelly if she wanted them to bring her back a box of popcorn or some JuJubes(tm).

"Certainly not candy," she'd replied with a smile. "And I guess I'll skip the popcorn, too. Thanks for the offer though."

•

The message light was on when Kelly entered the room. She dialed the front desk and learned Judy Wilson had called and left word to call her back. *She probably has an idea for tomorrow's meeting to bounce off me,* Kelly thought. She started to dial Judy's number and then changed her mind. *I think I'll have a shower first,* she thought. *I might be on the phone with her for a while.*

The shower felt wonderful. As Kelly turned her face up into the spray, she thought over all that had transpired since breakfast. No wonder she felt so mentally and physically drained. *Hopefully, I'll have enough energy left to jot down a few of my thoughts. Maybe I'll get a second wind.*

•

After toweling herself off and getting into her nightgown, she sat down on the edge of the bed and dialed Judy's number. As the phone began to ring, Kelly glanced up. Her eyes focused on something that had been slid under the door, a slip of paper or an envelope. Judy answered her phone.

"Hi Judy, it's me, Kelly, returning your call."

"I recognize your voice; thanks for getting back to me. I'm surprised you stayed out so late. I'm exhausted, myself."

"You should be. I heard you make a great bag lady. Larry Martino raved about your performance."

"He did, did he? Well, it didn't do much good. Maybe I should have dressed like Lady Godiva," Judy added with a laugh.

*Poor Judy,* Kelly mused. *Try though she did to be one of the boys or one of the girls, she seemed to irritate her cohorts rather than winning their acceptance. Like now, saying she recognized my voice, sort of reprimanding me for introducing myself. A hint of criticism for being out late, having difficulty accepting a compliment and a corny joke.*

"Let me explain the reason for my call," Judy was continuing. "I've had some thoughts and I was wondering if you'd had similar ones. They're about Kath."

"Can you hold for a minute, Judy? Someone just slipped something under my door. I just want to check it out."

"Sure, go ahead, I'll hold."

Kelly set the receiver down and crossed the room. It appeared to be a business size envelope and she reached down to retrieve it. Something in the hidden end made the envelope too bulky to pull it under the door. Still leaving the security chain on, she opened the door and looked out into the corridor. It appeared to be empty. Glancing down she saw a "Go Blue" sticker on the end of the envelope which protruded into the hall. "Go Blue" was one of the major cheers to root U of M teams on to victory. Perhaps the envelope has something to do with tomorrow's game, Kelly thought, an advertisement of some kind. However, as she glanced down the hallway she didn't see similar envelopes under anyone else's door. She kneeled down and grabbed the envelope, working it toward her, sliding it along the underside of the door. The exterior of the envelope had no markings or identification other than the Go Blue sticker. Holding the envelope up as she stood, she could tell something other than just a letter or note was inside. She shook the contents down to one end and opened the envelope by tearing off a portion of the opposite end. Squeezing the envelope open, she peered inside. She could see a handful of yellow and blue panned candies, similar to M&M's$^{(tm)}$. She poured them out into her hand. They *were* M&M's$^{(tm)}$. Kelly recalled the hype a short time ago when a blue color was added to the M&M's$^{(tm)}$ color mix. Looking down into the envelope again she saw a small photograph. Reaching inside, she removed it. She was startled to see it was a photograph of her as a youngster. She must have only been thirteen or fourteen years old when it was taken. There was nothing else in the envelope.

Her first thought was McConnell had discovered it in her apartment and was now sending the message he somehow knew where Kath and she were staying. No, that couldn't be it, she reasoned. She didn't have any of her childhood school things at her apartment. A shiver went through her body as she realized they were still at her parents' home. Her fears mounted as she tried to determine how someone – with the candy it has to be McConnell – had obtained the photo.

She raced back across the room to the phone.

"Judy, I'll have to call you back."

"What's wrong? Something to do with what was under your door?"

"Yes. It was an envelope with a photo of me as a young teenager. I think McConnell stole it from my parents' house. There was also some candy in the envelope. I need to call them to see if they're all right."

"I'll be up until eleven," Judy replied. "Remember to call me back."

Kelly almost slammed the receiver down. Seemingly, no concern by Judy for her parents' welfare. She nervously dialed their number. As the phone rang, she thought how easily it would have been for McConnell to have obtained her parents' address from the phone book. There were only the two listings under Travis.

The phone rang nearly ten times as Kelly waited with growing anxiety.

"Hello." It was her mother's voice.

"Are you okay, Mother?"

"Why yes, Kelly. Your father's in the bathroom, getting ready for bed. Sorry I took so long to get to the phone. Are you all right? I'm glad you called."

"I'm fine, Mom, I was worried about you."

"Now you know how we feel sometimes. Everything is all right here; we're just about ready to call it a day. I'm glad you called though, because I wanted to tell you about the visitor we had just after you left tonight. He's a former classmate of yours from Tappan Junior High. He says he had the biggest crush on you. He's here for the game tomorrow, from Indianapolis. He says he hasn't seen you since Tappan."

At least they're okay and safe now, Kelly thought as her mother continued. That was the most important thing.

"He loved seeing the current photograph of you we have on the mantle. He said he knew back then you'd turn into a beauty, but was delighted to see you're even more gorgeous now than he'd envisioned. He'd tried to reach you several times at your condo before coming here. He's anxious to see you, at least talk with you. Your father tried to call you several times while he was here, but you weren't in."

"No, we had dinner when we first arrived. I didn't get to the room until about nine-thirty."

"Let's see, I have his name here somewhere. His first name is Terry.

Here it is, Skcirton. Want me to spell it? S-K-C-I-R-T-O-N. Kind of an unusual last name. He's still single Kelly, and I think he's still in love with you. Do you remember him?"

Kelly had jotted down the name on the notepad next to the phone as her mother spelled it out.

"No, I don't remember him, Mother."

"Well, he remembers you. We had the nicest chat. We even rummaged up an old Tappan yearbook. He pointed himself out in one of the group pictures. He wears a beard now. You know I've never liked beards, but he was so nice, I may have to change my opinion."

"Did you give him a photograph of me?"

"Why yes, you must have – what do they call it – ESP. There was a cellophane bag in the yearbook with three copies of the same photo. Just those small ones. I hope you're not angry. He asked if he could have one."

"Did you tell him I was at the Sheraton, give him the phone number and room number?"

"Not until he was just leaving. Your father had kept trying to reach you. We told him about your work and also explained you were heavily involved in a major case and might not be able to see him. He so wanted to at least speak with you. Your father and I discussed it and finally decided to tell him how he could contact you. Was that wrong?"

Without answering Kelly asked, "Did he tell you where he's staying, or leave a phone number with you?"

"No, come to think of it he didn't. We should have gotten that information for you. I'm sorry. I would think you'd hear from him tonight."

Kelly had been staring at the name she'd jotted down earlier, Terry Skcirton, as her mother talked. She grimaced as the significance of the name became apparent to her. Skcirton spelled backwards read "no tricks."

"Mom, I can't go into all the details now, but if he, Terry, shows up again, don't let him in. Keep the door locked and call 911. I'm quite certain the young man you visited with is the man we're after – Joe McConnell."

"Oh my Lord, how could that be? Are you sure Kelly?"

"Yes. I'm one hundred percent certain it was him or someone working in collusion with him. Please warn Dad as well. I have to hang up now, but I'll either stop by or call you sometime tomorrow."

"I still can't believe it."

"It's true, Mother. I'm certain."

191

•

Kelly just sat for the next couple of minutes to collect her thoughts. McConnell was delivering a message, directly to her. If Kelly was involved in any attempt to apprehend him when the money was delivered on Tuesday, a party to any tricks, he could retaliate against her parents as well as her. He knew where they lived. He'd probably followed Mike's car when Kath and she were dropped off earlier this evening. Should she call Mike? No, best to think this out first. She didn't want to be taken off the case. Maybe special security could be arranged for her parents; get them out of town for a few days. Maybe she and Kath should move in with them. She could just picture McConnell with that sinister smile of his, smirking over the dilemma he'd placed Kelly in.

It was ten-twenty. She'd promised to call Judy back. What should she say to her? Shaking her head, Kelly picked up the phone.

## Chapter 28

"Hi. Sorry to be so late in getting back to you."

"I thought you may have forgotten about me," Judy responded. "How is everything? How is everybody?"

"Fine, except for the fact McConnell paid a visit to my parents."

"He what!? Are they all right? Did he threaten them?"

"They're fine. They didn't know it was him and he didn't threaten or intimidate them. To the contrary, really. He wowed them. He pretended he was an old classmate of mine from junior high. Here in town for the game tomorrow. A former boyfriend who was anxious to see me. He used the name of Terry Skcirton – S-K-C-I-R-T-O-N. He manipulated them into giving him my room number here at the Sheraton."

"That name. Do you realize in reverse it spells 'no tricks'?"

"Yes, though it took me a little longer than you to figure that out."

"Are you frightened?"

"Well yes, maybe concerned is a better description, though. He's clearly trying to intimidate me."

"Maybe it would help if I took over for you," Judy suggested. "I

192

could run that past David and Mike if you want me to."

"No, I don't think that will be necessary. There are other options. Possibly some protection for my parents. I'll let David and Mike know what's happened. I think they'll want to wait until the meeting tomorrow before making any changes, however. Sort it out some more."

"Okay. But remember, you can call on me if you need to."

"Thanks Judy. I appreciate that," Kelly replied, at the same time thinking that option would be far down her list.

"Well, let's get back to the purpose of my call to you earlier. I've been doing some thinking and had something to run by you, to see if you had similar thoughts. This latest instance might have a bearing on what I wanted to discuss with you. I've been concerned about McConnell's uncanny ability to seemingly stay just one step ahead of us. Not only does he seem to know what we're doing, I also get the feeling he knows what we're planning on doing."

"I know what you mean, Judy. I've had similar thoughts."

"I thought that might be the case," Judy said. "Maybe the same additional thoughts I've had. I wonder if we have a leak, if someone is feeding him information. That line of thought has pointed me in the direction of Kath. I've had vibes she might not be who we think she is. Remember all the confusion in getting the body identified? I was wondering if you had similar doubts or concerns?"

"No. None whatsoever," Kelly answered in surprise. "To the contrary, everything she's said and done has just reinforced my belief she's as anxious, maybe even more so if that's possible, to apprehend McConnell and bring him to justice, as we are. As a matter of fact, we played his tape this afternoon when you were out trying to nab him. David, Mike and I needed to settle her down. She was livid. She's at the movies now, with Rick. I persuaded her to get out and try to unwind. No, I don't share your thoughts or concerns. I've gotten to know her pretty well in the past few days."

"That could all be an act," Judy said. "Coming on strong to divert any suspicions. Remember her sister or she did an excellent job of acting in setting up those people for blackmail. Have an open mind."

"I think I do. But Judy, why would McConnell have gotten that man, Gary Tippel, to sit in on the media briefing this afternoon if he had an inside track or connection to learn what had been said? Have you considered that, factored that into your thinking?"

"Yes. It was a pretty cheap investment for him – fifty dollars – to divert any suspicions away from Kath. All I'm saying is don't immediately rule my suspicions out. Give it some thought. I heard that McConnell wants her to be present when he calls on Tuesday. What better way to stack the odds in his favor, arrange to get you in a position where it's two against one."

"Are you suggesting Kath shouldn't sit in on our discussions tomorrow?"

"I'm not sure what I am saying," Judy answered. "I guess I was hoping you'd had similar doubts or thoughts. I can see now that's not the case. But just think over what I've had to say. You're the first one I've confided in. I haven't shared these thoughts with Mike or David."

"As I said, Judy, my initial reaction is your imagination has gotten the best of you. She's legitimate. She's on our team. But I'll seriously consider what you've had to say. I'll be on guard. I really do appreciate you sharing your thoughts with me. Maybe we can find time to discuss this in more depth tomorrow. Let's both sleep on it."


## Chapter 29


Kelly sat on the edge of the bed for the next several minutes. It was nearly eleven o'clock. Kath and Rick would probably be returning in less than an hour. She'd hoped by this time to have completed several pages of notes in preparation for tomorrow morning's meeting. The fact McConnell knew where Kath and she were staying, the room they were in, was of relatively minor concern to Kelly compared to his involvement of her parents and Judy's suspicions. Due to the Indiana game, they were having to share a room tonight. A second room would become available tomorrow night. Should they even continue to stay at the Sheraton? Should she, they, be moving back to her condo, to her parents? Did McConnell still pose a threat? Would he have a change of mind about using them, or one of them, as a hostage? Just when she thought she'd be able to totally focus on the plans for Tuesday, a myriad of other concerns and questions now came into play.

She'd originally dismissed Judy's doubts about Kath. Now she was beginning to have some second thoughts. There were a number of unanswered questions about this afternoon's incident. McConnell had to of had the Zero$^{(tm)}$ bar with the smiley-face and 'long-gone' message prepared in advance – possibly the letter to her as well. Did he plan ahead for the possibility Tippel would be caught, or even plan in hopes he would be? Is that why he'd given him the eye-catching wig and thick glasses to wear? Another opportunity for him to needle the police with his letter to her containing the bars of Airheads$^{(tm)}$. Had that been his intention, rather than to discover what was said at the briefing?

All these thoughts and questions were simply distracting her from the really important work to be done, devising as close to a fool-proof plan as possible to apprehend McConnell on Tuesday. That could be part of his strategy now. Distracting them. Of course, he didn't have anything to do with Judy's suspicions. Or did he? What better way to confuse his adversaries. Plant seeds of doubt about Kath. Give the impression there was a leak, that he was privy to confidential, insider information. She didn't want to believe Kath was involved with McConnell, admit she'd been cleverly deceived these past few days. In trying to convince herself there were other reasonable explanations for his ability to stay one step ahead of them, she wondered if she was failing to look at all the facts in an unbiased manner.

She still believed that even though she'd have to agree he was very intelligent, McConnell had also enjoyed surprising luck. Hopefully, his string of luck would run out on Tuesday. Benton had shared with Kelly his reasoning for divulging the candy connection to the news media today.

"I'm hoping that by inflating his ego, we're able to get him to a point of being over-confident," David had said. "So sure of his abilities to outsmart us that he becomes vulnerable to making a mistake."

•

It was five minutes past twelve when there was a knock at the door. "Hi Kelly. It's us. Still awake?"

She recognized Kath's voice and walked over and unlocked the door. Greeting them with a smile, Kelly asked if they'd enjoyed the movie.

"Terrific! Right, Rick? We should have persuaded you to join us. I was really able to relax for an hour or so. I hadn't realized how stressed out I really was. It's a very funny, very romantic movie. Rick's promised me he's going to take you, see it again himself, once this is all over."

As Kath chatted, Rick noticed the nearby table with several sheets from a legal pad, filled with notes, scattered on it.

"Looks as if you've been productive in our absence," he said to Kelly. "Anything new?"

"Actually, yes," she answered, walking over to the desk between the beds. The yellow and blue candies were sitting next to the phone. She picked them up and, holding them up in the palm of her hand, said, "Compliments of McConnell."

"He's been here?" Kath asked with a look of surprise.

"Just to slide them under the door in that envelope," Kelly answered, pointing to the envelope with the Go Blue sticker still affixed to it. "I didn't actually see him."

"Are you sure it was him?" Rick asked. "How did he find out you were here? How did he know your room number?"

"You'd both better sit down. It's a fairly long story," Kelly answered.

Kelly proceeded to explain everything, showing them the photo and relating the conversation with her mother. As she discussed these details, Kelly studied Kath's reactions. Kath's face had flushed in anger and the concern she voiced for Kelly's parents appeared genuine. Kelly had a second sense this wasn't an act. She'd been truly shocked over Kelly's revelations, furious over McConnell's attempt to intimidate Kelly.

"Can you convince your parents to leave town for a couple of days?" Kath asked. "Do you have any relatives nearby?"

"My mother has a sister in Grand Rapids. They're very close. Maybe that would work."

"I'd be glad to chauffeur them," Rick volunteered. Grand Rapids was on the west side of the state, over a two-hour drive from Ann Arbor.

"Thanks Rick. I really haven't decided what would be the best thing to do. Except for Judy Wilson, you're the first to know. I thought about arranging for security guards, possibly you and I moving in with them, Kath. I was planning on discussing it with Mike and David in the morning. Get their input."

"I really think you should get them out of town," Rick said. "I know your mother's health is a problem. But you don't want to risk something happening to them."

"And there's no telling what that sick bastard might do," Kath said. "I agree with Rick. Get them out of town."

Rick smiled. "And to think your parents were trying to promote him as a potential suitor. I always sensed they weren't that enamored with me."

"That's not true, Rick," Kelly said, also breaking into a smile, relieved that he'd broken the tension.

The conversation continued for a few more minutes before Rick said he'd be leaving so they'd have an opportunity to get a good night's sleep.

"That might be wishful thinking," Kath said. "Were you planning to work a little longer?" she asked Kelly, pointing to the table.

"No. I really am ready to call it a day."

"Be sure to let me know if I can be of help," Rick said, "chauffeur you anywhere."

"We will, I'll be calling you," Kelly said, giving him a hug. "Thanks for everything."

•

Following Rick's departure, Kelly and Kath wasted little time in preparing for bed, engaging in only minimal conversation. After the lights had been turned off and they'd both been resting for a few minutes, Kath rose up and rested her head on her elbow. "I just had a horrible thought."

"What's that?" Kelly asked.

"I'm sorry, I shouldn't have said anything. I'll tell you in the morning."

Kelly laughed. "You'd better tell me now. Otherwise, I could be up all night wondering what you were going to say."

"I should have just kept my mouth shut. While we were waiting for the movie to begin tonight, I was following Mike's advice to the letter. Stretching my imagination to the limit, trying to determine what may happen on Tuesday. I thought of the possibility that Joe might plant a bomb somewhere on campus. With a timing device. And then promise to tell us where he'd hidden it and how to defuse it after he had the money and had distanced himself from Ann Arbor. As I was lying here, I thought of the possibility he might plant some explosive device in your parents' house, to convince you to cooperate with him. Kelly, you have to get them out of there."

Kelly nodded. "It's certainly a possibility, I guess. I think you're right, I'll have to convince them to move out for a couple of days. I'm glad you shared your thoughts with me. Thank you."

She rolled over on her side and closed her eyes. It was nearly an hour before she was able to fall asleep.

197

## Chapter 30

The clock read six-thirty-five when Kelly awakened from a surprisingly sound sleep. Kath was still sleeping. It was just a week ago today when this whole thing began, Kelly recalled, with Mike's call informing her a body had been discovered in the Arboretum. She remembered her feeling of elation. Her excitement over being involved in a homicide investigation. So much had happened, in some ways it seemed it had been far longer than a week since Mike's call. In other ways, far shorter – a blur of events. She decided to get up and dress and go down to the lobby. She could get a cup of coffee and also see how the papers had covered yesterday's events. She could also take her legal pad along and make some additional notes.

•

Sipping her coffee, Kelly had a copy of Saturday morning's *Detroit Free Press* spread out on the table in front of her. There was an article in the lower left-hand corner of the front page with the headline, "Sweet Side To Ann Arbor Murder Investigation." The article detailed some of the points Benton had made at yesterday's briefing, including McConnell's use of candy in his blackmail scheme and to taunt the police.

The article continued with a few paragraphs describing yesterday's incident at City Hall during the media briefing session. Tippel was not identified by name, just as a man in his early thirties who'd been wearing a wig and thick glasses. The chase from the briefing room through the parking lot was described in detail. The article stated the man had been taken into custody. The police had reported the man had no media credentials. He was still being questioned concerning his motives for attending the briefing. No relationship to the murder investigation had been established.

The article concluded with a quote from Benton, saying there was reason to believe the suspect, McConnell, had fled the area and that other law enforcement agencies, including those in Chicago, were cooperating fully with the Ann Arbor Police Department.

The *Ann Arbor News* had also featured an article on its front page, along with a photo. It pictured Mike and Kelly returning to City Hall, followed by Tippel with a police officer on each side. In the photo the *News* had selected, Tippel's head was bowed, making any identification difficult. The content of the article was reversed from the *Free Press*'s coverage, with the lead paragraphs dealing with the fact McConnell may have fled the Ann Arbor area. Kelly knew Benton had spoken with Greg Collier and was certain that conversation had a bearing on the thrust of the article.

The headline read, "Suspect May Have Fled A2" with a sub-heading "Commotion At City Hall." The content of the article was very similar to what had been reported in the *Free Press* with the exception of the major emphasis the *News* had given to the Hot Line which had been put into place for this case. Again, Kelly could sense Greg's involvement. Though saddened for the reason, Kelly was pleased they now had a strong ally at the paper in Greg Collier.

Kelly spent the following forty-five minutes making additional notes in preparation for the meeting. Glancing at her watch, she tucked the newspapers under her arm. She purchased two cups of coffee to carry back to the room.

•

Kath was in the shower when she returned. Kelly shouted through the bathroom door, "I have a hot cup of coffee out here for you."

"Wonderful, I'll be out in a minute. Thank you!"

Kath must have awakened just after she'd left the room, Kelly surmised as she saw a couple of pages of notes on the bed in Kath's handwriting. Glancing at them, she saw where she'd made notes on the possibility of McConnell planting a bomb somewhere on campus. Kelly didn't see any notation in regard to her parents; the likelihood of him planting an explosive or incendiary device in their house. Kelly smiled as she read a paragraph suggesting the possibility of Joe wiring himself up with explosives. She's getting a little bomb-happy, Kelly thought.

A note in the upper left-hand corner of one of the pages caught her eye. It was a phone number, 663-6321, preceded by the initial J. Kelly reached in the pocket of her blazer for a pen so she could jot down the number. It wasn't Judy's number. Kelly had dialed that number a couple of times last night and remembered it began with the 971 exchange. The door to the bathroom flew open and Kath bounded out, wrapped in a bath towel, with a second, turban-wrap towel covering her hair.

She grinned at Kelly. "One of life's simple pleasures; I love a shower in the morning. Are you a night-time shower person?"

"I suppose so," Kelly answered. "I guess I use one more to unwind than to charge up my batteries to begin the day. But I'm not real choosy; I do both."

Kelly hadn't had time to write down the phone number. She was attempting to recall it so she could in a few moments. Could the J refer to Joe, Joseph McConnell? Who else would she be calling? She hadn't indicated she'd been in touch with any friends here in town. It was a local number. The best way to find out whose number it was would be to place a call. She couldn't really confront Kath and risk alarming her about her suspicions. Try as she might, Kelly couldn't recall the last four digits of the number she'd seen. Maybe I'll get another chance to see the number, either now or even during our meeting later this morning, she thought.

While Kelly's mind was racing, Kath had continued to chat. "Oh, this coffee tastes good! Thanks again. I see you bought some newspapers. The *Free Press*. Good! I really enjoy its comic pages. Do you follow 'For Better Or For Worse'? I just love it when the little girl's involved. Oh, I see they have an article on the case on the front page. Any surprises?"

Kelly smiled and shook her head no. Kath was in an upbeat mode compared to yesterday. Kelly liked her, finding it hard to even think she could be involved with McConnell.

"No, I don't think you'll find any surprises. You'll find it interesting though, the different approach the *Ann Arbor News* takes compared to the *Free Press* in reporting the same essential facts. Is the shower still on? I think I hear it."

"I'm sure I turned it off – positive," she answered. "But I'll check."

As Kath was looking in the doorway of the bathroom, Kelly quickly looked at the sheet of notes on the bed on which the phone number had been written. She repeated it to herself, 663-6321, hoping to commit it to memory.

"No, it's off. What's our schedule, by the way? Should I be getting dressed?"

"Mike should be here to pick us up in about an hour," Kelly answered. "I thought about calling him to tell him about last night, about McConnell's visit to my parents. But I think I'll just wait. I thought I'd have breakfast. How about you?"

"Sounds good. I'll just be a few minutes. Casual dress okay?"

"Fine," Kelly answered. "I'm just dressed the way I am because I don't have the option. Maybe we'll get time to swing by my condo so I can get something other than business garb to wear. We still have to decide, find out what we're going to be doing, where we'll be staying tonight. Tomorrow night and Monday night, too."

Kath nodded as she pulled on her underpants and adjusted her bra. Kelly noticed a birthmark on her left buttock, the size of a silver dollar. She didn't recall any mention of it when the body was being identified.

"I'm just going to put on a touch of makeup and get my things to-gether," Kelly said. "We can probably leave right from breakfast, unless you want to come back to the room. I'll get us a table and meet you in the dining room."

"Fine, I'll only be a few."

•

Kelly went to one of the phones in the lobby, inserted a quarter and dialed the number she'd seen. The phone rang over half a dozen times and Kelly was just ready to hang up when an answering machine came on.

"Hi. Sam and I are unavailable to answer your call just now." It was a young woman's voice, a voice Kelly didn't recall having heard before. "Please leave a message. We probably won't get back to you until late Tuesday or Wednesday. Go Blue! Or if you're calling after the game, let's hope we're celebrating a victory."

Whoever it was had left town for the weekend, not due back until Tuesday. Could it possibly be McConnell was staying in this couple's apartment or house? They needed to get the listing and address for the phone number. Check that possibility out.

•

A few minutes later Kath joined Kelly at a table in the Sheraton's restaurant. Kelly had a legal pad in front her and was making some additional notes.

"I see you're still readying yourself for the meeting," Kath said as she seated herself. "I don't know exactly why, but I'm getting optimistic about Tuesday. I think Joe's going to slip up some way, that we're going to be able to nail him. Just a gut feeling."

"I hope you're right. I wish I could get myself in that frame of mind. I'm still frightened – maybe concerned is the better word – that we might be the ones who make a mistake. And we can't afford to."

Later in the conversation Kelly worked a question in, trying to be as casual as possible.

"Have you been in touch with any of your friends these past few days, since you returned to Ann Arbor?"

"I really haven't had time, we've been so busy," Kath quickly answered. "Most of my closest friends are no longer here. My former roommates, for example. I did call one of them and filled her in."

Kelly let the subject drop. She'd been wishing for a simple explanation for Kath's notation.


**Chapter 31**

They were just finishing with their breakfast when Kelly spotted Mike standing near the hostess stand, scanning the room. She raised her hand and waved. Mike saw her and came down the stairs. Navigating between tables, he broke into a smile as he approached them.

"Good morning," Kelly said. "Looks as if you're ready to get started. We are too. I'm glad you're a little early. How about a cup of coffee? We have some news to share with you, and I need your input and advice."

Mike nodded and pulled a nearby chair over to their table. "Sounds like a good idea to me. I also have some news for you. You first, go ahead."

Kelly explained to Mike the details of yesterday evening, the discovery of the envelope under the door, the conversation with her mother, and even Kath's concerns. As she talked, she handed Mike the envelope containing her photograph. He grinned and commented over what a knockout she was as a teenager and added she'd only improved with age. Kelly blushed as Kath chuckled.

"Our boy had a busy evening," Mike said. "He also paid a visit to Gary Tippel. About midnight. I'll fill you in on the details – we didn't catch him – but first let's talk about your parents."

A thought flashed through Kelly's mind. Why would McConnell risk calling on Tippel if he was in touch with Kath?

"I think Kath is right," Mike said. "We have to get your parents out of the house, out of town is even better. Are there any relatives close by they could visit, probably just until Wednesday? Does your father drive? I can arrange for transportation."

Kelly told him about her aunt in Grand Rapids and Rick having volunteered to drive them.

"You still haven't talked to your parents about this though?" Mike asked. Kelly shook her head. "That's probably the first step, getting them to agree. Think they'll be up so you could contact them now?"

"I'm sure they're up and probably my aunt and uncle are, too. Give me about twenty minutes, maybe we'll be able to work everything out. But I'm curious about McConnell visiting Tippel. Should that wait or can you make it brief?"

"It'll be brief, there's not that much to tell. But why don't we leave it for when we're driving downtown. Contact your parents first."

Kelly rejoined Kath and Mike in the lobby a few minutes later. She was all smiles.

"We're in luck. I spoke with my dad. Mom's sister called on Thursday and invited them to visit for a couple of days. They'd declined, but Dad's sure the invitation is probably still open. He's going to call her. Either way, he says they'll be out of the house by noon today, on their way to Grand Rapids, staying at the Amway Plaza if arrangements can't be worked out with my aunt. He also wants to drive. He was highly insulted," Kelly added with a giggle, "when I suggested we could get someone to chauffeur them. All he wants me to do is to keep in touch, let them know what's happening."

"That's great!" Kath said. "I thought you'd have more difficulty persuading them of the need to move out."

"Frankly, I did too. We still have to decide where we'll be staying for the next few days."

"I suggest you continue staying right here," Mike said. "I'm sure we can get the room changed and I think we can get you separate rooms, too, if you'd prefer. I believe we already made arrangements for two rooms, didn't we? Even though he knows you're here, I'd rather have you here than back at your place. But we could change you over to another hotel or motel if you'd prefer."

"What do you think, Kelly?" Kath asked. "Fine with me to stay where we are. We should probably let the front desk know now if we want to change rooms. Maybe we'll have to check our stuff. One room suits me, but it's your call."

"That's fine with me, too," Kelly replied, thinking she'd prefer that in order to keep a close eye on Kath.

•

A few minutes later, just after nine o'clock, the three were in Mike's car on their way to headquarters. Mike wasted no time in filling them in on the details of McConnell's visit to Gary Tippel. At about twenty minutes to twelve last night, an anonymous 911 call had come in to the Ypsilanti Police Department. The caller alleged he'd overheard a conversation discussing plans to rob the Perry Drug Store on Washtenaw at midnight. The caller explained at least six men were involved.

"The store is only about eight blocks from where Tippel lives," Mike said. We made arrangements with the Ypsi police to have two of their people watching Tippel's house last night. We thought it was a long-shot that he'd show, but they were willing to cooperate."

Mike went on to explain why the Ypsilanti police were involved, the jurisdiction problem and also to provide a buffer for them with McConnell if the Ypsi police attempted to apprehend him and failed.

"We could tell him it was the Ypsilanti police who screwed up and that we were honoring his demand to hold off in our efforts to capture him.

"A couple of minutes before midnight, the police received word the

Perry Drug Store had lost its power. One squad car had already been directed there as a result of the 911 call, and was still a few blocks away. The officers on duty at Tippel's house were notified to suspend their surveillance and immediately go to Perry's. Other units were also dispatched. At about this same time, Tippel received a call from McConnell, informing him to meet him with the tape at his back door in five minutes. He told him not to turn on any exterior lights. About five minutes later McConnell arrived, handed Tippel a fifty dollar bill, thanked him in a crisp, English accent, and departed through the backyard.

"I think Tippel was motivated by his desire to get himself out of hot water. Regardless, he followed McConnell through his neighbor's yard and saw him enter a car. He was able to obtain the license number and the make and model, a dark blue Pontiac Bonneville. He immediately notified us and we ran a trace on the car. The plates were stolen from a Lincoln Continental in Livonia this past Thursday. We still have an alert out for the car and the license plate. We might get lucky, if not today, Sunday or Monday. Hopefully, he won't dump the car before then."

"What happened at Perry's?" Kath asked.

"Nothing. It was a diversion. We're sure it was orchestrated by McConnell. Power was restored in about ten minutes. Last I knew, they still weren't certain how he'd accomplished that. The good news is, we've been put on alert he might attempt some similar diversionary tactic on Tuesday, and we know about the car. The bad news is, he outwitted us again."

"Why would the tape of the media briefing be so important to him?" Kath asked.

"I'm having difficulty with that, too," Mike replied. "As near as I can surmise, he might think that holds some clue about whether we're going to try to entrap him on Tuesday or going to go along with letting him take the money and run. Whether or not we're intimidated by his threat and want to put the matter behind us. He also may have been curious as to whether we'd mention the possibility of someone other than him being responsible for your sister's death. I just don't know."

As Mike spoke, Kelly was considering what this all meant in relation to Judy's suspicions about Kath and the discovery of the phone number. She'd have to get Mike away from Kath in some way this morning so she could brief him and get his input. They also needed to trace the phone number.

205

**Chapter 32**

Judy Wilson, Steve Rentz and Larry Martino were already gathered around the conference room table when the three of them arrived. Looking up as they entered the room, Judy said, "David will be joining us in about five minutes. Steve and I are just updating Larry, getting his input on how we should handle McConnell's tape."

"Good," said Kelly. "That gives me time to get some notes from my office. I'll be back in a few minutes."

Kath had taken a chair and Kelly motioned to Mike to follow her. In the hallway on the way to her office, she explained to him, "There are a couple things I need your input and help on." She went on to tell him about the conversation she'd had with Judy the previous evening.

"I was skeptical at first. I've grown fond of Kath over the course of these past few days. Gotten, I thought, to know her quite well."

She then went on to explain about finding the notation on a page of Kath's notes, the phone number with the initial J. She told Mike about calling the number and the answering machine message she'd heard.

"Combined with Judy's suspicions, this added development has my imagination in overdrive. I gave Kath a couple of opportunities to let me know if she'd been in contact with anyone over the past few days and she didn't volunteer anything about her notation. I'm wondering if McConnell could possibly be headquartering at that couple's house while they're gone for the weekend."

"I can run a quick check on the listing for that number, hopefully an address we can check out. I'll get on it right away," Mike said. "My gut feeling is in sync with yours. It won't be the first time my opinion has been at odds with Judy's. She's been known to go off on tangents before. We're forewarned, however. We'll need to keep a sharp eye on Kath. At this stage, until we have something more definite on the phone number, I wouldn't recommend excluding her from our meeting. Would you?"

"No. But I think we should also tell David about this."

"I intend to. We'll have a break in a couple of hours and I'll brief him then. Hopefully, by then we'll also have something on the phone number."

•

David was there when Kelly and Mike returned to the conference room. A discussion was already underway over the pros and cons of getting the people McConnell was blackmailing together to hear his taped message. The opinion was quite evenly divided. The arguments which had been articulated yesterday were further expanded on. The intervening hours did not appear to have changed anyone's initial thoughts.

It was actually Larry Martino's comments, Kelly believed, which finally led to a decision. He'd suggested that McConnell appeared to have a second sense for what was taking place, that he might attempt to verify in some way whether his message had been shared with those who had the greatest interest in keeping the flyer, photos and other information under wraps. As Martino spoke, Judy caught Kelly's eye. Kelly nodded and glanced over toward Mike, who had observed this non-verbal exchange of thoughts. Was Kath the viaduct for McConnell?

"At this stage, I don't think it would be wise to do anything, not do anything in this instance, which would prompt him to alter the current plan," Larry said. "Being second-guessed if we fail to apprehend him on Tuesday, if we botch up and prompt him to circulate his garbage, is a whole other issue. I'm in agreement with those of you who think he'll go ahead and distribute the stuff regardless of what happens Tuesday. I'm just suggesting we don't do anything before then which would decrease our chance of catching him."

Mike, who had been one of those fervently arguing the case to do nothing, to just sit on the tape, conceded Larry's point. "Let's not waste too much more time on this," Mike said. "That was my major argument to begin with. We'd be devoting too much time to the process of getting them together to hear the tape, explaining our plans. We need to get to the real crux of this meeting. I'm willing to buy into Larry's reasoning if it will get us off dead-center."

David, who had for the most part just been listening to the views of the others, intervened, saying, "Enough said. Mike's right, we have to move along. We'll try to arrange a meeting so they can all hear the tape. We need to begin by contacting the Jamesons to see if they're still available and still willing to host a meeting at their house, early tomorrow morning if possible."

Kath spoke up. "I can make the necessary calls, beginning with the Jamesons. That will save the rest of you some time and besides, of anyone, I probably have the least to contribute in making plans for Tuesday."

Kelly observed the look of surprise and concern on Judy's face. However it was Mike who replied to Kath.

"Thanks Kath. We appreciate your offer, but I think it's best if Kelly contacts the Jamesons. Once that's done, we can hopefully split up the other four calls among ourselves. We could make them during our break. You should probably try the Jamesons right now though, Kelly."

Kelly pushed her chair back as she said, "It shouldn't take long. Why don't the rest of you get started."

Mike had turned to Kath again and said, "Thanks again for your offer. I just think that we're the ones who should be making those contacts. Make them official." He smiled. "We're the ones being paid to do it."

Kath returned Mike's smile. "That's okay, you haven't hurt my feelings. I just thought it was a good way to help Kelly and the rest of you."

●

Kelly was fortunate to reach the Jamesons just as they were preparing to leave for a tailgate party. She spoke briefly with both of them. They would be happy to host an eight-thirty meeting on Sunday morning. Kelly explained that in addition to the other four being blackmailed, David Benton, Mike Cummings and she would probably be present.

"Oh, and one other – I think we'll have Kath Edwards with us as well," Kelly added as an after-thought, remembering she needed to be almost a shadow of Kath's the next couple of days. It would be easier to include her than to arrange for someone else, such as Judy, to keep an eye on her. The conversation ended with comments about how nice the weather was for the game, and whether Kelly would be attending.

"I'm afraid not. We're having a meeting now and it will likely continue well into the afternoon. I envy you; bring us a victory."

"We'll do our best," John Jameson replied. "Go Blue!"

As Kelly hung up the phone she smiled, recalling finding the envelope with the Go Blue sticker under her door last night. Hopefully, by Tuesday night, she thought, her world might begin to get back to normal. But there was a downside. This had been the most exciting week of her life, what she'd always dreamed of when she made her decision to pursue a career in law enforcement.

# Chapter 33

It was nearly one o'clock when David suggested they take a break and begin again at two-thirty. The past few hours had been spent in giving everyone the opportunity to air their ideas. There were various lists affixed to the walls of the conference room. David had asked each of them to put themselves in McConnell's shoes and describe the plan they'd devise to take possession of the money. It had been a fun process, with many of the more outlandish ideas prompting laughter. That helped to break the tension, as none had to be reminded of the seriousness and importance of these deliberations. Reputations were at stake – individuals', the University's, the police department's and their own.

The notations under the heading, "Location For Delivery" listed the wide range of possibilities which had been put forth. From Disney World to the Windsor gambling casino in Canada, across the river from Detroit; from Toledo's airport and Zoo to Chicago's O'Hare terminal and Museum of Natural History – there were nearly fifty sites on the list.

Mention of possible locales outside the Ann Arbor area had been accompanied by comments that McConnell would probably select a spot where local or state law enforcement officials would have difficulty setting up and coordinating a plan to apprehend him. Several Chicago locations were suggested because of his familiarity with the area. Toledo's frequent mention was due to its location, less than an hour's drive from Ann Arbor, and being the closest large, metropolitan area outside Michigan.

Kelly was surprised that Ann Arbor locales accounted for nearly a third of the sites appearing on the list. Those suggestions had been accompanied by statements about McConnell's perceived mind set. "He's overconfident, thinking he can easily outwit us." "He thinks he's intimidated us into agreeing not to pursue him." "The deal's with us rather than every police agency." "He's still playing a game, enjoying taking high risks." "He has an immense ego and needs to stick it to us, so to speak, on our home ground to satisfy it." "He doesn't want to risk the FBI being brought in if he should cross state lines." "He'd rather risk his chances with us than with the Detroit or Chicago police. They have far more manpower and resources at their disposal."

Possible Ann Arbor sites on the list ranged from the Briarwood shopping center south of town, to the Law Quad; from the Michigan League to the University Hospital complex.

Another list appeared under the title, "Disguises." The group had also stretched their imaginations on this question to come up with a very diverse range of possibilities. Several suggested McConnell's possible use of a uniform – dressed as a police officer, a Catholic priest, a UPS driver, or a doctor in a white coat with a stethoscope hanging from his pocket. There were a number of descriptions on the list which would give him a vanilla appearance, to enable him to easily blend in with a crowd. These ranged from traditional, casual student attire to the formal coat and tie of a businessman. Comments had been made suggesting he'd probably avoid any type of disguise which would draw attention to himself – bright colors or unusual garb – unless it were on the order of a baseball cap or an afro wig, which could quickly be cast aside.

There were also suggestions McConnell might try to make use of props which could easily and quickly be disposed of, such as crutches, a bicycle or roller blades. Several of them had mentioned he might attempt to disguise himself as a woman, perhaps dressed in a warm-up suit with a wig and sunglasses. Judy had provoked some laughter when she suggested he might disguise himself as a bag lady. Kath raised the question of whether he might arrange for one or more people to be accompanying him – such as a couple of young children or a female companion; even an elderly woman – to throw off attention or suspicion.

Under the heading, "Diversions," Kath's input had provided nearly half the possibilities listed. She'd enthralled the others with her discussion of how he might decide to detonate a bomb at some popular campus landmark just prior to the delivery of the money.

"Destroying the President's house would be a fitting way to top off his objective to get back at the University. Maybe even the University Carillon," Kath said, referring to the historic tower which graced the Ann Arbor skyline, not only of the University of Michigan campus, but the city as well. She also suggested he might plant a bomb somewhere, communicate the fact he had and that it had a timing device. If he received delivery of the money and escaped, he'd tell the proper authorities where it was located and how to disarm it. She stressed he could do this anywhere, the casino in Windsor, Detroit Metropolitan Airport, anywhere. Her zinger was the further suggestion that he might wire himself up with some type of explosive device.

Kath had briefed Kelly on several of these possibilities earlier, when they'd discussed the possibility of him planting a bomb in her parents' house. As a result, she wasn't as surprised by Kath's input as some of the others were.

Other possible disruptive or divergent tactics which had been added to the list included the use of tear gas and 911 calls, which would result in the police being called off their surveillance of the delivery site, similar to what had happened last night.

Steve had joked, "The possibilities are really endless. He could put a python or other large snake in one of the dorms, pay some students to instigate a massive food fight in one of the residence halls, or to streak across the Diag."

There were another half-dozen lists on the walls of the room. One was titled, "Electronic Devices," with Kath's and Kelly's names in parentheses underneath. Ideas ranged from the obvious – a homing device on the car they'd be driving – to the exotic – microphone earrings and bras and panties which gave off electronic signals. During this discussion, David had shown them the attaché case in which the money would be carried. It was designed with a hidden microphone as well as an electronic homing device. David also showed them four stacks of money which would be blended in with the other stacks of money on Tuesday. He cut one of the stacks in half, similar to a deck of cards, revealing a hole or indentation with a small, less than the size of a pea, microchip. He explained that all four stacks had a similar transmitter. They each would emit a short transmission once a minute, timed so a signal was sent every fifteen seconds.

"If he has a scanner of some type to detect a homing device or hidden mikes, which from our previous experiences he probably will, the fact signals are being sent intermittently will greatly lessen the chance of him detecting these micro units," David explained. "Discovering others might also lead him to believe he's found all the devices we've planted. We'll need to get lucky."

Under the heading, "Deceptions and Disguises To Be Used By The Surveillance Teams," was another list of suggestions ranging from the use of various delivery and service vehicles – Federal Express, Michigan Bell, a Triple-A Tow Truck – manned by police personnel in appropriate dress, to the use of solo personnel impersonating joggers, an elderly person with car trouble, a young hot-rodder out joy-riding, or a leather jacketed type on a Harley-Davidson with a ponytail.

Before calling the break, David had suggested the afternoon should be spent in narrowing down the various lists, planning for the most logical possibilities. Over the course of the morning, the group had reached a consensus of opinion on several points. Among them was a shared belief that McConnell would want to remain armed. Therefore, the transfer of the money would probably not take place inside the security area of an airport. Another shared opinion was in regard to his use of a bomb. After going to such great lengths in claiming he wasn't responsible for Elizabeth Edwards' death, all agreed it was doubtful if he'd detonate a bomb where there was risk of killing or seriously injuring someone. However, if he should plant a timed explosive device or wire himself up with explosives, they also were in agreement he'd do it in a densely populated or heavily traveled area to maximize his threat and the consequences if they should fail to meet his demands.

•

As the group began to depart the conference room, Mike spoke to Kelly and Kath.

"Are the two of you planning to go out for lunch?"

They exchanged looks before Kelly suggested, "I thought we might just pick up something at Zingerman's and bring it back to the office. Does that sound all right to you, Kath?"

"Fine with me. I don't want much, I'm not used to such a big breakfast."

"Why don't you give me about ten or fifteen minutes and I'll walk over with you," Mike said. "I just need to check on a couple of things and speak with David for a minute or two. I'll buzz you in your office when I'm ready, okay?"

Kelly nodded in agreement and she and Kath headed for her office.

"That will give us a chance to use the ladies room, too," Kath said to Mike, looking over her shoulder with a smile on her face.

## Chapter 34

About twenty minutes later, Kelly's phone rang. It was Mike.

"Good news, Kelly. I'm relieved and I think you will be, too. I'll just explain briefly now, rather than saying anything in front of Kath."

"Fine. She's sitting across the desk from me now. We'll meet you at the main entrance in about five minutes."

"I understand, I'll do the talking. The phone number is listed under the name J. Stevens. Some further checking discovered the J is for Jill, a free-lance writer living in the Burns Park area. She has an excellent reputation, winning several awards for some of her stories. She's also co-authored two books which drew good reviews and made considerable money. One was on the child custody case involving the lesbian couple. You might recall it."

"I do," Kelly replied.

"Now comes the surprise. I just finished speaking with David. Kath spoke with him yesterday about Jill Stevens contacting her following one of the media briefings. Stevens is attempting to get her to agree to sign a contract, to do a book together about this case. She talked in terms of considerable dollars with a cash advance. Kath spoke with David because of her concern about entering into any type of agreement which would give the appearance she was cashing in, financially benefiting from her sister's murder. David says it was really Kath's decision not to do anything until McConnell was apprehended, tried and convicted. She was particularly sensitive about you and I not knowing she'd even contemplated signing an agreement with Stevens. That's why he didn't mention anything to us about it."

"You're right, I am relieved," Kelly said.

"I thought you would be. I don't think it's really necessary, but I am going ahead with checking Jill's house out. Seeing if there's any sign of activity there. We verified she's out of town for the weekend. By the way, Jill's single and lives alone. Sam is a large house cat."

Kelly smiled. "Thanks for the update, Mike. We'll see you in a few minutes."

As Kelly hung up the phone, Kath commented, "I don't know what that was all about, but you seemed pleased."

"I am. Just a loose end Mike was checking out," Kelly replied, looking at her watch. "We're due back in session in less than an hour. We'd better get moving."

•

The break had benefited everyone. The afternoon flew by quickly, and Kelly found it surprising how the group's thinking had begun to mesh.

213

Differences of opinion were quickly resolved and the master plan for Tuesday began to take shape.

There was considerable discussion about the possibility McConnell would send Kath and Kelly on something similar to a scavenger hunt. Being sent to one location only to find a clue or receive another communication from McConnell to go elsewhere. This would strain the department's resources, build frustrations and perhaps cause them to get sloppy in their surveillance, creating a window of opportunity for McConnell to approach Kath and Kelly and disappear with the money. The discussion focused on how they could stay one step ahead of McConnell, anticipate his moves without too thinly spreading their resources.

All available personnel were being called on to implement the department's plans to capture McConnell on Tuesday, including even parking enforcement personnel and clerical staff. Only a skeleton crew would be manning the ship, the basics, on Tuesday. Most of those on the night shift would be brought in early on Tuesday afternoon. As Steve Rentz put it, "If I was going to get in trouble in Ann Arbor, Tuesday afternoon would be the time to do it."

At about four o'clock, David called a twenty minute recess. He predicted the way things were progressing, they should be able to wrap up by six-thirty or seven.

"That should avoid the need for getting together tomorrow. Some of us, of course, will be involved at the Jamesons' tomorrow morning."

With the exception of Tim Masterson, all the others had been contacted in regard to the meeting at the Jamesons' and had agreed to be there. Masterson still hadn't been reached, having been involved all day in his coaching duties. The group had just been told that Michigan was leading Indiana, 35-17, late in the fourth quarter. Mike would be phoning Masterson later this evening. Hopefully, he'd be able to arrange his schedule to also attend the breakfast meeting.

•

When the group returned to the conference room a short time later, they found David sitting at the head of the table flanked by a floral bouquet and a box of Lady Godiva chocolates. He smiled as he explained their significance.

"The card's addressed to me as 'Team Captain.' It reads, 'Sorry you felt you had to miss the game. Enjoy the remainder of the weekend. You'll hear from me on Tuesday.' Signed with a smiley-face."

"Don't let looks deceive you," David continued, lifting the lid from the box of candy. He turned the box upside down and a dozen or so Nestle 100 Grand<sup>(tm)</sup> candy bars fell on the desk top in front of him. "It's a good sign. He's still in town and getting cockier than ever."

Sliding a couple of the bars over the table top toward each of them, David continued. "Chelsea Flowers delivered the bouquet and candy about an hour ago. A very polite Englishman came into the shop around noon and placed the order. He hand-wrote the message card and paid them an extra five dollars to deliver the box of chocolates along with the flowers. I already ate one of the bars. Pretty good! I don't think he's intending to poison us, just ruffle our feathers again."

•

Over the remainder of the afternoon, specific responsibilities were assigned along with projects each was to complete prior to their next meeting, at one-thirty on Monday.

"Be sure to let me or Mike know if you run into any difficulties, for example, not getting the cooperation you need. Any problems whatsoever. We don't want to wait until Tuesday before we hear about them."

There was a knock on the door as David was finishing his comments. Steve opened the door and was handed a small box. He carried it to the head of the table and handed it to David. David removed the box lid and smiled, saying, "Oh, good, we want to test these this weekend. Make sure they all work."

He first removed two small jewelry boxes, handing one to Kelly and asking Mike to pass the other down to Kath.

"You'll find a fairly attractive set of earrings in each box. One in each set contains a tiny microphone. We believe we'll be able to pick up any conversation by the wearer from a range of several miles. That's one of the things we want to verify this weekend. If you'll turn them over so you're looking at the bottom side," David said, glancing at Kath and Kelly, "on one of the two earrings you'll see a small hole. That's the one with the mike. By inserting the point of a pencil or pen you can activate the mike."

Reaching into the box again, he removed two pens. "One for each of you. They have a fine enough point to use. We'll make sure the earrings

215

are properly switched on before you leave these premises on Tuesday. Hopefully, they'll stay on until he's apprehended. Knowing how to switch them on and off is just a precaution in case things get dragged out, so the battery doesn't run down. You'll want to switch them off tonight, too. We'll discuss how we want to go about testing them before you leave today.

"The pens also have another purpose. They're charged with tear gas. Very effective if aimed directly into a person's face at a range of eighteen inches or less. Two quick clicks on the top of the pen will trigger the discharge. Two knocks on a hard surface will have the same initializing effect.

"While you're in the car, we'll have two-way communication with you on the car phone. You're also familiar with these units," David said, reaching into the box and holding up a miniaturized walkie-talkie unit about twice the size of a Zippo lighter. "You'll each be equipped with one of them. You'll also each have a tube of lipstick," he continued, reaching into the box again. He handed one tube to Kelly and gave the other to Mike to pass down to Kath.

"You'll see they work similar to any other tube of lipstick. Remove the cap and twist the tube and the lipstick emerges. The difference is in the color or shade of the tube. We can send a signal which will cause the current dark brown color of the cylinder to change to a lighter amber shade. We can also transmit a beeping signal. If for some reason the hand-held walkie-talkie units aren't available, the change in color of the tube will send you the message we need to communicate with you. You'd immediately access the nearest phone and call our direct number.

"I'd suggest you both wear warm-up suits with comfortable, athletic shoes on Tuesday. Rather than a purse, you'll have plenty of pockets in which to carry these devices. Preferably, each one in a different pocket.

"And now," said David, reaching into the box for the final time, "the grand finale. I don't want to shock or embarrass either of you, but these may prove the best safeguard of all."

David held up two sets of lacy bras and panties, one white in color, the other black. Even though somewhat forewarned and remembering the mention of wired undergarments in the conversation earlier that morning, Kath and Kelly were both taken aback as David held the lingerie aloft. Kath gasped and turned crimson. Kelly also blushed and laughed.

"You're not too subtle, David," Kelly said. "Maybe you could go to

216

work for Frederick's of Hollywood." Now it was David who was blushing while the others laughed.

"I'm sorry, I didn't mean to spring this on you. I didn't know if we could come up with these in time or not. Before you think too ill of me, let me explain their purpose."

David spent the next few minutes describing the virtually-invisible network of wires in the garments, which transmitted a signal with power generated by body heat.

"We believe the range is well over a thousand yards. Furthermore, we'll know from which of you we're picking up the signal."

Kath had gotten over her initial embarrassment and now looked over at Kelly. "Shall we draw straws to see who gets which color?" she asked with a wink.

"The winner gets first choice?" Kelly asked. "Maybe that's not necessary. Which do you prefer?"

"I can remember my mother warning me when I first started dating, that I could save myself and my parents a lot of grief and trouble if I'd always remember to keep my underwear on," Kath said. "I guess that's what you're telling us too. Right David?"

Considerable tension had built up during the long day of discussions. In hindsight, Kelly reasoned, David couldn't have planned the introduction of the bras and panties into the equation any better. A little laughter and change of pace had been necessary.

Across the table, Kath was silently mouthing the word, 'black.'

"Guess we'll have to draw straws then," Kelly told her with a grin.

•

During the earlier break that afternoon, Kelly had been able to have a short conversation with Judy. She explained finding the phone number on Kath's notes preceded by the initial J. Judy's eyebrows had raised in alarm. Hurriedly, Kelly filled her in on the rest of the story. She also told her that Mike and David had been appraised of Judy's concerns. And while appreciative of her for communicating those thoughts, they didn't share her concern.

"They have even fewer doubts about her than I have, and I'm ninety-eight percent certain she's legit," Kelly concluded.

Judy readily seemed to accept her statement. Almost too quickly,

Kelly thought.  Judy ended the conversation by cautioning Kelly to still keep a close eye on Kath.

•

Kelly was on the phone with Rick when Kath returned from the restroom.  She cupped her hand over the mouthpiece and said, "Rick suggests we walk over to Champion House and he'll meet us there.  Does that appeal to you?"

"The table top cooking or the regular Chinese?" she asked.  There were two restaurants in one at Champion House.

"I suppose either.  Do you have a preference?"

"Not really.  I enjoy both.  Let Rick decide."

Kelly resumed the conversation with Rick, telling him he could make the decision as to which side of the restaurant they'd dine in.  He'd responded by saying he automatically thought of the table top cuisine when he thought of Champion House.

"In about half an hour then," Kelly suggested.  "Let's say eight o'clock.  We'll see you there."

Kath already had the earrings on and had changed into the black set of underwear.  Drawing straws hadn't been necessary as Kelly really did prefer the white.

"I'll just be a couple minutes," Kelly said to her as she slid the bra and panties into the pocket of her blazer.  "Would you let Mike know where we'll be having dinner?"  The plan was for them to wear the earrings and undergarments until at least ten o'clock tonight.  The communication specialists would be doing their testing, driving various distances from the restaurant and the Sheraton to test the signal and range.  They'd also experiment with the lipstick tube contact device.  We'll have to remember everything we'll be saying tonight is being heard by others, Kelly thought as she headed down the hall to the ladies room.  I'll have to remind Kath and Rick of that.

•

Their dinner had been enjoyable, even though the conversation had been somewhat stilted.  Several times one of them had started to say something, only to remember the conversation was being overheard, and then changing the subject. They'd been instructed to attempt to have a constant flow of talk so they could easily be monitored. They'd been fortunate to have been assigned one of the more personable and talented chefs. Much of the conversation was commentary on his skills in juggling his cooking utensils, flipping food onto their plates and catching trimmings in his hat.

During the course of the dinner, Kelly had reached into her pocket several times to check for any color change on the tube of lipstick. Just after her most recent check, she heard a tiny beep and reached in her pocket again. Sure enough, the shade had changed.

"I'll make the call," Kath volunteered. "I'm about finished eating anyway. I noticed a phone near the front door when we came in."

Kelly and Rick continued to make small talk during her absence. During a lull in the conversation she related a joke Steve Rentz had told the group earlier in the day. The joke wasn't all that funny, but it continued the conversation. Kelly checked her watch. Kath had already been gone for over ten minutes. Maybe someone else had been using the phone. Her call to check in shouldn't have taken hardly any time. Their chef had long since departed and the waitress asked if they'd be needing anything else. Rick ordered some pineapple sherbet for them to share, since they were having to wait for Kath anyway. Their dinner companions, two other couples, had paid their checks and were beginning to leave. Kelly had a premonition something might be wrong. And then another thought. Could Kath be calling McConnell?

There had really been no need to even call in. They could have just mentioned contact had been made in their conversation. No, I guess that's not true, Kelly reasoned. They may have had something to tell us.

"I'm going to check on her. Why don't we meet you at the front door," Kelly said, rising from her chair. Rick nodded.

She nearly bumped into Kath in the short aisleway connecting the two sections of the restaurant as she was rushing back to their table.

"Oh, excuse me. Sorry that took so long. A man was using the phone. He kept holding up a finger, indicating he'd only be another minute, but he seemed to be having difficulty winding up his conversation." Kath said, smiling. "I think it was a girlfriend and she'd forgotten their date. Anyway, everything's fine."

"That's good, we were beginning to worry about you."

"I'm sorry. It was just one of those things. They say they're getting excellent results. Our conversation didn't start to fade until they were nearly

219

a mile beyond the Territorial Road exit north on US-23. They had no difficulty hearing us from the Plymouth/23 area either. We didn't start to fade out until after they'd reached Dixboro."

Rick came up to them, interrupting the conversation. "There you are. We were getting worried."

"I know, I'm sorry. I just explained the reason for the long delay to Kelly."

"I'm parked in the structure. Why don't I drive you back to your car," Rick suggested to Kelly.

Earlier in the evening Kelly had explained rather than having Rick drop them off tonight at the Sheraton, she'd prefer to drive her car so they'd have it to drive to the Jamesons' in the morning. Kelly also wanted to use it to stop by her condo after the breakfast meeting to pick up additional clothes.

As they were exiting the restaurant, Kath grinned and said, "By the way, they enjoyed your joke, Kelly."

Rick laughed. "I think they're just being polite," he said, winking at Kelly.

They'd just started towards the parking structure when Kelly exclaimed, "Oh darn! I've lost an earring. Luckily it's not the one with the mike."

"I'll go back with you and help you look," Kath volunteered.

"No, why don't you go on with Rick. I'll meet you out front. It should be right near my chair."

Kelly went back inside the Champion House. While they were going out the door, she'd removed the missing earring and slipped it in the pocket of her blue blazer. She wanted to speak with the hostess outside of Kath's presence, to verify if Kath had really had a long wait for the phone.

The hostess was just returning from seating a party.

"Excuse me, I'd like to ask you a question," Kelly began. She could tell by the expression on the young woman's face that there might be a language problem.

"The woman I was with, do you remember her using your phone?" The girl nodded yes.

"Did she have to wait before using it?"

"Yes, another man on phone."

"How long did she have to wait?"

"Not long."

"Five minutes, ten minutes?"

The girl shrugged her shoulders, replying, "Not sure."

"Did you notice how many calls she placed? How many times she dialed the phone?"

Again the girl shrugged her shoulders.

"Do you recall how long she used the phone, how many minutes?"

The girl shook her head as she replied, "Not long."

This conversation was going nowhere. One more chance. "Is the man who was using the phone still here?"

"No, he left. Ten minutes ago," she added, smiling.

Another couple was waiting to be seated and the hostess was reaching for some menus. Kelly thanked her and stepped outside to wait for Kath and Rick.


## Chapter 35


During the short drive to the City Hall parking structure, Kath supplied Kelly and Rick with further details on her conversation with the team who was monitoring them. It appeared their conversation was being picked up in all directions to a range of five to eight miles, from south of the Briarwood shopping center to west of Weber's on I-94.

"I told them we'd be heading to the Sheraton in a few minutes. They say the range should be even greater outside the downtown area."

"What about our underwear? Are . . . "

Rick glanced back at Kelly in the rearview mirror with a look of surprise on his face. She giggled, remembering they hadn't told him about it, just about the earrings and lipstick tubes. Kelly quickly informed him about the wired underwear they were wearing, and the fact that signal was also being monitored.

"In answer to your question Kelly, they've been receiving a strong signal. From both of us. Over the next hour or so they hope to have a fix on the range. Thus far, they've been concentrating on the earring mikes."

Rick said he wanted to follow them to the Sheraton, see they were safely in their room before bidding them goodnight.

"I know you've had a strenuous day. I won't stay. You're probably both looking forward to a good night's sleep."

"Amen to that, and a nice, long, hot shower, too," Kath said. "They're going to signal us via the lipstick tubes after they've completed their testing. Maybe you want to join us for a nightcap, Rick. We'll have to keep our sexy duds on a while longer. The showers will have to wait. Maybe you can talk Kelly into a style show," Kath teased Rick.

"If you're serious about the invite, the nightcap not the style show, we could swing by Food & Drug Mart on the way to the Sheraton and pick up some cold beer . . . or a chilled bottle of wine."

"Sounds good to me," Kelly said. "Beer's fine for me, just one can."

"Either's all right with me – beer or wine. You decide Rick," Kath said.

"I'm getting to make all the really important decisions tonight, aren't I? Where to eat, what to drink. Let me make another offer. I'll buy the champagne Tuesday night to celebrate McConnell's arrest."

Almost in unison, both replied, "Let's hope we'll be able to take you up on that offer!"

•

Their room was a little more spacious than last night. Mike had probably pulled some strings. They were able to catch the last few minutes of Larry King Live and had then switched over to Headline News. Kelly and Rick were having beer while Kath had opted for a glass of wine. Rick had purchased both, explaining he could take any leftovers back to his apartment.

Kelly and Kath had placed their lipsticks on the small table between the beds so they could quickly observe any change in color. Just before ten-thirty, the color on both began to lighten to an amber hue. The process was fascinating to watch, taking less than a minute.

Kelly placed the call. The man she spoke to was ecstatic. The pickup of the signal from their clothing ranged from a quarter to half a mile, over double what had been anticipated. The testing was complete. They could switch off their earrings and, the man had hesitated. Kelly could tell he was slightly embarrassed. "Get naked I guess is the easiest way to put it," he said with a laugh.

"Understood," Kelly replied. "Thanks for checking everything out. We'll keep our fingers crossed everything works as well on Tuesday.

"Oh, I'm sure they will. And good luck."

・

Rick left a few minutes later. "You can be first in the shower since I got the black undies," Kath said, smiling.

"That's nice of you," Kelly replied, returning her smile.

Just before stepping into the shower, Kelly had a premonition and walked back to the bathroom door and stuck her head out. Kath was sitting in the easy chair watching television.

"I thought I heard the phone ring," Kelly said.

"No, I don't think so. You must be imagining things."

As Kelly climbed into the shower she thought about Kath's comment. She certainly hoped she was just imagining things. She had a sense of guilt over thinking Kath had offered her the opportunity to shower first so she could use the phone while Kelly was in the shower. Her thoughts then turned to tomorrow morning's breakfast meeting as she turned her face up into the hot spray.


## Chapter 36

David, Mike and Tim Masterson were already at the Jamesons' when Kath and Kelly arrived shortly after eight-fifteen. John and Marion Jameson both greeted Kath warmly, each giving her a lengthy hug as they expressed their sorrow over the death of her sister. Tears welled in her eyes as she told them how sorry she was they'd become entangled in this mess. She apologized for being indirectly responsible. Kelly noticed this exchange as Mike explained to her how pleased he was to have heard all the communication devices had tested so well. More than ever, Kelly was convinced of Kath's innocence.

Over the course of the next ten minutes, the other three arrived – Clare Singleton, Liz Hernandes and Dr. "Bill" Broadstead. Though everyone knew who each other was, it was apparent that most were actually meeting for the first time on an informal basis, with the exception of Liz Hernandes and John Jameson, who'd served on committees together.

Marion Jameson had prepared a variety of juices, sweet rolls and muffins in addition to coffee. Benton let them mingle for the next ten minutes before asking them to be seated. Kelly noticed Liz Hernandes appeared especially nervous, seemingly avoiding eye contact. Kelly surmised it was probably due to her belief many in the group had already seen the photographs McConnell had sent her. Kelly had to smile at Clare Singleton. If she could get her hands on McConnell, they wouldn't have to worry about a lengthy legal process before his punishment began.

David provided about a five-minute background before playing the tape. As they heard the tape, Kelly attempted to be very subtle in her attempt to observe the reactions of the five, particularly when McConnell alleged it was one of them, rather than he, who was responsible for Elizabeth Edwards' death.

Following the playing of the tape, David explained the department, while not completely ceasing their efforts to apprehend McConnell, had been cautious not to do anything which would prompt him to circulate the flyers, and possibly copies of the photographs as well, prior to Tuesday's payment of the $100,000. He then explained the goal of the police was to apprehend McConnell on Tuesday, as he was taking delivery of the money or shortly thereafter. David then voiced his opinion – explaining it was shared by all his associates – that McConnell would probably attempt to circulate the flyers, photographs, and perhaps make other charges or allegations regardless of what happened on Tuesday.

"The chances of paying him off and never hearing from him again are virtually nil in our estimation."

David then told them about receiving the bouquet of flowers and box of 100 Grand(tm) candy bars during yesterday's planning session. He asked Mike and Kelly if they had anything to add before opening up for questions and comments. Both shook their heads no.

Over the course of the next half-hour, Clare Singleton must have used the expression "pardon my French" at least half a dozen times in prefacing statements such as, "I hope you nail his ass," "It's too bad Michigan doesn't have capital punishment so we could fry the bastard," and "Hope you can put the screws to that son-of-a-bitch."

Liz Hernandes, in particular, cringed as Clare aired these comments. Her outbursts also shocked others. Even Kath blanched. Her outspoken remarks in the past seemed tame in comparison to Clare's.

Dr. Broadstead also came on strong in his endorsement of the plans to "apprehend that S.O.B." During his comments, he asked the question of how much credence the police were giving to McConnell's allegation someone else other than he was responsible for "that girl's death."

David in response raised his hand, holding his forefinger and thumb about an eighth of an inch apart. "About this much," he said.

Broadstead laughed. "I thought so. You mean none of us are suspects then?"

"What I probably should have said is that our top priority right now is the apprehension of McConnell. Whether he's guilty or not of the murder of Kath's sister, he's still a criminal. There are several felonies he can be charged with – blackmail, assault and battery – without getting to the question of murder. With our main objective being to get our hands on him, we've delayed exploring, investigating, any other potential suspects."

Dean Jamesons' comments came from the heart. The circulation of the incriminating photos, the false allegations and the resulting publicity, would wreak havoc on all their lives, Jameson had said, directing his comments to the other four who had been blackmailed.

"Tim, my heart goes out to you. You're on the threshold of a banner career in coaching, on the verge of signing a multi-million dollar contract. You have a wonderful wife and family. You have by far and away the most to lose financially in this whole affair. You have the highest profile, the most unblemished reputation of any of us.

"Liz, you've been a symbol of the American dream. Coming from the most adverse environment one could imagine, a world of poverty and abuse. You've literally climbed the mountain. You've become one of the foremost advocates and spokespersons in the human rights area in the country today. If your reputation is tarnished or destroyed at this juncture, it will be a set-back for everything you've strived for, everything you believe in.

"I've just had a taste of the amount of injury one damaging allegation can cause. This further publicity, even though they're totally false allegations, would, I'm certain, result in my being fired or forced to resign. An embarrassment to my family, an embarrassment to my race, an embarrassment to the University.

"Bill and Clare, I don't want to minimize the potential damage to your careers as well as ours. The stakes are high. We all have much to lose. But if Chief Benton, Detective Cummings and Detective Travis and their associates in the law enforcement field can be successful Tuesday in apprehending McConnell, successful in preventing circulation of the false, slanderous materials – all five of us will have a new lease on life.

"I have to admit I had some mixed thoughts as I heard the tape. In fact, I was putting together an argument to convince the police to back off

– in fairness to us – the ones who had the most to lose in this affair. I'd be surprised if some of you weren't having similar thoughts. The thought that McConnell would take the money and never be heard from again is an appealing one.

"I'd even gone so far as to think I might be able to pay him off on my own, maybe convince one other to join up with me. Not confide in the police, try to work with McConnell on our own. No one would be the wiser when he just disappeared from the scene.

"But as I've mulled it over, I've chastised myself for even harboring those thoughts. It would be wrong. Wrong for me, wrong for us, wrong to have the police compromise their principles.

"There's no guarantee, that's been made abundantly clear. No certainty he can be stopped, that the allegations won't be publicized. But I'm certain we're making the right decision, really the only possible decision."

There were tears in Jamesons' eyes, his wife's, too. Glancing around the room, Kelly could see it was an emotional moment for all of them. In a trembling voice, he concluded by saying, "God bless the police. God bless us."

After a few moments of silence, Tim Masterson began to speak. "John, I wish I had the ability to voice my thoughts the way you have yours. I just wish to thank you. You verbalized my thoughts as well. The goal is to bring McConnell to justice. I'm in full support."

Kelly felt sorry for Liz Hernandes. She knew and Liz knew all eyes were focused on her now, waiting for her comments. Liz sat staring at the floor for a few moments before looking up. Kelly was amazed. There had been a transformation in her appearance. The nervous look of anxiety and defeat had now been replaced by a defiant look and a touch of a smile.

"You're going to be successful," she said, looking at David, Mike and Kelly. "I thank all of you for reminding me to find courage to . . ." Liz bowed her head and Kelly could hear her sobbing, the only sound to be heard. Then Liz's head popped back up, a radiant smile on her face and tears in her eyes. "Thank you!" she whispered.

Broadstead was first to break the silence; even Clare Singleton was subdued after hearing the others' comments.

"Can you share with us any of your plans for Tuesday? Can any of us help you in any way?"

"I'd prefer to address your second question first," David said. "I can't express how much you've already helped, by in different ways endorsing our actions. We're extremely sensitive to the fact the five of you have the most to lose if our plans for Tuesday are not successful, if our actions prompt McConnell into doing something he's promised not to.

"I do want to caution you again, remind you, warn you – there is the possibility that he might have plans to mail the flyers, copies of the photographs and perhaps other letters or communications of some type. He might even have them in the mail on Tuesday, before he even makes contact with us. Whether he's in jail, as we hope, on Tuesday night, or on his way to some destination in let's say, South America, there is the possibility his false allegations might make headlines. We pray that won't be the case. You can count on everyone involved doing their damndest to prevent that.

"As to your question about the plans for Tuesday, I can't go into specific details. Considerable time and thought has gone into our preparations. You should know that Kath may also be involved. He's specifically requested that she be present when he calls us on Tuesday afternoon. At one time, there was the possibility he might use her as a hostage to further insure we'd meet his demands. Possibly use Kelly as a hostage, too."

David went on to explain how McConnell had taken the two of them as hostages on Friday, threatened them, and driven them to Gallup Park. He described how Greg Collier, the reporter covering the story for the *Ann Arbor News*, had accidentally interrupted them as McConnell was releasing the two women. He also told them of Collier's dog being shot and the fact McConnell had driven Kelly's car back and forth over the dog's body. All of them were wide-eyed, hearing these details for the first time.

"We're dealing with a volatile personality," David continued. "A sick person, a psychotic with a violent bent. He's also very intelligent. He's still treating this as a game, matching his wits against ours. We've been attempting to feed his ego, get him over-confident so he'll drop his guard and make a mistake. That's our strategy. I'm sure you all read yesterday's article in the *Ann Arbor News*. I was quoted about McConnell's use of candy in taunting us. I went public with that information as part of our strategy. To inflate his ego. The article also suggested we had reason to believe McConnell had left the area. To the contrary, we have reason to believe he's still here. We want him believing we're buffoons, easy pickings. Why? So he'll arrange to obtain the money here in Ann Arbor, where we can employ all our resources, rather than having it delivered elsewhere – Chicago, for example.

"As you might imagine, Greg Collier is as eager as we are to see

McConnell's caught. He's cooperating with us in his articles. The one in this morning's paper," David said, holding up a copy of Sunday's *Ann Arbor News*, "is a continuation of our strategy."

Kelly had only had time to read the headline and the initial paragraph of the story. She reminded herself she'd have to find time to read the complete article.

David asked if there were additional questions. Clare Singleton asked when he thought they'd be advised on what happened Tuesday.

"Will we have to rely on television or the newspapers?"

"Definitely not," David answered. "One of our first priorities will be to personally contact each of you and advise you of any major development in the case. You have our promise on that."

After answering a couple other minor questions, David wrapped up the meeting by once again promising the police would be doing everything possible to bring this episode to a happy conclusion – the arrest, prosecution and conviction of Joseph McConnell. "We'll try our best to keep the flyer and photos out of the trial, have that evidence sealed. That's our hope."

Liz Hernandes began to clap her hands and the others quickly joined in. Words of appreciation were voiced to David, Mike, Kelly and Kath, concerning all they'd done and would be doing. The meeting ended on an upbeat note, with warm handshakes all around.

•

Following the meeting, Kelly and Kath swung by Kelly's condo without incident. She picked up fresh clothing, including a warm-up and running shoes. As she unlocked her car for the drive back to the Sheraton, Kelly asked Kath if she'd ever visited the nearby University of Michigan's Matthaei Botanical Gardens. She hadn't. It was a beautiful, sunny day, chilly with the temperature in the forties.

"I think we should stop by," Kelly said. "It'll be a nice unwinder for us both. Especially since you've never been there."

### Chapter 37

The decision to visit the Matthaei Botanical Gardens proved to be a good one. Even on a Sunday, due to the season, the two of them virtually had the place to themselves. As they strolled through the observatory, they had an opportunity to discuss the meeting at the Jamesons'.

"I was able to chat with Clare Singleton a little at the end," Kath said. "She really is a sweet person. She's terrified, as well she should be. I think her anger and harsh words are a front to mask her fear. I really feel for her, all of them."

"Me, too," Kelly said. "They're under an immense amount of stress. And the sad thing is, they have little control over what's going to happen. They have to feel frustrated. As David said, we have to be delighted with the support they voiced for our efforts. The ball's in our court now. I hope we don't let them down."

"We won't," Kath replied. "I'm starting to get some good vibes. I was really down a couple days ago. But now I'm turning into an optimist. We'll catch him; I just know we will."

They exchanged small talk for about another hour. Kath suggested being in touch with nature was as refreshing as if they'd gone to church. Kelly had hoped the meeting this morning would be over in time for her to take Kath with her to the ten-thirty service at First Pres. But the meeting had gone on longer than she had anticipated.

Kelly glanced at her watch. "Can you believe it? It's nearly noon. I want to stop by my parents' on our way back to the Sheraton, bring in their mail and papers. Getting hungry? Maybe we could stop by Wendy's next to the Sheraton, for a trip through their salad bar."

"Sounds good to me, let's do it," Kath replied with a smile.

•

As they were entering the side door at Kelly's parents' house, Kath nervously asked, "Do you have your gun handy, Kelly? Joe's probably not here, but let's be on the safe side."

Kelly nodded, handing Kath the pile of mail and newspapers she was carrying and reaching into her purse for her revolver.

The house appeared to be empty. Her parents had left Kelly a note on the kitchen counter, wishing her well and reminding her to call them. The phone number of Kelly's aunt and uncle was written on the note.

Kelly spread the front page of her parents' *Ann Arbor News* out on the counter so they could both read Greg Collier's article. As David had indicated, the content had been structured to send McConnell the message he was in total control – calling all the shots.

"Let's hope it works," Kelly said as they finished reading the article. Kath pulled out the *Detroit Free Press* comic section from the other paper. Giggling, she shared 'For Better Or For Worse' with Kelly.

•

Entering their room at the Sheraton, Kath said, "I was really dreading today. I thought the time would drag, but it's already nearly two-thirty. Do you want to take in a three o'clock movie at Briarwood?"

Kelly smiled. "Good idea, but if it suits you, let's make it the five o'clock show. Rick might want to join us, if he's not too involved with studies. I think he has an exam tomorrow. I also want to get everything organized for tomorrow."

Kath nodded. "Fine. Anything special you've been wanting to see? We should have brought the entertainment section from your parents' paper so we could check the times. Why don't I go down to the lobby and get another paper while you're doing your thing?"

Kelly nodded, but an alarm was sounding. Was Kath seizing an opportunity to contact McConnell? I have to stop this, Kelly thought. I keep wavering in terms of my confidence in her. Kath had been so genuine in her emotions and comments today. I need to shelve my suspicions, she reasoned. Unless, she smiled to herself, something major happens to reinforce them.

As Kath was talking and Kelly was mulling over her thoughts, Kelly had been cleaning out the pockets of her blazer. She noticed the color of her lipstick tube was now amber. Kath was just heading out the door.

"Hold up for a minute," Kelly said, holding up the lipstick so Kath could see it. "It might be a mistake, but I'd better check in."

Kelly dialed the contact number and was told Mike Cummings wanted to speak with her. She was transferred to his extension.

"Hi, Kelly. We've just had an interesting new development. McConnell's still in town. At least he was, up until an hour ago. This will take a few minutes. Do you have time now?"

"Certainly. Just a minute," Kelly replied, holding the receiver out so Kath could also hear and motioning her over. "Go ahead."

"About two hours ago a customer came into Wenk's Pharmacy and purchased some candy bars."

Kelly knew Wenk's well, a small drug store near the intersection of Washtenaw and Stadium. Her parents had their prescriptions filled there.

"He wanted PayDay$^{(tm)}$ candy bars. He purchased thirteen of them."

"Do you read anything into that Mike? The fact he purchased thirteen?"

Mike laughed. "There were only thirteen left in the display box. He asked the clerk if he had any in back-up. He checked, but it was the last box."

"The customer was very personable, a nice English accent. Get this; the clerk remembered him from a couple of days earlier, when the man purchased about a dozen or more Nestle 100 Grand$^{(tm)}$ bars."

Kelly and Kath exchanged looks, breaking into smiles.

"The clerk put the Paydays in a bag and the man paid for them, making small talk with the clerk about the weather and the fact he had a number of friends who were candy fanatics. Another customer, an older woman, came into the store about then and approached the counter. The man nodded at her, said good afternoon in his crisp, English accent, and backed up to give her more room to pass. He backed into a floor display and a number of items on the display tumbled onto the floor. The man swore and bent down to pick them up. The clerk came out from behind the counter to assist him.

"The man angrily told him it was a stupid place to put a display. The clerk told him not to worry, he'd clean up the mess. A glass jar of nuts had broken. The man then screamed at him, 'You should, it's your own damn fault to begin with,' and stomped out the door. Those final comments were made without any sign of an accent."

"It was him, all right," Kelly responded. "Did the clerk get a license number or see the car he was driving?"

"I'm just getting to that."

"Sorry, I didn't mean to interrupt. Go ahead."

"The man didn't have a car in Wenk's' lot. He crossed over Stadium by foot."

Kelly knew the Lamp Post shopping center was across the street, to the east of Wenk's.

"After waiting on a couple of other customers and cleaning up, the clerk called 911. He'd recalled reading the article about the candy connection in yesterday's paper. Our people jumped on it right away. They saw

231

the significance of the PayDay<sup>(tm)</sup> bars immediately. Sorry to say, not many people were told about the 100 Grand<sup>(tm)</sup> bars McConnell sent us. Can't say that anything would have been handled any differently if the operator or investigating officer had known.

"A police cruiser was at the scene within five minutes. There aren't any detectives on duty today because of next week's schedule. We also have just one officer to a vehicle today for that same reason. Anyway, the officer was able to get a description from the clerk. The last he'd seen of the man was when he was crossing Stadium. He hadn't seen which direction he headed.

"The officer was on the ball though. He remembered the notice out on the dark blue Pontiac Bonneville with the stolen plate. He drove around the Lamp Post Plaza looking for the car and also questioned a few people to see if they'd seen the man. No one appeared to have. Being a Sunday with many of the stores closed, the parking lot was less than half full.

"The officer walked over to the motel just east of the shopping center, the Lamp Post Inn. And low and behold, he spots the Bonneville in the lot. He immediately went into the motel office. If his vehicle hadn't still been next door at the shopping center, he'd have probably called in for assistance.

"The desk clerk at the motel ushered him into the manager's office. The manager was very cooperative and from the officer's description, knew immediately who the man was. He'd just checked out fifteen minutes ago. There had been a big argument about a refund. The man had paid cash in advance. The officer dashed out into the parking lot and the car was gone."

Kelly and Kath were both shaking their heads. It appeared McConnell's string of luck was continuing.

"The officer reported in on the motel's phone and a further notice went out on the car. Nothing yet; the number of cruisers available is limited. One was immediately dispatched to the motel so the officer would have assistance in checking out the room and in further questioning the motel manager and clerk.

"Nothing was found in the room with the exception of a PayDay<sup>(tm)</sup> wrapper left on the dresser. He'd registered under the name Charles Underwood. He paid cash so the clerk or motel manager didn't see any identification or credit card. Next to the signature on the registration card is a space for entering the planned date for checkout. That was Tuesday's date. It took a few minutes before the officer made the connection. The initials for Charles Underwood are C.U.  He signed with a flourish, so the C and U were much larger than the other letters.  He's still up to his tricks.  'C. U. Tuesday' is his message."

●

After hanging up, Kath and Kelly just sat for a few minutes, mulling over what they'd just learned.  Kath broke the silence.

"I was so elated when Mike told us Joe was only able to buy thirteen bars.  I thought, great, his luck has finally changed.  But that wasn't the case.  We've sure come close, haven't we?"

Kelly nodded.  "It has been a roller coaster ride.  As Mike indicated, if there had been two officers rather than one, things might have turned out vastly different.  One would have been watching the car while the other was talking to the motel manager."

"His luck is going to run out.  I'm still optimistic," Kath said.  "By the way, in regards to a movie.  I noticed last night there are some fairly good ones we could watch in the room.  Want to do that instead?  We won't need a paper then."

"I guess I'm old-fashioned," Kelly replied.  "I seem to enjoy a movie twice as much in a regular theater.  We could also have a snack afterwards at Ruby Tuesday's if we go to Briarwood."

"I'd actually prefer that, too.  I'll get a paper then."

After Kath had left the room, Kelly continued to sit, deep in thought.  Maybe my suspicions about her aren't warranted.  She'd been willing to forego going down to the lobby.  But that may be because she now knows she can't reach him at the motel.  I continue to vacillate, Kelly thought as she stood and walked over to the small suitcase she'd brought from her apartment.  She lifted it onto the bed and began to unpack.

●

The movie had been a bummer.  Kath and Kelly both found it hard to understand why the critics hadn't panned it.  Maybe because the leads had done such an excellent job in spite of the virtually non-existent storyline.  Maybe the disappointment was a result of thinking how it could have so easily been a good movie, Kelly thought.  The scenery was incredible, but they hadn't gone to see a travelogue.

233

It wasn't a wasted evening, though. They'd had a delightful dinner at Ruby Tuesday's and shared a carafe of wine. They'd also shared some intimate thoughts. Close as they had been physically for the past week, there had been little time to really get to know one another.

Kath reviewed her childhood, the relationship with her family, in particular with her sister, Beth. She was having difficulty dealing with her death. Their relationship had deteriorated over the past year and she was depressed over things not done – words not said.

She also shared her fears and anxieties. Not about Tuesday – that subject was being put aside for a few hours. She had worries about her future, sadness over the fact she'd never had a true boyfriend. While she had good friends of both sexes, she didn't seem to have any best friends, truly close friends.

"You sometimes think it's something that's wrong with you," Kath said. "You expect and hope the future will look brighter tomorrow. But the tomorrows come and go, leaving you more confused."

Kelly tried to perk her up. She said many of her thoughts and fears were normal. She herself had often had similar doubts and questions.

"I often found someone else's grass isn't necessarily always greener; the person you think most has their life together frequently has more problems and doubts than you. Time and time again, I've been surprised. What I thought, what I thought I saw, was just a façade. A relationship or a marriage I envisioned to be perfect, I later found crumbled when a stressful incident occurred."

Kelly discussed her relationship with Rick, a wonderful, true friend. "But the sparks aren't there; he knows it and I know it."

Kath nodded and then said, "You know Mike's in love with you, don't you?"

"Now why do you say that? You hardly know either of us."

"It's easy to tell. The way he looks at you. The way he delights in hearing you talk, his enthusiasm over your suggestions or ideas. And his true concern when he believes you're being exposed to some potential danger. I think his biggest fear about Tuesday is the fact something might happen to you."

Kelly blushed. She teased Kath by saying, "For someone who's having trouble understanding herself, you certainly think you have Mike figured out."

•

It was going on ten o'clock when the two returned to their room. The message light on the phone was blinking. Kelly dialed the front desk and was told Mike Cummings had called and left word for her to call him at home. He'd left the message at 7:10 p.m.

Kelly began the conversation by apologizing for the delay in getting back to him.

"Probably just as well, Kelly, in that I just spoke with David and have some additional information to share with you. How was your evening?"

Kelly told him about going to the early movie, the fact he could pass on that particular one. She then described the enjoyable time at Ruby Tuesday's, getting to know Kath better.

"We just blanked Tuesday out of our minds for a few hours. It was great."

"Sounds wonderful. I wish I could have been there with you."

Kelly found herself blushing and smiled at Kath.

"The reason for my call is two-fold. First, McConnell's car, the Bonneville, was found late this afternoon in the Church Street parking structure. He'd backed into a spot, no doubt to conceal the license plate. That proved his undoing, maybe his luck is changing. In that particular area, that's prohibited. Posted and enforced. The parking ramp attendant ticketed him. A short time later he discovered the car and license number matched the description on the notice he'd received earlier.

"We have a surveillance team watching the car. Thus far, there's been no sign of McConnell. The car's empty. He's possibly abandoned it, but we aren't taking any chances. We'll rotate teams through tomorrow."

The Church Street parking structure was just south of the South University campus town area, four blocks of stores, largely restaurants, east of the central campus. No motels or hotels were located in that area, Kelly thought, wondering where McConnell might be spending the night.

"He may have stolen another car. I'm sure you've checked," Kelly said.

"We have. There have been no reports of thefts from that parking structure or the South U area since McConnell left the Lamp Post Inn. Even if he stole another car, it could be well into next week before someone realizes it's missing or reports it. A couple of cars did turn up missing in the area of South Quad and the Michigan Union, not all that far away.

Hopefully, we're keeping on top of it.

"The second reason I called was to update you on another matter. I didn't say anything this afternoon because I knew Kath was listening in. She isn't now, is she?"

"No. She's in the bathroom getting ready for bed."

"At the motel this afternoon, the officer involved inquired if McConnell, Charles Underwood, had had any visitors or phone calls the desk clerk or manager could remember. Neither remembered visitors, but the manager remembers there had been a couple of calls for him. A woman's voice."

Kelly was glad Kath wasn't there to see her expression. Mike, seeming to sense her reaction, was saying, "Don't jump to any conclusions until you hear everything. When the night clerk came on duty around six, we learned something more about those calls. He'd taken a call from a woman yesterday evening asking to be connected to Underwood's room. When there was no answer, she asked him to verify whether Underwood had checked out. She said she was trying to contact him about some reservations he'd made and that she'd tried a couple times earlier in the day to reach him. She started to give him an 800 number and then said something about the difficulty he'd have getting through to her and that she'd better try again later. She didn't give her name or identify the company she represented. Not much to go on, but it could explain the calls."

Kelly wasn't so sure as she continued to listen.

"I didn't have that information when I tried to reach you earlier. I jumped ahead a little. What I was going to brief you about then was in regards to Judy. She was aware that McConnell had received a couple calls at the motel from a woman. Without saying anything to me or David, she went off on her own to do some investigating. She obtained the phone records for outgoing calls – from your office, from your hotel room, not just the Sheraton, the Crowne Plaza and Campus Inn as well. She even ran a check on your personal phone. She was looking to see if a call had been made to the Lamp Post Inn from any of those phones. There hadn't been.

"Then she went one step further. She ran a query on the pay phones in the lobby at headquarters. She discovered two calls to the Lamp Post had originated from those phones – one yesterday and one the day before. Of course, that's when he was staying at the motel. They were also times when Kath could have conceivably had access to those phones.

"She immediately contacted David with her findings. Maybe I was unavailable; I doubt it. She reviewed her suspicions about Kath with him. It's probably just as well she spoke to David. He asked her to expand her query on the pay phones to include the last two weeks of October. She's amazing, I have to give her credit – getting the phone company to cooperate with her so quickly, on a Sunday no less. She has a friend there. She found out a half-dozen calls had been made to the Lamp Post Inn over that time frame, prior to McConnell's stay. By the time she'd informed David on her findings, I'd already briefed him on what I'd learned from the night clerk.

"David told me he reprimanded Judy for going off on her own without first discussing it with him or me. He was particularly angry she'd obtained records on your phones, invaded your privacy, without first clearing it with you."

"In fairness to Judy, I'm sure she thought she was doing the right thing," Kelly said. "She was probably right in assuming Kath had access to those phones while out of my presence. I don't think she thought she was snooping. Maybe she'd tried to reach me."

"I personally doubt it," Mike said. "The problem goes deeper than that, though. There are procedures for accessing phone records. If her friend turned on her, the department could be in deep trouble."

"I realize that," Kelly said. "But the only way David learned about this was being told by Judy. If she hadn't learned of the calls from the pay phones, we'd probably have never known what she'd done. All I guess I'm saying is that I think her intentions are sincere and David should let it rest. There's no sense letting something hinder our cohesiveness at this stage. We'll need everyone's full attention, including Judy's, focused on apprehending McConnell on Tuesday."

"I tend to agree with you, Kelly. As a matter of fact, Judy did call me a few minutes ago to apologize. Though she sounded contrite, she did want to make the point Kath shouldn't be underestimated. Though she professes she'd like to believe Kath's true blue, she suggests the woman's talk of a reservation and an 800 number could have been done to throw off suspicion. She warns us, you in particular, to be on our guard.

"I also spoke with David again about supplying Kath with a gun on Tuesday. We've decided against it. More out of concern she might be tempted to use it in a fit of rage, than because of any doubts about her. You'll be the only one armed. Be sure . . . I don't have to say that, do I. And that's about it. Enough for you to mull on tonight. We'll let you know

237

if anything further develops."

Kath had returned from the bathroom. "Anything wrong?" she mouthed. Kelly smiled, shaking her head no.

"I'll brief Kath, she's here now. Thanks for the update. We'll be in by nine tomorrow."

•

"That was a long call," Kath said as Kelly hung up the phone. "What's up?"

Kelly told her about finding McConnell's car. She elaborated as much as possible, embellishing the facts with stories about the makes and models of other cars stolen in the past few hours and how the car was being staked out.

"What actually took so long," Kelly said, grinning, "was telling him of your comments tonight and asking him if there was any truth to them."

"I bet," Kath said with a laugh. "It's okay, I don't, I didn't expect to be appraised of all the plans for Tuesday. I'd probably just get more nervous if you clued me in on everything."

## Chapter 38

Kelly had been awake for hours, tossing and turning, before finally falling into a deep slumber. She awoke to the aroma of coffee. She was surprised to see Kath was already dressed, sitting in a chair at the table with a newspaper spread out in front of her. Kelly glanced at her watch. It was a few minutes after eight.

"Good morning. I thought I'd do the honors today," she said to Kelly. "You were really zonked. Are you feeling all right?"

"Just still sleepy. I'm fine," Kelly said with a smile.

"We didn't even make the front page today. Page six, saying no new developments and that an intense search for Joe is underway outside the state. Let's hope for headlines Wednesday, announcing his arrest. A sweet ending for him," Kath joked.

•

As Kelly brushed her teeth, she found her thoughts turning to Mike and the conversation she'd had with Kath last night.

When Kelly had first joined the department, she viewed Mike as one of those people for whom everything in life had clicked. Tall, slightly over six-feet with an athletic build, light brown hair and blue eyes, and nearly always with a grin or ready smile. He was one of those people who always seemed to have a light tan. Not what you'd call handsome, Kelly thought, but very attractive and appealing, very masculine. Intelligent and articulate and seemingly with time for everyone, he was a natural leader. People gravitated to him. Kelly couldn't recall anyone ever having spoken ill of him.

In addition, he had a lovely wife. A southern girl, a beauty with a bubbling personality. Kelly had met her several times, mostly at department functions. Their romance had begun when Mike was in the service, stationed in the Carolinas.

Kelly had been in their home. It was an older house on the west side of town which Mike and his wife, Caroline, had restored and immaculately decorated over the years. A real charmer.

Then, shortly after celebrating their tenth anniversary and just after Mike had been promoted to head the Detective Division, it became public knowledge they were in the process of a divorce. There were a number of rumors as to the cause. Caroline's desire to move back closer to home, her desire to get Mike out of law enforcement work, and her preference for a career rather than children. She'd started a very successful interior decorating business in Ann Arbor. Mike had never confided in Kelly; they'd both avoided the subject. She knew there were two sides to every squabble. His friends and co-workers had sympathized with him and blamed Caroline

239

for the break-up.

Kelly remembered that over that period of time, Mike's trademark grin wasn't as much in evidence. It had only been over the course of the past six months that Mike had regained his former spark. Kelly recalled several times, walking in on him as he was sitting at his desk, seeing him deep in thought.

"How are you doing in there? We should be leaving in another ten minutes or so."

Kath shook Kelly out of her reverie. She smiled at herself in the mirror. I'd better start getting focused on what's going to be happening tomorrow, she said to herself. The future will take care of itself.

Kath was continuing to read the newspaper as Kelly dressed. "What's your birth date, Kelly? I'm just reading my horoscope."

Kelly smiled as she replied, "July third."

Kath giggled as she read Kelly's and looked up. "Right on, I'd say. Listen to this. 'Prepare yourself for some exciting developments which will occur soon.' Want to hear mine?"

Kelly nodded.

"'Something you've been waiting for will happen sooner than you expected,'" Kath read. "I'm not generally superstitious. I treat horoscopes similar to the comics. But in this case, I'm wondering if this is a warning that Joe might jump the gun, advance the time-table."

Kelly smiled again before she said, "Could be. Actually, David and Mike have been worried about that possibility. That's why David was so anxious to get the essentials of a plan in place so soon. Arrangements have already been made to get everyone involved on a moment's notice. The reason nothing was mentioned to you about their concerns is that they didn't want you primed for an earlier contact, getting yourself all worked up and then being exhausted Tuesday afternoon when he's said he'll call.

"There are plenty of reasons to think he might advance his time-table. To catch us off guard, make his move before we've had time to finalize our plans. He has to be concerned we're playing along so that we can trap him. He's probably rightly assumed we'll have the cash together before the day's out. Frankly, I wouldn't be at all surprised if he contacted us sooner.

"That's why David reminded us to bring everything with us this morning, the earrings, the pens, the walkie talkies, our warm-ups, even the bras and underpants. Not necessarily having everything on, just with us."

"I remember him emphasizing we bring everything," Kath said. "I assumed it had something to do with further testing. Thanks for cluing me in on the main reason."

## Chapter 39

There was excitement in the air as Kath and Kelly walked in the front door of City Hall. Steve Rentz spotted them and rushed over. "Good morning, ladies. Kelly, I need your car keys for an hour or so. We need to make those minor modifications for you." He winked as he made the latter statement. Even though there was no certainty Kelly would be driving her car, it was being fully prepped. McConnell might mandate a taxi, another car or even a bus. Kelly had joked at the meeting on Saturday that she'd think she was 007 with all the James Bond features being added to her car. In addition to an array of electronic devices, there were a number of other enhancements being made, ranging from a hidden flare gun to an ear-shattering alarm, from a switch to immobilize the car's engine to a button to inflate the passenger side airbag while the car was being driven.

"I'll come up and get you around ten-thirty and take you down to demo everything. Okay?" Steve asked. Kelly nodded.

•

The next hour was spent with Mike going through their master checklist. It appeared the two of them had all their gear, and even more importantly, from the earrings to the underwear, everything was properly working.

Mike reviewed the special codes which would be used to protect Kath and Kelly from being fooled by one of McConnell's voice imitations. It was still fresh in Kelly's mind how she'd been deceived into thinking she was talking to Rick during the Campus Inn incident. In all their communications to them, team members would be identifying themselves with various words and phrases to guard against any deception. In like manner, Kath and Kelly had their own codes to use when communicating back to the team. Ways in which to send a message, for example, that a gun may be pointed at one of their heads and McConnell was forcing them to say what they did. Ways to communicate whether what they were saying was true or false.

Kath had needed to use the restroom. While she was gone, Mike took advantage of the opportunity to supply Kelly with a special code to let them know if Kath proved not to be on the up and up, if she'd turned against Kelly and was actually acting on McConnell's behalf.

Kath had still not returned when Steve arrived, ready to show Kelly her car.

"Why don't you go on ahead with Steve," Mike said. "I'll keep Kath occupied and we'll join you in a few minutes."

•

Kelly was amazed at how quickly the morning had gone. It was eleven-thirty when she and Kath and Mike returned from having been shown the car. David had made arrangements for a buffet lunch for everyone, to make it easier for all and also to keep them together in case something came up. Mike suggested they be among the first to go through the line.

"David wants to spend a few minutes with the two of you before we all get together this afternoon. About one o'clock, in his office."

•

As they were eating in the conference room, Judy Wilson came in. "Good, I was hoping I'd find you here. We just received a call from the Lamp Post Inn. The woman who'd placed those calls to McConnell called back again today, about an hour ago. This time they were able to get her to identify herself, a Northwest reservations agent. They also obtained her name. They didn't think of asking her what she was calling about, what reservation he'd made or was attempting to make. We've tried to contact her, but she's on a lunch break. Even worse, she might also be off this afternoon. We don't know that for sure. We already have her home number, just in case. What we do know is there aren't any Northwest reservations in Underwood's name or McConnell's."

Kelly was delighted to hear the mystery woman caller had finally been identified. She was relieved and could tell Judy was too, having shared the news in front of Kath.

"When is she due back from lunch?" Mike asked.

"About twelve-thirty. That is, if she comes back."

"I know you'll stay on top if it," he said. "How do other things stand?"

242

"I think we're all set. We're double-checking now. We still have a few more calls to make."

Kelly realized Judy had been assigned a long list of 'to-do's' to have completed by today and had been extremely busy behind the scenes. She sensed and could identify with Judy's frustration over not being in the front lines, so to speak, with Kath and her.

"Does anyone besides me need to use the restroom before we go in to see David?" Mike asked.

"Good idea," Kelly said, standing and beginning to clear her place.

"I'll take care of that, I think I'm fine," Kath said. "Should I just meet you in David's office?"

•

In addition to visiting the ladies room, Kelly had been able to have a brief chat with her parents before heading to David's office. Kath and Mike were already seated across from David's desk as Kelly arrived.

"Good. We can get started," he said, smiling warmly at Kelly and motioning her to a vacant chair. "I wanted just a couple minutes with you before our general meeting to finalize things. I realize you've been busy and your heads are probably bursting with all the information you've been fed. I guess you could call this my 'No Heroes' speech. No heroines, in this case. What I want to say, and I couldn't be more serious, is we don't expect – we don't want – either of you to take any unnecessary risks tomorrow."

David spent the next five minutes or so detailing some of the pitfalls they could encounter. "We know from past experience that McConnell has a short fuse. You'll need to be extremely careful not to do anything which could trigger impulsive, irrational and possibly violent, behavior on his part. Neither of you should attempt to use the tear gas pens, for example, unless an ideal set of circumstances arises.

"I'm sorry we aren't in control of the situation, that he's positioned to call the shots. Mike and I wish we could take your places, be the ones to confront him. Hopefully, before the end of the day tomorrow, that may occur. We want you to keep your cool. Don't be tempted to act or react without considerable forethought, even if you think he's slipping out of our grasp. We'd rather regroup for another attempt than to have either of you risk being injured. And remember, you're a team. A mistake by one could result in disastrous consequences for the other.

"I don't want to paint too dire a picture, just caution you." David said, breaking into a smile. "I'm very optimistic we'll be celebrating his arrest tomorrow night. Remember, you'll have a vast number of people behind you, all dedicated to your welfare and safety. Anything further you want to add, Mike, before we go into the conference room?"

"What was the expression you said your mother always used, Kelly? attaché,' is that it?"

Kelly was flattered Mike remembered. She didn't even recall mentioning it to him. She nodded at Mike as she broke into a smile.

"That's my advice also, to both of you," Mike continued. "We're doing everything we can think of to prepare you. Now let's hope luck smiles on us, on the two of you."

•

They were preparing to start the general meeting a few minutes later when Judy came bursting into the room.

"You aren't going to appreciate hearing what I have to say," she exclaimed to everyone, her face flushed. "Kath and Kelly are booked on a Chicago flight. Not tomorrow, this afternoon at four-thirty. He's already purchased the tickets and they're holding them at the gate." She checked her notes. "Gate C10, it's a Northwest flight."

There was an instant, collective reaction. Mike slammed his fist on the table top. Larry Martino placed his palms on the table and leaning down, bounced his head on the table surface a couple times. "Damn it," Steve said, slamming his fist into the palm of his hand. Kath and Kelly simply stared at each other for a second or two before glancing around, observing the others' reactions. David was shaking his head, with a startled look of disappointment. Mike opened his mouth to ask a question.

"Done," Judy said, anticipating the question. "There were two seats left on the flight. I've booked both spaces."

Their strategy had been to steer McConnell in the direction of making plans to take possession of the extortion payment in Ann Arbor. The fact he was planning to have Kath and Kelly come to Chicago didn't come as a total surprise. It was one of the options they'd considered, actually high on the list. Their feeling of frustration was more the case that all of them now realized their chances of apprehending him had been greatly reduced. Many of their preparations would have now been for naught. Kelly's car, for example. The apparent change in his time-table didn't come as a complete surprise, either. That possibility had been considered, factored into their plans.

There was a jumble of conversations underway as David held up his hands. "Hold up, we have to get organized. The good news is we have a little time to do it. We could have learned of his plans an hour before takeoff."

Judy had taken a seat at the conference table. "It's my fault we don't have even more time," she said. "I apologize. I should have thought of checking earlier whether he'd booked a flight for Kath and Kelly. I'm sorry."

"None of us suggested doing it either, Judy. Don't blame yourself," David replied.

"I did research other flights," Judy said. "Northwest has one at two-thirty. That cuts it pretty close though. Southwest has one at three-thirty."

"I think they fly in to Midway," Steve said. "I don't think there would be time to get over to O'Hare to meet their flight," he added, gesturing at Kath and Kelly.

"I think there's a helicopter service between airports," Larry said. "That might work."

"We have a plane available here at the Ann Arbor airport," Mike said. "We reserved it in anticipation of a need such as this."

"You're right, Mike, it's probably best to use that option," David said.

Steve jumped up. "I'll alert the pilot now. How many of us will be going, Mike? You, me, who else do you have in mind? I'll let them know. We could leave here by three, schedule departure for about three-thirty. Should I notify Chicago, too?"

Mike smiled. "Slow down, Steve. We've plenty of time. Let's make sure everyone knows how they'll be involved, their responsibilities."

David nodded. "Why don't you lay it out for us, Mike."

Over the next twenty minutes, plans fell into place. With the help of Mike's direction and suggestions, the group agreed on who would be best suited to be involved in various aspects. Care was taken to avoid using people who McConnell might recognize for certain assignments. The two chosen to accompany Kath and Kelly were detectives, a man and a woman, who'd been working on other cases. Two of the six people flying down on the chartered plane would be strangers to McConnell. They'd be stationed at Kath's and Kelly's arrival gate.

"I'm sorry we haven't been able to determine if he's already in Chicago. My guess is, he is," Judy said. "He could have driven there."

"Sounds logical," David agreed. "I'm sure he's not going to risk being on the same plane with Kath and Kelly. I would think he'd definitely want to get there ahead of them. He'll probably be cautious about meeting them at the airport, too. He may direct you to some nearby hotel, anywhere for that matter. We'll need to get the Chicago police involved."

Steve was poised, ready to swing into action as Kath raised her hand to indicate she had a question. To the chagrin of the others, she suggested another possibility. "Has anyone considered this may be just another trick of Joe's? To get everyone moving in one direction while he's heading in another? I'd hate to see Mike and Steve on a plane bound for Chicago as he's sending Kelly and me off to Toledo. For that matter, maybe he's still considering Ann Arbor as a delivery site."

"Good point, Kath," Mike said. "You're right, those reservations might be just a smoke screen. Maybe he hasn't even advanced his time-table. But I'm inclined to think he's going to contact Kelly at the last minute, just in time for the two of you to catch the flight. Minimize the time we have to react."

Kelly was delighted that Kath had spoken up. The same thoughts she'd voiced had crossed Kelly's mind. More important, any suspicions she still had about Kath were being cast aside. As recently as when Judy had told them about the woman calling the Lamp Post and identifying herself as a Northwest reservations agent, she still had a slight doubt, thinking perhaps Kath could have made the call to throw off suspicion. The call to the Lamp Post Inn had been made at about the same time Kelly had excused herself to supposedly go to the ladies room. Kelly wondered if Mike had also made that same connection. It was a mute question now, Kelly thought. Or was it? Was Kath trying to distract them now? Raising this possibility so Mike and Steve wouldn't be in Chicago ahead of them? Still, Kath had been the one this morning to come up with the suggestion McConnell might accelerate things.

As these thoughts flashed through Kelly's mind, David was saying, "Maybe we should give a little more thought as to who will be assigned where, and when." The others nodded in agreement.

•

During their further discussions, Judy had checked on later flights and had found seating available on a five p.m. Northwest flight. The decision was made for Mike and two other officers to take this flight if Kath and Kelly were airborne on the four-thirty flight. Steve and three others would take the chartered flight at three-thirty. Judy Wilson was still assigned to supervise all communications, from and to headquarters. She'd be taking direction from David as would Larry Martino, who'd be responsible for coordinating activities in the field. The latter might only entail getting Kath and Kelly to the airport; Steve Renz would take charge in Chicago. Mike would be on standby, ready to spring into action when and where needed.

It was nearly two o'clock when the meeting ended on an upbeat note, the participants having accepted and adjusted to the fact the major scene of action might well be in Chicago. David gestured to Kelly that he'd like to see her as the group was exiting the room.

"I'm going to try to arrange to get you through airport security with your handgun," David told her. "Failing that, we'll find some way for the Chicago police to get a firearm to you after you arrive there. I hope to advise you on which it will be within the hour. You should anticipate receiving a call from McConnell in the next hour or so. I think you should assume you'll be on that plane for Chicago this afternoon. I'd suggest that you and Kath get yourselves prepared, dressed for battle so to speak. Get into your warm-ups, including those special undergarments, put the earrings on, load your pockets, get fully prepared.

"I'm going to inform the switchboard to be expecting a call. After you and Kath are set, why don't you come back here to the conference room. I'll tell them to notify us as well when the call comes in. I don't think we'll put him on speaker phone though, unless he suggests it."


## Chapter 40


A call came in for Kelly at half past two. Mike and David came scrambling into the conference room as Kelly picked up the receiver.

"Hello."

"Hi. I'm just checking in to see how things are going and whether we'll be getting together for dinner tonight."

It was Rick – Rick's voice at least, Kelly thought as she answered. "I don't think that's going to work. How did your physics exam go?"

"Physics? It was Statistics. It went pretty well, actually."

Kelly smiled. "I thought it would, and I really knew what exam it was. I just wanted to verify it was really you. We're somewhat in the air right now, Rick. McConnell may be pushing his timetable ahead a bit. I'll have to cut you short. I'll be in touch."

"I understand. Let me know if I can help. Good luck."

The four of them exchanged smiles as Kelly hung up.

•

McConnell's call came in just before three. David, Steve and Mike were already there, chatting with Kath and Kelly, no doubt trying to lessen the tension which had begun to build, Kelly thought.

"Hello," Kelly said.

"Surprise, it's me." It was McConnell's voice, no trace of an accent. "I was hoping I'd be able to reach you. I'd like to up our schedule, get the money today. Is Kath nearby, available?"

"She's actually sitting right across from me now. But I'm not sure we even have the money assembled yet. They thought they'd have it later today – if not, first thing in the morning."

"Don't try to play games with me, Kelly. I know you have it. Listen up, this call's going to be brief, so pay attention."

"We're all ears. Can I put you on speaker so Kath can hear?"

"Don't get smart with me," McConnell screamed in anger. "I don't have time to screw around with you. Sure, put me on speaker."

A walking time-bomb, Kelly thought. The others had also recoiled in reaction to his angry retort, hearing him scream.

"I have a little trip planned for the two of you. You're booked on Northwest flight 54, departing for Chicago at four-thirty this afternoon. Leaving from Gate 10C. There are two tickets in your names at the departure counter. To show you I'm not all bad, I already shelled out the dollars for them. Coming home, you're on your own. I want Mike Cummings to drop you off at the airport. Have him drive his car, not yours, Kelly."

Steve was shaking his head. All the hard work to equip Kelly's car was down the drain.

"I'll also need the number for his car phone, in case I have to reach you. Do you have it?"

"No," Kelly replied. "But it shouldn't take long for us to get it."

Speaking so McConnell could hear, Kelly said, "Kath, could you see if you can come up with it in a hurry, while we're talking?"

Mike was jotting the number down on a slip of paper and sliding it over to Kath.

"When you arrive in Chicago, Kelly, please check in at the arrival gate. I'll have a message waiting there for you. You should get started right away, I don't want you to miss the flight. Does Kath have the number of Mike's car phone yet?"

"Yes. She's just coming in the door now. Here it is. 610-2460."

McConnell repeated the number and thanked her. "I'll be looking forward to seeing you," he said, "and the little token of esteem you'll be bringing with you. Cheerio!"

They could hear him laughing as he hung up the phone.

Mike immediately lifted the receiver and dialed an intercom number. "Were you able to get a trace?" he asked. After listening for a couple of seconds, he said, "I thought not. Thanks for trying anyway." He looked around the room, shaking his head. "They think it was a local call, though, or possibly a car phone. They don't think it was a long distance call."

•

Steve was the first to speak. "Do you think we could arrange to have the Chicago police watch the arrival gate counter, possibly apprehend him when he drops off the message?"

"It's worth a try," Mike said. "My guess, however, is he'll just call in with the message. Make up a story about his flight being delayed and that he was supposed to meet you. He might not even be there ahead of you."

"Maybe we could – you could – learn the contents of the message before our arrival," Kelly said. "Maybe we could have a letter typed up that I could sign, authorizing the bearer to pick up the message. We could fax it."

"Maybe the message is already there," Steve suggested.

"I doubt it," David said. "We could send a fax, but my assumption is the Chicago police will figure out a way to get their hands on the message. I'll call and brief them."

"One other point, not really a question," Kelly said. "I don't know

249

about the rest of you, but his request for the number of Mike's car phone sounded a note of alarm with me. I think he may call us while we're on our way to the airport, telling us there's been a change in plans, have us make a detour along the way."

"That's a legitimate concern, Kelly," David said. "I definitely agree that we should have someone following you to the airport, maybe even two cars involved, one ahead of you and one behind you. But I don't have quite the suspicions you do. I think he wants to use Mike as the chauffeur to limit the time he can be personally involved in orchestrating our reaction to his call. I think he wants to call and make sure Mike's in the car with you."

"If he's thinking along those lines, he's overestimating my role and importance," Mike said.

"I'm glad you're the one to suggest that," Steve said with a touch of humor. "But I'm inclined to agree with David. He might have suspicions we've done some things to Kelly's car, valid ones; but I don't think that's his prime motivation for getting you to drive Kelly and Kath in your car. Removing the enemy's general from the battle, if only for an hour or two, is a good strategy."

Mike glanced at his watch. It was five after three. Looking over at Kath and Kelly, he said, "We'll have to be leaving in the next five or ten minutes, in case you need to use the restroom. Larry, you should probably be in the vehicle tailing us. Set a team up for the lead car. We'll keep it simple, south on Main to I-94 and straight to the airport. With their ear-rings switched on, you'll be able to pick up everything we say, including McConnell's call as well, if he makes one. I'll just stay out there for the later five o'clock flight, if all goes as anticipated. You or one of the other officers can drive my car back to Ann Arbor.

"Steve, you need to be getting started, too. I'll either see you at my arrival gate in Chicago or wait there for a message or contact. It might be a little more complex than we wanted, but we're still going to succeed. Right?" Mike said, glancing around the room.

•

Kath was in the front seat next to Mike, with Kelly in the back. They were waiting for the traffic light at Main and Packard when the car phone rang. Mike switched on the speaker phone so all could hear, including the officers listening in.

"Hello," he said.

"This is the second time I've had to call," McConnell said. "You're a little late getting started, aren't you? Where are you now?"

"We're on Main at Packard, heading out to I-94. Stopped for the light. It just changed."

"Good," was McConnell's only comment before hanging up.

"I think he must be outside or in a car with the window down," Kath said. "I could hear traffic in the background."

"I sensed that, too," Kelly said.

"Maybe he's not on his way to Chicago after all," Mike said. "Possibly somewhere on 94 waiting for us. I'd like that."

The phone rang again. Surprised, Mike switched on the speaker phone again.

"Hello."

"It's me again. Have you come to the stadium yet?" he asked.

"In another minute or two," Mike replied. The U of M football stadium loomed ahead on their left.

"I want you to turn left onto Stadium Boulevard," he said. "Listen carefully. I want you to enter the U of M Golf Course parking lot. Stop just inside the gate. Understood?"

"Yes, but I'm not sure we want to," Mike replied.

"Don't be a smart-ass," McConnell snarled. "I've warned you of the consequences."

He'd hung up. "Everybody heard that, I hope. I'm just about ready to get in the left turn lane. The golf course entrance is a couple hundred yards east on Stadium on the right. The first entrance is Ann Arbor Golf & Outing's. Larry, why don't you pull in there. Bruce, you'll have to come back. Pull into the lot next to Crisler, across from the golf course entrance."

Bruce Van Nuesen was driving the lead car and had already passed through the intersection of Main and Stadium. He'd have to make a U-turn or get turned around some other way. The parking lot Mike referred to was just east of Crisler Arena, where Michigan's basketball team played its games.

Kelly and Kath noticed Mike pull his revolver out of his shoulder holster and place it on the car seat. Kelly reached into a pocket of her warm-up suit and removed her handgun. She reached behind her back and slid it under the elastic waistband. Mike had made the turn onto Stadium and their car was now passing the entrance to Ann Arbor Golf & Outing.

251

Mike had flicked his right-hand turn signal on.

•

Mike stopped the car just inside the open gates, which were framed by two large, brick pillars. A man in golf attire was standing just to the right of their car. A golf bag, resting on a pull cart, was standing next to him. The man's head was tilted towards the ground, and the wide brim of a black, Greg Norman-style golf hat hid his face. He reached into the golf bag, quickly removing an assault weapon of some kind. Lifting his head as he pointed the gun in their direction, held with both hands, McConnell grinned.

"Move," he yelled. "Out of the car now, on your stomachs, hands behind your heads."

He was waving the barrel of what looked to Kelly like one of the automatic weapons which were now banned. The golf course lot was almost empty, perhaps a half-dozen cars at the opposite end near the clubhouse, nearly a hundred yards from where Mike had parked. The time of the year, the beginning of the second week of November, and the temperature, high forties, would explain that. Mike had started to react swiftly, reaching for his gun. Then reconsidering, he quickly tucked his revolver under his belt and buttoned his blazer to hide it. It was obvious to Kelly that if she and Kath hadn't been present, Mike's reaction would have been different.

They quickly scrambled out of the car as McConnell gestured for them to position themselves in front of the car on the asphalt surface of the parking lot, prone with their hands clasped behind their heads. Kath was in the middle with Mike stretched out to her left. Kelly felt the barrel of McConnell's weapon pressed to the back of her head.

"Did you leave the keys in the ignition?" he asked. Barely giving Mike time to answer, he began screaming. "Damn it, I asked you a question. Where are the keys?"

"In my pocket," Mike replied, raising his head slightly.

"Keep your head down," McConnell shouted. "All of you." Then in a softer voice, he said, "I have my gun pointed at Kelly's head, so let's not have anyone try to be cute. Understood?"

All three remained silent.

"Understood?" McConnell screamed.

Kelly shuddered at the ferocity of his tone. They all mumbled, "Yes."

"That's better," he said, once again lowering his voice. "Mike, I want you to reach in your pocket for the keys. Very carefully."

Mike removed the car keys from his pocket and held them aloft in his hand.

"Now toss them over this way. Again, very carefully," he instructed.

Mike tossed the keys and they landed a few yards from Kelly's head. McConnell moved forward and leaned down to retrieve them, the gun still aimed at Kelly.

"Where's the money?"

Before he could react violently again, Kelly volunteered, "It's in an attaché case in the trunk."

They heard the sound of the trunk being opened as McConnell asked, "Is the case locked?"

"Yes," Kelly replied.

"Do you have the key?"

"Yes," she replied, reaching into one of her pockets and then holding up the key.

"Give it to Kath. Kath, I want you to get up and walk back and open the case. The trunk's open, thanks to Mike's high-tech key chain. As soon as you've opened it, come back and," he chuckled, "resume the position."

The possibility of rigging the briefcase containing the money had been discussed in the planning meetings. Thoughts of installing a device to trigger a small explosion or burst of tear gas to stun the person opening the case were considered. Thinking McConnell might anticipate this and have Kath or Kelly or someone else open the case – exactly what he was doing – the decision was made not to rig the case.

Judy had suggested incorporating a feature whereby the case could be disarmed by Kelly or Kath if one of them was asked to open it. In lieu of that, it was decided to install a switch in the lock that Kath or Kelly could turn on. It would start a thirty-minute timing device. At the end of that time, a deafening, high-pitched siren would go off. Kelly hoped Kath remembered and would also recall how to go about switching it on.

Kath had only needed a few seconds to open the case. As she was kneeling and getting ready to stretch out on the parking surface again, McConnell said, "Now it's your turn, Mike. I want you to shut the gates. You'll see a chain and a padlock. Use them. Just one catch – I want you on the outside looking in, understand? Lock yourself out."

Mike slowly stood, nodding his head. Pressing the end of the gun barrel against Kelly's head, McConnell raised his voice. "I didn't hear you, Mike. Kelly didn't either."

Mike glared at him, his face flushed as he said, "I understand."

Keeping his gun trained on Kelly and Kath, he watched as Mike shut the tall, wrought iron gates and began to affix the chain.

"Remember to shut the padlock," McConnell said, reaching in his pocket. "Good job, here's a little treat I almost forgot about."

In an underhand motion, he threw the object he'd removed from his pocket high in the air and over the fence. It landed a few feet in back of Mike – a 3 Musketeers[(tm)] candy bar.

"Don't worry, I have one for each of the ladies, too."

He told Kath and Kelly to get back in the car – Kelly in the driver's seat, Kath on the passenger side.

"Kath, before you get in, I'd like you to do two things. Toss my golf bag in the trunk, forget about the cart, and shut the trunk."

McConnell had climbed in the back seat with his gun pointed at Kelly. He handed her the car keys.

"We'll be going for a short drive. No tricks."

The trunk slammed shut and Kath opened the car door and climbed in the passenger side of the front seat. Too bad he hadn't loaded the golf bag himself, Kelly thought. She was sure Mike might have shot him, disabled him, as he did so.

McConnell tossed a 3 Musketeers[(tm)] bar in each of their laps as he asked Kelly, "Have you ever played the U of M course?"

Kelly shook her head.

"Well, we're heading to the eighteenth tee. There's a beautiful view of the campus from there. You're in for a treat. Just drive up that service drive to your right, straight ahead. Quickly now, we're a little behind schedule."

Mike watched his car drive off as he began removing the chain from the gates. He'd only pretended to snap the padlock. He turned and waved across the street in hopes that Van Neusen's car had arrived, motioning them to come over. Removing the walkie-talkie from his inside jacket pocket, he called for Martino to come in.

"Yes, Mike, we're here. We heard everything," Martino said.

"He just drove off with Kelly and Kath. Bring your cars around, I'll have the gate open. They're on the golf course somewhere. Get your rifles out."

"We're a step ahead of you, Mike. There are already two more cars here. We'll come around, but we already have three men headed towards the fence bordering the golf course. McConnell said they were headed to the eighteenth tee. That will be in the range of our people. They all have rifles."

Mike was pleased, but concerned. "Remember that Kelly and Kath are there. Be careful."

•

Kelly followed McConnell's directions as they drove up the service road to the eighteenth tee.

"Park here. Leave the keys in the ignition and push the button to open the trunk. Now both of you, get out and on your stomachs, your arms extended out above your heads. Move!"

As Kelly exited the car, she saw and heard a helicopter approaching overhead. Great, she thought. Steve and the others were probably at the airport when they heard the news we'd been detoured. They'd moved fast, already up above them in the chopper. If in some way she and Kath could avoid being used as hostages, they'd have him.

"Eyes right on the ground," he screamed at them as he bent over the open trunk. A minute or two later, he lifted out the attaché case and looked up.

The helicopter was coming down, a rope ladder was being lowered and another rope with a hook was dangling in the air. It now hovered just above McConnell, who stood with the gun in one hand and the case in the other.

"A little lower," he shouted above the noise.

Kelly realized what was happening. The helicopter's arrival had been orchestrated by McConnell. She lifted her head and saw him attaching the hook to the briefcase. He glanced back at them before slinging the gun over his shoulder and starting to climb up the rope ladder.

Kelly was reaching behind her back for her gun, finally seeing an opportunity to use it with McConnell in a vulnerable position. She was considering where she should aim to immobilize him when she heard several shots. Bullets ricochet off the helicopter and one of its windows shattered. Kelly hugged the ground with her body as she felt the gun and removed it from her waistband at the pit of her back. There was suddenly a puff of black smoke emitting from the copter and with a roar, it started to climb. Everything was happening so quickly. Kelly glanced over at Kath, who was also cringing close to the ground. Her head was slightly raised and she had a wide-eyed expression on her face.

"Drop it, Kelly," she heard McConnell scream as she was bringing her hand around with the gun, trying to dislodge the safety switch. He was flat on his stomach with his gun pointed directly at Kelly. He'd jumped from the ladder and while rolling, had somehow grabbed his gun to now be in this commanding position.

Kelly dropped her gun as McConnell shouted above the roar of the rapidly ascending helicopter. "Leave it there, in the car, both of you."

He moved to use the car as a shield, in a crouch on the side opposite from which the bullets had been fired. As Kelly and Kath stood up to re-enter Mike's car, they could see two cars speeding up the service drive towards them, still some two or three hundred yards away.

"Damn it, hurry," McConnell screamed, already having opened the rear door and now crawling into the car. The keys were still in the ignition and he directed her to turn the engine on and get moving. "I'll direct you."

Kelly debated for a second or two, wondering whether she should pretend the engine wouldn't start, try to flood it. That thought vanished when he said, "If you want me to make a point, I'll blow Kath's head off right now. I've got nothing to lose. No tricks, Kelly. Turn left just beyond that clump of trees and floor it."

The car raced down the middle of a fairway heading east, down one hill and up another. As they crested it they saw two carts of golfers on the fairway in front of the green. Seeing them barreling down the fairway toward them, one of the golfers jumped out, waving his fist. He was not going to sit idly by while his golf course was being damaged.

"To the left of them, keep flooring it. Watch this," he said.

He shifted to the opposite side of the back seat, behind Kath, and lowered the window. He stuck the nose of the gun through the window and fired a round of bullets in the direction of the two golf carts. The golfers were shocked and terrified. The man who'd been shaking his fist scrambled to get behind his cart as its driver also quickly crawled to get the cart between him and their speeding car. In the other cart, the two men were tumbling over one another in their haste to get out of the cart and hide behind it.

McConnell laughed. "Down that cart path, Kelly. See that large tree along the fence? Pull up there and park."

Kath spoke, the first words she'd said, Kelly thought, since they'd confronted McConnell.

"We're on one of the fairways bordering State Street?" she asked.

McConnell glared at her. "What did you say? You're wired, aren't you? That's it, no talking from here on out, by either of you."

He slammed the stock of his weapon into the back of Kath's head, knocking her forward in the seat. "Don't try my patience," he yelled.

Kelly had stopped the car in front of the tree. He motioned them out and grabbed the keys from Kelly, pushing the button to open the trunk. He pointed out the direction he wanted them to walk, to the right of the tree towards some bushes. He went to the trunk and removed the golf bag, carrying it in his left hand with the gun in his right, following them. He pointed to show them where an opening had been cut in the fence and motioned them through it. A blue-green four-door Saturn was parked next to the opening.

"Inside, hurry," he said to Kath as he motioned for Kelly to take the golf bag. He reached into his pocket and pulled out a set of keys and proceeded to open the car's trunk. Kelly wondered why he was keeping the bag, possibly there were additional guns packed in it. Her eyes widened as she glanced in and saw it was stuffed with packets of money. Was the helicopter just a ruse? Had he emptied the case before attaching it to the rope? These questions flashed through Kelly's mind as he directed her to place the bag in the trunk and to get in the driver's seat of the car. She still had a vision of the helicopter rising, with the case dangling from below, being pulled up into the copter.

Kelly turned on the motor and McConnell directed her to drive to the edge of State Street, only a few feet away. Traffic was heavy and Kelly had to stop and wait for a gap between cars. McConnell had pointed they'd be going south. Kelly had a momentary thought of perhaps driving into the side of one of the passing cars. Remembering the blood she'd observed on the back of Kath's head, she felt it was too risky. She had her to worry about, in addition to herself. They drove south on State and he instructed her, "Keep it around forty to forty-five. We don't want any unnecessary attention, do we?"

As the street widened he motioned her to stay in the left-hand lane. "We're going to make a turn up here in a little while."

The next intersection was Eisenhower. Left turns weren't allowed. Maybe he didn't realize this. They could attempt to gain attention with an illegal turn, Kelly thought with a note of optimism. Sirens could be heard in the distance. Kelly thought she could see a flashing light far in back of them as she glanced in the rearview mirror. He tapped Kelly on the shoulder and pointed to the large 777 Group office building coming up on their left. He leaned up and started to whisper in her ear. A note of alarm appeared on his face. Rather than saying anything, he motioned Kelly to get in the left-hand turn lane. He reached over her shoulder and flicked the turn signal on. Kelly thought of slamming on the brakes, but again decided it was too risky. Kath, rather than McConnell, might be the one to slam into the windshield.

"Turn there," McConnell said, pointing to the entry drive to the parking lot, north of the office building, less than a hundred yards short of the Eisenhower and State major intersection. He gestured she should just keep driving down the lane which was abutted by parking areas filled with cars. There was a stop sign along with a couple of traffic humps to slow the speed of cars on this stretch of the service drive. The sound of sirens had become louder and Kelly noticed in her rearview mirror, two police cars with flashing lights, racing south on State.

"We're cutting it close," McConnell said with a chuckle. It was still a game for him, thought Kelly, but possibly a deadly game.

They reached the end of the drive, where it exited to Boardwalk, and McConnell motioned for Kelly to turn right, or south. He gestured for her to just go through the green light at Eisenhower and Boardwalk. On the south side of the intersection were a number of hotels and motels, including the Sheraton, where Kath and Kelly had been staying. There must be six in this area, Kelly thought. As they passed the Sheraton on their right, just after Wendy's, with the Marriott on their left, Kelly wondered what McConnell's plans were. For a second, she thought he might be bold enough to take them to their room at the Sheraton. Getting them through the lobby, without drawing attention to themselves, would have been too much of a challenge, Kelly surmised as they drove past.

At the end of Boardwalk, McConnell had motioned for her to turn right. Towards the end of the street they were now on, on the left kitty corner to a Burger King, was the Wolverine Inn, next to a Bill Knapp's restaurant. It was an economy motel. Kelly believed it offered room access without going inside. Perhaps that was their destination.

Instead, just after she turned, McConnell pointed for her to turn into the Residence Inn driveway on her left, motioning for her to continue to the rear of the complex. Tapping both of them on their shoulders, he held his finger to his lips.

Pointing to their earlobes, as the car came to a halt in one of the empty parking places, he indicated with an outstretched palm that the two should remove their earrings and place them there. "Unless you'd prefer I yank them off," he snarled.

They complied and he closely examined the earrings. To Kelly's consternation, there didn't appear to be any people around. She glanced over her shoulder towards the registration office, but saw no one. His amazing luck continues to hold, she thought. She could sense Kath was having similar thoughts.

He motioned for them to get out of the car and directed Kath to open the trunk. He laid his assault weapon on the floor of the back seat and showed them he had a handgun. He didn't want to risk someone seeing him with the automatic weapon trained on them, Kelly thought. He placed the earrings on the pavement next to the car and stomped on them several times.

"Maybe that will make conversation a little easier," he said with a twinkle in his eye. Then he quickly changed expressions and said, "Still, no talking. Understood?"

They nodded.

"Bring that inside with us," he said to Kelly, motioning to the golf bag. "You two lead, right over there."

He directed them to one of the ground level units and handed a room key to Kath as they approached.

"Sorry about your head," he said.

## Chapter 41

The car in which Mike was riding, closely followed by the one driven by Larry Martino, had screeched to a stop alongside Mike's car. They'd quickly discovered the opening which had been cut in the fence. Stooping, Mike and another officer maneuvered through it. They couldn't be far behind, Mike reasoned. Directed by Kath's message indicating McConnell was on a fairway bordering State, and the golfers who'd pointed out the route Mike's car had taken, the two pursuing vehicles had been just minutes behind McConnell.

"He must have had a car parked here," Mike said, glancing up and down State – hoping, but not expecting, to see the three proceeding by foot. "Let's check over there to see if anyone saw something," Mike said, pointing to the Produce Station across the street. Per usual, Mike thought as they darted across State during a break in the traffic, the parking lot of one of Ann Arbor's most popular retail outlets was swarming with activity.

Mike was fortunate to quickly discover one woman who'd seen three people entering a car on the opposite side of the street just minutes before. "Right over there, by the fence, next to the large tree," she'd said. She was unable to remember the make or model or even the color of the vehicle. After questioning several other people with no success, they were ready to give up and return back across the roadway.

Mike was a little annoyed as he observed the young officer he was with stopping an attractive young woman coming out of the store, her arms filled with two large bags. Timing was critical; they needed to hurry. The officer waved to Mike, motioning for him to come back.

"She remembers seeing a car parked over there about ten minutes ago, before she went into the store," the officer called out. They hurried toward Mike as the young officer said, "Please tell him what you told me."

"I noticed the car because it was identical to mine. A '93 Saturn, four-door, that color," she said, pointing a few yards away to where her car was parked. "I didn't see anyone in it or near it."

Thanking her, Mike and the other officer dashed back across State. Larry was standing on the opposite side of the fence with another officer.

"We know the make, model and color of the car they're in," Mike announced to them as he and the young officer ducked through the opening in the fence. "Have you been able to get a read on where they're headed?" Mike asked.

Larry nodded. "Yes, they appear to be bound for I-94, possibly the Ann Arbor Airport. The signal's similar to the one we're getting from the money. Bit of bad news, though, Mike. It appears he's discovered the earrings. The last bit of conversation we picked up was a remark of McConnell's about yanking them off. I'm sure he was referring to the earrings. Immediately after that comment, there was a crunching sound and a burst of static. Nothing since."

Mike nodded, disappointed but not surprised. He'd been afraid

McConnell would stumble onto the earrings after Kath had been a little too obvious in giving the clue as to where their car was headed. We'll just have to work around it, he thought as he said, "We need to call in a description of the car, Larry. Get the message to those cars headed for the airport."

While Mike and the other officer had been questioning people at the Produce Station, two police cars had roared past, headed south on State Street. They were the two units who'd been at Ann Arbor Golf & Outing with Martino. He'd left word for them to head to the airport, prior to his driving over to the U of M Golf Course entrance to meet Mike. They'd been on their way seconds after the two officers who'd been successful in scoring some direct hits with their rifle fire, had entered their respective squad cars.

Mike, in the passenger seat of Martino's car, watched the monitor screens as Larry called in the car's description to headquarters. It appeared the signal emanating from Kelly's and Kath's undergarments was holding steady, suggesting the car had stopped. Mike had expected to find the signal moving either east or west on I-94, or continuing south on State towards the airport. The intermittent signal, originating from the money, was also giving a steady reading. A dreadful thought came to Mike. Could it be possible the helicopter had landed somewhere else, between them and the airport, a secondary rendezvous site in case something went wrong at the golf course? Maybe he's boarding it right now, possibly in the large parking area surrounding Briarwood, Mike thought.

Larry was just hanging up. "Good news! Steve just called in. They'd been able to contact him a few minutes before he was ready to board the plane for Chicago. They surrounded the helicopter at the airport as it landed. They're questioning the pilots now."

That is good news, Mike thought, breathing a sigh of relief, his worries uncalled for. "Do they have the attaché case and the money?" Mike asked.

"I forgot to ask, and they didn't mention they had. Should I call back?" Larry asked.

"Yes, but let's do it while we're driving," Mike responded. "While we're getting a fix on the signal from Kelly and Kath. By the way, did you find anything in my car?"

Martino shook his head no. "Empty, the trunk too, except for this," he answered, handing Mike a 3 Musketeers(tm) candy bar. "It was on the passenger side of the front seat."

Mike took the bar from Martino and slipped it into the pocket of his jacket. "Let's hope we're able to stuff it down his throat before the day's over," he said as he pounded his fist on the dashboard. "Since you have the monitoring equipment, I'll ride with you. I'll tell one of the other officers to take my car and follow us."

## Chapter 42

McConnell herded Kelly and Kath into the room. Still pointing the revolver at them, he gestured towards a nearby table.

"Empty your pockets. Very carefully. Everything."

As Kelly and Kath proceeded to do so, he reached down into the golf bag and removed a hand-held scanning device, similar to those used at

airport security check-points. Switching it on, he inserted the hand-held device back into the bag.

"Good," he said with a look of surprise and a smile. "I halfway expected you'd doctored up the money. Maybe I over-estimated you."

Kelly was delighted the intermittent signal from the money hadn't been picked up by the scanner. The process of emptying their pockets completed, Kelly and Kath stood awaiting further instructions. Kelly had left the tear gas pen in one pocket of her warm up, wedging it in as deeply as possible. There was a moment of doubt, wondering if she should be taking this added risk.

"Okay, hands above your heads," he said as he brought the scanning wand over to the table and passed it over the items the two had placed there. Receiving no reading, he nodded in satisfaction. He next proceeded to move the instrument up and down Kath's warm up. The scanner began to beep and a small, red light flashed, blinking on and off. He repeated the process with the same result. Raising his eyebrows, he shifted his attention to Kelly, moving the scanner up and down the sides of her warm up with similar results. Rather than being upset and angry, McConnell's response had been simply a smile. "I thought it was getting too easy," he said as he motioned for them to enter the bedroom. Still keeping the gun pointed at them in a threatening manner, McConnell walked over to the dresser and pulled open the top drawer. With a show, he removed two sets of hand-cuffs.

"You first, Kelly. Turn around and place your hands behind your back. That's right, good girl." He quickly cuffed Kelly. "Now I want you to just stretch out on that bed," he said, pointing to one of the two double beds in the room. "On your back."

After Kelly had maneuvered herself into that position, McConnell turned to Kath and in the same soft-spoken, confident tone, in the belief he was in total control of the situation, said, "Now I want you to completely strip."

He pulled open the lower drawer of the dresser and removed what appeared to be a heavily insulated, small carrying bag. Kelly and Kath sensed it was fairly heavy as he hoisted the padded bag and tossed it onto the empty bed.

"Put everything in there," he said. Kath still hadn't moved. His face flushing, McConnell raised his voice. "I don't have all day, so don't try my patience. Strip. Now."

As Kath began to disrobe, sitting down on the edge of the bed, beginning with her shoes and socks, McConnell reached into the lower drawer of the dresser and pulled out what resembled a fisherman's vest, only longer.

It was covered with pockets. Still holding the gun, he slipped it on. It reached to his mid-thighs.

Kath had removed her warm up jacket and pants along with her shirt, and was now standing clad only in her bra and panties. Glancing over at Kelly, she said, "See, what did I tell you, he's a pervert, a real creep."

McConnell's reaction was as if Kath had just struck him. His face flushed in anger.

"Why, you little bitch," he screamed. He raised his right hand, in which the gun was held, across his face and stepping forward, viciously backhanded Kath on the side of her cheek, sending her reeling and falling to the floor between the two beds. He pointed the gun at Kelly, yelling, "Just stay where you are," as Kelly struggled to sit up.

He stepped back and grabbed the other pair of handcuffs in his left hand. "Get up," he said to Kath. "Hands behind your back. Turn around."

As he talked, his voice began to return to a more moderate level, as he appeared to regain control over his emotions. Blood was dripping out of the corner of Kath's mouth, and she moved a little unsteadily as she rose to her feet. She turned around with her hands behind her and McConnell quickly had the handcuffs on.

"Now get into that bed, the same position as Kelly," he instructed her as he reached in the drawer and pulled out a roll of adhesive tape.

"Stay still, no more wise cracks," he said as he began to bind Kath's ankles with the tape. Kelly could sense Kath had been tempted to kick him in the face. Thank heavens she hadn't, Kelly thought. With her hands cuffed behind her, the end result would have only been further abuse, an additional beating by McConnell.

After binding Kath, McConnell had lifted the bag he'd had her place her clothes in. Kelly could see the walls of the bag were insulated in some way. Probably the same principal as the aprons X-ray technicians use, a leaded material to prevent exposure, Kelly thought. Articles such as their underwear placed in the bag would probably be neutralized, Kelly surmised. Thanks to Kath, that still wasn't a worry. Maybe Mike and the others were homing in on them now. He'd taken the bag into the next room, first having cautioned them to stay put. He was probably putting the items they'd removed earlier from their pockets into the bag, Kelly thought.

McConnell returned a couple of minutes later, carrying the golf bag. He removed the clubs and stood them in the corner. He then dumped the remaining contents of the bag, the packets of money, onto the surface of the dresser. He stuffed a few of the packets into the pockets of the vest, seemingly testing to see how they would fit. He appeared satisfied with the result as he looked up at Kelly and said, "Now it's your turn, Kelly. Turn over, I'll remove the cuffs."

As Kelly undressed, McConnell continued to stuff packets of money into the pockets of the vest with one hand, while directing the gun at Kelly with the other. When Kelly had stripped down to her panties and bra, he picked up the scanner and passed it down over her chest and stomach. The beeping noise sounded as the light began blinking. McConnell jumped back as if he'd been bitten.

"Damn it, I should have guessed," he said. "I hope for your sakes it's the panties and bras. Otherwise," he laughed, "I might have to do a little probing."

Kelly shuddered at the thought as she unfastened her bra. She then turned her back on McConnell, shrugged the bra off and slid the panties down over her hips and stepped out of them.

"Toss them here," he said.

Kelly leaned down and picked the garments up. Looking over her shoulder, she tossed them underhanded in McConnell's direction. He ran the scanner over them and smiled as it beeped.

"Hands behind you, Kelly. I need to put these back on," he said, the cuffs dangling in his left hand. He quickly slipped them on and ordered Kelly back on the bed. She was more angered than embarrassed as she stretched out on her back. He smirked as he passed the scanner over her nude body, getting a negative read.

He reached for the adhesive tape and began to bind Kelly's ankles. How she'd love to kick that smirk off his face, she thought. She restrained herself, realizing it would be counter-productive. He cut the tape with the pair of scissors he'd previously used when binding Kath, and stepped back as if to admire his work. Hopefully, Mike and the others will locate us soon, Kelly prayed, sensing Kath probably had the same thought.

"You have a beautiful figure," he said to Kelly. "I would have loved having you in some of my photo sessions. Too bad I don't have my camera now." He laughed, thumping his chest, which was now padded with packets of money. "Your photos would have probably earned me a few extra shekels, too."

"Pervert! Creep! Slimeball!," Kath shouted at him. "You know you're going to be caught, don't you?"

265

McConnell recoiled from the verbal attack Kath had launched. For a second or two his face was livid. He started to shout back at her and then regained his composure, sensing he was in control and needed to maintain his cool.

"Don't you wish. You're dreaming." He continued talking as he moved toward Kath with the scissors. He'd placed the revolver on the dresser. Kelly was worried he might be about to injure Kath, but instead he carefully cut through the fabric of her bra and underpants. Laughing, he reached down and viciously ripped them off.

"Feisty as your sister, aren't you? I should snip your nipples off. Too bad I don't have more time," he said as he slid his hand over her left breast and down her stomach. She bucked and twisted, sneering as she said, "You're sick!"

He laughed again. "Now be quiet, both of you, or I'll have to tape your mouths shut. Understand?"

The two quietly glared at him. He laughed again as he carried their underwear into the adjoining room. Kelly guessed he was putting it in the bag. Were Mike and the others close to locating them? What would happen now? Kelly hoped Kath would heed his demand and remain silent for now. The thought of being gagged had occurred to Kelly earlier; not a pleasant one.

McConnell hurriedly completed the process of stuffing the money into the pockets of the vest. He reached into the bottom drawer of the dresser and removed a large, colorful, floral-patterned dress. He slipped it over his head, pulling it into position over his now bulky figure. He then stood in front of the mirror hanging over the dresser and removed a carrying case of cosmetics from one of the drawers. He began to apply lipstick, rouge and eye shadow. Reaching into the dresser again, he removed a black wig, with a pill box-style hat affixed to the top. He placed it on his head, made some adjustments while looking in the mirror, and then spun around, saying, "Ta da! How do I look?"

Kelly and Kath were both awed by the transformation, even more so as he put on a pair of thick-lensed glasses. Standing before them was a full-figured, matronly woman. Heavens, thought Kelly. He could walk through the lobby of City Hall and nobody would guess. It was still a game for him, and he was on center stage.

# Chapter 43

The three cars, with Larry and Mike in the lead car, had retraced their route over the golf course. Larry tried to keep to the fairway rough as much as possible, to minimize damage to the course. Mike dialed headquarters to verify whether Steve Renz and his people had recovered the money. He spoke with Judy. She explained, as of their most recent communication with Steve, they hadn't. They had the case, she said, but it was empty. Steve had people searching the copter and was questioning the pilot and the young man who'd also been in the copter.

"Thus far, they've been maintaining their innocence and denying any knowledge of the money," Judy said. "It's strange, the pilot claims he was involved in a sort of dress rehearsal . . . Just a second, Mike, Steve's on the other line. I'll have him call you. You're in Larry's car, right?" Mike acknowledged he was.

Their car was nearly halfway down the service drive, headed for the parking area and entrance gate. Mike turned to Larry, saying, "You heard?" Larry nodded. "Steve should be calling us right away with a later update," Mike said.

As they pulled into the parking lot, Larry and Mike saw a small truck parked next to the entrance gate. A man, probably one of the grounds keepers, was standing next to it. The gates were closed. Mike lowered his window as they drove up alongside the man.

"What the hell is going on?" the man asked in anger. "Do you . . ."

"Hold on," Mike said, holding up his right hand. "We're all police, tracking down a killer. He has two hostages, women. He's just ahead of us. Please get these gates open as quickly as you can."

"I'm sorry, I didn't . . . " the man stammered as he hurriedly turned toward the gates.

The man seemed dazed by the news and seemed to take forever unlocking the padlock, removing the chain and finally pulling the gates open. He waved and shouted, "Good luck," as Larry, seeing the traffic was clear, sped out onto Stadium Boulevard.

Seconds later, the phone rang. "Hi, Mike, it's me," Steve said. "Judy said she filled you in about finding the empty attaché case. There's no sign of the money in the helicopter, either. They're doing another search now, but I'm not optimistic. I'm thinking the money may have been transferred to a container of some sort and dumped during the flight back to the airport. That, or the possibility he emptied the case before sending it up."

Either could explain the reading they were currently getting on the scanner, Mike thought as he asked, "What does the pilot say?"

"Strange, I don't know how much Judy told you. He claims he's innocent, of course. His story's so far-fetched I'm beginning to believe him. He says he was contacted by the University to be involved in a unique acknowledgment of a multi-million dollar gift a prominent alum had made. Part of the money was for a new club house at the golf course. The man would be flying in on his private plane next week. University officials would be meeting him here in a limo and driving him to the golf course. Following his arrival there, he'd be taken in a golf cart out to the eighteenth tee where they expected to have nearly a hundred people gathered. President Robinson would present him with a large painting of the University campus as seen from that vantage point. The finale would be the arrival of the helicopter. The alum would climb up the lowered ladder into the copter. The painting would also be hoisted up and they'd ferry him back to the airport. A quick thirty minutes – arrival, award and departure. That's the gist of the story. Today was to be a trial run, a dress rehearsal. The pilot and the boy he had with him in the copter allege they were terrified and surprised when the gunfire erupted."

"What was their reaction when they saw McConnell holding a gun and the two women on the ground? Didn't that make them a little suspicious?" Mike asked.

"We confronted them with that question, too," Steve answered.

"And what did they say?"

"They thought the girls were in some way indicating the spots where the ladder and rope should be lowered. They say they realized the man had a gun at about the same time the shots were fired. They claim they thought it was a flare gun or launcher of some sort, perhaps to send up some flares as part of the award presentation. They believed that part was also being rehearsed. I told you their story was strange, farfetched. What's your reaction?"

"I'd suggest you keep the heat on. Shake them up a little. But from what you've said, they're shell-shocked already. Tell them if they don't cooperate, they could be charged as accomplices to extortion, kidnapping, even murder. I can't believe they're totally innocent. But why don't you have one of the other officers continue the questioning, Steve. We're headed your way, on State just north of the expressway. I think you should come and meet us. Have those two other cruisers double-back, too. They've probably just arrived in the past few minutes. The readings we're getting on the scanners indicate Kath and Kelly are somewhere between here and the airport. They don't appear to be moving. The signals we're receiving from the money seem to coincide with the ones we're receiving from them. That's been true for the past few minutes.

"It could mean he's retrieved the money, which was possibly dropped from the helicopter at some previously-agreed to spot, or as you suggested, maybe he never gave up possession of it. We've just crossed I-94. We'll either meet you, or if by chance the signals lead us off this route, we'll drop off one of the other officers and he'll flag you down and advise you which direction we headed."

"Got it," Steve replied. "We'll leave here in two or three minutes. See you soon . . and good luck."

Mike could sense Steve shared his concerns over the welfare of Kelly and Kath. Larry was pointing to the scanner screens and pulling over to the side of the road.

"I think we've come too far, Mike. They have to be back on the other side of the freeway. I don't know if you noticed it or not, but there's about a one-hundred-yard stretch over there, just north of the expressway, where we're getting considerable interference. We were having trouble pinpointing the signals. They're clearer now, but both signals indicate they're originating north of us now. Maybe from one of those hotels or motels over there."

Larry jumped out of the car and walked back and spoke to the officers in the two cars which were following them. While he was gone, Mike mulled over what he'd just learned from Larry. Had McConnell realized there would be a problem with sensor tracking equipment in this area? Is that why he's holed up somewhere over there? Or is he just lucky once again? With all this manpower, it won't take us long to check out those hotels and motels, Mike reasoned, especially with Steve coming to meet them, plus another two teams. Attempting to locate the car, questioning desk clerks . . .

Larry opened the car door, interrupting Mike's train of thought. "I've briefed them, Mike. After we get turned around, the officer in your car is going to stay here and wait for Steve and the other units. Van Neusen and Parker are going to be checking out the Crowne Plaza, seeing if they can spot the Saturn and checking with the registration desk to see if anyone has spotted McConnell and Kelly and Kath or anything suspicious. I told them we'd be doing the same at the Wolverine Inn."

"Good, except for one change," Mike replied. "I'd rather we head directly to the Sheraton. His style has been to challenge us head on. I'm thinking he might just be crazy enough to be holding Kelly and Kath hostage in their room at the Sheraton."

"I think you may be right," Martino said. "Should I have everyone come there?"

"No, why don't you tell Van Neusen and Parker to go ahead with a check at the Crowne Plaza and then work their way toward us, to the Wolverine Inn and the Residence Inn. Steve and the others can meet us at the Sheraton. If I'm wrong about the Sheraton, we can split up and check out the Courtyard Marriott and Hampton, as well as the Atrium office buildings."

## Chapter 44

McConnell was standing in front of the mirror, admiring his appearance. He'd slipped off the eye glasses to have a better look as he adjusted the wig and dress. He whistled at his image and laughed.

"Ladies, it's time to bid you adieu. I'll call in a couple hours to let . . ." he hesitated, "I think I'll call one of the television stations, let them know where to find you. Clips of the two of you would really spice up the eleven o'clock news tonight," he added with a chuckle.

"Just a couple more details," he said, reaching for the roll of adhesive tape and scissors. "I know you'd promise not to yell or shout after I leave, but I want to be on the safe side. Consider yourselves lucky I'm not going to tape your eyes shut as well."

Kath was whimpering and there were tears in her eyes as he walked towards her with a strip of the tape.

"Are you all right?" Kelly asked. "Can't you see she's in pain?" she said to him.

"And I'm supposed to feel sorry after her lipping off? No way," he said.

"I think I broke my wrist," Kath said, a grimace of pain passing over her face.

If that's the case, the pain must be unbearable, Kelly thought, knowing her own pain with her hands cuffed behind her back.

"Can't you take her handcuffs off, maybe tape her hands in front of her?" Kelly pleaded. "You've won the game for now. There's no reason to leave her in agony. We could be here for hours. Even handcuffing her to the pipe under the bathroom sink would be better than having her hands behind her back."

His initial reaction was to leave things as they were, tape their mouths shut and keep moving. He glanced at his watch. "Damn," he said, sticking the end of the strip of tape on the corner of the dresser and pulling up the skirt of the dress. He reached in his pant pocket and pulled out his gun. He placed it on the dresser as he reached into his pocket again, feeling for the key to the handcuffs.

"Okay, sit up," he said to Kath. He reached behind her back and gingerly felt her wrist. She flinched in pain and groaned. Tears continued to well up in her eyes.

"Be gentle," Kelly cautioned him.

He turned toward Kelly. "Just shut up. I shouldn't even be taking the time to check on her."

He unlocked the cuffs and slipped them off her wrists. She brought her hands around in front of her as she sat on the bed.

"Thank you," she mumbled, trying to keep from crying.

He bent down to take a closer look at her wrist. "Just the left one?" he asked.

Kelly saw her nod and then a blur of action. Kath had extended her thumbs. Exerting every bit of strength she could muster, she lifted her arms, jamming her thumbs into his eyes and twisting her hands, attempting to gouge his eyes with her thumbnails. Kath's quickness had taken him by surprise. He staggered back a couple steps. Wiping his hand across his eyes, he growled and lunged forward, his hands outstretched, reaching for her. Kelly watched in horror as Kath rolled off the bed onto the floor, using her arms to quickly slither across the floor to the dresser. Rising to her knees, she reached up and grabbed the revolver. McConnell was swinging his arms, crawling across the bed she'd been on, screaming profanities. Kelly saw blood streaming from at least one of his eyes. He'll come for me, she thought as she wriggled to the side of the bed and rolled off onto the floor, between the bed and the wall.

He lunged again, landing on the bed where she'd just been, as he yelled, "You two bitches are dead meat! I can't see!"

271

Kelly heard the roar of a gun shot and a moment later, a second shot as she struggled to right herself. McConnell was lumbering toward Kath, who held the gun in both hands, pointed directly at him, preparing to pull the trigger again. He lashed out with his arm, managing to deflect her aim. Her third shot hit the mirror and Kelly cringed as broken pieces fell onto the dresser top. Resembling a huge bear, McConnell staggered toward the bedroom doorway. Feeling blindly with his hands, he located the door frame and fled into the next room. Turning and reaching back, he groped for the door knob and pulled it closed behind him. A fourth shot sounded and the closing door splintered. Kelly thought she heard a groan.

With the gun still in her hand, Kath was sliding her body across the floor to the door. "I should've aimed for his face," she screamed. From her sitting position, she reached for the door knob as Kelly shouted, "Wait, don't open the door! Remember, he may have another gun in there. See if the phone's working."

Kath pulled her hand back and slid across the carpet on her haunches to the dresser. Reaching up, she groped for the scissors among the shattered pieces of mirror. Locating them, she cut the tape binding her ankles. She quickly walked over to where Kelly was sitting on the floor. Bending down, she cut and removed the tape from Kelly's ankles. She next went over and picked up the phone. "It's working," she said, dialing 911. With her hands still secured behind her back, Kelly managed to stand and walk over to the phone. Kath placed the receiver so Kelly could cradle it under her chin and be able to talk as well as listen. "I'll try to locate the key to unlock your cuffs while you're on the phone."

Within seconds Judy was on the line. Kelly quickly explained where they were, what had happened, and the fact McConnell was either in the next room or in the process of fleeing.

"He might be blinded, at least partially. He's bleeding." As Kelly talked she was fearful McConnell might be charging through the door at any moment.

"Thank God you're not seriously injured," Judy said. "We'll brief everyone right away."

"Remember to mention how he's disguised himself. And warn them he could have the gun he used on the golf course."

"Will do, talk to you soon," Judy replied.

Kath had located the key and was unlocking Kelly's cuffs. "You took a big risk," Kelly said to her. "Are you okay?"

She nodded as she removed the handcuffs. Putting them on the dresser top, she handed the revolver to Kelly, saying, "You'd better be the one with the gun. Let's see if he's still here."

"Be careful," Kelly cautioned her as Kath started for the door. "You open the door and stand back there next to the wall. I'll peek out from this side."

Both tensed as she turned the knob and yanked the door open, quickly positioning herself behind the door as Kelly had instructed. Kelly glanced into the next room – no sign of him. Cautiously going through the door in a crouched position with the gun in her hand, Kelly viewed the area of the room she'd been unable to survey from the doorway.

"Looks as if he's gone," she called back. Rising up, she walked into the kitchen area, spotting blood stains on a damp dish towel in the sink. Kelly turned and saw Kath behind her. She couldn't help but smile. She'd nearly forgotten her own nakedness over the course of the past few minutes. Kath, interpreting Kelly's smile, grinned and said, "Revenge of the amazon women. If our friends could see us now."

"I think our clothes are on the table in that bag," Kelly said. "Let's get them on before we venture outside."


## Chapter 45

"I think you have it figured right," Martino said as he turned off State onto Victors Way, past the Wolverine Inn, heading towards the Sheraton. "See how strong the signals are?"

Accelerating past the Residence Inn, Martino braked to navigate the left turn onto Boardwalk, then accelerated again prior to reaching the Sheraton's entrance drive. As he turned in, Martino started to say, "Strange, I think the signals . . . "

"Look over there," Mike interrupted, pointing. "A Saturn four-door in the same blue-green color as hers was. Drop me off at the main entrance. When Steve and the others arrive, have them split up and watch the rear and side exits. You can keep an eye on the Saturn and the main entrance."

Mike hurried through the Sheraton's front door. He proceeded directly to the registration desk, recognizing the young man he'd spoken to previously, when he'd arranged the room change for Kelly and Kath. He remembered Mike. In answer to Mike's question as to whether he'd seen Kelly and Kath in the past half hour, the clerk shook his head no.

"Could you give me a room key?" Mike asked as he moved to the end of the desk and dialed their room number on the house phone. As Mike listened to the phone ring, the young man approached and held out a keycard. After the tenth ring with still no answer, Mike hung up.

"Those women are being held hostage," Mike explained. "There's a strong possibility they're somewhere here on the premises. In a few minutes we'll have officers at all the exits. Could you brief the rest of the staff? The man who's holding them hostage is armed and dangerous. There's no need to sound an alarm just yet, but it may come to that. I'll let you know in a couple minutes."

As Mike left the desk and started down the corridor, he heard Larry call out to him.

"Steve and the others arrived and are in the process of securing the exits. I have another officer watching the Saturn and the main entrance. By the way, it has an Ohio plate."

•

The two of them flanked the doorway with their guns drawn as Mike inserted the keycard in the door and twisted the handle. The room was empty. There was no indication anyone except for housekeeping had been inside the room since Kelly and Kath had left early this morning.

"They could still be here at the Sheraton, in another room," Mike said. "He could have planned in advance, possibly obtaining a room yesterday or earlier today."

"When I was waiting for Steve, I was monitoring the signals," Larry said. "I think they're originating just south of us, the Hampton Inn or Residence Inn. Maybe one of the Atrium buildings. I should have said something earlier."

Mike raised his eyebrows. "You'd started to say something as we drove up. I should have heard you out. Let's leave someone here watching the car, have everyone else start checking out those other facilities."

•

Steve was standing in the center of the Sheraton lobby. He spotted

Larry and Mike as they approached.

"No luck?" he asked.

"No, their room's empty," Mike answered. "And Larry thinks the signals are originating from down the street, near the Hampton or Residence Inns. Before we do any further checking here, we should canvas that area. The office buildings, too."

Steve nodded. "Two things. I just spoke with Judy. She says we've lost the signals from Kelly and Kath. She's just getting the intermittent signal from the money."

Not good news, Mike thought as Steve continued.

"We also discovered two more cars, one near the rear entrance and the other parked on the south side of the complex, which match the Saturn description you gave us. Do you think we should leave people to watch all three cars, while the rest of us move on or what?"

Mike nodded, disappointed, but not surprised to find they'd found multiple cars which matched the description.

"Better keep an eye on all three, I guess." To fail to do so and later discover one of the cars had been the one he escaped in would be a disaster, Mike reasoned.

"Larry and I will head to the Hampton Inn, Steve. You start at the Residence Inn. You might run into Van Neusen and Parker. They're working their way in that direction after checking out the Crowne Plaza and the Wolverine Inn. I'll get the others involved at the Atrium office buildings and parking lots."

Steve nodded as the three exited the Sheraton. "Reid and I will catch up with you at the Hampton Inn after we've scoped out the Residence Inn."

•

Steve had Terry Reid drop him off at the registration office at the Residence Inn.

"Drive through the lot and see if you spot the Saturn or notice anything suspicious while I'm asking questions inside."

The desk clerk was on the phone when Steve entered the office. Steve removed his identification as he stood waiting for him to finish the call.

The clerk was saying, "I'm sure it's probably just someone watching a video, maybe one of those "Die Hard" films, with the volume turned up. We'll check it out, though. Sorry you've been disturbed. Thanks for notifying us."

The clerk smiled as he turned to Steve, saying, "All in a day's work, I guess. Can I help you?"

"I hope so," said Steve, showing the clerk his identification. "We're looking for a man and two women. The man's in his mid-thirties and . . . "

The phone rang again. The clerk held up a finger, indicating he'd only be a minute. After listening for a minute or two, the clerk responded to the caller by saying, "You're the second one who's called. I have the police here in the office right now. An officer, a detective, will be down to your room in a couple minutes. Yes, we think it may just have been someone's television set, too."

Could this be related? Steve thought, his interest building as he heard the conversation. The clerk had hung up and turned to Steve again.

"As you heard, that's the second call, the second report of hearing shots and the sound of breaking glass." Steve winced, hoping Kelly and Kath were alive and well. "It happened about five minutes ago. Both had hesitated to call, thinking it may have been someone's television."

"Which building? Do you have a master key?" Steve interrupted him. "We're looking for a suspected killer who's holding two women hostage. It may be him . . . them."

Wide-eyed, the clerk blurted out the building number and nervously reached for a key.

"Should I call 911 for additional help for you?"

Steve was darting for the door. "There's another officer out in your lot, but yes, call in and tell them Steve Renz needs help here at the Residence Inn."

•

As he drove slowly through the parking area, Terry Reid spotted a Saturn four-door in the blue-green color, parked at the rear of the complex. He pulled up behind the car and climbed out of his so he could take a closer look. A woman was just coming out of one of the rooms in the building to the left of where the Saturn was parked. A huge woman, in a flowered dress with an old-fashioned, small hat perched on her head. Terry observed she was having some difficulty with her eyes. She stopped and rubbed them with her right hand and then squinted, staring at him. She then continued toward him. Terry was surprised at how quickly she was able to move for such a large woman. As she approached closer she asked nervously in a trembling, squeaky voice, "Are you here to investigate the gunshots? Are you a policeman?"

Terry nodded as he reached for his gun and removed it from his shoulder holster. "Yes, I'm with the police. What's this about gun shots?"

She smiled. Seemingly relieved, she rubbed her eyes again before saying, "Thank goodness, I thought you might be with them. I think someone may be injured. There were three or four shots."

The woman was breathing heavily as she continued to speak in the same high-pitched tone and move closer toward Terry.

"There was a scream, I think it was a woman. From that room," she said, pointing out the room next to the one she'd just come from a moment before and moving within inches of Terry's side. As Terry glanced in the direction she'd pointed, he failed to see her raising her arm. She lowered it in a flash, delivering a karate chop to Terry's shoulder. The pain was awesome, a bone must have been shattered. Dazed and stunned, he was able to turn his head to see a balled fist coming at him a second before it slammed into his nose. Though the gun was still in his hand, he'd lost all control of his arm. His knees had begun to buckle as he was struck in the face again. The last thing he remembered before blacking out was collapsing onto the asphalt parking lot and being viciously kicked in the head as the woman tried to pry the revolver from his clenched hand.

•

Kath was still tying her shoe laces as Kelly opened the door. Peering out, she saw the Saturn, still parked in the same spot they'd left it.

"The car's still there," she called over her shoulder as she started out the doorway toward it with the gun in her hand. Kelly froze as she saw what appeared to be a body lying behind the car. Kath, who'd been just behind her, nearly stumbled into her. They were temporarily distracted by a loud sound of crunching metal. Startled, they looked up and saw a car had crashed into another vehicle, parked near the entrance to the complex. The backup lights came on as the car reversed and then quickly started forward again, weaving in an erratic fashion, moving toward the exit onto Victors Way. Turning their attention back to the body they'd seen, they saw it was a man's body.

"Oh, no," Kelly said, "it's Terry Reid."

Seeing Kath's questioning look she added, "A fellow detective, he must have tried to stop him."

Both grimaced as they saw his bludgeoned face, blood streaming from his nose.

"Get a couple towels from the room," Kelly directed Kath, as she dropped to her knees next to Terry feeling for a pulse.

•

As Steve dashed out of the office, he heard the screech of brakes. He looked toward the street where a car had nearly been broadsided as it exited the Residence Inn lot, making a left turn onto Victors Way. Steve recognized the car which had nearly been hit as either his own, or a similar department vehicle. Looking in the opposite direction he saw someone kneeling in the rear of the parking lot next to what appeared to be another person lying on the pavement. Hesitating for only a moment, he ran towards them.

•

Kelly, hearing the sound of someone running, glanced up and saw a man approaching them. As she started to stand, she recognized Steve. Kath, coming out of the doorway of their room with a handful of towels, also saw the man racing toward Kelly. Steve's face lit up as he drew close enough to recognize Kelly and then spotted Kath. Seconds later he was standing next to them, quickly taking in the scene.

"Am I glad to see you," he said to them as he kneeled down next to Terry. He reached for one of the towels Kath was holding and cleared the blood from Reid's nose and mouth. He folded one of the towels and carefully lifted Terry's head, sliding the towel underneath.

"Is there a working phone in there?" he asked, pointing to the open door of the room Kath had come from.

Two police cruisers had just turned into the drive of the Residence Inn. As he headed for the room, Steve spotted them and raced back into the lot, waving his hands over his head to get their attention.

"We can call for an EMS unit from one of the cars," he explained to Kelly and Kath. "I think McConnell's in my car, headed towards State Street."

The car in which Mike and Larry were riding screeched to a halt next to Steve. Mike had his door open as the car came to a standstill and leaped out.

"Kelly and Kath are okay?" he asked.

Steve nodded. "But Terry Reid's been badly injured. He really worked him over. Can I use your phone to call for an EMS unit?"

Mike spotted Kelly on her knees next to Reid, adjusting the towel which had been placed under his head. He walked over and placed his hand on her shoulder.

"Judy provided us with some of the details," Mike said. "What an ordeal! I can't tell you how relieved we were to hear you were safe. Both of you," he added, looking over at Kath.

He gave Kelly's shoulder a squeeze as she looked up at him. Kath observed both their expressions, thinking how right she'd been in her belief Mike was in love with Kelly. She could sense Kelly was aware of this as well as she caught the two's exchange of eye contact. Mike glanced over at Kath again, aware she'd been watching them.

"I hear you took a stupid risk," he said to her. "Thank God it worked. I couldn't be prouder. I'm anxious to hear all the details, but first we have to track that bastard down."

"He's in my car," Steve volunteered, having completed the call requesting emergency medical attention for Reid. "Five minutes ahead of us at the most, headed west towards State Street. Maybe on I-94 by now. We can set up roadblocks."

"We saw him crash into a car on his way out of the lot," Kelly said. "It might mean he's having trouble seeing. It could slow him down."

"Good!" Mike replied. "We need a break."

Looking over his shoulder at Martino, he asked, "Are we getting any kind of a read on which direction he's moving?"

Larry shook his head. "We still have considerable interference. Near as I can pinpoint it, he's just west of here. Possibly the Briarwood area. It doesn't appear he's on the expressway or heading south on State or north into the campus area."

"One of the problems we have," Mike reminded them, "is the fact he's in your car, Steve, with access to any communications we make on our

279

current frequency."

Two more police cars had pulled up as Mike was speaking. "I'll phone David and Judy and get us on another frequency. Before we split up, we'll inform everyone what it is. Then we'll blanket the Briarwood area in hopes we'll soon have a better fix on his position or the direction he's heading. Maybe we'll spot your car in one of the Briarwood lots. Make sure everyone knows the license number, Steve."

While he'd been talking, Mike had been dialing headquarters. He was able to get David and Judy on a speaker phone and quickly brought them up to date. He also was given a new frequency band to use so McConnell wouldn't be privy to their communications. Meanwhile Steve had drawn out a grid of the Briarwood shopping center area on a slip of paper and was making assignments of the geographical area each team would cover. Guests from the Residence Inn, including the two who'd called the office reporting hearing gunshots, were now mingling with the police in the parking lot. Kath and Kelly returned to the room they'd been held hostage in to retrieve the items they'd been forced to remove from their pockets. In their haste, they hadn't taken the time to bother with them when they'd put their warm ups on. Kelly hesitated before stuffing the wired bra and panties she'd been wearing into her pocket.

Kath noticed and said, "Might as well take them, a great souvenir if nothing else. He cut mine, but wouldn't you love to ram them down that S.O.B.'s throat?"

Kelly nodded as she said, "I'm sure we can make arrangements to drop you off at the Sheraton. You must be exhausted, a hot shower . . . "

"You have to be kidding!" Kath interrupted, a surprised look on her face. "My adrenaline's still flowing. Please don't cut me out now."

Kelly laughed. "Just thought I'd ask. I'm sure Mike will go along with us both staying involved. We better get back to them before they forget about us."

Kath smirked. "Mike's not about to forget about you," she said as Kelly blushed.

•

Several of the officers had already left for the Briarwood area in their cars. Mike was discussing an idea David had proposed with Larry and Steve. He'd suggested the possibility of broadcasting some erroneous information over their regular channel in hopes McConnell would hear it and relax his guard, expose himself. One idea was to announce that all available units were assigned to roadblocks on I-94.

"One problem I see is the fact we've already sent some units in readily identifiable cruisers over to Briarwood," Steve said. "We could also confuse some of our own people who still aren't aware of the change in channels."

Martino nodded, saying, "Let's not rule it out just yet, maybe the opportunity will present itself."

"Or someone could come up with a better idea that may work," Mike said. "Let's get ourselves over to Briarwood."

Kelly and Kath had returned, rejoining the group. Mike looked up. "Why don't the two of you ride with Larry and me. That is, unless you'd rather not. After all you've been through, you might . . ."

They were both shaking their heads. "We're ready when you are, we're not about to bow out now."

Mike grinned. "I thought that might be the case. I think we're set."

## Chapter 46

Marcie Steinfeld was coming out the door of Jacobson's department store at the Briarwood Mall, accompanied by her four-year-old daughter, Melissa. Marcie smiled down at her daughter, who was experiencing considerable difficulty in carrying a large Jacobson's bag. Among the purchases in the bag was a new dress for Melissa to wear when they visited Marcie's parents for Thanksgiving.

"Careful, don't let it drag on the ground," Marcie reminded her daughter.

The two walked into the parking lot towards their white Dodge minivan. As Marcie removed the keys to the van from her purse, she noticed a woman staring at them. The lady was huge, in a flowered-print dress with a tiny white hat perched on her head. She was squinting as she walked towards them. Marcie hoped her daughter wouldn't make a comment which might prove embarrassing. A few weeks ago in the grocery store, Melissa had asked a man why his nose was so big and red. He'd laughed it off, but Marcie had been mortified. She'd had a lengthy discussion with Melissa after that incident. This would be a good test to learn whether Melissa had benefited from that experience.

Marcie had her key in the door lock when the woman said, "Pardon me, I need your help."

The woman had a deep baritone voice. Marcie smiled as she turned around, facing the woman.

"I need you to chauffeur me, just a couple minutes of your time."

"Which direction are you headed?" Marcie inquired. "We live towards Saline. We'll be going south on Main Street. Will that help?"

"No, I need to go up to the central campus area. You can just drop me off near Hill Auditorium."

"I'm sorry, maybe you can find someone else headed that way. We really have to be headed home. We're late as it is," Marcie replied, somewhat angered at the brashness of the woman, boldly assuming they'd go out of their way to accommodate her.

Melissa was looking up at the woman. Marcie glanced around to see if there were any other people nearby who might be able to oblige the woman.

"Sorry, but I really do need your help," the woman said. The tone of her voice had changed – it was clearly a man's voice. The woman lifted her dress and Marcie could see she was wearing pants, rolled up to just below the knee. The woman had reached under her dress and removed a handgun which had been tucked in her waistband.

"No one needs to get hurt. Get that door open. I need your full cooperation; your daughter's safety is in your hands."

Horrified, Marcie saw the woman had aimed the gun at Melissa.

"Is that a real gun?" her daughter asked. Marcie nodded as she opened the car door.

"You two in front," the woman said, reaching for the Jacobson's bag in Melissa's hands. Melissa stepped back a couple steps and pulled the bag closer to her chest.

"Let her have the bag, sweetheart," Marcie said, a tremble in her voice. "Jump up into the seat, I'll buckle you up."

"Remember now," McConnell said, "no screaming, no beeping the horn. Don't try to attract anyone's attention. You'd just be asking for trouble."

Melissa was still staring wide-eyed at the woman as her mother strapped her in the car seat. "She talks the same as Daddy."

Marcie nodded. "We have to do what she, he says, Melissa. We're going to take a short drive with him before we head for home."

McConnell smiled as he lifted his skirt and climbed into the side door of the van. "You're right, this won't take long. You're doing just fine."

As he sat down behind the little girl, he pointed the revolver at the back of her head so her mother would see what he was doing as she walked around the front of the van and then stepped up to seat herself behind the steering wheel.

"Remember, no one needs to be hurt. I want you to just drive as you would normally and remember, don't get any ideas. A fender bender could prove disastrous."

McConnell explained to Marcie the route he wanted her to take, around the west end of Briarwood and then north on Main, towards the central campus. As they proceeded around the shopping center, he noticed a couple police cars to their right, driving slowly up and down the lanes of the parking lot between the rows of cars. He rubbed his hand over his eyes, in an attempt to clear up some of the blurring. They might be searching for the car I was driving, he thought, happy with his decision to abandon it so soon.

A few moments later, as they were stopped waiting for the light to change at the intersection of Main and Eisenhower, McConnell squinted, seeing two police cars coming south on Main, approaching the intersection. He could tell the woman had also spotted them.

"Don't even think of trying to attract their attention," he whispered in her ear as he lowered himself to the floor of the van, so he wouldn't be seen. "Remember where my gun's pointed."

•

The car in which Kelly and Kath were riding along with Mike and Larry was driving past the entrance of Sears on the north side of the shopping center.

"He's close by," Martino said, nodding to the monitor which was picking up a strong, intermittent signal. All of them were poised, staring out the windows of the car, hoping to catch a glimpse of McConnell or the car at any minute. In the parking area on their right, they could see one of the other teams slowly driving down an aisle.

"They've found the car!" It was Judy's voice over the speaker. "Abandoned, just to the west of Jacobson's entrance."

283

Martino swung the car around in a quick U-turn and accelerated around the east end of the center in the direction of Jacobson's.

"People are being questioned now," Judy continued. "So far no one's been found who's seen him. If you're there Mike, call in and let me know if you want us to continue on this new frequency or go back to our normal one."

Steve waved at their car as he saw them headed to where he stood, in front of Jacobson's. They all lowered their windows as Martino pulled to a stop next to Steve.

"We're in luck," he began excitedly, leaning down towards Mike's open window. "We just talked with a man who'd been standing outside Jacobson's, having a cigarette. We think he saw McConnell, a large woman in a floral-patterned dress wearing a hat, talking to a young woman and a small child over in that area of the lot a few minutes ago. He says they all entered a white-colored van. He doesn't know the make. They drove off in that direction."

Martino was bending over the monitor. "The read we're getting indicates the signals are originating north of here. Take a look Mike. I'd guess he's headed towards town, on Main rather than State Street."

•

Glancing in her rearview mirror, Marcie could see their passenger was once again sitting on the back seat. He'd dumped the contents of the Jacobson's shopping bag onto the seat to his left and had hiked up his dress. He was removing objects from underneath the dress and tossing them into the Jacobson's bag. McConnell noticed his actions were being observed in the rearview mirror and broke into a smile. He leaned forward and held out a couple packets of twenty-dollar bills so the woman could see them.

"Do you like candy?" he asked the little girl. Melissa looked back at him, her face in a frown, holding her lips tightly together. Marcie gasped as she turned to stare at the money. He must be a bank robber, she thought.

"This is enough money to buy heaps of candy for you and your friends. And I'm going to give it to your mother. You should be smiling young lady."

The van was passing the U of M golf course, nearing the traffic light at the intersection of Main and Stadium.

"The money's yours on one condition. An easy way to earn over

$1,000. You first have to forget about me and this side-trip after I leave you."

Marcie was scared and remained silent as she looked back at McConnell.

He smiled again. "That's probably too much to ask or expect, isn't it?" he asked. "Why don't we agree you'll just drive home first after you drop me off, before you contact the police or say anything to anyone about me. That's easy enough, isn't it?"

Marcie nodded, with a glimmer of hope Melissa and she would be able to escape this ordeal without harm.

"Agreed?" he asked again.

"Yes," Marcie quickly answered.

"Good, I trust you," he said as he gently tossed the two packets of money next to her on the seat.

They'd driven through the intersection and were passing the Michigan football stadium on their right.

"I want you to turn on Hoover and go over to State Street. In another ten minutes, I'll be history."

Sensing her mother's anxiety, Melissa has begun to sob. "Tell her to stop," he said to her mother. "I don't want anyone noticing us, wondering why your little girl is crying."

Marcie spoke to her daughter in soothing tones, assuring her everything was going to be fine and this man in the funny outfit would be getting out of their car in just a few minutes.

"Please don't cry Melissa. We'll be home soon."

As they passed the U of M's swimming and diving complex on their right, he instructed Marcie again.

"Make a left turn onto State. We're headed for Hill Auditorium."

They had to wait for the light to change before making the left turn. At this time of day, traffic was heavy. They also had to wait for the light at the intersection of State and Packard. They were the third car in line waiting for the light to change. McConnell was continuing to empty his pockets, placing packets of money in the bag. The light changed and the small sports car, two cars in front of them, sped forward into the intersection, its driver failing to see the Ford Explorer speeding south on Packard, accelerating as the light changed. There was a screech of brakes and the thunderous sounds of the crash as the utility vehicle broad-sided the tiny sports car. Shocked, Marcie bolted upright in her seat. A man who was a passenger in the car in front of them already had his door open, ready to leap out to see if he could be of assistance. The driver was already talking on his car phone, probably calling 911 to report the accident. Over a dozen pedestrians, mostly students, were staring in awe at the wreckage, some beginning to move toward the two heavily damaged vehicles.

"Damn it! We're going to be tied up here for a while and I can't wait," McConnell said, sliding open the door of the van. "Remember your promise!"

He climbed out of the van and slid the door closed. The Jacobson's bag was in his left hand. He raised the index finger of his right hand to his lips and moved alongside the van to the passenger front seat window. He grinned and blew a kiss to Melissa and then waved to Marcie. He quickly turned and hurried through the parking lot of the Bell's Pizza outlet on the corner. Marcie watched him as he glanced to his left to view the accident scene before stepping off the curb to cross Packard. There was no traffic in the southbound lane due to the accident. Cars heading north were waiting in line for the accident to clear. McConnell maneuvered between two of them, the fourth and fifth in a line, which now numbered over twenty-five vehicles.

•

Joe Lindstrom, a third-year engineering student who'd been on his bicycle heading south on Packard, had heard the sound of the crash from over two blocks away. He'd stopped and stared back to see what had happened. There appeared to be two vehicles, one a sports car, at odd angles in the middle of the intersection of State and Packard, both badly damaged. He turned his bike around and crossed over to the other side of Packard. Speeding up, he headed back towards the accident. A long line of cars was waiting for the intersection to clear. Joe flew past them. He was standing up to pedal, proceeding at a fast clip, when a large woman stepped out from between two cars directly in front of him. Though he tried to swerve to avoid hitting her, there wasn't sufficient distance or time to do so. His bike slammed into the woman, sending her sprawling onto the pavement between the line of cars and the curb. Joe sailed over the handlebars of his bike, tumbling onto the street next to the woman, his head bouncing off the curb.

·

Martha Roberts was sitting in her car wondering how long it might take for the accident scene up ahead to be cleared. She hoped no one had been seriously injured. She glanced at her watch. She still had twenty minutes until her dental appointment. Looking in her rearview mirror, she saw a large-bodied woman in a floral print dress crossing the street, making her way between the bumpers of her car and the car behind her. The woman appeared to stop and look to her right in the direction of a boy on a bicycle who was speeding toward her on the strip of pavement between the curb and the line of parked cars. Either her eyes were bad or she'd had her mind on other things, Martha concluded, as the woman walked directly into the path of the bike. Martha gasped as the cyclist collided with the woman. Both fell to the pavement. Martha lowered the window on the passenger side and slid across the seat.

The woman was struggling to get to her feet. Her dress was soiled and torn. Her hair, Martha saw it was a wig, was in a cockeyed position on her head and the woman was attempting to adjust it, along with the small hat attached to it, back into place.

Martha assumed she must have been carrying the large Jacobson's shopping bag which had ripped open and was now resting on the street a few feet in front of her. Martha's eyes widened as she saw what appeared to be bundled stacks of money scattered on the pavement around the bag.

The boy, who'd been riding the bike was groaning, holding his head in his hands. He also appeared to be bleeding from cuts on his forehead and elbow. Dazed, he was attempting to sit up as he mumbled to the woman he was sorry. She'd picked up the Jacobson's bag and had it clutched to her chest. A boy who'd been walking down the sidewalk a few feet ahead of where the accident occurred, had come to the woman's aid. He'd leaned down and picked up two of the packets of money. Martha saw his look of surprise as he realized what he was holding and that there were additional bundles of money still in the street. He reached out to hand the money to the woman.

"Stay away from me," the woman screamed. The boy jumped back, surprised at her reaction and also the masculine tone of her voice.

"It's yours!" the woman said to the boy, pointing to the additional stacks of money which had fallen from the bag. "Just don't try to follow me."

Hearing the commotion, other bystanders, mostly students, were coming to investigate what was happening as the woman turned and began to run, crossing the sidewalk and disappearing between two houses. Martha and the others would later recall how surprised they were to see how quickly she'd moved for such a large woman.

•

Martino's car was just passing the U of M Stadium when the report of the car collision at the intersection of Packard and State came over the speaker. Moments before, Judy Wilson had relayed the information a road block had been set up on North Main just south of the entrance to M-14 and US-23, the expressways north of town.

"The signals from the money appear to have changed," Martino noted. "Northeast now, rather than due north. Actually in the direction of State and Packard, where that accident occurred."

"Wouldn't it be something if he was involved in a car crash?" Kath asked. "After the string of lucky breaks he's had, it's about time for a turn."

•

Kelly and Kath had supplied Mike and Larry details of their ordeal at the Residence Inn, explaining how the stacks of money in McConnell's vest had allowed him to avoid being injured by Kath's gunfire. Either that or his gun had been loaded with blanks, but that hadn't been true as bullets had shattered the mirror and the door. Kelly expressed her belief that McConnell may have been wounded by the latter shot. She thought she'd heard him groan in anguish after yanking the door shut behind him.

•

"Let's cross over to State on Hoover," Mike said. "I'll let the team ahead of us know what we're doing and have them continue on Main," he added, picking up the phone. "We'll direct the others to work their way over to the State Street area."

Let's hope he doesn't reverse his tracks now, Mike thought. Possibly head back south on State to I-94 or Saline. When they reached State Street,

288

Larry turned left onto the south-bound lane, which was empty due to the accident, and drove the short distance to the Packard intersection. A police cruiser, an EMS vehicle, and a crowd of spectators were there to greet them. The four of them exited the car and quickly moved through the crowd toward the accident scene.

"Looks as if that small sports car and that black, I think, Ford Explorer are the two that collided," Martino said with a note of disappointment, hoping to find it was the white van McConnell was believed to be in.

Larry and Mike had moved a few yards ahead of the two women when Kath tugged on Kelly's arm and said, "Was I the only one who noticed that white van waiting in line when we drove by?" She pointed it out to Kelly.

"Glad you were noticing," Kelly replied, seeing a woman behind the wheel and what appeared to be a young child, a little girl, in the passenger seat.

"It's certainly worth checking out," Kelly said as they moved towards the van. "I'm surprised none of us spotted it. Maybe you're going to end up with a permanent job."

Kelly suddenly remembered that she no longer had her gun. There was the possibility McConnell might be armed and hiding in the van. She held up her hand, signaling for Kath to wait, saying, "It may be best for us to get Mike or Larry, to be on the safe side."

Kath nodded as Kelly walked back towards the accident. She spotted Mike and called out to him. Hearing her, he turned and saw her motioning for him to come join her. She briefed him as they walked back towards Kath. Mike complemented them for not having investigated on their own. The woman behind the wheel of the van saw them approaching and lowered her window. When they were about ten yards from her, she called out, "Are you with the police?" She was staring at the gun in Mike's hand.

Even Kath was nodding yes as Mike replied, "Yes we are; detectives, in case you're wondering about lack of uniforms."

"Oh, thank goodness." There were tears of relief in her eyes. "My daughter and I were kidnapped by a woman, a woman I think was really a man, I . . ."

"Where is he now?" Mike asked.

"I think we were saved by the accident. He just left us, a couple minutes ago, headed in that direction," she said pointing to her right. "The last I saw of him, he was crossing Packard."

Reaching down next to her she picked up the two stacks of twenty-dollar bills she'd been given. "Here," she said handing them to Mike. "He gave me this money and tried to get me to promise I'd drive home first before I tried to contact the police. He wanted to be dropped off near Hill Auditorium. That's where we were headed until this accident. Thank heavens for it, even though I'm sorry about the people involved. Whoever was in the sports car might be seriously injured. But at least my little girl's safe now," she said reaching over and placing her arm around her daughter's shoulders.

"You're right, the accident was probably a blessing," Mike said, nodding in agreement. "The man's armed and dangerous. I realize it must have been a harrowing experience, but consider yourselves lucky. We'll need to have your name and phone number so we can be back in touch with you. Right now, we need to try to catch up to him. Was he still wearing the dress when he left you?"

The woman nodded. "He was also carrying a shopping bag of ours from Jacobson's. He'd stuffed several stacks of money, like those I gave you, into it. He had them hidden under the dress and . . . "

Mike interrupted her, turning to Kath. "Hear that? Find Larry and have him call in. Tell him where he was last seen, the fact he's carrying a Jacobson's bag. Kelly and I will head over to see what we can find out. Someone in one of those cars held up in line over there must have seen him."

Kath hurried toward the accident scene to try to locate Larry as Kelly and Mike headed across Packard, their attention drawn to a cluster of students on the opposite side of one of the cars waiting in line. A heated discussion was in progress, including some pushing and shoving. Mike shouted out as he darted between the bumpers of two of the cars.

"Hold it! We're police officers."

Mike had removed his identification and held it over his head as he surveyed the group of approximately ten students.

"What's going on?" he asked as he observed at least two of the men had one or more stacks of money in their hands. At least three more packets of money were scattered on the pavement next to where the young men were standing. One boy tossed the packet he was holding back onto the pavement, while another boy hurriedly attempted to stash the money into the pocket of his jacket. All ten, including the two women in the group, began answering Mike, seemingly at the same time.

Mike raised his hands to quiet them. "We're after the man who dropped this money. Did any . . . "

"It was a woman," one of the girls said, interrupting him.

"A man dressed as a woman," Mike answered. "Did any of you see which way he headed?"

"Between those two houses," one of the boys answered as he pointed. "He threatened us and Ginny, here, thinks she saw a gun."

Mike and Kelly nodded as they noticed a uniformed officer approaching the group from the intersection, accompanied by a woman. Turning to Kelly, Mike said, "I'll have him try to sort out things here while we go after McConnell."

Mike recognized the officer, Bill Tway, and quickly briefed him on the situation. They learned the woman accompanying him had been the driver of the car next to where they were standing. She'd sought out the officer and told him about the woman being hit by the bicycle and the packets of money tumbling out of the shopping bag. Tway asked the woman to describe to Mike and Kelly the injuries to the woman she'd observed.

"There was a cut just above her left eye," she said pointing to her own forehead. "A small one, not much blood. She had a pavement burn, some deep scratches on her left cheek. Some bleeding there, too. I knew she was wearing a wig. It was knocked off kilter when she fell. When she screamed at those boys, she sounded like a man."

"Yes, she's actually a man in disguise," Kelly explained. "The suspected murderer you've probably read about in the paper."

The woman had smiled when Kelly explained, yes, it had been a man in women's clothing. But she'd turned ashen white when Kelly explained who he was.

Kelly turned to Bill Tway. "Let the others know in case you need assistance here. Also try to locate Martino and advise him the direction Mike and I are heading. Tell him we think he's headed toward campus, possibly the Hill Auditorium area."

•

Kelly and Mike hurried up the driveway between the two houses along the route they'd been told McConnell had taken. Mike held his gun partially concealed alongside his leg. Kelly was deep in the thought as they hurried on and suddenly placed her hand on Mike's left arm.

"Mike, I have strong vibes he might be headed to Kath's apartment.

It's only about three blocks away. He needs a place to clean up, attend to his injuries."

Mike glanced at her and nodded his head. "I think you're on to something, it would make sense. Maybe we should split up. You could go back and round up Larry and Kath and whoever else is there. Do you think Kath has a key with her?"

"I doubt it," Kelly answered. "He had us empty our pockets and I didn't notice one, but she may have a key hidden. I'd be surprised if she didn't."

"You're probably right," Mike said. "Chances are, I'll meet you at the apartment. If not, you'll know I've been able to track him in another direction, possibly talked to someone who spotted him."

Kelly nodded, turned and darted back between the houses as Mike turned and headed for Kath's apartment.

## Chapter 47

The temperature seemed to have dropped at least ten degrees in the last half hour. Kelly calculated it must have dipped into the thirties as she jogged toward the intersection. She waved to Bill Tway and shouted she was going to try to find Larry and call in a report. She noticed he had a half-dozen of the banded packets of money clutched in his hand. She shivered as she glanced up at the sky, now dark and filled with ominous-looking storm clouds. She sighted Larry and Kath a few yards from the car they'd arrived in, walking towards it. They were already in the car by the time they noticed Kelly running toward them. Kelly quickly briefed them, explaining how McConnell had been struck by the boy on the bike and describing his injuries.

"Wish it were worse," Kath said. "That damn vest has been a shield for him. If I'd only aimed for his face, we wouldn't . . . "

Kelly shook her head. "Forget that, Kath. We think he may be headed to your apartment. We'll head over there, I'll report in on our way."

Martino backed up and swung the car around, driving a couple blocks south on State before turning left on one of the side streets to work his way over to Packard to Kath's apartment. Kelly reached Judy on the phone and brought her up to date. After hanging up, she told Kath and Larry about the money which had spilled out of the shopping bag.

"Those kids thought they'd discovered buried treasure. At least one packet had broken open and those twenty-dollar bills were blowing in all directions. Mike and I spoiled the party when we explained finders-keepers wouldn't apply. Most of the students realized the money wasn't theirs and were doing their best to retrieve it. But one or two were trying to take advantage of the situation. A fight had nearly broken out when we arrived. Kath, I forgot to ask, do you have a key to the apartment with you?"

Shaking her head no, she replied, "But there should be one there, hidden in the porch light." She frowned. "Joe may know about it. If he's gone to the apartment, and I think you may be right, he might use it to get in. He could still have Beth's key though. I'd given an extra one to her."

Kath's voice had lowered as she finished speaking, a wistful look in her eyes. The three remained silent the last few minutes of the drive. Kelly's mind was racing, hopeful she'd guessed right in predicting he'd headed to the apartment to tend to his injuries and possibly change clothes. She didn't recall having seen any men's clothes in the apartment, though. The woman who'd been taken hostage along with her daughter had told them McConnell had said he was headed to the central campus area. Near Hill Auditorium. He could of said that knowing she'd eventually be talking to the police, as a red herring to throw them off his trail. But if true, why? They hadn't given any credence to his claim that one of the people being blackmailed was responsible for Beth's death. But was there something to it? Was he headed to campus to deal with that person, possibly Jameson or Hernandes? The other three didn't have offices in the campus area. Perhaps more likely, Kelly reasoned, it was an attempt by McConnell to make some sort of statement. Kath had suggested he might set off a bomb or explosive device of some kind in or near one of the campus landmarks, his final act of revenge on the University. She crossed her fingers. Let's hope he's at the apartment and we can capture him before he does more damage, before more people are injured or killed.

Larry had turned onto Packard and was headed toward the driveway next to Kath's apartment, less than fifty yards away. As he pulled into the drive they saw Mike standing in the parking area at the rear of the house talking to a young man. Larry tapped on the horn to draw Mike's attention, letting him know they'd arrived. He immediately realized he'd made an error and swore at himself. If McConnell was there, hopefully he hadn't heard the horn beep or identified it with them.

Larry stopped the car a few feet from Mike. Kelly recognized the young man standing next to him as one of the boys they'd seen and spoken to on the Saturday morning Beth's body was found. Seems like ages ago Kelly thought, as she climbed out of the car.

Mike still had his gun in his hand. He put a finger to his lips so the three of them wouldn't slam their car doors. In a lowered voice, Mike said to Kelly, "You remember Steve." Turning to Larry and Kath as Kelly nodded and shook hands with Steve, Mike informed them, "Steve's a tenant, he's in one of the apartments up front. He just arrived a few moments ahead of me and noticed a light on in your apartment Kath. I think I startled him coming up behind him with my gun drawn."

Steve nodded his head vigorously as he said, "I was going to call. You'd asked me to be on the lookout for anyone." He was staring wide-eyed at Kath. "This is eerie, I thought you were dead. It's your apartment isn't it?"

Kath nodded as she pointed and said to Mike, "There should be a key in that light fixture. I have to stand on the railing to reach it."

Mike looked over at Kelly. "I think you were right."

She nodded, replying, "The reading we've been getting from the money indicates he's here, too."

"Larry and I will go up and see if the key's there and if we can get inside," Mike said. "Call Judy, Kelly. Have her pass the word on in case we need help. I'd suggest you go out front Steve, there could be some bullets flying."

Larry had also drawn his gun, starting up the stairs to the apartment.

Turning to Kath, Mike said, "Go out front and be on the lookout for any patrol cars. Wave them over if you see any."

Kath opened her mouth to object. "Can't I watch from here? Steve can be on the lookout without my help."

"No time to argue," said Mike mounting the stairs behind Larry. "I don't want you being struck by a stray bullet or in any kind of position where he can seize you as a hostage or threaten to shoot you. Out front!" Mike said, waving his hand in that direction.

•

A few sprinkles had started as Kelly re-entered Larry's car. Before reaching for the phone, she turned on the windshield wipers so she could better observe the two men as they reached the top of the stairs. Standing on tip-toe Larry was able to open the top of the porch light and reach down, probing for the key. His face lit up as he felt it and removed it. The two were conversing in whispered tones, plotting their course of action, as Kelly dialed the command center at police headquarters. Judy answered after only one ring. The sprinkles had now turned into heavy raindrops and Kelly was temporarily startled by a bolt of lightning, quickly followed by a peal of thunder. She turned the wipers up to maximum speed as the rain began to fall in torrents, splashing off the hood of the car and thundering on the roof.

"Hi Judy, it's me, Kelly again. Can you hear me over this rain?"

•

Larry turned the key in the door lock and nodded to Mike. He shoved the door open as the two framed the doorway, guns raised in their hands. There was no overhang over the door and both were becoming rapidly soaked as they peered around the door casing into the apartment. They saw the flowered dress on the floor in the center of the room with the hat and wig McConnell had been wearing laying next to it. There was no sign of him, but the door which Mike remembered having led into the bedroom was shut.

Mike charged into the room first, in a crouch and rolled to the floor surveying the kitchen area of the apartment which had been hidden from their view. Still no sign of him. Mike motioned Larry inside as he stood and walked to the sink where a pile of dish towels sat. The water was still on and Mike held up one of the towels to point out the blood stains on it. He tossed a clean one to Larry so he could wipe the rain from his head and face as he mouthed the words, "He's here," pointing to the door of the bedroom. Moving alongside one another they discussed their next step in whispered tones. "I think the element of surprise is probably past," Mike said. "Let's position ourselves on both sides of the door and I'll announce we're here and ask him to give himself up." Larry nodded in understanding and agreement.

"We're outside the door, Joe. We're armed and the apartment's surrounded." Mike hoped this was now the case, that the backup units had arrived or soon would. "Come out with both hands on your head," Mike shouted. "Now! You have one minute to comply. Otherwise, we'll be using tear gas. Save yourself some grief."

Mike smiled and shrugged his shoulders, realizing his threat of tear gas was a bluff. A good idea, but a bluff, unless one of them went back down to Larry's car to get some canisters or another unit arrived equipped with some. Reading Mike's mind, Larry shook his head, indicating there were none in his car.

Mike mouthed the words, "On the count of three" before shouting, "You have thirty seconds." Mike tried the door knob and found it unlocked. He shoved the door open as they once again hid behind the door frame. Peeking into the room, they saw no sign of McConnell. What they did see, however, was distressing. The bed had been stripped with blankets strewn on the floor next to it. The window was open with the curtains blowing. The bed had been moved next to the open window and a roping of sheets was tied to the metal bed frame, draped over the window ledge and out the open window. Larry's face flushed in anger as he headed toward the window. Mike grabbed his sleeve and pointed to the door of the bathroom which was closed. A closet door next to the closed door stood open and the closet appeared to be empty.

Still whispering Mike said, "It may be another trick of his. He may be hiding in there hoping we'll assume he went out of the window and we'll charge off after him. Either that or attacking us while we're both leaning out the window with our backs to him.

"We know you're in there, Joe," Mike called out. "Last chance. Come out now."

There was only silence. Mike tried the door and found it was unlocked. Shoving it open, they could see the bathroom was empty. But Larry pointed toward the bathtub and closed shower curtain as he said to Mike, "Stand back and cover me." He walked over and pulled the curtain aside. The tub was empty.

## Chapter 48

Kelly's face reflected her disappointment as Mike briefed her on what they'd found. Rain was still falling heavily as they sat in the front seat of Larry's car.

"Do you remember what he was wearing under the dress?" Mike asked her. "We'll check with Kath and have her look over the apartment to see if any clothes are missing, but chances are he's still wearing the same clothes he had on under the vest and dress."

"You saw him, too," Kelly answered. "Except he was wearing a golf sweater then. The pants are tan and the golf shirt was plain white. It could have been a Polo or possibly Brooks Brothers. Just a small logo, nothing unique about it or the pants. Nothing special about his shoes either that I recall. Possibly Reeboks, a sports shoe of some kind, white."

Over Mike's shoulder, Kelly saw Kath and Larry approaching the car. She was drenched, her warm up was soaked and her hair was matted to her head. Kelly pointed for them to climb in the back seat. In response to Mike's question of whether she'd seen any sign of McConnell, Kath simply shook her head no, her disappointment was obvious.

"What I'd like you to do, Kath is go up to the apartment with Kelly. See if you can see anything missing, particularly clothing, which McConnell might have taken, be wearing now. Also try . . . "

Two police cars were pulling up next to them, two officers were already out of their cars coming toward them. They were dressed in raincoats. Mike lowered his window and spoke briefly to the officers before turning back toward Kelly and Kath.

"Why don't you go ahead and check out the apartment. Can you find some dry clothes for yourself up there, Kath? Maybe an extra raincoat for Kelly?"

•

The search of the apartment proved futile. Even though there were several articles of clothing belonging to Kath that he might have been able to use, such as bulky sweatshirts, nothing appeared to be missing. While Kath changed clothes, Kelly had tried to clean up the apartment a little, pulling the sheets back inside and closing the window. She was mopping up the puddle in front of the window with the dry portion of the sheet which had been tied to the bed frame when she heard Kath cry out.

"Finally! It's the first thing I should have thought of, an umbrella is missing. A big one, yellow and blue."

Kath saw Kelly's initial excited expression fade from her face. She could read her mind. There must be over a thousand yellow and blue umbrellas, U of M's colors, on the streets of Ann Arbor at this moment.

Kath smiled. "I know what you're thinking, but the one missing is a little unique. There's a logo of Mr. Peanut$^{(tm)}$, you know the Planter's

Peanut[(tm)] character in the top hat with a cane. It's not a Michigan umbrella. Joe had given it to Beth."

Kelly smiled in return. "At least it's something. We could possibly put out a public announcement, radio and TV in addition to getting the word out internally. I'll go tell Mike while you're finishing getting dressed."

"Hold on, here's a raincoat for you. I also have these two other umbrellas."

As Kelly took the raincoat she looked at the two umbrellas. One was in a floral pattern, but the other was black. Why wouldn't he have taken the non-descript black one, instead of the one he chose? Still playing games, Kelly thought.

•

Mike nodded as Kelly told him about the missing umbrella and smiled.

"We may be in luck. We've had the other officers checking out the neighborhood to see if anyone spotted him. One just reported talking to a woman who remembers seeing a man who matched our description – the tan pants, white golf shirt, mid-thirties and so forth. He had a blue and yellow umbrella and was carrying a black trash bag. The woman recalled seeing him because she'd mentioned to her friend, the man must be freezing in his short-sleeved shirt. We'll check back with her to see if she remembers a logo on the umbrella. It could have been him. He was heading up toward Hill Street, jogging through the puddles."

Kath had opened the rear door of the car and was climbing in as Mike tooted the horn to get Larry's attention. He was standing next to one of the patrol cars with another officer.

"Get Judy on the phone and tell her what we have," Mike said to Kelly. "Suggest we get the campus area saturated with patrol cars as well as a foot detail from Hill Street north, State Street to Washtenaw. The complete area south of Huron."

As Larry quickly jumped in the car, Kelly could sense the mood of depression, which McConnell's escape had left them all in, reversing itself. She updated Judy as Martino drove out of the drive onto Packard. The accident had been cleared and traffic was moving normally, though heavy due to the time of day, just past five-thirty. Kelly halted her conversation for a moment and turned to Mike who had just given Larry directions to drive up to Hill Street and make a couple passes through that area.

"Should I suggest putting out an alert over the radio, TV, too, with a description of him, how we think he's dressed, a description of the umbrella and the fact he has a cut on his forehead?"

Mike thought for a moment before answering her. "It's going to be getting dark in a few minutes. We don't want some student to risk injury trying to apprehend him, any civilian for that matter. Our first priority should be to alert all law enforcement personnel – the campus police, the sheriff's department – get them all involved. Then, yes, let's suggest pulling out all the stops. Go ahead, have Judy run the idea past David."

•

Professor George Jurkow was proceeding toward his car which was parked on the second floor of the parking structure on Hill Street, behind the Business School. A staff meeting had run a little later than expected. He glanced at his watch. He'd promised his wife he'd be home before six, to be ready to entertain some good friends of theirs from out of town. He planned to swing by the Big Ten Party Store on his way home to pick up some wine. Glad I brought my raincoat this morning he thought, having observed the torrential downpour on the way to his car.

Jurkow pressed the button on his keychain to unlock the car door. He sensed someone or something behind him and turned as he reached for the door handle. All he saw was the top of a large yellow and blue umbrella for a brief second before he was slammed into the car. Winded, he gasped for air as someone grabbed his hair and turned his head to the side. The muzzle of a gun was being forced against his teeth. A man of approximately the same size and build as him was whispering in his ear, his face inches from his own. This can't be happening he thought, his fear mounting as he stared into the eyes of his assailant.

"No noise, no resistance, or you're a dead man. Understood?"

Jurkow, still gasping for breath, tried to nod his head. The pain from nearly having his scalp ripped off was intense. The man lifted Jurkow's head a couple inches off the roof of the car and then smashed the side of his head against the surface. Jurkow felt the man's grip relax. The pressure of the gun barrel against Jurkow's jaw was reduced as the man spoke again.

"I need your raincoat. I'm going to step back. Take it off slowly, put it on the hood and then get in the car."

Jurkow did as he was told, still trembling in hopes the worst was over.

299

Don't provoke him into using the gun he said to himself, as he stood and struggled out of his raincoat. The man's crazed expression terrified him. Don't stare at him, he reminded himself. He'd noticed the man's face was scratched, with a Band-Aid on his forehead. Evil was the only adjective he could think of to describe the look in the eyes of the man pointing the gun at his face. Jurkow saw the umbrella, still open, resting on the cement surface behind his car. As he placed his raincoat on the hood, he heard another car just coming down the ramp from the third floor of the structure. His assailant had also heard it.

"Just relax and act normally. Any tricks and whoever is driving that car is a goner too. I don't want to kill anyone. Don't make me."

Jurkow was frightened. Rather than viewing the approaching car as a blessing, he saw it as the possible factor which would push this madman over the edge. But to his surprise, the man's expression changed, a friendly smile spreading over his face. He'd shifted the gun to his left hand and was holding out his right hand extending a handshake to Jurkow. Even more amazing was the change in the tone of the man's voice to a lilting English accent.

"Sorry, ol' chap, about having to meet under such unfavorable circumstances. I'd deem it an honor if you could return my smile."

The car slowed as it approached them and the driver had lowered his window. Jurkow had turned his head toward the car and recognized Paul Tiblet, a fellow professor at the Business School.

"Looks as if you'll need that umbrella, George. It's coming down pretty hard."

Jurkow was attempting to smile, but realized he had a frozen expression. The man also smiled at Paul and raised his hand with a wave of acknowledgment. Paul nodded and said, "Hope you have a good evening in spite of the rain. See you tomorrow, George."

Jurkow nodded and watched as Tiblet raised his window and drove off. He turned back towards the man who still had a broad smile on his face.

"Good show!" he said reaching out his hand again to shake Jurkow's. Instead, in a quick motion the man had balled his fist and driven it into the pit of Jurkow's stomach. Jurkow gulped for air and leaned over. The man had taken the barrel of the gun he'd been holding into his right hand. Raising his arm he brought the gun down towards the back of Jurkow's head. Jurkow remembered trying to twist his head and duck to avoid being struck before he felt the blow and blacked out.

•

Martino turned off State onto Hill Street and slowed the car to a crawl. In the gathering dusk with the rain continuing to fall, the four of them had their eyes close to the car windows in hopes of sighting McConnell. Across from the Business School parking structure, Martino had stopped and waved for the car following them to pass. There was a burst of excitement when they caught sight of a yellow and blue umbrella a block ahead, at the South University and Hill Street four-way stop intersection. Martino accelerated, and then quickly slowed down again, as they saw it was a young coed and the umbrella had a large block "M." A patrol car had just pulled up to the intersection proceeding south. It turned on Hill towards them and they exchanged waves as the two cars passed.

"A couple more blocks, Larry and then let's turn around and double back over this stretch," Mike said. "If we strike out again, go up State to South U and we'll comb that area."

Martino had just eased to a stop at the intersection of Church and Hill. A block and a half ahead of them, another patrol car was headed toward them, prompting Kath to comment, "You'd think with so many of us looking for him, someone would be bound to see something."

A block ahead, a car had pulled over to the curb and the driver, a man, had jumped out of his car. Standing in the middle of the street, he appeared to be signaling the patrol car coming toward him to stop. Martino drove past the Kappa sorority house and the man's car, and swung left into a driveway behind the now-stopped patrol car. One of the officers was out of the car talking to the man. He turned and vigorously motioned to Martino, apparently having recognized him as they'd driven past.

"I'll see what this is about," Larry said opening his door. "I'll just be a minute or two."

They watched through the rain as Martino walked over to the officer. After only a moment or two of conversation, the officer opened the rear door of his squad car and motioned for the man they'd been talking with to get in as Larry darted back towards them. In excitement, Larry explained they thought the man, a professor at the Business School, had seen McConnell moments ago on the second floor of the Business School parking structure.

301

"We're going to follow them," Larry said as he backed out onto Hill. "This man just turned on his radio and as luck would have it, caught the tail end of the news flash about McConnell. He'd just seen an umbrella with a Mr. Peanut[tm] logo open on the floor next to a fellow professor's car in the parking ramp behind the Bus Ad School. He says the professor whose car it was appeared to be having a friendly conversation with a man whose description matches McConnell's, wearing light brown pants and a white polo shirt. He said something seemed strange about the scene when he slid his window down and mentioned something about the umbrella to his friend. Then when he heard the news bulletin over the radio, he realized George – George Jurkow is the name of the other professor – could be in danger. You saw the rest. He spotted the patrol car and flagged those officers down."

•

The two cars drove into the parking ramp. The officer driving the lead car stopped at the turn leading up to the second floor and parked at an angle to block any vehicles from exiting the structure. After a brief conversation, the two officers from the patrol car, guns drawn, hurried up the ramp while Larry and Mike, followed by the three others, crossed the parking lot to the stairwell. As they climbed the stairs, Tiblet described Jurkow's car, a dark blue, four-door Olds 88 or 98, and where it had been parked. As they exited the stairwell, they saw the other two officers approaching from the opposite direction, but no sign of McConnell or anyone else. The two officers already had the door of Jurkow's car open as they arrived at the car.

"He's alive, but unconscious," one of the officers said, pointing to Jurkow's body which was sprawled on the back seat. Papers – letters and memos – were scattered on the front seat.

Jurkow's eyes fluttered open. One of the officers had a handkerchief and was wiping some blood off Jurkow's forehead. Jurkow appeared startled for a moment as his eyes began to focus. Catching sight of Tiblet, he seemed to relax, opening and closing his mouth, trying to say something, but with no words coming forth. Finally he was able to say the word raincoat and in another moment or two, with the help of one of the officers, he managed to sit up. In a halting voice he tried to tell them what had happened. In addition to having taken his raincoat, it appeared McConnell had also taken Jurkow's briefcase. Kelly had spotted the empty black trash bag on the floor of the front seat. He must have dumped the contents of Jurkow's briefcase and filled it with the money and whatever else he'd been carrying in the trash bag.

## Chapter 49

Roy Wilbanks, a member of the University of Michigan's Campus Security Force, was standing next to the front door of the Law Library. He'd taken a position just underneath the overhang to avoid some of the downpour. He had a full view of the courtyard inside the Law Quadrangle. He was casting his gaze to and fro in hopes of seeing the man who he and

his partner had been informed about a few minutes earlier. They both knew who McConnell was. The Campus Police had been fully involved for the past few days in attempting to find and apprehend him. Roy and his partner had parked their patrol car just outside the arched entryway on the north side of the Law Quad, directly across from where he was standing. His partner had stationed himself near the University President's residence. Roy had just spoken with him on his cellular phone.

A number of students had been exiting the library during the past several minutes, dodging the raindrops as they darted through puddles on their way to their rooms in the complex, or the dining hall to Wilbank's left.

Other clusters of students were also crossing the Quadrangle on their way to dinner. Several were carrying yellow and blue umbrellas. While seeing plenty of tan colored pants, Roy didn't see anyone who matched McConnell's description. While several of the umbrellas had logos, banks and eateries in addition to U of M logos, he hadn't spotted one with a Mr. Peanut[tm]. He worried over how easy it would be for McConnell to blend in with these students in the dusk and rain. The students were laughing and shouting, most seemingly enjoying the thundershower. A couple of coeds screamed and giggled as a flash of lightning lit up the sky closely followed by the sound of thunder.

To his right, Wilbanks saw a man entering the courtyard from the southeast corner of the complex, carrying a large yellow and blue umbrella. He was wearing what looked like a fairly expensive London Fog raincoat and carrying a briefcase. He also appeared to be a little older than a normal student, maybe a professor, more likely an MBA graduate student coming from the Business School. The man was wearing athletic shoes of some sort, not surprising with the rain. Besides, everyone seemed to be into sport shoes these days, Wilbanks thought, as he stared down at his leather shoes which were taking a beating from the rain.

The man had nearly reached the center of the courtyard when Wilbanks caught a glimpse of an imprint on the umbrella. He squinted. Was it his imagination or was it, in fact, the Mr. Peanut[tm] character? Continuing to squint, he hurried down the steps to see if he could get a closer look. The man had now reached the center of the Quad and had turned toward the archway across the way. Wilbanks' heartbeat increased as he saw the design on the umbrella was the Mr. Peanut[tm] character.

"Hold up a minute! You with the yellow and blue umbrella," Wilbanks called out, breaking into a run. A group of students in their rainwear, some with umbrellas, was approaching the man on his right along the walk on the north side of the Quadrangle. Hearing Wilbanks' shouts, they looked and saw him running in their direction.

"Hey mister, he's talking to you," one of the students called out to the man who was now glancing over his shoulder back towards Wilbanks. The man broke into a run toward the archway. Wilbanks remembered they'd been warned McConnell was armed and reached for his gun. He hoped none of the students would try to confront the man as they watched what was happening. As the man ran, he maneuvered the umbrella into his left hand which held the briefcase. Suddenly he swung around, a gun now in his right hand, and fired a shot at Wilbanks. The bullet struck his left shoulder, spinning him around and sending him stumbling to the surface of the slate walkway. The man turned toward the cluster of students only a few yards away and pointed his gun at them as he screamed, "You're too young to die! Stay away from me!"

The students had frozen in horror and disbelief over what was happening. The man was now entering the archway leading to South University.

•

Martino was driving north on Tappan between the Law Quad and Martha Cook, one of the women's residence halls on campus. He was just beginning to brake at the stop sign where Tappan dead-ended into South U when the report of the shooting in the Law Quad came over the car's speaker. Turning left, he accelerated past Clements Library and the President's residence. In seconds, he'd reached the archway on the north side of the Law Quad.

A University of Michigan Campus Security patrol car was parked on the side of the walkway leading into the arch. Martino turned and drove over the curb next to it and slammed on his brakes. As the four of them quickly exited the car, they could hear the sound of a siren a few blocks away. A police car, its dome light flashing, came toward them on South U from the direction of the Michigan Union. Running through the archway, they saw a yellow and blue umbrella, still open, propped against the south wall of the short corridor.

"It's his!" Kath shouted. "See the Mr. Peanut(tm)?"

A few feet ahead of them, just into the courtyard beyond the archway, a group of what appeared to be mostly students was gathered around a body. As the four of them drew closer, they saw it was a man lying on the walk, dressed in the uniform worn by the University's Campus Police. The man, kneeling down next to him, wore an identical uniform. What appeared to be a folded sweater had been placed under the prone security guard's head. The students stepped back to let Larry and Mike pass, sensing their official capacity. The kneeling guard looked up.

"He's going to be all right. I think maybe his shoulder's been shattered though."

Hearing his partner's voice, the injured man opened his eyes and started

305

to nod his head.

"Just lie still Roy, the medics will be here in a minute. You're gonna be fine."

One of the students was sitting on the wet grass next to the walk, his knees up with his head resting on them. A girl saw Kelly noticing him and said, "He tried to stop the man who shot the guard. As he started to tackle him, the man slammed his briefcase into the side of his head."

"Did you see which way the man headed?" Kelly asked the girl.

She nodded. "He was running. He crossed South U and headed up that path behind the Art Museum. He dropped his umbrella as he hit Jamie. He didn't take time to retrieve it, just dashed on across the street. A couple of the other guys started to chase him, but we yelled to them they could be shot, too. They came back to wait for the police."

Mike and Larry had heard most of the girl's statement. Mike turned to Larry and said, "We need to get some people, at least two units, in front of the Union. Make sure he doesn't grab a cab or bus, possibly the airport shuttle."

Larry nodded. "I'll get on it right away. Get everyone else surrounding the campus proper to conduct a search."

"You got it," Mike answered. "We'll see what else we can find out here while you're working on that."

The EMS unit had arrived and the team was now working with Wilbanks, about to place him on a stretcher. Mike took a couple of the other officers who'd arrived on the scene off to the side. He briefed them on the route McConnell had taken and sent them off in pursuit.

"Hopefully, you'll be lucky and run into someone who's seen him. Remember, he's wearing a tan raincoat, no hat and carrying a cordovan colored briefcase. Watch yourselves."

Coming back toward Kelly and Kath, Mike shook his head saying, "It's too bad in a way he doesn't still have the umbrella. It probably means he'll try to find some cover until the downpour lets up. He can't be far off. I think we've learned everything we can here. Let's head out."

•

Martino was just hanging up when Mike, Kelly and Kath returned to the car.

"All set," Larry said. "We should have the central campus pretty well surrounded in a few minutes. David spoke with Robinson and was also able to reach four of the five being blackmailed and provide them with an update. Jameson's at his office, working late. David has a couple officers on their way there now."

"Good thinking," Mike replied. "McConnell's headed in that direction and we know he's been in Jameson's office before. He was probably driving the car which struck Jameson and may be targeting him again."

Larry nodded as he continued. "Jameson is headed to the Michigan League in a few minutes for a cocktail and dinner bash they're having for some of the U's largest financial givers. Robinson will be there too. David instructed Jameson to wait until our people get to his office before heading to the League. They'll escort him. Seems Jameson brought his change of clothes, formal wear, to the office. Robinson has two people from the campus security force with him. Seems as if we're covering all the bases."

"What about the others?" Kelly asked. "Have we offered them protection?"

"Clare Singleton and Masterson and Broadstead are at their respective homes or condos. None of them want or think they need any special protection. David's left messages for Liz Hernandes, but hasn't spoken directly with her."

"I just recalled the Boston Pops Orchestra is playing at Hill Auditorium tonight," Kelly said. "It's a sell-out. It means in another hour or so there will be crowds of people in that area."

"You're right, Kelly. I forgot to mention that," Larry said. "The shindig at the League is tied in with the concert. David also said there's nothing scheduled at the Lydia Mendelssohn at the League tonight, but the "Capitol Steps" are performing at the Power Center. It's close to a sell-out, too. Our best bet, of course, is to nab him before the crowds hit."

"And that doesn't give us much time," Kath said.

"Right, let's get moving," Mike said. "Larry, why don't you take State up to North University. We'll park up there, across from Hill and the League."

As he drove up State, Larry continued to fill them in on what was taking place. "There should be upwards of twenty officers fanning out through this central campus area now. You can see a couple of them there on the steps of Angell Hall. They're all equipped with earphones in addition to their regular cellular phones. If he's spotted, we can immediately notify everyone."

As they approached North University, they saw another team of officers in the area north of Angell Hall. The rain showed no sign of easing up and Martino had the car's wipers working at peak speed.

•

Two officers, Renee Overton and Keith Bartels, had just parked in a no parking zone on North University in front of the Michigan League. They'd been investigating an accident on Washtenaw near US-23 and had been delayed in getting involved in the search. As they'd driven back on Washtenaw toward campus, they'd learned the latest developments. McConnell no longer was carrying the yellow and blue umbrella, discarding it after he'd shot a University security guard. The raincoat he was wearing was pretty non-descript, they saw five or six men in their range of sight now, wearing similar raincoats. All had umbrellas and were wearing hats. Though he was believed to have neither, that could have changed by now. The cordovan colored briefcase was the best thing they had to work with.

Two of the men they saw did have briefcases. Though it was very difficult to determine their colors through the downpour, one was definitely a light tan in color and the other appeared to be black. The man carrying the latter was far too short to be him.

Through the rearview mirror, Renee caught a glimpse of a man dashing across North University toward the Michigan League. He must have come out of one of the University buildings on the south side of the street, opposite the League. Renee and Keith were able to get a good look at him as he stood on the medium waiting for a car to pass, before resuming his dash across the street.

"It could be him," Keith said looking at Renee. "See the briefcase?"

Renee, who'd been driving, grabbed the door handle and quickly exited from the car. The man was only a few yards from her and glanced up, flashing her a smile.

"Hell of a night isn't it?" he said, making a waving gesture to her. Keith had also climbed out of the car on the passenger side. The man was running towards the overhang at the door to the League.

"Hold it, we need to speak to you," Bartels called out to the man, who turned, a grin on his face.

"Me?" he answered, pointing at his chest with his finger, seemingly surprised by the request and continuing towards the door to the League. The two officers had closed to within twenty yards of him and nodded.

"Let's do it out of the rain. I'll wait for you inside," the man said, nearly to the door. It opened as a young couple came out and the man ducked past them and entered the building.

"What do you think?" Bartels asked, turning to Renee.

"Doubtful if it's him, but his briefcase is the same color. We need to check him out," she said reaching for the handle of the door.

Bartels had reached for his gun as he'd asked the man to halt. Making sure the safety was off, he held the door open for Renee. The couple who had just come out the door, was giggling over how hard it was raining and asked Keith if he knew when the shower was supposed to let up. He shook his head, indicating he had no idea, and stepped inside the entrance behind Renee.

There was a small vestibule area inside the entrance where they assumed the man would be waiting, but it was empty. Through the windows of the second set of double doors in front of them, they could see a number of people, but no sign of their man. Most of the people were standing in line, waiting to get into the League's cafeteria. With the storm, it appeared many people had the same idea, grabbing a bite to eat there before possibly heading over to Hill Auditorium or the Power Center. Their concerns mounting, Renee and Keith pushed through the second set of doors. They split up and began questioning people in hopes of finding someone who remembered seeing the man. Keith lucked out immediately, the first couple he asked having recalled seeing him. Keith called out to Renee.

"They say he headed up those stairs just inside the door, two steps at a time," Keith explained. "One of us should report in. Suggest they get people at every possible exit, immediately surround the building."

Renee nodded. "I can do that. Maybe rather than going up after him, you should head down to the north end of the building and make sure he doesn't escape out that door. I can keep an eye on this door while I'm calling in."

"Good idea," Keith replied already turning. Looking back, he said, "Maybe I can convince that couple to help us for a few minutes until help arrives. Have them watch the main entrance on the west side."

Renee looked skeptical, but Keith continued. "I'll make them promise not to confront him, just report if they see him."

Renee smiled and nodded her approval before turning and dashing out the door to their patrol car.

•

Frank and Alice Woodbridge were waiting for the elevator on the third floor of the League. They'd just come from one of the guest rooms. Major contributors to the University, they'd driven down from Saginaw earlier that afternoon, having been invited to attend the Boston Pops Concert and the cocktails and dinner beforehand, hosted by the University's Development Office. Woodbridge had been a very successful auto parts manufacturer, with several plants located throughout the state. He'd sold the company ten years ago and come into substantial wealth. A generous couple and both graduates of the University, they'd shared their good fortune over the past few years with the University. Now in their late seventies, they still remained very active.

Tonight was a particularly festive evening they'd been looking forward to for months. They made a handsome couple, dressed in formal wear, Frank with a tux and Alice with a full-length gown. They were running a little behind schedule, having been delayed driving through the rain. Cocktails had been scheduled for six o'clock, with dinner at six-thirty. It was almost six-thirty now. Alice had just mentioned to her husband that he might be wise to limit himself to one drink so he didn't fall asleep during the performance when the elevator door opened.

They could tell the man standing inside the elevator had just come in out of the rain, his raincoat drenched and his wet hair plastered to his head. He was holding a briefcase in front of his body and grinned at the two of them as he moved out of the elevator. Though much younger, thirty or so, the man was about the same height and build as Frank Woodbridge.

"You look nice, all set for a party," he said to them as he stepped to the side to allow them to enter the elevator. They were smiling as the man suddenly wrapped his arm, while still holding the briefcase, around Mrs. Woodbridge's waist and pointed a gun at her head.

"No screaming," the man said. "We're going back to your room. Quickly." He spoke quietly, a menacing tone in his voice.

Frank Woodbridge started to lunge forward to come to his wife's aid. McConnell pulled Woodbridge's wife back a couple steps, shaking his head no, the barrel of the gun pressed firmly into her cheek. Frank caught himself and stepped back.

"Don't hurt her. We'll do as we're told. She's . . . "

"No one needs to get hurt. Now quickly, lead the way," the man said, glancing up and down the corridor, which was empty.

●

Martino drove slowly past Hill Auditorium which was on the left and continued down North University toward the Michigan League.

"Why don't you pull over to the curb here," Mike suggested. "Is it my imagination or is the rain actually letting up? I think . . . "

Judy Wilson's voice on the speaker phone interrupted him. In an excited voice she was repeating her initial statement.

"I repeat. We're quite certain McConnell's been sighted entering the entrance at the south end of the Michigan League and is still inside the building."

Mike and Kelly had already reached for their door handles as Judy continued, directing all units to converge on the League and secure all exits.

"Renee Overton and Keith Bartels sighted him and have stationed themselves at opposite ends of the building. We believe they recruited a couple to watch the main west side entrance. The University is . . . "

"Call in Larry and let them know we're heading into the League right now," Mike said opening his car door. "Catch up to us inside after you've assigned teams to every conceivable exit."

Kelly and Kath were just behind him as Mike dashed across North University. The three did their best to avoid the many puddles in the street. As he held the door open for the two women, Mike glanced back and saw Martino was already out of the car, waving to two officers who had just rounded one of the buildings across the street from the League.

Renee recognized Kelly and Mike as they entered the League with Kath. She'd been standing a few steps up on the stairway McConnell had used and headed towards them. After Renee greeted them and was introduced to Kath, she quickly explained that McConnell had last been seen racing up the stairway.

"Keith Bartels is down at the north exit. Someone needs to relieve the couple he recruited to watch the main entrance as soon as possible," she added, pointing down the hall.

Mike was about to assign Kelly and Kath that task when he remembered they were unarmed. He certainly didn't want to risk placing one or both in the position of being taken hostage once again or injured.

"Wait here," he instructed Kelly and Kath. "Larry will be here in a minute or two. I'm sure he'll have several other officers with him. Renee and I'll go down and spell that couple. Don't challenge McConnell! Wait for Larry and come join us at the west entrance. One or more of the officers he's with can guard this exit. Be careful and don't venture off on your own."

•

"He's treating us like a couple of school children, a little over-protective don't you think?" Kath said after Renee and Mike had left them.

Kelly smiled. "His intentions are sincere. He's under enormous stress, the one being second-guessed."

Kath's eyes twinkled as she interrupted saying, "When anything goes wrong, and there's been an abundance of that. Guess I shouldn't be surprised you'd come to his defense."

Seeing where she was headed, Kelly attempted to change the subject. "I've been up those stairs dozens of times," Kelly said. "You probably have too."

Kath shook her head. "Never have as a matter of fact. The ballroom's at the top of the stairs isn't it? I've just been to the theater at the other end of the second floor. There are a number of other beautiful meeting rooms up there though, in addition to the ballroom, aren't there?"

Kelly nodded. "Mom and Dad used to come to the St. Joe's Christmas Gala every year. The entire second floor would be decorated, sort of a winter wonderland. They brought me once," Kelly reminisced. "I think the last time I was in the ballroom was at a United Way gathering."

"Maybe you can . . . " Kath began as they noticed Larry opening the door, followed by at least a half a dozen other officers.

"Finally!" Kath said. "Now we can catch up to Mike and see how we can help."

Holding up her hand with her fingers crossed, Kelly replied, "Let's hope we're successful and nobody else gets hurt in the process."

•

Immediately after entering their room, McConnell directed Frank Woodbridge to take off his clothes.

"Shoes, socks, everything down to your undershorts. What size shoes do you wear?"

"Size ten," Frank answered as he started to untie his tie.

McConnell smiled as he said, "Perfect."

The Woodbridge's suitcase was sitting on a stand at the foot of the bed. "Is this unlocked?" McConnell asked.

Alice Woodbridge shook her head no. She was sitting in a chair in front of the small desk in the room, her hands on her head in accordance with McConnell's instructions.

"Open it," he said.

She stood up and walked over to the end of the bed. Lowering her hands she nervously worked the combination and unsnapped the lock. Frank Woodbridge had removed his jacket and shirt and was unbuttoning his pants as the phone rang.

"Ignore it," McConnell said. Directing Alice Woodbridge back to the chair, the man peered into the suitcase.

"You can leave on your underwear and socks, I see you have extras here."

The phone was continuing to ring. McConnell turned to stare at it, seemingly reconsidering his decision not to answer it. He finally turned to Frank and said, "Better answer it. Be careful of what you say."

He'd walked over next to Mrs. Woodbridge and was once again holding the gun with the barrel pressed against her forehead.

"Hello," Frank said. "Oh, hi Beth."

Beth Elkins was one of the coordinators of tonight's event. The Woodbridge's had seen her when they'd checked in less than an hour ago.

"I'm sorry we're running a little late. We often skip the cocktail portion of these functions. Elaine's just finishing up with her make-up."

McConnell held up his hands, raising and lowering his fingers to flash the number ten twice. Frank nodded as he continued speaking.

"We'll be down in about twenty minutes. Thanks for checking with us and certainly don't delay President Robinson's remarks for us."

"Very good," McConnell complimented him as Frank hung up the receiver. He instructed Alice Woodbridge to turn around in the chair and straddle it. It proved to be a difficult task in her long dress. He then had her place her hands around the back of the chair as he removed a pair of pantyhose from the suitcase and tied her wrists together. He stretched one of the loose ends down and knotted it around one of the legs of the chair. He then stepped back as if admiring his ingenuity.

Frank Woodbridge was completely undressed except for his socks and underwear. He appeared older and frailer than he'd looked fully dressed in his tux. McConnell was continuing to rummage through the suitcase. He'd previously removed a set of underwear and a pair of socks. His face broke into a grin as he spotted a gray wig nestled in the corner of the suitcase. With a surprised expression he looked over at Mrs. Woodbridge and said, "You're wearing a wig, aren't you? And I'd thought you'd just had a new perm for tonight's affair."

He removed the wig from the suitcase and held it out, giving it a shake and then fluffing it into shape with his hands.

"I think I might borrow this one for the evening," he said, tossing it on the bed.

•

Strange, thought Beth Elkins as she placed the receiver down. She'd seen the Woodbridge's when they'd checked in. Their conversation then was the complete opposite of what she'd just heard. After the strenuous drive through the rain, Frank Woodbridge had said he couldn't wait to down his first Manhattan. He'd also suggested the University could hold its costs down if it wasn't too late for them to cancel their dinner reservations. He'd indicated that at their age, cocktails and hors d'ouevres generally met their needs and they often skipped dinner. Now he'd just reversed himself.

She recalled the time her father had experienced a mini-stroke. Her mother and she first realized something had occurred when he voiced some thoughts totally contrary to those he'd verbalized moments before. In his case, there was an element of confusion in his speech, a hesitation. She hadn't noticed that with Mr. Woodbridge. His speech was very clear and deliberate. She glanced at her watch. If the Woodbridge's didn't show up in the next twenty minutes, she'd send someone up to check on them.

Beth had come down to the office next to the registration desk on the first floor of the League to place the call to the Woodbridge's room. As she left the office and started toward the stairs across the hall, she noticed two policemen standing at the main door on the west side of the building. She smiled to herself, just like Jeff, her boss, to arrange for something like this, a police escort to Hill Auditorium for the donors, without, to her knowledge at least, having told anyone else on the staff.

Halfway up the stairs, another thought came to her. She'd been a little irritated when Woodbridge had placed the blame on his wife for their being delayed. Something else about his statement had struck a sour note, too. She remembered now, he'd referred to his wife as Elaine. Beth flipped through the pages of the listing of guests for tonight's affair. She'd thought so, she had her listed as Alice. She'd handed them their name badges earlier. They'd appeared to read them and hadn't mentioned that there was a mistake with Mrs. Woodbridge's. As Beth reached the top of the stairs, she spotted her boss, Jeff Martin, talking to a police officer. Two young women, dressed in warm ups, and another man were also engaged in the conversation. Should she interrupt to tell Jeff her concerns about the Woodbridges? Behind them, a few guests were still proceeding from the cocktail party area into the adjacent room for dinner.

"Oh, there you are, Beth," she heard a voice call out. "We need you. There's a mix-up in the seating."

Ginny Edwards was speaking to her. Beth held up her hand indicating she needed to say something to Jeff first. Jeff noticed her and said, "I'll be another minute or two, Beth. See if you can help Ginny, I'll catch up to you."

Beth nodded. "I do need to talk with you," she replied. "We might have a problem with the Woodbridge's."

"We're just wrapping up here, I'll be right in," Jeff said, turning back toward the group with whom he'd been conversing.

"If you agree, I'd like to delay any announcement until after dinner," Jeff said to them. "Hopefully, you'll have apprehended him by that time. I'm certain none of those people saw him. They were all in there having cocktails. I'd rather not alarm them, throw a damper on Robinson's brief talk."

Five other officers were coming down the hall in their direction. Mike noticed them as he began his reply.

"That's fine with us, but don't let anyone leave the room, even to use a restroom, until we get back to you. We'll leave one officer at that side door."

Mike then turned and began delivering instructions to the other officers who'd now arrived. "You two are staying close to me," he explained to Kath and Kelly.

315

•

In the Woodbridge's room, McConnell had hurriedly stripped and re-dressed himself in Woodbridge's clothes while Frank Woodbridge was in the bathroom with the door closed. His wife had pleaded with McConnell not to tie him up, explaining he was not well and needed access to his heart medicine. McConnell had finally relented, warning Woodbridge to sit on the toilet seat and be quiet. He'd removed the small bottle of Nitroglycerin tablets from a pocket of the tux and handed it to Woodbridge before pulling the door shut.

As McConnell adjusted the bow tie and reached for the tux jacket, he began to brief Mrs. Woodbridge. "You're going to be leaving with me in a minute or two. I'm the guest conductor for tonight's concert and you're my mother," he said, breaking into a smile. "We're Russians, you don't speak or understand any English. I just want you to smile and nod, don't say a word, I'll do all the talking. Understand?"

He looked in the mirror above the dresser as he adjusted the wig on his head. He pulled strands of the hair out to give him the appearance of a man with an unkempt, bushy head of hair which hadn't seen a comb in some time.

"Remember, cooperate and you and your husband will be just fine. In less than an hour, this will all have simply been a bad dream."

He was looking himself over in the mirror again, buttoning the jacket of the tux. He'd removed the Band-Aid from his forehead earlier and applied some rouge and powder from Alice's purse to mask the cut and the scratches on his face. He studied his face in the mirror and used his hand to rub off the excess make-up. Stepping back, he appeared satisfied with his appearance. The Woodbridges' name tags were setting on the dresser top. The man picked up Alice's and turned toward her, a furious expression on his face. He swore as he strode across the room toward the door of the bathroom.

"He called you Elaine on the phone!"

"Don't hurt him! I can help you. I'll cooperate," Alice shouted. The man's hand froze on the door knob. He glanced over his shoulder at her and then stepped away from the door. Still livid, his face flushed, he walked to the bed where he'd previously emptied the contents of his pockets. His briefcase was also on the bed, next to his gun.

316

Alice cringed, assuming he'd come back for his gun. He appeared to read her mind as his face relaxed and broke into a grin. He reached for the briefcase, opened it and dumped a pile of stacks of money onto the bed. Alice watched as he went to the closet and removed a plastic laundry bag from the shelf. Shaking it open, he began to fill it up with the banded packets of money.

"I hope this won't be too heavy or clumsy for you, Alice," he said to her, his voice rising as he sarcastically spoke her name. "In a minute or two I'm going to untie you." He continued to fill the bag as he talked. "I'm going to put this extra belt of your husband's around your waist, under your gown, and attach this bag to it. It's going to be dangling down between your legs." He grinned again. "I'm going to have to get under your skirt. You'll have to shed your modesty for a moment while I make sure it's securely tied. Understand?"

Alice blushed as she nodded her head. "Remember, I have no intention of hurting you. Walking might be a little awkward and you may have to shorten your steps. We'll see after I get it attached."

McConnell untied Mrs. Woodbridge's hands and had her stand, instructing her to hoist her skirt and slip up above her waist. She cringed as the man attached the belt. Her body was trembling. As he attached the plastic bag which held the money in place he reminded her, "You'll have to relax, Alice. I don't want you to appear nervous, just a big broad smile, confused because you can't speak or understand any English. Remember I'll do all the talking. You'll just hang onto my arm and smile. We're going to be walking over to Hill Auditorium."

McConnell assisted her in adjusting her gown, pulling the slip and skirt back into place. He had her walk back and forth across the small room a couple times to make sure the bag now hanging between her legs wasn't noticeable and that there was nothing out of the ordinary in her walk to attract attention.

"I think we're about set," McConnell said, glancing at his watch and also at his image in the mirror once again. He fluffed up the wig and then reached for the gun and placed it in the inside vest pocket of the tuxedo.

"I'm just going to explain to your husband that we're leaving, but that he can expect to see you soon, safe and unharmed, providing he stays in the bathroom for the next half-hour. You just stand there by the door, it'll only take a minute." He smiled. "Remember you promised to cooperate. I don't want you to get any wild ideas, have any thought you can alert someone without dire consequences to you and your husband."

McConnell then walked over to the bathroom door and opened it. Frank Woodbridge had been sitting on the toilet seat and jumped up, somewhat taken aback by McConnell's appearance.

"You better not have injured my wife," he said, staring at the wig. "I . . ."

McConnell held up his hand. "Take a look, she's just fine. And if you continue to do as you're told, she'll continue to be. Now step back in there, we need to talk."

McConnell stepped into the bathroom and closed the door behind him. Alice Woodbridge was engulfed by a sense of panic and fear as she wondered why the man had closed the door. She started towards the bathroom door and then stopped as another thought came to her. Maybe he's testing me, she reasoned. Seeing if I'll try to use the phone or attempt to escape. She could hear the man speaking, but could only make out every third or fourth word being said.

•

As McConnell closed the door behind him, he was explaining to Woodbridge he had a few things to tell him. Though smiling, Frank Woodbridge could see a menacing, evil look in the man's eyes.

"Your wife and I are going to be . . ."

The blow to Woodbridge's abdomen caught him by surprise. As he gasped for air, bending over, McConnell delivered a karate chop to Woodbridge's neck. While continuing to talk, he caught Woodbridge's body as he collapsed in his arms. And still speaking in a loud voice, he maneuvered Woodbridge to the side of the bathtub and stretched his body out on the floor of the bathroom. Standing up and seemingly admiring what he'd just done, McConnell reached down for Woodbridge's eyeglasses which had fallen to the floor during the scuffle. Placing them on, he looked at himself in the mirror above the sink.

•

"You'll have Alice and your glasses back, intact, safe and sound, in just a few minutes," McConnell was saying as he came out of the bathroom, looking back over his shoulder as if talking to Woodbridge. He'd opened the door just enough for him to edge out. Alice started forward to see if she could get a glimpse of her husband, but he'd quickly closed the door.

"We're on our way," he said to her, moving across the room toward her. "Remember, you're my mother, no speak English. Try not to react to anything I or anyone else says. Just continue to smile."

Though Alice Woodbridge was nodding in understanding, her only reply was, "Is my husband all right? You didn't hurt him, did you?"

McConnell grinned. "Why of course not. He'll be staying in there until you get back." McConnell was opening the door to the room as he asked, "Do you want to check for yourself? You think I'm lying?"

Before Alice could answer, he was nudging her out of the door, saying, "I'm afraid there isn't time, we need to hurry. We'll take the elevator. Grab my arm."

They proceeded to the elevator door and as McConnell pressed the button he flashed Mrs. Woodbridge a smile. "One last reminder . . . smile."


## Chapter 50

The first and second floors of the League had been thoroughly searched with no sign of McConnell. Close to thirty law enforcement personnel were now involved, a dozen or so spread around all the possible exits from the building, the rest inside, working as teams. Master keys had been made available. With the exception of the three teams sent to check out the basement areas, the rest had been directed to move up to the third floor. Mike, accompanied by Kelly and Kath, was now on the stairway leading to the third floor, preceded by half a dozen officers with their guns drawn. Though there had been no sign of him yet, all were fairly certain he was still in the building. People who had been in the vicinity of the main exits before they'd been secured had been questioned. None remembered seeing anyone leaving the building who came close to matching McConnell's description, a white male, approximately six-feet tall, one-hundred-and-seventy pounds, thirty years of age and probably carrying a briefcase.

"Someone just got on the elevator," one of the officers called down to Mike. "The door just closed."

"Thanks, I'll alert them downstairs," Mike replied, lifting his portable phone.

"I'll check to see if anyone gets off on the second floor," Kelly said, turning and starting down the stairs.

"Remember he's armed and you aren't," Mike called out to her. "Don't confront him!"

"I'll go with her," Kath volunteered, turning to follow Kelly.

"No you don't," Mike said, breaking into a smile. "You stay with me." He was still grinning as he passed the word on that someone had just entered the elevator on the third floor.

•

Beth Elkins had finally been able to corner Jeff to tell him of her concerns about the Woodbridge's. As she told him of her phone conversation and how it conflicted with the earlier one she'd had with the Woodbridge's on their arrival, Jeff, who had only been halfway listening, suddenly looked at Beth in alarm.

"We need to let the police know immediately. What's the Woodbridge's room number? I didn't want to alarm people, but the police are here because they believe there's a suspected murderer hiding here in the League."

Beth stood frozen in shock, grasping the implication of what Jeff had said. She'd previously just been concerned Mr. Woodbridge might have experienced a stroke. Now, she realized he and his wife might be being held hostage. Why didn't I say something sooner, she thought, realizing Woodbridge was probably trying to send her a distress signal by calling his wife a different name.

"They're in 308. Jeff, he was trying to tell me they were in trouble. He referred to his wife as Elaine rather than Alice."

"Good Lord! I hope they haven't been harmed. The police just headed up to the third floor a couple minutes ago. I'll try to warn them."

Jeff walked hurriedly to the side door of the banquet room. Beth saw him break into a run in the hallway as he headed toward the central staircase.

"What's that all about, Beth?" She turned. It was President Robinson, who was due to begin his remarks in another few minutes. She hesitated a moment, not sure of where to begin.

"I'm aware the suspected murderer of the girl who's body was discovered in the Arb might be in the building. Maybe we should go out into the hall," Robinson suggested as he nodded and smiled at some of the guests at nearby tables who were looking in their direction. "Has he been caught?"

"I don't think so," Beth replied as they moved toward the door through which Jeff had departed. "There's a possibility he's in the Woodbridge's room. Jeff went to warn the police."

Out in the hallway, Beth attempted to explain as quickly as possible her conversation with Frank Woodbridge. President Robinson listened intently, shaking his head in concern as Beth spoke, closing his eyes for a moment at one point.

•

As Jeff reached the top of the stairs, he saw Mike Cummings standing in the middle of the hallway with the two women he'd met a few minutes before. They were facing in the opposite direction, in front of two guest room doors which were standing open. Hearing his footsteps, they glanced over their shoulders.

"Room 308," Jeff blurted out as he approached them. "He may be holding an elderly couple hostage."

Mike immediately shifted his gaze down the hallway where two officers were just about to enter another guest room. One of the officers was fitting a key into the lock.

"Hold it a minute," Mike called out to the officers, and then turning back toward Jeff he asked, "What are you saying?"

Still trying to catch his breath after his dash up the stairs, his anxieties mounting, Jeff attempted to tell them the reasons for his suspicions as quickly as possible. He was interrupted when a message came over Mike's receiver advising him it wasn't McConnell who'd come down in the elevator.

"It was the guest conductor for tonight's concert at Hill and his mother. I think they're from Russia," the officer from downstairs informed him.

Kelly, Kath and Mike were fascinated by Jeff's story as he explained why he believed Frank Woodbridge was trying to send a message of distress to Beth Elkins.

"You stay here with them," Mike said to Jeff as he started down the hallway. The officers had been about to enter room 307. He whispered a brief explanation to them, before they cautiously moved on down the hallway to room 308.

•

Alice Woodbridge held on to McConnell's arm as they walked past the now turned off courtyard fountain outside the League's west entrance toward Hill Auditorium.

"You were just perfect," McConnell mumbled to her, referring to the confrontation they'd just had with the two policemen at the door as they exited the League.

McConnell had done an amazing job of convincing them he was tonight's guest conductor for the Boston Pops, Alice thought. His accent and halting English had been perfect and she had just smiled and nodded her head as he'd instructed her. She could feel the plastic bag bouncing against her thighs as she tried to keep up with McConnell's strides.

"It'll all be over for you in another few minutes. Remember, you're unable to comprehend anything that's being said."

•

They'd found Frank Woodbridge, clad only in boxer shorts, an undershirt and socks, on the bathroom floor. One of the officers was kneeling down next to him, checking his pulse. Woodbridge groaned as his eyes opened. He stared at the two officers and Mike in confusion and then tried to raise his head trying to talk. The officer kneeling next to him, attempted to help him.

"Get Kelly," Mike directed the other officer. "Have her call for some medical attention."

"Alice," Woodbridge struggled to talk. "Did he hurt her? Is she all right?"

"We don't know," Mike replied. "You're the only one here."

Mike and the two officers had seen the open briefcase on the bed when they'd first entered the room and quickly concluded Jeff's assumption had been accurate.

"He's wearing my tuxedo." Woodbridge closed his eyes for a moment, still finding it difficult to talk. With assistance from the officer, he was able to prop himself up, with his back against the tub. "And Alice's wig and my glasses."

The guest conductor, Mike immediately thought as he turned and quickly walked into the main room.

322

"The man and woman who were on the elevator," Mike blurted out. "They could be McConnell and Mrs. Woodbridge. We need to check!"

•

The young coed, stationed at the side door at Hill Auditorium, was new to the role of a ticket-taker. Her supervisor had been emphatic during her brief indoctrination session that no one be allowed entry unless they had a ticket. She was holding fast to that instruction as the man who claimed he was the guest conductor for tonight's performance heaped verbal abuse on her. She told him he and his mother would only have to wait a minute or two until she'd checked with her supervisor and reminded him the concert wasn't scheduled to begin for another hour. But the man didn't understand, or didn't want to. He continued his tirade, attempting to push her out of the way. The nervous mother knew there was some type of problem, but just continued to nod her head and smile.

The young woman finally relinquished and let them in as other theater patrons, who had also arrived early, began to bunch up behind the irate man and his mother. McConnell and Mrs. Woodbridge hurried down one of the center aisles toward the front of the auditorium. He leaned over and angrily whispered, "Can you believe that damn bitch? She almost screwed up everything. I want you to take a seat in about the fourth row, there. You're going to have to remove that bag for me. Quickly! And then I'll bid you farewell."

He was beginning to simmer down and actually grinned at her as he added, "I don't think you'll mind that a bit, will you. Just stay in your seat, don't try to attract anyone's attention."

•

Accompanied by Kelly and Kath, Mike had charged down the two flights of stairs to the main floor of the League. He'd used his phone to advise everyone of his suspicions, as they'd raced down the steps. He instructed them not to halt the search or pull teams off the exits until they were able to verify if the man who'd represented himself as the guest conductor was actually McConnell. There was only a single officer at the west door of the League. As he pushed the door open for them, he told them two officers had already headed for Hill Auditorium. They nodded in acknowledgment and Mike asked the officer to see if he could get someone right away to assist him in securing the exit.

"We might need everyone over at Hill in a minute or two. Get on your phone and prepare everyone for that possibility."

Darkness had now settled in. They could hear the chimes from Burton Tower in the background as they dashed toward Hill Auditorium. Only a handful of people were milling about in the plaza between the League and the Auditorium. They turned to stare at the three as they raced past them. Kelly saw Mike had his gun out, holding it in one hand as he attempted to remove his identification from the pocket of his jacket with his other hand. As they reached the side entrance, he flashed it at the ticket-takers, who nodded with frightened, wide-eyed expressions on their faces, stepping aside to let them enter.

Less than thirty people were seated in the Auditorium as they hurried down the center aisle toward the two officers they saw talking to a woman seated near the front of the Auditorium. As they approached closer, they could see the woman was in tears.

"Mrs. Woodbridge?" Mike asked.

She nodded.

"Your husband is going to be just fine. An EMS unit will be with him in a minute or two. He's worried about you."

Alice Woodbridge, her face brightening, as one of the officers, who'd been hesitating to interrupt, spoke. "She's described a man who has to be McConnell, armed, dressed in her husband's tuxedo and wearing a wig of hers. Posing as the Boston Pops' guest conductor. She said he went back-stage, in that direction."

Mike nodded. "Kelly, here, take my phone. Notify everyone we need the Auditorium surrounded. Any extra bodies should come inside and check in with you. The three of us," Mike said, indicating the other two officers, "will see if we can locate him while the two of you remain here with Mrs. Woodbridge."

## Chapter 51

Sam Potts had the responsibility to keep an eye on the musicians' instruments while they were out, grabbing a bite to eat before tonight's performance. Ann Arbor was the next to last destination on their tour.

Tomorrow night, they'd be in Toledo. Sam was relieved the tour was winding down. They'd been on the road for nearly two weeks and he'd be happy to be back in Boston.

He glanced at his watch, just past seven. The musicians should be straggling in any minute now, he thought, time to unlock the backstage entry door. He'd felt more secure keeping it locked while he wandered about backstage. As he walked toward the door, Sam saw a man approaching him from the stage. Dressed in a tuxedo, Sam assumed the man was associated with the University. Sam smiled as he observed the man's unkempt hair, typical of some of the arty weirdoes they encountered on the tour. In their own orchestra, for that matter. Seeing Sam, the man grinned.

"Are you the only one back here?" he asked.

Sam nodded. "But I'm expecting company soon, they . . . "

The man's expression changed as he removed a gun from the pocket of the tux and leveled it at Sam.

"It's loaded, and I'm in a hurry," he said in a menacing tone. "Just do as you're told and you won't get hurt." McConnell then grinned again. "Don't worry, I'm not going to be touching or damaging any of these precious instruments," he sarcastically said.

Sam had been associated with the Boston Pops going on twenty years. He'd never experienced anything like this. He gulped and felt his knees buckle slightly as he held up his hands, saying, "Anything you say, don't get nervous."

McConnell replied with a sinister laugh. "I'm not the one who needs to be nervous." He motioned with the hand holding the gun for Sam to move further backstage.

•

Accompanied by the two officers, Mike had climbed the stairs to the stage. With guns drawn, they started backstage.

"Do you want to use this, Mike?" one of the officers said, holding up a miniature electronic mike, a new piece of technology which replaced the megaphones frequently used to broadcast a warning to someone barricaded in a house or building. Though tiny in size, the device magnified a person's voice tenfold.

"Good idea, thanks," Mike said, taking the mike from the officer. Switching it on, he held it to his lips.

"McConnell, this is Mike Cummings. You can avoid injury by surrendering now. We have the auditorium surrounded. We'll give you three minutes. Throw your weapon down and place your hands on your head."

The two officers nodded at Mike, acknowledging he'd given the right message, as they cautiously moved past the curtains with Mike and into the open backstage area. They saw dozens of musical instruments and carrying cases scattered about, but no sign of any people.

"I'll try one more time," Mike said to the officers, as he put the mike up to his mouth once again.

"It's the police, Joe. Your luck's run out. We have you surrounded. We'll give you two minutes to show yourself, to surrender. You've been warned. Save yourself from possible injury. In two minutes we'll be coming in after you."

"I think I hear something," one of the officers said. "Someone pounding, a knocking noise back there in that direction."

"I hear it too," the other officer said as Mike nodded, acknowledging he'd also heard the noise.

The three spread out and walked in the direction from which the thumping noise was originating, cautiously with their guns drawn. One of the officers stepped on something and jumped. He leaned down and picked a crushed Hershey's Kiss<sup>(tm)</sup> off the floor.

"Just some candy," he said, smiling at Mike and the other officer who'd both noticed his startled reaction as he'd stepped back.

Mike, sensing its possible importance, immediately retraced his steps, coming back to the officer's side. He saw three or four other Hershey's Kisses<sup>(tm)</sup> scattered on the floor in front of a storage locker with its door ajar. Mike opened the locker door. A black leather carry-all was sitting on the floor of the locker, unzipped. Mike leaned over and peered inside. His eyes widened on seeing the bag contained a stack of the flyers McConnell had threatened to distribute. More Hershey Kisses<sup>(tm)</sup>, and what were they called, Hershey Hugs<sup>(tm)</sup>, the new companion piece, were scattered on and alongside the stack of flyer sheets. His alarm mounted as he also saw some electrical wire and what appeared to be an explosive device of some kind toward the bottom of the bag. Remembering Kath's prediction that McConnell might try to set off a bomb at some campus landmark, Mike stepped back, pushing the locker door closed. We'll have to get a team here right away to check it out, Mike thought. As he turned to the other two officers to tell them of his findings, one of them called out, "Freeze!"

Mike looked up to see a man dressed in a tuxedo, who'd just entered the door leading outside on their left, not far from where Mike and the two officers were standing. Both officers had their guns aimed at the man.

"Place your hands on your head," shouted one.

"It's not him," Mike told the officers, as two more men and a woman edged into the doorway behind the man. All three were dressed in formal wear.

"They're probably members of the orchestra. They'll need to stay outside, we may have a bomb here."

Mike started toward the doorway where the startled musicians were standing. Still with their guns drawn, the other two officers were continuing farther backstage to see if they could locate the source of the noise they were still hearing.

"Sorry," Mike said to the first man who'd entered, who was now lowering his hands. "I'm Detective Cummings of the Ann Arbor Police Department. We're searching for an armed fugitive, who may be hiding somewhere in the auditorium. I'm going to have to ask you all to wait outside for a few minutes. It's stopped raining, hasn't it?" Mike asked, looking beyond them, out the door.

There were nearly twenty-five people mingling there and he saw more coming across the street. Mike also spotted three or four officers, one of whom was jogging up to the doorway. The handful of individuals who'd been in the doorway had backed out as Mike had attempted to answer their questions. No, there was no need to return to the Campus Inn or the Bell Tower, he told them. The wait should be minimal. If the delay proved longer than expected, he'd probably have them use the front entrance and they could wait upstairs in one or more of the rooms located there. No, their instruments didn't appear to have been touched. The officer had arrived at the entrance door. Mike asked for his cellular phone and called David, asking him to immediately send a team of demolition experts. David assured Mike they'd be there in ten minutes or less.

Turning his attention to the officer, Mike explained where things stood. "We aren't sure if he's still inside or not. We need to have you and the others question all these people to learn whether anyone's seen him. It's likely he's carrying a bag or container of some sort, could even be something like a violin case, I suppose. He may have removed the wig. You know his description. Let me know the minute . . ."

"Mike," one of the officers checking on the source of the noise they'd

327

heard called out. "You'd better come here."

Mike hurried over, seeing the officer who'd called to him next to the other officer, both kneeling down over a man lying on the floor. They appeared to be untying his hands and feet.

One of the officers stood up and stepped forward toward Mike as he approached as the other officer helped the middle-aged man to his feet.

"This could be bad news for us, Mike," the officer said. "He's told us he was just heading over there to unlock the entrance door when a man confronted him, it had to be McConnell. The fact those musicians were able to get in means McConnell or someone else must have unlocked the door."

Mike nodded as the officer continued. "He says no one else was back here with him. McConnell must have opened the door and left it unlocked as he left the building."

The other officer interrupted, saying, "But he could still be here, inside. Maybe he only unlocked the door in order to have a quick escape route in case it was needed."

"They're questioning people now," Mike replied. "Some of them may have seen him leave as they were returning from dinner."

Turning to the man, who was still rubbing his wrists, Mike asked, "Did you see what he was doing before he confronted you?"

There were still traces of adhesive around the man's lips from the tape McConnell had used to gag him. Shaking his head no, he replied, "He seemed to have just come from the stage area. I assumed he was connected with the University. He caught me by surprise and as I told these officers, he had a gun. He threatened me and warned me not to make any noise. I didn't until I heard you fellas broadcast the warning to him, the second time. Then I started kicking and pounding on the door as loud as I could."

"Would you like us to arrange for a doctor to check you over?" Mike asked.

The man shook his head. "No, I'm fine. Maybe still shaking a little, though. I guess I'm lucky. He murdered someone?"

"We believe so," Mike answered.

"And severely injured several others," one of the officers added. "We're sorry about what happened to you, but count your blessings."

"Oh, good!" Mike said, noticing members of the bomb squad coming through the side door with scads of equipment. He went over and directed them to the locker where he'd found the leather carrying bag.

"You'd better vacate this area," one of the team suggested to Mike. "Is anyone else here in addition to the four of you?"

"The man who left this bag might still be here, hiding," Mike said. "Other than that possibility, no just us."

Remembering he'd left Kelly and Kath with Mrs. Woodbridge near the front of the theater, Mike said, "I'll go out by way of the stage. The three of you could probably help with the questioning outside," Mike suggested to Potts and the two officers. "We'll have to postpone any additional search for McConnell until they're done."

Turning to the three officers who were now in the process of donning padded, protective gear, Mike asked, "You're armed, aren't you? There's a possibility he could come out of hiding while you're defusing that apparatus. Maybe he didn't have enough time to arm it. He may have heard or seen us coming and stopped before it was properly set, left or hidden somewhere."

The officers assured him they were armed. They'd have one serve as a lookout while the other two were occupied with the possible bomb. They promised to get word to Mike the minute they'd defused the device. They'd also let him know if they ran into any kind of problem which might delay them.

•

Mike was standing in the lobby of Hill Auditorium next to Kelly and Kath. He'd updated them and informed the ushers that no one was to be seated until they were notified otherwise. The presence of so many policemen had sparked many rumors among the increasing number of concertgoers. Mike and other officers had been forthright with the theater staff in advising them the delay in seating was due to the fact an armed fugitive that the police were attempting to apprehend might be hiding in the auditorium. This same story was being relayed to the crowd of theater patrons. Nothing had been communicated, however, about the possibility he'd planted an explosive device of some kind. President Robinson had been kept fully informed and had been advised to keep the University's guests at the League until he was advised of an all-clear – an arrest and/or a defusing of the explosive device. Mike had also arranged for one of the officers who'd been outside in front of the auditorium to escort Mrs. Woodbridge back to the League.

329

"He must have had this all planned in advance," Kelly said. "He had to have hidden the candy and the flyers early this morning, maybe even yesterday – the bomb, too."

"I'm not certain it's an actual bomb," Mike said. "Possibly just some type of propulsion device to launch the candy and flyers, scatter them through the auditorium."

Kath arched her eyebrows. "That makes sense. How would it work?"

"No idea, not a clue, and it might not make sense at all. The experts might have an answer. My point was it's not necessarily a bomb per se. Some of the ideas you floated in our meeting the other day made me think bomb when I saw the wires and other materials in the bag. We should know one way or another in a couple minutes. Maybe something more in regard to McConnell, too," Mike said as he spotted the officer who he'd put in charge of the questioning of the Boston Pops personnel coming through one of the front doors, heading towards him.

They walked over to meet him. "We've talked to four or five people who we've reason to believe may have seen McConnell," he explained with excitement. "The gray wig was missing, but you were right in your hunch about the instrument case, Mike. The man they saw was carrying a small horn or flute case. He caught their attention because he was a stranger in their midst, so to speak, trying to blend in. He was doing his best to give the impression he was waiting for some of the other musicians to catch up and join him. Two people think he sauntered into the Thayer Street parking structure. One last remembered seeing him as he appeared headed north toward Washington Street. There must be close to fifty men dressed in tuxedos milling about outside the auditorium. You can easily see why an officer would have had a problem identifying him in the group."

As Mike started to ask a question, the officer held up his hand and said, "We already have at least half a dozen officers combing the parking structure. We also . . ."

Mike felt a tap on his shoulder and turned to see the officer heading the team which was checking out the potential bomb.

"It wasn't a bomb. Some explosives, but nothing was set, armed. Everything's in here," he said as he handed Mike the black zippered bag.

"Have they allowed anyone backstage yet?" Mike asked.

"No. They're under the impression you wanted to keep everyone out until you were able to determine whether or not McConnell was still inside."

"We're fairly certain he isn't." Turning to the officer who'd just informed him of the probable sighting of McConnell, Mike said, "On your way back, notify the musicians they're free to go in. We'll inform the ushers that they can begin seating people and catch up with you in a couple minutes. Get any spare officers over to search the State Street area."

At Mike's direction, Kelly left to inform the Hill Auditorium staff and also arrange for an officer to head to the Michigan League to update President Robinson and advise him his group could come over now.

Mike then turned his attention back to the officer who'd just informed him the bag hadn't contained a bomb. "I've a few questions for you."

The officer grinned. "I assumed you would. You want to know what he was up to."

Mike nodded.

"As near as we can figure, he planned to fill the paper bag in there," the officer said, pointing to the leather bag in Mike's hand, "with those flyer sheets, the candy and these cards. Did you see them?" he asked, handing Mike a small, one-inch by two-inch card. "They're at least a couple hundred of them."

Mike read the card as Kath looked over his shoulder. Printed in blue ink on heavy stock yellow paper was the message, "Hugs and Kisses from a True Blue Fan."

"There's also over a hundred loose twenty-dollar bills in there," the officer continued. "He no doubt planned to have them in the paper bag, too. You've seen those little party poppers? You pull a string and they explode with streamers and confetti. We think he was trying to come up with the same effect or result on a magnified scale. Maybe even a better example would be one of those Mexican straw animals, I forget what you call them, that children smash at birthday parties and toys and candies tumble out?"

Kath and Mike both nodded.

"We think he was going to launch the bag in some way and explode it in mid-air, scattering the contents. Maybe hurl it above the audience from one of the stage wings. This is just conjecture. He'd probably tested it, but we think he underestimated the weight of those flyers. Everything he'd need is in that bag. It would have been a rather spectacular feat if he could have pulled it off."

Mike and Kath exchanged glances, both envisioning the sight of Hershey's Kisses[tm] and the little yellow cards falling onto theater patrons

331

as the twenty-dollar bills and the flyers fluttered down.

"You and Kelly had it figured right," Kath said. "He never intended to honor his promise not to circulate the flyers if the blackmail was paid. This was all planned in advance."

Kelly rejoined them as Mike replied. "You warned us, Kath. I think everyone had their suspicions, too. That's why no one argued against trying to entrap him. One of my concerns now is just how extensive his planning was. I think he may have left a car close by to be used for his getaway. The Thayer Street parking structure is restricted to University personnel. He would have had to beg, borrow or steal a pass, or I guess simply steal a car with a window sticker. There's no reason to be optimistic, but let's hope we're able to corner him inside or catch him leaving the structure."

•

The last of the Boston Pops contingent was just entering the west side door of Hill Auditorium as Mike, Kelly and Kath hurriedly walked toward the Thayer Street parking ramp. Kelly smiled as she noticed the tuxedo-garbed men entering the building. Mike, who'd just finished a phone conversation with David Benton and Judy Wilson, noticed her smile and asked, "What's so funny?"

"Sorry," Kelly replied with a grin. "Guess it's my way of dealing with stress. Seeing those men in their tuxedos and imagining the difficulty of trying to pick McConnell out of the group reminded me of that Dr. Seuss story, *Sneeches on the Beaches*[c]. Finding a Sneech with a star on its belly button. A silly thought."

"I remember the story," Mike said.

"Me, too," said Kath.

"Hopefully, there aren't many men in the parking structure or wandering through campus town dressed in a tux," Mike said. "It'll work against him now."

Two officers with their guns drawn were just checking over a car which was about to exit the parking structure. They'd had the driver open his trunk and one of the officers had the rear door of the car open, checking the back seat.

•

Steve Renz spotted Mike, Kelly and Kath standing across the street from the parking structure as he rounded the southwest corner of Hill Auditorium. As he neared them, he could see the disappointed looks on their faces. Though hardly necessary, he asked the question, "No sign of him?"

The three shook their heads.

The four stood for a moment, silently sharing one another's frustration, before Steve asked a second question.

"Have you been briefed on the blow-up with Jameson?"

Mike and the two women looked up in surprise. "No, nothing," Mike replied. "We don't even know what you're referring to."

"He went ballistic when he learned we'd let McConnell escape our net again. He was standing next to President Robinson when the officer arrived to explain what had happened and advise them the University group could be brought over to Hill.

"Even Robinson was surprised and embarrassed over Jameson's behavior. I just finished talking to him. Jameson lashed out at the entire department, calling us incompetent, a bunch of monkeys, and an insult and menace to the community because of our lack of smarts and how easily McConnell's bamboozled us."

A small smile surfaced on Steve's face as he commented. "Came on rather strong, don't you think?"

The three of them exchanged looks of surprise, all astounded at Jameson's reaction and comments, in light of their previous contacts and conversations with him.

"In fairness to Jameson, we goofed," Steve continued. "The two officers assigned to escort him over to the League got way-laid in the search. They never got to his office. After a long wait, he came over on his own. The wait and walk over on his own must have been very stressful, perhaps in fear of being attacked again, possibly killed. When he learned McConnell was still on the loose, something snapped."

"Where is he now?" Kelly asked.

"He headed home to be with his wife. She wasn't planning on joining him for the affair at the League, or the concert."

"We should get some of our people over to their house to guard them," Mike said.

"The officer offered to do that and it set Jameson off again. He said he didn't want any imbeciles coming near him or his wife. He stomped off, saying it was safer for them to look after themselves."

"Maybe there's more to it than just breaking down under stress," Mike suggested. "McConnell's still alleging he wasn't responsible for Beth's death. He threatened the one who was."

"I still don't buy into that," Kath said. "I worry the poor man may have had a nervous breakdown. It happens."

"I hope it's only a temporary thing," Kelly said. "It's so out-of-character; maybe there was something else that was said or happened that triggered him off, something we don't know about. Maybe I should go over and talk to him and his wife."

"Let's hold on that for a few minutes. Maybe David will want to be involved," Mike said, glancing at his watch. Ten past eight.

In addition to a thorough search of the structure, scores of other law enforcement personnel had been canvassing the area within a three- to five-block radius, to no avail. They saw Greg Collier from the *Ann Arbor News* approaching them. During the course of the past half-hour, Mike had given a pat answer to several other news media people who had tried to question him.

"No comment."

"It appears that S.O.B. has eluded you again," Greg commented. "I realize you're not making any statements," he said, referring to Mike, "but I've pieced the day's events together fairly well, I think. I believe it would be in both our interests if you could look over my story later this evening or first thing in the morning. I still want to help, but I also have a job to do, an obligation to the paper."

Mike empathized with Greg. In addition to admiring him as a good reporter, Mike felt a sense of responsibility for his dog's death.

"I'll have to clear it with David, there's an issue of undue favoritism. But if he agrees, I will. I'm not committing myself to provide you with any additional facts, just to make sure there aren't any glaring errors. Knowing you, there probably aren't. You're aware it's been a hell of a day. Give me your card; I'll call you tonight."

Greg handed him his business card, jotting down his home phone on the back.

"Could I talk with you in private for a minute, Mike?" Greg asked.

Mike nodded, turning to the others and saying, "Sorry, I'll just be a minute," as he moved off to the side with Greg.

# Chapter 52

"While we're waiting for Mike to finish up with Greg, I'll give David and Judy a call," Steve said. "They've probably been briefed about the incident with Jameson, but I'll make sure."

The search of the parking structure appeared to be winding down. As Steve dialed headquarters on his cellular phone, several officers were milling about across the way.

"He's been sighted!" Steve exclaimed to Kelly and Kath. "At Marty's clothing store over on State Street."

Steve adjusted the receiver volume control and held the phone so Kelly and Kath could also hear Judy's voice.

"Martino's there now questioning the owner," Judy was saying. "Seems McConnell rapped on the alley entrance door about thirty minutes ago, dressed in the tux. The owner and one of his employees had stayed late to unpack a shipment of Christmas merchandise which they were anxious to get on display. Marty's, you may know, is one of the largest suppliers of formal rental wear in town and they first thought it was a customer needing a last-minute alteration of some kind."

"Where's McConnell now?" Kelly asked, interrupting her.

"No idea," Judy replied. "He left the store about ten minutes ago."

"Was he walking or did he have a car?" Steve asked.

"Again, we don't know. He'd locked the owner and his employee in the basement. He told them he'd lost his luggage and needed a complete outfit. Joked about hoping they were like the Men's Warehouse chain and could supply his emergency needs in a hurry even though they weren't open for business. They don't know if he had a car in the alley. The owner does remember he'd tapped on the door with a set of keys, though. He was worried the man might crack or scratch the glass."

"Did he change clothes? Do we have a description of what he's wearing now?" Kelly asked.

"Yes and no," Judy answered. "He changed clothes, but we don't know how he's dressed. He locked the owner and the other employee in the basement and they weren't able to see what he finally changed into. Larry might be able to get a better handle on that and we can get a description out right away. Inform all the hotels and motels in the area to notify us if anyone resembling McConnell checks in this evening. Get the word out to all the cab and bus drivers, too."

"Good!" Steve said. "We should also keep track of any reported car thefts in the State Street area. He might go that route, too. He could have walked to Marty's."

"We will be. We've already notified all the 911 operators to keep us informed. Let me finish, I'll try to be quick. When McConnell was in one of the dressing rooms trying on a pair of pants, the owner picked up his tux jacket. As he shook it out getting ready to put it on a hanger, he noticed something bulky in the pocket, a gun. The one he took from Terry. He'd thought the man's face looked familiar. The gun triggered his memory, he recalled the face was similar to the sketch of McConnell that's been in the papers. He was picking up the phone to call 911 when McConnell came out of the dressing room. The owner explained that he was just calling his wife to tell her he'd been delayed. He was proud of himself for quickly figuring how he could still handle notifying the police with McConnell listening. He hoped the 911 operator had Caller ID. He was going to say, 'Hi honey, it's me. I've been tied up with a customer who lost his luggage. He needs a whole new wardrobe – shirt, sport coat, slacks, shoes – the works.' He'd even planned ahead to hang up as he dialed a seven-digit number and make the last three digits, 911. As he was dialing, McConnell became suspicious. He said he couldn't believe the owner wouldn't have his home number on speed-dial. He went over to his tux jacket and re-moved the gun, locked them in the basement."

"How long were they there, in the basement?" Kelly asked.

"About twenty minutes, they estimate. There's a phone down there too, but he'd dismantled the system in some way so that was of no help. Though he'd threatened them to stay put, they forced the door open after about twenty minutes, which the owner says seemed like an hour. McConnell was gone. You'll find this next part absurd," Judy said with a laugh. "They found the tux – tie, shoes and all – on a hanger next to the counter with a note pinned on it saying it should be returned to Frank Woodbridge at the Michigan League. There was a stack of twenty-dollar bills on the counter next to a pile of price tags. They could be helpful in piecing together the outfit he finally decided on. Prior to being locked in the basement, they'd shown him where all his sizes were located. The owner says it had to have taken him a minimum of ten minutes, probably more like fifteen, to accomplish what he did. Fitting himself out in a com-pletely new wardrobe."

"He's still playing games," Steve said. "Probably disappointed he didn't have some candy to leave on the counter along with the money."

"Was he carrying an instrument case when he came in the store?" Kelly asked.

"No. He could have left it just outside the door, though, possibly hidden, or in a car if he'd had one."

"I think we'll head over to Marty's," Steve said to Judy. "See if Larry's learned anything else. Mike's just finishing up a conversation with Greg Collier. By the way, I almost forgot. The reason I called was to see if you and David were aware of the ugly incident with Jameson."

"Yes, only very sketchy details though. David wants the lead team to meet here at headquarters as soon as possible to review and plan where we go from here. Martino's already been told, he'll be heading here from Marty's. Let Mike know and we'll see you all here in a few minutes."


## Chapter 53

The entire group, with the exception of Larry Martino, was assembled in the conference room. He'd just called in to report he was on his way. There had been no further sighting of McConnell. Benton speculated that he was probably thirty miles away by now.

"If he'd been planning to stick around," David reasoned, "I don't think he would have made it so easy for us to determine what he's wearing. We know he's not stupid. Larry just described the hat and coat McConnell took from Marty's. If he hadn't left the sales tags, it would probably have been hours, maybe days, before the owner and his staff could have determined what was missing. I think Larry has the full description of everything he's wearing except for the color and design of the tie. He should be here soon. Why don't we discuss the Jameson incident while we're waiting. Can you give us a full briefing, Steve?"

"Excuse me, David, I know we need to get to that," Mike said. "But could I tell you about my conversation with Greg Collier first? It sort of relates to your prior comments, and there's a tight timetable if we want to follow through on his suggestion."

"Go ahead, Mike, unless it's something we should delay until Larry's here. What do you think?"

"I'm sure he can provide some valuable input, but I'd just as soon get into it right away. It could be a lengthy discussion; his idea entails some

337

risks."

Mike had said very little to Kelly, Kath and Steve during the drive to headquarters. He'd appeared to be in deep thought, mulling over his conversation with Greg.

"I'm still uncertain of my own position regarding Greg's idea," Mike continued. "I'll try to lay it out as simply as possible. Greg has thoughts similar to yours, David. Even without the benefit of knowing what took place at Marty's, he thinks McConnell's on his way into the wild blue yonder or soon will be, to possibly lick his wounds, but also to plan a return, months from now or even years from now. Collier's emotionally caught up in this case. He wants to see McConnell arrested as quickly as possible, punished for having killed his dog in addition to everything else. He believes something needs to be done to change McConnell's mind about fleeing the area now, or in case he already has, something to motivate his immediate return. What he proposes is to . . . "

Someone had knocked on the door and Mike hesitated.

"It's probably Larry," Steve suggested, standing and walking over to the door and opening it. Rather than Larry, it was one of the 911 operators.

"Sorry to interrupt, but we just had a call that I'm sure will be of interest to you," she said to the group.

"Come in, Pam," David said. "Go ahead, fill us in."

"It was from a young woman who was rear-ended about half an hour ago at the corner of Maynard and Liberty. There was minimal damage to her car, far more to the man's car who ran into her. He jumped out of his car, saw there was only slight damage to hers, and explained besides being in a hurry, he didn't want his insurance company informed about the accident. He gave her two-hundred dollars in twenties and said he was sorry. There were two policemen coming down Liberty from State in their direction. The woman was worried there might be some hidden damage to her car and suggested the man wait and they could have the two officers write up an accident report. He jumped back in his car and quickly drove off before she could get the officers' attention."

Everyone's interest had escalated when Pam mentioned the twenty-dollar bills in conjunction with the Maynard and Liberty location of the accident. The alley behind Marty's exited onto Maynard, a half block south of Liberty. Maynard was a one-way street, running north.

"She finally did get the officers to notice her and come over to where she was standing next to her car. She started to explain what had occurred

338

and one of the officers held up his hand and asked if the driver was wearing a tuxedo. When she shook her head no, he explained they were in pursuit of an armed fugitive and couldn't take time to write up a report. He suggested she call in a report. Which she did, after first driving back to her apartment."

"Did she provide you with a description of the man, what he was wearing?" David asked.

Pam nodded. As she began to give the description, Larry Martino entered the room. As Pam continued, his eyes widened and his mouth dropped open.

"Someone's spotted him!" he exclaimed. "Where?"

Pam briefly went over her story again for Larry's benefit.

"Was she able to provide a description of the car he was driving? A license plate number?" Steve asked, phrasing the latter question in a way that suggested that was almost too much to hope for.

But Pam broke into a smile as she replied, "Yes, to both questions. And we already ran a check. The car belongs to a University professor. He reported it stolen yesterday afternoon. He had it parked in front of a convenience store with the keys in the ignition and the motor running."

Steve shook his head in disgust. "Probably has a University parking permit decal, too."

Pam nodded. "On the front window."

"He had it all planned in advance," Kath said, voicing the thoughts of all. "He probably had the car parked in the Thayer Street structure, waiting for him."

"The fact he rear-ended that woman's car might indicate he's still having problems with his vision," David suggested.

"Not necessarily," Pam replied. "The woman didn't blame him for the accident. She said she had just moved forward from the stop sign to turn left onto Liberty when a student stepped out in front of her, forcing her to slam on her brakes. That's when the man's car struck hers."

"I'm glad you interrupted us," David said. "Would you take charge, Pam, and make sure this information gets out immediately to everyone in the field?"

Pam nodded and disappeared out the door.

"Might be a break for us," Mike said. "About time a bit of luck flowed our way. He's smart, but he's been damn lucky, too."

"Amen!" Steve said, as the others nodded.

"Guess it's back to you, Mike," David said. "Take a second or two to bring Larry up to speed."

•

After updating Larry, Mike launched into an explanation of Collier's proposal.

"Greg wants to orchestrate a news story to humiliate and infuriate McConnell. He wants to portray him as a buffoon, a blunderer, a mentally deranged, frightened little boy. He has some truly vicious taunts in mind, painting him as a vicious, cruel bully who . . . "

"Right on!" Kath exclaimed, breaking into a smile. Though the others, including Mike, smiled over Kath's comment, they'd also become serious, sensing the direction Collier's proposal would be taking them in.

"Collier believes, and I tend to agree," Mike continued, "that simply having an institution such as the Police Department, the University or the *Ann Arbor News*, as a source for these quotes, won't be sufficient. He believes we have to pinpoint an individual who he can focus his rage and frustration on. A person to retaliate against to show he's not the stupid psycho that person alleges he is.

"Collier goes one step further. He makes a strong case for the person to be a woman. A woman who's questioned – challenged – this macho guy's manhood, bravery and intelligence. Greg suggests the ideal would be one of the women he's attempted to blackmail. I thought of Liz Hernandes, but we don't even know where she is."

"Yes, we do," Judy Wilson said. "I'm sorry I forgot to say something earlier. We finally were able to trace her down. She's been taking heavy doses of sedatives the past week or so and then had more than a couple drinks last night. She checked herself into a mini-rehab program at St. Jo early this morning. The prognosis is good, but they'll be keeping her there a few days. I think you'd have to rule her out."

Mike nodded in agreement. "Collier and I agree the timing is critical. He thinks tomorrow afternoon's edition of the *Ann Arbor News* might even be too late. He's hoping we can make a decision so that there could be front page coverage in tomorrow morning's Detroit papers. That virtually means less than two hours to put everything into place in order to make those editions. He's working on the release now, leaving a blank for the name of the person being quoted."

"What about me?" Kath asked. "Collier's thoughts match mine. I think I'd be the ideal choice."

"Or me," said Kelly. "There are numerous risks involved. We think he's killed one person already. Sorry, Kath, but your family's suffered enough already. For me, it's my job."

Kath started to respond, but Mike interrupted her. "Greg and I discussed the possibility of using one of you, even both of you." He hesitated.

"And?" Kelly asked.

"We both concluded neither of you would be ideal. For one thing, he already knows you both despise him. Knowing he's already assaulted both of you, twice in your case, Kelly, had you both at his mercy, he's more liable to just laugh off either of your statements. We need someone who he believes has been awed by his cleverness, his ability to avoid our entrapments. Someone who should be intimidated by his exploits. Someone whose ridicule will totally send him into orbit. Earlier, a week ago, I would have agreed that either of you would be perfect. I don't think that's true now."

"I tend to agree," David said. "But we're running out of options. I don't believe Clare Singleton is a good choice either. She certainly doesn't fit the role of the demure woman who's been awed by him, frightened by him."

"That's for certain!" Steve said. "I think the person we're seeking is someone who can insult his manhood. Having already raised questions about her sexual orientation, he's not apt to be riled up over what she has to say."

"So where does that leave us?" David asked, voicing the concern of all. "What's Greg's opinion? Is there a reporter on the *Ann Arbor News* staff who could and would be willing to be involved?"

"We did discuss that possibility," Mike said. "One of the problems there is getting the other papers, the rest of the media, radio and TV, too, to pick up on the statements of another reporter."

"I think I have a solution," Judy said with a smile. "Me."

Steve laughed. "A sweet, demure young lady who's been awed by his prowess?"

"Hold on a minute," Judy said. "Remember, I don't think he knows who I am. I don't think he's ever seen me, except maybe when I was posing as a bag lady. You have to admit I did that pretty well. I think I could surprise you."

•

Over the course of the next few minutes, Judy had not only won over the group to the idea, but also had prompted several of them to suggest she was ideal for the role and they should have considered it sooner.

With a twinkle in his eye, Steve said, "Let's hope you'll need to carry on the charade for a while, it's certain to boost morale in the department."

Steve was disappointed his chauvinistic comment prompted only a shaking of heads, rather than the laughter he thought was warranted.

"Steve's comment does raise an issue that I wanted to get into," Mike said. "It deals with the risks involved. The sole object of this endeavor is to forestall him from leaving town, to enhance our chances of apprehending him, to infuriate him to such a degree he'll feel the need to immediately retaliate to prove the allegations are false.

"But we know McConnell's no dummy," Mike continued. "He could easily see through this ruse right away. That doesn't mean it isn't worth a try, though. But I want all of us, especially Judy, to realize the potential risks. For example, what if he decides to delay any retaliatory action until next month, next year? To just brood and work up his anger for a period of time, planning his act of revenge? We can arrange for tight security for a short period of time. But we don't want to have created the terrifying possibility Judy will have to be looking over her shoulder, fearing him for years to come, wherever she is, whatever she's doing."

Mike held up his hands, delaying comments until he'd presented an additional thought. "I think you're all aware there doesn't appear to be any previous criminal record for McConnell. At least that's what the Chicago police have told us. I don't know who his source is, but Greg thinks he may have stumbled onto something. He has someone trying to get hold of McConnell's juvenile records. McConnell grew up in Chicago. Collier's source was able to trace down his childhood home. His parents are both dead now, but his source had an interesting conversation with a neighbor, an elderly woman who remembers McConnell as a youngster, nearly twenty-five years ago. Her memory's faded, but she told Greg's source she wasn't surprised to hear Joe was in some type of trouble.

"She went on to tell Greg's source a couple stories. Although she was vague on many of the details, she says McConnell was accused of torturing and killing a neighbor's cat. He was also caught in his garage with a young neighborhood girl. Very young, five or six years old. She says McConnell was just into his teens. He'd tied her up."

The room was totally silent as members of the group exchanged knowing looks as Mike continued. "As I said, Greg hopes to get more details. But he thinks we can use what he already has to our advantage, by having the person who we decide on, hinting she'll soon be divulging facts about McConnell's childhood which help explain his current behavior. It's an added incentive to prompt him to stay in this area and take some action. But we can't predict what that will be. His reaction might be to just do something such as fire-bombing your house, Judy. Whether you're there or not. Or possibly, wire your car with an explosive device of some kind. There are enormous risks if he decides not to confront you face-to-face. And even if we're successful in prompting the latter, our track record has been none too good in keeping people from being injured."

"What about the possibility of creating a fictitious person for Judy to portray?" Steve asked. "If McConnell doesn't make an appearance in the next couple days, we just kill her off. I'm sorry, that was a poor choice of words. You know what I mean. We'd let the person disappear as if she'd never existed."

"There's also the option of later publicizing what we've done," Kelly suggested, "if McConnell fails to surface. Air the details of the hoax we'd planned, and take Judy off the hook. He'd be infuriated at the entire department, rather than just isolating in on Judy."

"This group never ceases to amaze me," David said. "You'd certainly think with our collective smarts, we could devise a plan that will work and minimize the risks. I personally think he'll want to confront the individual who's made the allegations, to show her how wrong she was to ridicule and minimize his talents and intellect, to see the fear in her eyes when . . . "

There was a knock at the door and Pam came into the room again.

"I felt I had to interrupt, we've found the car. Parked near the rear entrance to Toys 'R Us at Arborland Mall. We've already communicated this news to the field and additional units are already on their way to canvas the area."

"Keep an eye pealed for any reports of stolen vehicles, not only from the lot behind Toys 'R Us, but from the entire Arborland complex," Martino instructed Pam. "It might be wise to have a unit check out the motel on Washtenaw across from Arborland. The former Holiday Inn East; I think it's a Ramada now."

Pam nodded as she made notes.

"I know the cab and bus drivers have been alerted," Larry continued, "but we should contact them again, specifically about the possibility of him having boarded a bus or taken a cab from Arborland this evening."

"The team watching Jameson's house just called in a few minutes ago, too," Pam advised them. "Nothing suspicious, no sign of McConnell."

"Thank you, Pam," David said. "We'll be wrapping up here in just a few minutes and I'll be out to join you."

"We still haven't had time to discuss Jameson," David continued after Pam had departed. "When you first presented Collier's suggestion, Mike, I thought of him as the logical choice for many reasons."

"You'd have ruled him out in a hurry," Steve said, "if you'd witnessed his outburst at the League. We'd be playing with fire, totally unreliable in his present mental state. Besides, I don't think we'd be able to convince him to be a sitting duck, not with the lack of confidence he expressed about our abilities."

"So it comes down to me again, doesn't it?" Judy said. "How much time before we need a decision, Mike?"

He glanced at his watch, twenty to ten, before replying. "Ten minutes probably, if we're going to make the morning papers. The rest of the night I suppose, if we kick it off at a news conference early tomorrow morning."

"I'm aware and sensitive to the risks," Judy said. "Kelly's idea to air everything in case we don't get immediate results, an instant reaction from him, might be a good possibility to limit the window of exposure. I still want to go ahead with it; I think it will work. And of course, if we can nab him tonight, so much the better. I don't think we have the time to do a good job of carrying out your suggestion, Steve. Creating a bogus person, identity, even if I played the role. McConnell will probably do his homework, do a little research. My name and address are in the phone book, for one thing. The . . . "

"You're right," Steve said. "I more or less ruled it out as we've been sitting here for many of the same reasons. What do you think, David? Systems go for Judy?"

Glancing around the room, David nodded. "Give Greg a call, Mike. Have him fax everything to us to review, though, before he turns it loose to the media." David grinned. "I'm optimistic!"

•

While Mike was out of the room contacting Collier, David asked the others for input on how best to handle the Jameson incident.

"We need some follow-up, and I should probably be the one to do it," Benton suggested. "It's getting late, but it should probably be face-to-face, rather than over the phone."

"You'd better phone first to advise him you're coming," Steve said. "Otherwise you might risk being shot. I'm not exaggerating when I say Jameson went absolutely bonkers. You might also want to contact Robinson; he was present when Jameson sounded off. He might provide some input on how best to proceed."

"This may be out of order," Judy said, "but I always had my doubts about that hit-and-run incident. Doubts over whether Jameson staged it to throw suspicion away from him."

"What are you saying?" Kath asked. "You aren't being taken in by Joe's allegation someone else killed my sister, are you? He's just floating a red herring to distract you. Don't fall for it."

"The question needs to be asked though, Kath," Martino said. "I think there's more behind Jameson's behavior than we're privy to."

"I can't explain his explosive behavior," Kath replied. "But please, please, don't get taken in by that lying, no-good scumbag. Joe's nothing . . . "

"Hold on, Kath," Judy interrupted, "we all know your opinion. But doesn't common sense dictate that any one of us should feel comfortable enough to raise an issue for discussion without fear of being read the riot act? If you want to know the truth, I had my doubts as to whether you were in cahoots with McConnell."

"You what?" Kath swung around in her chair to face Kelly. "Were you aware of that?"

Kelly nodded.

"I can't believe this!" Kath said. "Now I can understand why Jameson blew his cool. He probably got wind of the fact you people are viewing him as a suspect. Unbelievable!"

"Calm down, Kath," David said. "We wouldn't be having you privy to all our discussions if we had any doubts about you. I wouldn't be making arrangements to get you a gun. Our job, our mind set, as law enforcement personnel, is to examine all avenues, no matter how remote or incredulous they might seem. That's all we're doing – all we have been doing. Our goal right now is to apprehend McConnell. Now let's get this discussion back on track. Everyone's under considerable stress. I'd like to wrap this meeting up in another fifteen minutes if possible. It was a good suggestion, Steve, to contact Robinson. I'll do that as soon as . . . "

Mike opened the door and stepped into the room. "You missed the fireworks display," Kath told him with a grin. "I apologize," she said with a more somber look, slowly glancing around the room at the others.

Mike shrugged his shoulders with a questioning look on his face. "I'm sure I'll be filled in, but let me tell you about my call to Greg. He's enthused about the choice of Judy. He'll have the press release, with Judy being quoted, to us in about five minutes. I promised we'd be back to him in short order. Pam's going to bring it in to us, a half dozen copies, as soon as it arrives.

"Greg thinks we should announce a media briefing for around ten a.m. tomorrow. Have Judy conduct it. He'll be here to meet with her and us at eight to go over some suggestions he has for it. He'll have a front-page story in tomorrow afternoon's edition of the *Ann Arbor News*. Hopefully, the radio and TV stations will play up the story tomorrow after the briefing. This will all be a follow-up on the articles he hopes to arrange in tomorrow morning's *Detroit Free Press* and *News* editions. He's had his contacts holding space in hopes we'd give him the go ahead."

•

A few minutes later, everyone was gathered around the conference table reading Collier's fax. He had a gift with words. He was also a man carrying out a vendetta. The quotes attributed to Judy were zingers. There were chuckles, intermixed with gasps, as they reviewed the content of the story. Greg had provided details of the gist of what had occurred earlier in the day, interspersed with Judy's response to reporters' questions. In answering the question of whether the Ann Arbor Police Department had considered approaching the FBI for assistance, Judy was quoted as having replied with a laugh, "Heavens no! We've actually seriously considered recruiting four or five nine- to ten-year-old boys, and not too smart ones at that, to assist us. Our problem has been trying to predict the behavior of a man who's never grown up. We're certainly not being outsmarted. The difficulty is trying to duplicate the mind-set of a not-too-bright little boy."

Another question was whether the police considered McConnell a master of disguises. Judy's quoted response was, "He's actually still a little kid playing dress-up. Maybe a wretched childhood stymied his physical and intellectual development."

In response to a question about McConnell's use of candy in his escapades, Judy was quoted as saying, "Perhaps if he'd had more 'Hugs(tm) and Kisses(tm)' as a child, there wouldn't be this sick fascination with candy now. He's a frightened, mentally unstable man. The problem is, he's also vicious and cruel, a menace and danger to anyone who gets in his way."

"Want to change anything?" David asked the group in general. "How about you, Judy? Are we comfortable over how you've been quoted? Does it sound like you? Or should I say the new you?"

Judy laughed. "He's done a great job. I just made a couple of very minor changes, with the slang and in one instance the grammar. Other than that, perfect! I'll have problems embellishing these quotes tomorrow."

Suggestions for changes from the rest were few and minor, too.

"Be sure to let Greg know how great a job we think he's done," Kelly said. "I think he's pushing just the right hot buttons."

"I certainly will," Mike replied. "I'll call him right after I fax the pages back with our notations."

•

The next few minutes were spent in tying up loose ends. Kelly and Kath were both given cellular phones and guns. They would be staying at the Sheraton again tonight, but in a different room. David had already taken care of having their clothes and other personal belongings moved to the new room and he handed each of them a key.

It was decided it wouldn't be necessary for anyone to be with Judy tonight at her home on the west side. David was going to have a hair stylist and a make-up specialist at Judy's shortly after six-thirty a.m. She was due in the office to meet with Collier at eight. Calls and faxes, notifying media of the ten o'clock briefing, were being attended to.

When Kelly and Kath left David's office at close to ten-thirty, David was still conferring with Steve and Larry on preparations which would have to be made at Judy's home, motion detectors around the parameter, hidden floodlights, cameras and microphones, outside and inside, and more.

Mike caught up to them as they were heading out the door to Kelly's car. "Tomorrow's going to be a better day," he said. "The two of you have to be exhausted. Pleasant dreams, both of you. You'll probably want to be here for Judy's . . . performance. I think I'll just follow you back to the hotel, make sure you're in your room safely. Our prayers were answered earlier today, finding you . . . safe and relatively unharmed." He reached out with both hands, gripping one of Kath's hands with his left and one of Kelly's with his right. Later, after they were in the car, Kath teased Kelly.

"You did notice he held on to your hand a wee bit longer."

## Chapter 54

After the two of them had taken turns lingering in a hot shower, Kelly and Kath had wasted no time in climbing into bed and switching off the lights. Kelly had made brief calls to her parents and Rick while Kath was showering, and Kath had spoken to her mother while Kelly had her shower.

Rick had some exciting news to share with Kelly. One of the companies he'd been interviewing with was flying him out to California for a final interview this Wednesday and Thursday.

"They know I'm not married, but they volunteered to also pick up expenses for any significant other if I wished to bring someone – you – along with me. I'm thinking I'll accept if they do offer me the job. Living in San Diego has a lot of appeal."

"Oh, Rick, I'm delighted to hear they're interested. I know they were at the top of your list. As far as me, though, you know everything's up in the air. Even if that wasn't the case, though, I don't think my tagging along would be a good idea."

"Can't say I'm surprised," Rick replied. "Disappointed, yes, but not surprised. I haven't been blind; I've noticed the way you look at Mike."

"Oh no, Rick. What are you saying? That's not it at all. This has nothing to do with him. There's no one else in the picture. It's just that . . . "

"You don't have to explain," Rick interrupted. "You've been a great friend and that's probably all we'll ever be. Like I said, I'm not surprised."

"Oh, Rick, I'm sorry. I want to continue to be friends. I'll have my fingers crossed for you on Wednesday and Thursday. I'll try to see you, at least call, before you get away. Don't be hurt. I love you."

There are many levels and kinds of love, Kelly thought in the moment or two before Rick spoke again.

"I love you, too. And I'm delighted you survived today's ordeal. Good luck. I hope you're successful in catching him. I'll touch base when I get back."

He hung up before Kelly could say anything further. Not that she knew what she would or should say. There was a feeling of sadness as she hung up the receiver.

They were just dozing off when the phone rang. Kelly looked at the bedside clock as she picked up the receiver – eleven-thirty-five.

It was Mike, hoping he'd managed to catch them before they'd fallen asleep.

"Thought the two of you would be interested in hearing the latest development. One of the teams of officers reported in from Arborland a few minutes ago. They ran into a man whose wife is missing. She'd gone to Arborland, to Toys 'R Us, around seven-thirty, planning to be home by nine. When she still hadn't returned at ten, he recruited a neighbor to look after his daughters while he drove over to Arborland to look for his wife. The girls are nine and seven, and he realized his wife might have been delayed, waiting perhaps for one of the toys to be assembled, to save him some grief. He did say she was very good about phoning when she was going to be late, especially when she was out by herself at night. He also explained they usually parked in the lot behind the store and he was certain she'd probably done that tonight, as she planned to make a number of bulky purchases. Early Christmas shopping, and she'd be able to get packages in her car easier from the back entrance."

Kelly had the phone held out so Kath could also hear Mike. The two exchanged fearful looks, anticipating where Mike was headed with the conversation.

"The husband didn't find their car in the lot and went in the store to see if he could find anyone who remembered seeing his wife. He was in luck. Two of the clerks did. She'd needed two carts to hold all her purchases and they'd remembered joking with her about the head start she and her husband would have in assembling some of the toys. They remembered the time, around eight-forty-five, because they remembered his wife had looked at her watch, saying she'd promised her husband she'd be home by nine. The clerks explained to the husband that there were a number of police officers in the complex, searching for the man who'd been pictured recently in the papers. They told him the man's car had been found a little earlier this evening in the lot behind the store. One of the clerks accompanied him into the mall, where they spotted an officer.

"There aren't any witnesses, but we assume McConnell may have confronted her in the parking lot, possibly offering to wheel one of the carts and help her load her car, a Jeep Wagoneer by the way, white. There's an alert out on the car, also a description of the woman, with mention of the fact the Wagoneer might be loaded with toys. The motels in the area have been informed to be on the lookout for a couple now, rather than just McConnell. We'd already advised them that he would probably be paying cash, rather than using a credit card. That fact alone narrows it down. Yet there's always the possibility he has a credit card in some assumed name. He's planned ahead in the past."

"I'm glad you took time to call us, Mike," Kelly said. "You probably realize how much we're identifying with that poor woman. I know you're not certain they're together, but all the pieces appear to fit."

The conversation ended with Mike assuring them he'd keep them informed of any further developments.

"By the way, Greg's article was too late to make the outstate editions, but it will be in the metro editions. That includes Ann Arbor. I question whether McConnell would head upstate with her, but they could be in Ohio or on their way to Chicago by now. Let's hope not."

•

David Benton tried to reach John Jameson, but kept getting a busy signal. He'd spoken with James Robinson, who'd been as surprised and shocked by Jameson's outburst as the others.

"I'm sure it's nothing that a speedy arrest of McConnell wouldn't solve in a hurry," he'd said. "A good night's sleep might do wonders for him, too."

After the phone company verified the Jamesons' phone was off the hook, David decided to call it a night.

## Chapter 55

Kelly and Kath arrived at headquarters just before nine a.m. Mike was one of the first people they ran into and the three briefly discussed the newspaper articles which Kelly and Kath had read and discussed during breakfast.

"There's no way he can miss them if he sees the papers," Kath said.

"I loved their choice of headlines."

Both papers had featured the story on their front pages. The *Free Press* chose "'Kandy Kid' Continues To Elude Police," as its headline. The *News'* choice was "A2 Police Tell Fugitive To Grow Up."

"Have you seen Judy yet?" Mike asked. He grinned when they indicated they hadn't. "She's back in the conference room with Greg Collier and David. Even knowing what to expect, I was amazed. Come on and see for yourselves."

Mike knocked before opening the door and gesturing for Kelly and Kath to enter the room. Judy was initially hidden from their view and they didn't see her until after they'd entered the room, seated conversing with Greg and David. Both gasped, and started to giggle. Judy stood, smiling, turning in a pirouette for their benefit. Even with Mike's comment, they weren't prepared for Judy's transformation.

"You said you could do it," Kath said, giggling once again. "If word gets out, it'll be standing room only this morning."

To say Judy looked stunning would be an understatement. Glamorous would be a better adjective. She'd been transformed into a beautiful blonde. There was nothing cheap or gaudy in her appearance. Just a look which would cause heads to turn.

Judy was a brunette and normally wore her hair straight, using a minimum of make-up. Today her flowing blonde hair was swept back in a ponytail, tied with a bright red scarf. She wore a red blazer in the same shade of red over a high-collared, white silk blouse. She was wearing a black skirt with black high heels. Her lips were painted in the same shade of red as the scarf and blazer. Dramatic, yet tasteful, use of eye shadow, mascara and rouge reminded Kelly of those before-and-after ads for cosmetics. A beauty mark on Judy's left cheek focused attention to a dimple Kelly couldn't recall having noticed before. Dangling gold earrings and a number of gold bracelets added to her dramatic look, a look of wide-eyed innocence combined with the allure of a sophisticated woman. Judy must be in her mid-forties, Kelly thought. Today, she didn't look a day over thirty.

Judy smiled and fluttered her eyelashes innocently as she spoke in a raspy voice. "I think my own mother would have difficulty recognizing me. I think I'll give her a call in case clips of the briefing make one of the television channels."

Greg Collier laughed as he joked, "I think some of my cohorts will be hammering on you this morning, better check your calendar as far as availability for dates."

The next half hour with Judy was focused on rehearsing her opening comments and perfecting the sultry intonation in her voice, in addition to preparing her for some of the questions she might be asked.

•

At exactly ten o'clock, Judy strolled into the briefing room and made her way to the podium. As expected, conversations ended in mid-sentence as heads turned to stare.

Judy smiled, fluttered her eyelashes, and began by introducing herself. Her remarks reinforced the theme carried in the morning news article, once again portraying McConnell as a dangerous, frightened, confused young man. All was going extremely well, including Judy's answers to the first couple of questions asked.

Kelly and Mike exchanged looks and cringed as one of the TV reporters, a young woman, asked a question. The gist of it was why, if Judy's quotes of yesterday and comments this morning were accurate, McConnell was seemingly able to stay one step ahead of the police. Why did they appear to be unable to anticipate his moves?

Judy had smiled and said she was thinking how best to respond to the question. "Maybe a what if, is the best way," she said with a look of innocence. "What if, for example, we were to get word he'd just been spotted at the wheel of a car near the intersection of Division and Williams. In one of the center lanes on Division, driving about twenty miles an hour. For those of you not familiar with Ann Arbor and its street patterns, Division is a four-lane, one-way street, heading north between the central downtown area and the State Street campus town area. If we could mobilize quickly, we might be able to intercept him a couple blocks later, at the Huron and Division intersection. There would be the possibility he might turn west or east off Division onto Liberty or Washington. But being in one of the center lanes, we'd hope he'd be coming straight up Division. We'd know within minutes if he'd changed routes. We could then explore the other possibilities, maybe even one of the parking lots off Division."

Still speaking in a raspy voice, Judy had captivated her audience. "Assume we do everything right, we're there waiting for him at the Huron intersection. Minutes pass, still no sign of him. We fan out and check the other possibilities without success. Does everyone here remember the story of 'Wrong Way Corrigan'? He's the man who began a flight from Boston to the west coast. He ended up in Scotland. He claimed his compass froze.

"What does that have to do with McConnell? In my what-if example, the witness had failed to mention he was driving the car in reverse, towards Packard rather than Huron. That's the type of thing we've been encountering with McConnell, unpredictable behavior.

"You've all heard the expression, a person makes his own luck. And we all know it's easier to have a lucky putt when you're only six feet from the cup than when you're twenty feet away. We've been lucky to come within seconds of apprehending McConnell several times. We've been lucky because we planned and executed well. But there's such a thing as dumb luck, too. We think he's been blessed with it. Maybe he's carrying a rabbit's foot. He's been damn lucky, and we believe his string of luck is about to reach an end.

"He'd love to have you believe he's too bright and clever to be caught, that he's outwitted the vast number of dumb cops who've been trying to apprehend him. He'd also love to have you believe that the havoc he's brought to this community is the result of his noble attempt to expose the real villains in our midst. Don't be misled. The scared, confused, evil little boy I've described is the real McConnell. We'll need everyone's cooperation to get lucky and finally apprehend him. The psychologists among us are probably having a field day, explaining his behavior. All we know is he's an evil, dangerous person, and our department and the other law enforcement agencies involved are committed to bring his reign of terror to a speedy end."

Kelly tried to suppress a grin. Judy had done a beautiful job of handling a difficult question. Kelly could imagine the news coverage lead-in. "Wrong Way McConnell Continues To Baffle Police." Shortly before Judy had completed her lengthy answer, one of the 911 operators had poked her head in the door and motioned for Mike to come out and join her. Kelly wondered if Mike was learning anything of value.

Judy was continuing to speak. "I mentioned that a psychologist could probably do a real number on him. We're just in the process of obtaining some revealing information about a couple of incidents that occurred when McConnell was a young boy. Hopefully, I'll have the details for you at our next briefing."

The next question dealt with what precautions were being taken to protect innocent bystanders from injury, as McConnell was being pursued.

Judy answered that this was a major concern, highlighted by McConnell's concentration of activity in the central campus area, in the midst of thousands of students.

"We're always sensitive to this issue, but probably even more so in this instance. As I've suggested, he's a little boy playing games. We can't send the message that within a quarter mile radius of the Diag, the center of campus, it's a safe zone. We aren't playing Capture The Flag. Two people are dead, four or five others have been hospitalized as a result of injuries inflicted by McConnell. I repeat, inflicted by him. He's also responsible for physical and emotional injuries to several others. Law enforcement personnel have, thus far, not been the cause of anyone being injured. There have been no errant shots, no high-speed car crashes."

Judy closed her fist and pretended to knock on her head. "Knock on wood," she said smiling, "but I believe this is more than luck. We're all fortunate to have a professional, well-trained police force in Ann Arbor. I don't want this to sound like a PR spiel, but the public should have confidence the utmost priority is being given to effecting McConnell's apprehension without placing the lives and well-being of innocent bystanders in jeopardy."

Glancing at her watch, Judy said, "I'm sorry we have to bring this briefing to a close now. My hope is that the next time I'll be speaking to you, it will be to announce McConnell's arrest."

.

Mike had re-entered the briefing room as Judy was wrapping up. He whispered to Kelly. "The Jeep Wagoneer was spotted last night in the parking lot of a motel across the expressway from Detroit Metro Airport. It's gone now, but I'll fill you in on the details with David and the others in a minute or two. Let's congratulate Judy."

They went to the front of the room, along with Kath, where Judy was engaged in conversation with David and Steve.

"We need to get back together in the conference room," Mike said to them and also to Larry Martino who had also joined them. Mike raised his left hand with his index finger and thumb forming an "O", his smile telling Judy he'd been delighted over how well she'd handled the briefing.

"I hope Joe gets a full accounting of what's been said," Kath said.

"And is ready to wring Judy's neck," Steve added with a smile.

"I think you should audition for a role with Ann Arbor Civic Theater after this is all behind you," Kelly said. "You were perfect!"

## Chapter 56

A short time later, with the team regrouped in the conference room, Mike was briefing them on the sighting of the Jeep Wagoneer.

"A man who stayed at the Holiday Inn out by Detroit Metro Airport last night just called in. He was on I-94 headed to Kalamazoo when he heard the description of the Wagoneer over his car radio, including the mention it might be loaded with toys. It matched the description of the car he'd parked next to when he arrived at the motel late last night. He'd remembered the bags with the Toys 'R Us logo and pulled off at the next exit and called us. That's the good news. The bad news is the Wagoneer wasn't there when he left at just after nine-thirty this morning. We've ... "

They were interrupted by a knock on the door and Pam entering the room. "We've had a second report on the Wagoneer," she excitedly informed them. "It's been found in one of the airport parking lots out at Metro."

Steve banged his fist on the table. "Damn, I hope that doesn't mean he's hopped a flight to Lord-knows-where."

The others' expressions of disappointment showed they had the same concern.

"None of the shuttle drivers working the lot where the Wagoneer's been found – they call it the Green Lot, by the way – recall taking anyone resembling McConnell or the woman to any of the terminals this morning. We're having them check with the drivers who were on duty last night prior to six a.m., before the current drivers came on duty."

The same 911 operator who'd called Mike out of the briefing earlier, came to the door, a broad smile on her face. Looking over Pam's shoulder, she said, "The woman's been found, safe and unharmed. A housekeeper discovered her bound and gagged in a room at the same Holiday Inn where the Wagoneer was reported being seen. A Wayne County Sheriff's Deputy is holding on line five," she said, pointing to the phone in the conference room. "He's with the woman now."

Kath clapped her hands as David reached for the phone. "I'll put him on speaker," he said to the others.

"Hello, this is David Benton. We're delighted with the news."

The deputy introduced himself and explained briefly what the woman had been able to tell them.

"The man who abducted her left her approximately two hours ago, around nine this morning."

"Is she with you now?" David asked. "Could you put her on the line?"

"She's still a little shaken, as you might imagine. But we've already contacted her family; she's spoken with them. Here she is."

David called her by name and introduced himself. He told her how relieved they were to learn she hadn't been seriously injured, and then explained she was on a speaker phone with the team of law enforcement personnel in charge of the McConnell case – the man who'd kidnapped her. As David talked, Martino excused himself, whispering he'd inform the Airport Parking people they wouldn't have to worry about contacting the earlier shift drivers and also get Airport Security alerted to be on the lookout for just McConnell.

Mike accompanied Larry to the door. "Check to see if any cars have been reported missing from that Green Lot this morning," he instructed him. "Maybe, hopefully, he's just exchanged cars. Check with the cashiers to see if anyone matching his description exited the lot sometime after nine a.m. Also have them notify us right away if they get word of any missing vehicles." Larry nodded in understanding.

At David's request the woman, Beverly Paxon, was now telling them her story, describing in detail what had occurred the previous night. From time to time, David and others asked her to clarify or expand on portions of the story. As they'd assumed, McConnell had approached her in the Toys 'R Us parking lot and graciously offered to assist her in loading her car. He explained he was having difficulty starting his car and asked if she could drop him off at the Marathon service station at the entrance to the Arborland shopping complex. In the car, he'd removed a gun from his pocket and told her not to worry – he had no intention of hurting her. He explained he needed her to drive him to Metropolitan Airport. Throughout the drive, he kept apologizing for inconveniencing her, speaking in a soothing tone. As they neared the airport, he directed her to a Holiday Inn across the expressway from the airport. He had her park in front of the entrance and took the keys while he went in to register for a room. At that stage, he threatened her to stay put and not to do anything to attract attention. The consequences could be that she or some other innocent party could be shot and killed, he warned. She was terrified and explained that though she considered jumping out of the car and fleeing, the man had been able to keep her in view from inside the lobby, thwarting any attempt to escape.

After they were in a room, he apologized for not being able to allow her to notify her family. He explained his flight wasn't scheduled until the following morning. She spent the night in the bathroom. Although he'd given her blankets and pillows for use in the tub, she was too terrified to sleep. Throughout, he was a perfect gentleman, didn't abuse her in any way, continuously apologizing for putting her through this ordeal.

In the morning, when he let her out of the bathroom, she saw he'd already been out of the room, to get them coffee and rolls and the morning paper. He'd also purchased an assortment of candy bars. He explained he'd leave them with her to share with her family, so that her's and their memory of the past few hours wouldn't be totally negative.

"At that point he was almost cheerful," Mrs. Paxon continued, "saying he'd be out of my life in a few minutes. He handed me a section of the newspaper and suggested I might want to do the crossword puzzle to make the time go faster before he left. Then he sat down with his cup of coffee and began to read the front page. As he read, there was a total personality change. He became angry, swore a couple times and looked up, glaring at me. I began to get frightened again, especially when he jumped up and spilled his coffee. The deputies told me a couple minutes ago that there was an article in the paper about him. I didn't know it at the time. I knew it was something he'd read in the paper that had angered him; I just didn't know what it was."

"Can you tell us exactly what he said?" David asked. "It could be important."

"I'm sorry, I don't remember every word. I was too scared. He was swearing, cursing out someone. It was a woman. He referred to her as a dumb broad several times and as he jumped up he screamed out she had to be taught a lesson. Then he started to pace the floor; he was fuming. The words he used to describe her weren't nice ones."

There were smiles on the faces of everyone in the conference room. Steve had risen out of his chair with his arms extended and fingers crossed, nodding his head.

"In a couple minutes," Mrs. Paxon said, "his mood had completely changed again. He apologized for his outburst and told me I shouldn't be alarmed. He said he was going to have to tie me up, but it wouldn't be for long. He said he'd call in a few minutes to tell the motel staff where to find me, that in less than an hour, I'd be talking to my family.

"He had a roll of tape and some scissors in a briefcase. I think you're aware he taped my legs and hands together. He also wrapped a strip around my head, over my mouth. He apologized again before he left, saying he'd also let people know where to find my car."

"How was he dressed when he left you?" David asked. "Did he appear to have himself disguised in any way?"

"I don't think so. He was wearing a coat and tie. The jacket was a brown tweed, light brown pants. It was a dark tie, I don't remember much about it. I think he was wearing brown loafers."

"Did he take the briefcase with him?" Mike asked.

"Yes, he put the newspaper in it."

"Can you describe the briefcase?" Mike asked.

"Dark brown. It actually looked more like a small suitcase, rather than a briefcase."

David glanced around the room, to see if anyone had additional questions.

"Could you describe his hair?" Kelly asked.

"I guess you'd call it a medium shade of brown."

"How about the length?" Kelly asked.

"On the short side. Actually about the same as in the sketch the deputies showed me."

Steve smiled, knowing if they'd asked earlier if she'd seen the computer drawing of McConnell, it would have simplified things.

"The only real change from the sketch were his glasses," Beverly Paxon volunteered.

Everyone perked up as she revealed that piece of information and David asked her to describe them.

"The frame was a dark shade. I guess I'd call them old-fashioned, the tortoise-colored plastic frames that were popular when I was in school."

David concluded the conversation by thanking Mrs. Paxon and praising her for all she'd been able to remember and tell them.

Martino had returned just as David finished. Mike briefed him on the description of the clothes, briefcase and eyeglasses. Larry dashed out of the room again to pass on this additional information to the airport authorities.

For the past hour, David had been bringing everyone up to date on the preparations underway at Judy's house, the installation of sensors, microphones, floodlights and cameras. Judy's basement office was being outfitted as a command center. Panels had been installed over the basement windows to assure no light could be seen from outside the house. A tracking dog was on standby for the evening. Several of Judy's neighbors had had their vehicles commandeered, a panel truck and two vans, where officers would be in hiding.

"We need to be extremely careful to make the scene appear to be perfectly normal," David said. "If he shows, he'll probably do some advance work, canvassing the area out. Our people should be finished and out of there in the next few minutes."

"I was disappointed when Mrs. Paxon described how quickly he regained control of his emotions," Steve said. "Not a good sign."

"I'm sure they'll flare up again if he gets the opportunity to read Greg Collier's article in today's *Ann Arbor News*," David replied. "We all agreed this was worth a try."

"And the reaction Beverly Paxon described is just what we were hoping for," Judy said.

"You mean you were pleased to be referred to as a 'dumb broad'?" Steve asked, chuckling.

"You bet! And a bitch, too," Judy answered with a grin.

"We need to decide who is going to be where tonight and when," Mike said, focusing on the seriousness of their undertaking once again. "Larry, you need to . . . "

Pam opened the door to the conference room without having knocked, a big smile on her face.

"Good news, I just had to interrupt," she gushed. "The cashier at the Green parking lot is certain she saw McConnell leave the lot at around ten this morning. When she heard about the eyeglasses, it triggered her memory. She's a middle-aged lady who had a crush over a boy who wore similar glasses. She remembered having had that thought as a customer was paying her this morning. She's been shown the sketch and she's certain it was him. I know you were worried he may have taken a flight out."

"Great news, Pam!" David exclaimed. "It couldn't have come at a better time, either. Does the woman remember anything about the vehicle the man was driving?"

"That's the sad part – no. She's pretty sure it was a car, as opposed to a van or truck, but she really can't remember. You'll get a kick out of this, though. She said she'd be willing to undergo hypnosis, if we thought that might help her recall."

"Might not be a bad idea," David said, breaking into a smile.

"Have there been any reports of stolen vehicles yet?" Larry asked.

Pam shook her head. "I'll let you know the moment we hear anything."

•

Everyone was elated over the news, relieved to know that he was possibly still in the area. That was essential for their plan to work.

"I just had a thought," Steve said. "What if he calls your house and you're not there? You should have . . . "

"Done," said Judy with a grin. "I changed the message last night. Everyone might like to hear it, David."

As she talked, she'd risen from her chair and come to the head of the conference table where the phone sat, next to David.

"I'll put it on speaker," she said as she dialed her number.

After the sixth ring, the answering machine kicked in.

"Hello, I'm unable to talk to you now." Judy was speaking in the same raspy voice she'd used at the media briefing. "As you may know, my time's been devoted recently to trying to halt the antics of the man you've been hearing and reading about so much lately. A real creep! Hopefully, we'll soon have him behind bars, where the wacko belongs. If you care to, please leave a message."

"Oh, that's beautiful!" Kath said. "I love the voice."

"You're going to shock a few friends," Kelly said.

"Probably so," Judy replied. "I called my parents and brother and sister last night to alert them. Some of my friends might not be as surprised as you might imagine," she added with a wink, and a flutter of her eyelashes.

"Mike, you were just about to get into assignments for tonight, when Pam came in. Want to continue?" David asked.

## Chapter 57

Mike had made short work of assigning areas of responsibility. Kelly and he would be stationed in the command center in Judy's basement with two tech specialists. Larry and Steve would be directing activities around the perimeter of the property. Another detective, Ginny Stephenson, would be keeping Kath company at the Sheraton. That was the only controversial

City Hall

point. Kath made a very impassioned pitch for continuing to stay personally involved.

"Maybe if he's aware I'm staying at Judy's, he'll be even more motivated to try something, to take vengeance on both of us. Kill two birds with one stone."

The others flinched at this last statement. "A poor choice of words," Judy said. "You've been a big help, Kath, but you're not a professional. If something goes wrong, if you're injured or worse, the department is going to be second-guessed. I think Mike's right in keeping you out of the loop at this stage."

"But Judy, I know him better than any of you. How he's apt to react, how he thinks. I can be of help, I'll sign a waiver, I'll . . . "

David interrupted. "Why don't we wait on a final decision until after

361

lunch. Even though we don't think he'll make an appearance until after dark, Mike thinks and I agree, everyone should be in place by mid-afternoon. He may scout out the area while it's still light. It wouldn't be smart to have a parade of people entering Judy's house when there's the risk he might be in the vicinity. I think if he's still around, he's holed up somewhere and won't canvas things out until close to five o'clock, when traffic and activity in the area pick up.

"I'm going to be here in my office in case he's sighted elsewhere, to be able to immediately allocate resources. I have to admit, I'd rather be at Judy's. My vibes say this is going to work."

•

Outside in the hall, Steve questioned Mike as to how he believed McConnell had been able to obtain another car in which to leave the lot, as the Wagoneer was still there.

"I guess your guess is as good as mine," Mike replied. "Maybe he found an unlocked car with the parking ticket on the dash board. Maybe he assaulted someone, had or has the person locked up in the trunk of the car. I know what you're thinking. It's not as easy to break in or jump-start a car as it used to be. We can't assume he didn't have this all figured out ahead of time, maybe as a safety valve. He could have parked a second car there days ago, weeks ago. Maybe something will jog that woman's memory in regard to the car he was driving."

"That would be nice, but we'd better not count on it," Steve said. "Our best opportunity now is for us to catch him at Judy's."

"I think you're right," Mike replied. "I thought I'd go over to the *Ann Arbor News* and get a couple papers, see Greg's article. Want to tag along?"

"I better not, Mike. Larry and I have plenty to do in the next few hours. We're planning on having most of our people in plain clothes and in place by about two-thirty. We've even made arrangements for a couple porta johns next to two houses which are being remodeled in Judy's neighborhood. I'm worried they could possibly send up a red flag to McConnell. Larry thinks not."

"I'd side with Larry. We can't have it perfect. Hopefully, he'll be so inflamed and angered, he won't notice."

•

Kelly and Kath walked down to Maude's for lunch, approximately four blocks south of police headquarters. Though somewhat chilly, the walk had been good for both. Kelly had suggested Maude's, thinking it might be a while before they enjoyed another decent meal.

"You were pretty quiet," Kath said after they were seated. "I thought you'd be more vocal in supporting my involvement at Judy's. I know it's been tough and I've been an extra burden for you, but don't you think I can really be of help? An extra pair of ears and eyes, if nothing else, to spell you when you're trying to catch an hour or two of sleep tonight."

Kelly smiled. "I hope you aren't angry, but I'm the one who suggested to Mike we'd be exposing ourselves to criticism, let alone liability issues, if we continued to involve you as much as we have. David and I discussed it, you, at length. Believe me, there's no question you'd be able to be of help, I'm not saying you wouldn't be. You can probably tell, quite frankly I've grown rather fond of you, Kath. I admire your spunk."

"Let's not get too maudlin," Kath replied in a disgusted tone. "All I want is to stay involved. I think I could if I had your support."

"You're assuming I carry more clout than I do. David's not a totally by-the-book type leader as you've seen. He's the one who suggested a decision be postponed until after lunch. Let's wait and see what his answer's going to be. Now let's enjoy lunch; it's my treat."

•

The first bit of news Kelly and Kath learned, after getting back to headquarters shortly before two, was the fact Judy had received back-to-back phone calls during the past hour, on her home answering machine. Her long message had provided sufficient time to trace the calls, to a phone booth in Ypsilanti, a city a few miles east of Ann Arbor. The caller, hopefully McConnell, must have wanted to hear the message twice.

The second bit of news, which delighted Kath, was David's decision to let her stay involved. She would be keeping Judy company on the main floor of the house, while Kelly and Mike worked out of the basement with the tech people.

"There's a definite risk, Kath," David explained. "He might elect to obtain a rifle. Attempt to shoot Judy or you through a window. We don't think that's his style, but we can't be certain. We all seem to think he'll want to confront Judy face-to-face, see her fear, hear her beg for her life or not to be injured."

"I think you're right, although I also understand we can't be certain," Kath replied. Breaking into a smile, she said, "And of course he could also blow up the house, plant a bomb or set fire to it, to teach her a lesson."

David smiled. Over the course of the past few days, Kath had raised the possibility of him utilizing a bomb or other explosive device numerous times. The risk existed and it was no laughing matter, but there was a humorous side to Kath's continuing to be the one to suggest the use of explosives.

"The two of you need to get your clothes and personal effects together as quickly as possible," David said. "Mike plans to be at Judy's house before three. Judy won't be leaving here until about four. Her car's being monitored so we can hear everything she says. We don't want to tailgate her too closely, in case he's observing her leaving headquarters. We'll have people parked along her route. You're aware, of course, she only lives about twelve blocks from here, not far from West Park."

As Kelly and Kath turned to leave, they nearly bumped into Larry Martino.

"We're all set with these guns," he said to David, holding up a gun which resembled an enlarged squirt gun. "It's a Splat Gun," he explained to Kelly and Kath. "It's used in those War Games to spray a target with fluorescent paint. They may come in handy tonight."


**Chapter 58**


Kelly and Kath arrived at Judy's house shortly after three o'clock. They were dropped off by another detective, so they wouldn't have Kelly's car or another department vehicle parked nearby. Judy's house was a very attractive, one-story bungalow, probably nearly sixty years old, but well-maintained and updated over the years. It was light blue with black shutters and cottage-cut windows, either a fresh coat of paint or aluminum siding. There were several tall trees on the lot, which was attractively landscaped with numerous shrubs and bushes. Kelly could imagine it in the spring and summer with the flower beds in bloom. They were amazed to see a few flowers in a bed next to the unattached garage at the rear of the lot.

Kelly glanced up into the nearby trees to see if she could spot any cameras or floodlights. She saw nothing with her cursory look. The neighborhood appeared very peaceful, with little sign of activity. Three doors to the south, a paneled truck was parked in the driveway with the name of a plumbing and heating company painted on the side. Kelly wondered whether some officers were already inside the van. A large hedge separated Judy's lot from the two-story home to the north of hers. That house was also well-maintained, an attractive neighborhood in Ann Arbor's Old West Side.

Kelly and Kath entered the house through a side door next to the driveway, another sign of the age of the home. The door had been left unlocked for them. They entered a small hallway, an entryway to the kitchen on the left and another leading to the living room to the right. A quick look told them Judy was heavily into Early Americana. Very attractive, very immaculate. Kelly smiled, wondering if it was always like this, imagining Judy scurrying around last night in expectation of guests.

"That you, Kelly?" Mike called up from the basement.

"Me, too," Kath said with a grin. "Maybe David wanted me here to serve as a chaperone," she whispered to Kelly, who blushed and shook her head.

"Come on down," Mike shouted. "Both of you. I think you'll be impressed."

•

Mike introduced the two women to Frank Rabola and Billy Carter, the two electronic specialists who would be working with them. A real 'Mutt and Jeff' team, Kelly thought. Frank was no more than five-feet-six in height, and slightly overweight. Billy, an African-American, seemed seven feet tall by comparison, probably in reality six-feet-seven or -eight.

"Can you take a minute or two to explain what you've been able to put together here?" Mike asked them.

There were half a dozen television monitors on the counter in front of the men and a couple sets of headphones, each with a tiny mike attachment. On five of the screens, there were scenes of the yard surrounding the house. The sixth screen had a diagram of a square with what appeared to be the shape of the foundation of Judy's house inside the square.

Billy began the explanation. "The square here represents the area where we have sensors placed around the outside of the house. What we have is a sort of electronic wall or fence, from less than a foot off the ground to a height of approximately six feet. We're able to obtain a visual and audio reading if someone penetrates the area, or leaves too, for that matter. We can pinpoint where the entry has been made. If it's a squirrel, a cat or a bird, rather than a person, we'll know. There's a problem if it happens to be a large dog. We'd have to assume it was a person, until verified to the contrary.

"In most cases we could get a quick verification on the TV monitor covering the area of penetration. We have a control panel here to direct the angles of the cameras as needed. There's virtually no sound as we pan a camera, nothing at all like the whir of a motor with an old television antenna being rotated. We think we've done an excellent job of placing and camouflaging the cameras, too."

Frank took over the explanation from that point. It was refreshing to see the enthusiasm for their work that the two shared. As Frank spoke, he used the control panel to pan one of the cameras.

"It doesn't give us a total picture of the yard, but with the controls and the wide-angle lenses, we can cover eighty-five to ninety percent. Show them the zoom lens feature, Billy. As you can see, we can focus in for a close-up."

Mike started to open his mouth and Frank held up his hand, laughing. "Hold on, Mike, we're just getting started. The cameras have an infra-red or night feature, too. That's probably what you thought we'd forgotten to mention, right Mike?"

Mike nodded with a grin.

"You're probably aware it's going to be extremely dark tonight, cloudy, not a trace of the moon. We'll be able to generate a picture that makes it look as if it were dusk."

Billy now took over once again. They made quite a team, Kelly thought.

"These controls turn on flood lights. We have six of them placed around the yard. This master switch can turn them all on at once, or we can individually turn them on and off. Your people are all equipped with night goggles. If we see McConnell isn't, chances are we'll leave the lights off. Mike will be calling the shots.

"Inside the square, you see an outline of the house itself. If someone enters, or attempts to enter, we'll get a reading, again pinpointing the exact spot, door, window, whatever. We had a reading a few minutes ago when you came in the side door. That's why Mike knew you were here. We didn't hear you, just the alarm indicating an entry had been made."

Frank took over again, as if the two were playing catch. "We also have cameras inside, we're able to view every room, both the side and front doors."

"I'm amazed," said Kath. "He won't stand a chance. That is, if he shows."

"I'm just about done – I'll make it brief. The interior of the house and also the yard have both been monitored for sound. We can pick up a conversation or a peculiar noise originating from virtually anywhere in those areas. For example, if he penetrates the area and breaks a window in an attempt to gain entry, we'd pick it up and be able to tell quite closely which window it is."

It was another five minutes before Frank was finished. Kelly and Kath complimented the two men and thanked them again for taking the time to go through the features of the system with them.

"You can tell we get bored doing it," said Frank with a broad smile. "Both of us trying to shove an explanation off on the other."

Billy's eyes were twinkling, too. Kelly and Kath exchanged glances, each reading the other's mind, hoping the two men's work paid dividends.

"You're going to be using the guest room upstairs," Mike said to Kath. "We're lucky Judy has a bath and a shower down here. You can see we brought in a few cots so we can take turns getting a little shut-eye tonight. You'll have dinner, watch TV, read, just talk, whatever you want with Judy," Mike explained to Kath. "Just a reminder, we can hear everything that's being said. If by any remote chance he's able to get inside without alerting us, all you have to do is yell. We'll be there in seconds. I'm sure you remembered to bring the gun I gave you earlier."

Kath nodded.

Mike glanced at his watch. "Judy should be here in about half an hour or less. I'd suggest you not answer the phone until she's here, Kath. You're free to come down and see us for any reason, but we'll only come up in the case of an emergency. We don't want him to see anyone but Judy or you."

•

Over the course of the afternoon, Kelly learned there were even more features in the system Frank and Billy had assembled. They were on-line with Judy's phone, with instant access to a conversation or a message being left, and could automatically begin to trace a call if the need should arise. There was a direct line into David at headquarters or to a 911 operator if he was unavailable. They also had direct communication with the teams stationed nearby, direct lines to the two vans and the truck. Officers stationed outside were equipped with hearing aid-type receivers, a safeguard against a communication being overheard by someone nearby, such as McConnell. Officers could be communicated to individually or as a group. Each officer was equipped with a wrist-watch mike. The watch had four small buttons at the twelve, three, six and nine o'clock positions on the dial. If an officer was unable to use the mike because of fear of being heard, he could still send brief communications back to them by using the buttons – yes, no, I don't know, and contact me.

There were over a dozen officers within a hundred yards of Judy's house. Six were in the nearby vehicles. Neighbors on both sides had been moved out for the night, compliments of the police department, with poolside rooms at Weber's and complimentary meals.

Steve Renz and another officer were in the house to the south, with an excellent view of Judy's house and yard from a window near the rear of the house. Larry Martino was stationed in the house to the north, with his partner. Due to the hedge, they'd taken up a vantage point from a second-floor window. Two officers were in a garage across the street from Judy's and two others were in a storage shed located at the rear of the lot that backed up to Judy's.

•

Shortly after Judy arrived, the team in the panel truck reported a light blue Honda had driven past Judy's house a couple times.

"It appears to be an elderly gentleman, squinting through his glasses trying to get a fix on house numbers. Hold on, he just parked in front of the house to the north. He's just sitting in his car; he may be lost."

Mike asked Billy if he could reach that area with one of the cameras and Billy shook his head no. Mike contacted Larry Martino and his partner, and told them about the car parked in front of the house they were in.

"I'll go downstairs," Larry replied. "We can't get a view of that area from up here on the second floor."

The officer in the van came on again. "He just climbed out of the car. He's dressed like a priest, wearing a collar. Looks about seventy, bald-headed. He's just glancing around, he could be casing out the area. He's starting up the front walk toward the porch now."

"Hear that Larry?" They'd left Martino's line open so he could hear the officer.

"I heard and I can see him. If he knocks or rings the bell, how should I handle it?"

"We'll contact your partner and get him downstairs covering you. I'd invite him in and question him. Even with the bald head, it could be McConnell in disguise. Be careful!"

"He came halfway up the steps and then turned around," Larry reported. "He appeared to study Judy's house, but that could just be my imagination. He's walking back to his car now. Should we confront him?"

"I'm hesitant about doing that," Mike replied. "Chances are he's just an innocent passerby. I'd hate to have us confront him to find he isn't McConnell. I'd be fearful of doing so without advising you to have your guns out. We don't want to risk McConnell seeing that. Even if it is him, hopefully he'll return. I don't think it's worth the risk of possibly scaring him off."

"He's started his car," Larry said. "Just sitting there, though. He could be using the rearview mirror to study Judy's house."

"I agree you're making the right decision in not confronting him, if that's any help," Kelly said to Mike.

He smiled at her. "It is," he said.

"He's driving off," Larry said. "We could put out an alert and stop him a few blocks from here."

"Good idea, Larry. We're already running a check on the license plate. We'll keep you advised," Mike said.

While Mike was alerting headquarters, Kelly notified everyone about the incident, including Judy and Kath.

Judy said they'd been observing the man, too. "Just another piece of info for you to digest," Judy said. "It might not have any importance, but the couple next door aren't Catholic. They attend the Baptist Church on Huron near State Street."

Overhearing, Mike raised his eyebrows and shrugged his shoulders. Hanging up from his call, he informed them the car was titled in the name of a man with a Southfield address.

"They'll work on it from their end. They've put out an alert on the car. We'll see what happens."

"It would sure be nice if it were that easy," Kelly commented. "Apprehending McConnell . . ."

The phone rang. It was David. "You won't believe this. The airport parking officials at Metro called in a few minutes ago with the description of a car that's missing, probably stolen from the Green Lot. The two match. You probably saw him. We're putting out a red alert now, advising units the driver is probably McConnell, armed and dangerous. I'll let you know the minute we learn anything."

Mike immediately notified everyone of the circumstances and the missed opportunity.

Turning to Kelly and Frank and Billy, Mike said, "I think there's a good chance he'll be tracked down. Even if he isn't and providing he doesn't get scared off by the large number of police cruisers in the area, chances are good he may come back. That's only strike one. We're going to have another opportunity, I can sense it."

Knowing he was disappointed over the missed opportunity, Kelly walked over to where Mike was sitting. "I can too," she said. "All we can do now is relax and wait."

Standing behind Mike, Kelly began to massage his shoulders. He looked up with a strained smile on his face.

"Everything's going to work out," Kelly said. "It's just a matter of time."

She realized Mike was blaming himself, trying to present an optimistic picture, even though he was totally depressed, solely responsible for the decision which botched their best opportunity yet to catch McConnell. She wished there was something more she could do to alleviate Mike's distress. Only in hindsight could his decision be faulted.

At about six-thirty, Judy's phone rang. She answered, using the raspy voice she'd now perfected, in case it was McConnell or a member of the news media on the line.

"Oh, I'm sorry. I must have . . ."

"No you don't, Martha," replied Judy in her normal voice and laughing. "It's me, I've just been rehearsing a few voice imitations."

As Martha talked, Judy mouthed the words across the room to Kath, "My best friend didn't recognize my voice."

•

A microwave oven and refrigerator had been installed in the basement for the four of them to use, fully stocked with food and soft drinks. There was also an array of snacks, including three packages of microwave popcorn. The candy bars were a constant reminder to Kelly and Mike of why they were there.

About seven-fifteen, they divided into shifts for dinner, with Kelly and Frank being the first to eat. They monitored Judy's and Kath's conversation upstairs. Kelly had raised her eyebrows when she heard Judy offering Kath another glass of wine. Mike had smiled, explaining that, too, was part of the charade for McConnell. The two were sitting at the dining room table with a wine bottle filled with water. Seeing them drinking, he might make the assumption neither they nor anyone else was expecting a visit from him.

Kelly was impressed and smiled. "It appears to me you've thought of everything. Any feel for when he might return, if he does?"

"I would think prior to midnight, but not before ten. After midnight the streets are pretty deserted and he's more apt to be spotted. Prior to ten, there are still plenty of people awake and around, and that's a risk for him, too."

David had contacted them to let them know there was nothing new. There had been no sign of the Honda or McConnell. The car and priest appeared to have vanished.

•

At nine o'clock they initiated communication with each of the teams. No sign of him. When Mike spoke with David a few minutes later, in addition to learning there was nothing new on the Honda, David explained he had finally made contact with Jameson. Jameson had been very apologetic and embarrassed over his outburst the previous evening. He'd even asked David if he had any manpower available to keep an eye out for McConnell in his neighborhood. He attributed his blow up, losing his cool, to the fear he had that his wife, Marian, might be in danger. Jameson said it appeared McConnell had a vendetta against him and he wouldn't be able to relax his guard until he was in custody. He assured David he was convinced the Ann Arbor Police Department was doing everything it could.

371

David had explained to Mike that he hadn't confided to Jameson any details about the operation now underway.

•

Around ten-fifteen, Judy and Kath announced they'd be turning in, shutting off the lights.

"I think I've had too much to drink," giggled Kath.

"As if we could sleep," Judy said.

## Chapter 59

At approximately twenty to eleven, an excited Frank reported he thought someone was coming onto the property, penetrating the zone. He pointed to the screen as Kelly and Mike looked over his shoulders.

"Right here," Frank pointed. "It initially looked like a false alarm, a squirrel or a cat. But the break lasted too long."

"I think I have him!" Billy said. "I'll see if I can zoom in."

The four of them strained their eyes, staring at the television monitor. Suddenly there was movement. In front of the hedge to the north of Judy's house, a man dressed in a clinging black body suit, wearing a ski mask and goggles, was raising his body off the ground.

"He must have been slithering across the ground on his stomach," Frank said. "That's why I first thought it might be a small animal."

The man, they were certain it was McConnell, rose and dashed to the side door of Judy's house, the same door Kelly and Kath had entered earlier. Mike was on the speaker to all the teams.

"We have him sighted. He's at the side door on the north side of the house."

Frank tapped Kelly on the shoulder and directed her gaze to the portion of the screen which reflected the boundaries of the house. There was a slight flickering at the point of the side door. Mike noticed too.

"We think he's attempting a break-in, possibly in the process of removing one of the window panes. As soon as you're all in place we're going to turn the floodlights on. He's dressed all in black and appears to be wearing night goggles. Let us know the second you're in position. Kelly will be in charge here, I'm heading upstairs."

Mike removed his gun, checked to make sure the safety was off, and headed up the stairs two at a time. Several of the teams were already reporting in that they were ready, signaling in with the 'yes' button.

"A few more seconds and we'll turn on the floods," Kelly said to Billy, who nodded in acknowledgment, his hand on the master switch. With his other hand, he'd managed to direct one of the cameras at the side door where McConnell was hunched in the shadows, his back to the camera, with the storm door propped open by his leg. Another team reported it was in place and Kelly informed everyone, "He's still at the side door, we're turning on the lights."

Billy flipped the switch and McConnell was fully illuminated.

It's almost slow motion, Kelly thought, as the three watched him whirl, a gun in his hand, and then lunge into the bushes to the left of the side door. Three shots sounded and two of the floodlights shattered.

"There must be two of them," Frank said. "Or else he's a damn good shot."

Though the area on the north side of the house was now dark again, it was a little lighter than before with the glow from the other floodlights.

"Look!" Billy said. An object had been tossed from the bushes McConnell had dived into and was rolling across the driveway toward the hedge.

"Mayday, Mayday," Kelly screamed into the mike. "Take cover, he may . . . "

There was a tremendous explosion and the sound of glass breaking as the screen lit up. Billy was at the control panel, zooming in on the bushes where McConnell had hidden himself. Groans could be heard over the audio receiver. Some officers had been injured. On another screen, Kelly saw two officers in crouched positions, moving forward. Suddenly there was another explosion, directly in front of where Kelly had seen the two officers a moment before.

"Judy, Kath, take cover!" Kelly shouted into the mike. "He may throw a grenade into the house."

"He's making a move!" Billy shouted to her. Looking at the screen and through the haze of smoke created by the explosions, Kelly saw McConnell darting across the driveway and lawn and disappearing into the hedge next to where the initial grenade had exploded.

"My partner's badly hurt," one of the officers reported over his mike. Another voice said, "I have a man down, lots of blood."

Kelly recognized Steve's voice. "I'm calling for help," Kelly yelled into the mike. "He just ducked through the hedge next to where the first explosion was."

Kelly dialed David's direct line. He answered. "He showed and it's been a bad scene. He used hand grenades and several officers are injured. I'm not certain how many, at least two, maybe more. We need medical help right away."

"You'll have it in minutes, we've had two EMS teams on alert. Just a second, hold on."

David was back on the line seconds later. "What's the status in regard to McConnell, Kelly?"

"He may have escaped, we aren't sure. Mike went upstairs to confront him as he was breaking in Judy's side door. I think I saw Mike chasing him. I'll be in a better position to advise you in a couple minutes."

"Do you think we should get one of the tracking dogs out to you?"

"I just don't know, David. Sure wouldn't hurt. I'll call you shortly, after we know more."

Kelly picked up the microphone again. "EMS units are on their way. Does anyone know how many have been injured? Can anyone tell us if they've seen Mike?"

Judy and Kath had come down the basement stairs. Wide-eyed, Judy asked, "What's happened? Did we get him?"

"We don't know. A number of officers have been injured, though. Can you round up as many towels as you can and get outside to see if you can help?"

"It's Steve Renz," Frank said, handing Kelly a receiver. "He says at least five people are injured, three seriously. You can see two of them on this screen."

"Hi, Steve. I talked to David and help's on the way."

"Thanks, Kelly. In answer to your question about Mike. He charged through here just behind McConnell, a couple minutes ago. He paused to take the night goggles and a flashlight from one of the injured officers and then raced off after him. Larry and two or three other officers were just a few steps behind him. We heard a shot a moment or two ago. As soon as the EMS people arrive, I'll be going after them."

"You weren't injured then, thank God," Kelly replied.

"I didn't say that," Steve said. "My cuts are superficial though, the bleeding's nearly stopped."

"Judy and Kath should be there in a minute or two with some towels."

"That will help," Steve said, "but I'm going to have them get back inside the house right away. Martino cautioned us that McConnell might double back and I think it's a real possibility."

"What's the range on those earphones and wrist-watch mikes?" Kelly asked, hanging up from talking to Steve and turning toward Billy Carter.

"As much as half a mile," Billy replied. "I think you could probably still reach Larry, I don't think Mike was equipped with anything."

Billy flipped the switch to contact Larry Martino and motioned to Kelly to start talking.

"Larry, this is Kelly, if you can hear me please check in. I repeat, Larry Martino, if you . . ."

Billy clapped his hands and adjusted the controls as Larry's voice was heard. He appeared to be winded, perhaps still running.

"Hi, Kelly, how bad is it?"

"We still can't tell. The EMS units should be here in a minute or two. What's happened with you?"

"We're in West Park. Mike is a hundred yards or so ahead of us. McConnell's fired at him, at least a couple times that we're aware of, but we're fairly certain he hasn't been hit."

"What happened out there?" Kelly asked in frustration. "Couldn't any of you get a clear shot at McConnell?"

"My fault, Kelly, in hindsight we never should have turned on the floodlights. They confused us as much or more than they did him. We'd taken off our goggles and then had to get them back on in a hurry after he shot out the lights. I can't believe it was all luck. At first, we thought there might be a second person involved. But I'm sure that's not the case. He must be a hell of a marksman!"

"Since I was the only one with a silencer, I'd passed the word I'd take out McConnell. You'll probably find a couple bullet holes in the siding of Judy's house. I wasn't shooting to kill. I just wanted to wound him, incapacitate him. Damn, I still don't see how I could have missed. Several others were going to try and nail him with their splat guns. After the first grenade exploded, it took us a few seconds to reorganize. The second grenade is the one that undid us, caused most of the injuries. We were fearful there might be a third or fourth. I need to pick up the pace, Kelly, and I'm going to cut off our conversation for now. I don't think there's much chance McConnell will be doubling back your way, but take precautions anyway. Hopefully, he won't be able to elude us. I'll have Mike touch base with you when we catch up to him."

"Good luck," said Kelly. "We'll be anxious to get any news."

"You'll have it and we'll need the luck."

"Don't take any foolish risks. Caution Mike, too," Kelly said.

Larry laughed as he replied. "I hear you."

## Chapter 60

Mike stopped and strained to listen. Up until a few seconds ago, he'd been able to keep McConnell in his sights and also hear him up ahead, running through the underbrush. He'd skirted the south fringe of West Park, headed west, with Mike in close pursuit. Behind him, Mike could hear the other officers approaching, but up ahead, nothing.

Mike wondered if McConnell was waiting in ambush as he started forward again. Although McConnell had turned and fired a shot in his direction twice now, it appeared he was just trying to get Mike to slow down, rather than actually targeting him. He'd proven he was an excellent shot with his success in shooting out the floodlights. He doesn't want to get tagged with the charge of cop killer, too, Mike reasoned.

The bushes rustled to Mike's left and as he turned his head, he saw a tree limb heading towards his face. Reacting quickly, he was able to lean back. The limb glanced off his forehead. Stepping back, Mike stumbled and fell on his back. The barrel of a revolver was being pressed against his forehead, which had already begun to bleed. McConnell hovered over him, still wearing the ski mask and dressed entirely in black, including gloves.

"Take off those goggles and don't try to be a hero, I'd love an excuse to pull this trigger," he whispered. He removed the barrel of the gun from Mike's forehead and moved back a few feet to give Mike room to raise his hands and remove the goggles.

"Toss them this way, be careful. You bastards set me up, didn't you? Tell that bitch she hasn't seen the last of me."

He was continuing to speak in a whisper. Mike thought of what he might do or say to delay him. The officers who'd been behind him should be there any minute. They'd possibly stopped too, though, when they'd lost sight of the two of them.

"On your stomach, hands above your head," McConnell was instructing him. The blood from the cut on his forehead had dripped into one of Mike's eyes and he wiped it away as he rolled over. There was a moment of panic as he had the thought a bullet might be about to be fired into the back of his head.

"Why don't you just end this fiasco now," Mike whispered. "We're going to get you sooner or later. Stop now while . . . "

There was no reply. Mike glanced over his shoulder. McConnell had disappeared. He rolled over onto his back and rose to a sitting position, once again wiping the blood from his eyes.

"I'm here," he shouted out, starting to rise to his feet. "This way."

He heard the sounds of several people moving through the shrubbery, headed towards him.

"We hear you, Mike," Larry Martino's voice called out. A few seconds later they were by his side. They were alarmed, viewing the blood on his face.

"I'm okay," Mike assured them. He quickly described what had taken place. "I'm not even sure what direction he headed," he explained. "He knows he was set up, told me to pass the word to Judy she hadn't seen the last of him."

Larry and one of the other officers offered Mike their handkerchiefs. Larry instructed the other two to continue ahead. "Maybe you'll catch a glimpse of him. The border of the park is just up ahead."

As the two hurried off, Larry turned to Mike. "You need some medical attention. I'll call in and have a car meet us at the end of the park. Kelly will be relieved to hear you're at least alive," Larry said. "I spoke with her a few minutes ago."

"How bad were the injuries?" Mike asked.

"You can hear the update for yourself," Larry replied, switching on his watch microphone and raising it to his lips.

•

A cruiser was on the way. None of the other officers' injuries were life-threatening. Three officers, two males and one female, would be spending some time in the hospital. Another four had been taken in to have their relatively minor cuts treated. As Larry had indicated, Kelly was relieved to hear Mike's voice and learn he hadn't sustained any serious injuries.

The two officers who'd gone on ahead, met them as they were proceeding out of the park.

"We think we spotted him. Driving away, the car appeared to be the light blue Honda, but we weren't close enough to be certain. It raced off from that parking area over there," one of the officers said, pointing. "We ran ahead, but only caught a glimpse of the taillights. We think there was only person in the car, McConnell minus the ski mask. Whoever it was, was anxious to get away in a hurry, the car's tires were spinning on the gravel."

## Chapter 61

It was close to one a.m. when Mike arrived back at Judy's house. Ten stitches had been required to close the gash on his forehead. Kelly's eyes lit up when she saw him.

"You're sure you're okay; there's not a concussion?" she asked. "Did they do an X-ray?"

Mike smiled. "They say I'm going to be fine, maybe a slight headache for a day or two is all. What's been happening? Bring me up to date."

Judy and Kath had been in the basement with Kelly when Mike arrived. They'd exchanged glances and smirks as Kelly and Mike conversed.

"I just finished talking to David," Kelly explained to Mike. "There's been no sign of the car. He just had a call from Greg Collier, who told him the Detroit papers are using the same photograph of Judy that appeared in yesterday's *Ann Arbor News*, except it won't be in color." Greg had arranged for a striking, color photo of Judy in conjunction with his article. He'd had it taken shortly before yesterday's briefing.

"Next stop, *People* magazine," Kath joked, looking at Judy. "You're liable to get an offer for a modeling job."

"The main reason for Greg's call, though, was to discuss tonight's affair. By the way, Mike, those explosions attracted a crowd of onlookers. The last of them didn't leave until a few minutes before you arrived. There's no way we're going to be able to hide the fact of what happened. David was successful in keeping the television cameras away, but only because he promised to have a news conference on the entire incident later this morning.

"Greg's worried. For himself, for the paper and probably for us as

378

well. He says it's not going to take a genius to figure out yesterday's story was designed to inflame McConnell and provoke the type of response which resulted. He's fearful the *Ann Arbor News* is going to be lambasted for being used by the police, blamed for tonight's injuries and property damage. If word gets out, and it probably will, of the fact Greg fed those earlier stories to the *Detroit News* and *Free Press*, it could even get worse."

"If I didn't already have a headache, I'd be getting one now," Mike said, sitting down in one of the empty chairs.

"David said he thinks Greg's worried about the possibility of even being fired. That the *Ann Arbor News* might have to take that course of action to protect itself, its credibility. In addition to losing his job, he's concerned there's a risk of him being blacklisted."

"What about the possibility of covering up or down-playing the role of the police tonight?" Judy suggested. "Picturing it as sweet, innocent me being victimized by McConnell."

"How do we hide the fact three officers are in the hospital, and that several others, including me, required medical attention?" Mike replied to Judy. "Besides, I'd veto any attempt at a cover-up and I'm sure David would, too."

"You're right, of course," Judy said. "I didn't think it through. I'm just so angry that Greg and the department might come away from this pictured as the bad guys, rather than McConnell."

Frank and Billy were sitting at the master control panel, privy to everything being said. "The best solution," Frank suggested, "would be to catch him tonight, this morning, before all this news breaks."

The others turned toward Frank as Billy said, "That statement didn't require much of an IQ, Frank. You're right, though, maybe it's the only solution. The question is how? These people have been doing their utmost to catch the S.O.B. for over a week."

Mike smiled. "Thanks, gentlemen. You've put things into perspective. How right you are to prompt the question of whether we're doing everything humanly possible now to find him."

"Kelly and Larry told me about the message he told you to relay to me, Mike," Judy said. "It's probably wishful thinking, but we haven't given up hope that he'll pay me a second visit, have we? Possibly yet tonight – this morning. You're aware, aren't you Mike, that Larry and Steve are back in their positions and that there's a team of officers in one of the vans?"

"I was hoping they were," Mike replied. "And of course, we have Billy and Frank to assist us as well. But being realistic, I don't think any of us would bet much on the fact he'll be returning this morning. His message, his threat, could apply to sometime in the distant future. That was one of our worries going into this, of course. I . . . "

"I vote for sending you home, at least for a couple hours, Mike," Kelly said. "We can handle things, and as you suggest, chances are remote he'll show up again tonight. I could get Larry to come over here with us."

"Thanks, but no thanks," Mike said. "I might snooze a bit on one of those cots, though. Dream about McConnell being pulled over in that Honda Accord and arrested or shot. I realize I should be thankful he didn't kill me, he certainly had the opportunity. But I'm sure Larry and Steve and the others aren't going to be as hesitant about pulling a trigger as they possibly once were, and I'm not about to argue them into changing that mind-set."

•

Shortly after five a.m., Mike woke with a start. He glanced at his watch and shook his head. Kelly and Billy were sitting at the control panel and Frank was sleeping on one of the other cots.

"You shouldn't have let me sleep so long. I only intended to doze off for an hour."

Kelly turned and smiled. "You needed it."

"How about you?" Mike asked her. "Have you had a chance to grab any sleep?"

Kelly shook her head. "But I didn't get whopped in the head, either. I'm fine, right Billy?"

He nodded. "We've had time to solve most of the world's problems, except there's still been no sign of him."

"Did I miss anything?" Mike asked.

"David wants to talk with you. Why don't you wash up and then I'll explain. It's in regard to the media briefing, less than five hours from now."

•

A few minutes later, Kelly was briefing Mike on David's concerns. "Judy and David were talking earlier. One issue is who should handle the briefing, Judy again or David. If it's Judy, should she dress the same as she did yesterday, or in something similar? Use the same voice inflection?"

"That's the only good to come out of this, realizing what a gorgeous woman Judy is," Mike said. "Do you think we could or should arrange for the make-up artist and hair stylist again?"

Kelly grinned. "She says she can probably do a sufficient job on her own, if that's the decision. One problem is, if she reverts to her normal, by comparison sterile appearance, it accentuates the fact we orchestrated a show for yesterday. David thinks it important, and I agree, that Judy needs to make an appearance, for McConnell's benefit as well as the media's. Another issue is what the thrust of the briefing should be. One approach would be to play the incident down and ridicule McConnell again in the process, a confused little boy whose behavior has accelerated into playing war games."

Mike nodded as Kelly continued. "The other approach would be a complete airing of all the facts, from the highjacking and kidnapping in the Toys 'R Us lot to his escape from West Park. David could handle it with a comment or two from Judy, or you, or vice-versa."

"I better get David on the line," Mike said. "Did they reach any preliminary agreement? What are your thoughts?"

"I'm for biting the bullet, expecting and accepting the flack. Continuing to cast Judy in the role she's handled so beautifully. Prod McConnell, infuriate him, so he'll feel compelled to immediately try to retaliate against her again."

"I tend to agree," Mike replied, picking up the phone.

•

The discussion between David and Mike had been a lengthy one. David had been the devil's advocate in airing the risks involved by continuing to profile Judy. Mike could sense David and he were actually in close sync in their thinking, and that David's purpose was to have all the pros and cons considered. Toward the end of their conversation, Mike made the comment he hoped everything possible was being done to track down McConnell.

"I think we are," David replied. "We've had teams working throughout the night. Two-thirds of the force is on overtime. Every hotel and motel in Washtenaw County was visited. Officers spoke with desk clerks, bellhops and security personnel in addition to the managers. They searched every one of those lots for the Honda. We even went so far as to personally check out every male guest who registered in a name where the first and last initials matched McConnell's, J. M. Can you believe it, there were fifty-three?"

Mike was aware of the strange but seemingly true absurdity, that an individual frequently picked an alias which matched his or her initials. It was amazing how many times a person had been tracked down simply because of that simple mistake. McConnell was far too smart for that, Mike thought, but as David had said, anything and everything was worth trying at this stage.

"We've had cruisers patrolling the streets, checking out every parking lot in town, throughout the night. You tell me what we could be doing that we haven't already done."

Mike assured David that he hadn't voiced the question in a critical or negative vein. "I realize everyone's been doing their best, it's just so damn frustrating. As we've discussed, we came so close this last time to having him. One more shot, two more seconds, and he'd have been history."

"I know, Mike. That's why if we can get him to surface one more time, I don't think the same mistakes will be made. It's why I agree we need to keep Judy in the spotlight, keep needling him. It worked."

David laughed, breaking the tension. "As Casey Stengel said, it's not over till it's over. We can't lay back now, Mike. We have to have everyone believing we're going to nail him."

Mike couldn't help but smile. David seemed to be trying to psyche himself up, restore his own confidence.

"We will, we will," replied Mike, ending the conversation.

•

Judy had managed to fall asleep for an hour or so. She awakened shortly before six-thirty a.m. Mike immediately briefed her on his conversation with David and their decision. Judy was enthused, explaining that Kelly, Kath and she had been involved in a lengthy discussion until the wee hours of the morning and they'd reached a similar conclusion.

"It worked once," she said, "and maybe, just maybe, we'll be able to pull it off again." She grinned. "I think I can add a few new touches; I'll get Kath to help me."

While Judy and Kath were upstairs working on Judy's attire, Kelly and Mike were putting together their suggestions on points Judy could work into the briefing.

"I have a real concern about Greg Collier," Kelly said. "He's the one who came up with the idea to begin with, and it worked. But now he's the one who's apt to be the victim of the fallout because of our mistakes. It's not fair."

"I agree," Mike replied. "So does David. He suggested we might play up the fact Greg's dog was killed by McConnell, during the briefing this morning. But on second thought, we agreed that might backfire. People might allege his emotional involvement caused him to lose his objectivity, his professional integrity. We ... "

"We might have a problem!" Billy shouted. "Another grenade may have been tossed onto the front porch."

"Take cover!" Mike shouted into the speaker. "Get down – Judy, Kath!"

There was a moment of panic as everyone tensed, expecting to hear the sound of an explosion.

"I think it may be just the morning paper," Judy shouted. "The news-boy tosses it on the porch."

The four grinned in relief as the seconds passed with no explosion. "You're probably right," Mike shouted back. "But continue to take cover, we're coming up to check for sure."

Judy had been correct in her assumption. As Mike leaned down to retrieve the newspaper from the porch, he said, "At least this gives us a chance to see how the *Free Press* handled the story." Unfolding the paper, he said, "Okay, the alert's over, you made the front page again, Judy."

Kath had been in the middle of painting Judy's nails. Judy had a robe on and was holding up one hand with her fingers extended. "I'm switching to pink today. A light blue blazer and matching scarf. Rather than a skirt, I'm going to change to pants. That is, if I can manage to squeeze into them."

Kelly and Mike grinned. Whatever else happened, no one was going to ever forget Judy's transformation.

•

Mike notified Larry and Steve and the other members of the surveil-

383

lance team of the decision to have Judy conduct the ten a.m. briefing.

"Our strategy hasn't changed," Mike explained. "We hope to provoke him into surfacing again. Even though he's now aware of our plans, we're banking on the fact his ego won't allow him to let Judy's comments go unchallenged. He's a keg of dynamite and we think Judy can light his fuse again.

"Judy should be ready to leave in about an hour or so, around eight-thirty. I plan to be with her, hiding on the floor of the back seat. We'll have teams stationed along the route similar to yesterday and, of course, anything that's said in the car will be monitored at headquarters.

"We'll just leave a skeleton crew here at the house today. At this point I'm not sure when or if we'll need everyone in position again. Frank and Billy will be here with Steve throughout the day. Larry, you'll be driving Kelly and Kath down to headquarters. Give us about a five-minute lead, Larry, just in case he's watching. We don't want to scare him off if by chance he's planning to intercept Judy on her way into work.

"That about sums it up. We'll keep you all informed if any major development occurs. David and I are still confident we're going to be successful."

At about a quarter past eight, Kath informed them Judy was ready to give a little preliminary show.

"You fellas might as well come up, too," Mike said to Billy and Frank, "and voice your opinion. You saw the photo, but that really didn't do Judy justice."

The pink accents – hair ribbon, nail polish and lipstick – gave Judy even more of a dramatic flare than yesterday's outfit had.

"Did you paint those on?" Mike quipped, referring to the black pants.

Frank and Billy were wide-eyed and grinning, as if they'd just had the chance to meet a Hollywood starlet. They both whistled. Judy acknowledged their compliments with a couple wise cracks, in the same raspy voice she'd used so effectively yesterday.

"I didn't see how you could improve on yesterday," Mike said. "But I think you have. Are you about ready?"

"I'll just be a couple more minutes, Mike," Judy answered. "I need to get my car keys and purse."

"We need to get our things together too, Kath," Kelly said as she turned to follow Billy and Frank down the basement stairs.

"I'll be ready," Kath said. "We still have about five minutes or so?"

Mike was standing at the side door. Judy had just gone out to the garage for her car. As she backed out of the driveway, the plan was for her to stop momentarily next to the door and Mike would hop in the back seat as quickly and unobtrusively as possible. Judy had begun to back out of the garage. Mike had his hand on the handle of the side door when Kelly shouted out from downstairs.

"They think they have him! David's on the phone now."

"I'll be right there," Mike shouted back, opening the door and motioning to Judy to come back inside. Kath had also heard Kelly's shout and was coming out of the bedroom.

Within a few seconds, everyone was clustered in the basement, listening to David over the speaker phone. The blue Honda had been found parked on a street in the Burns Park area. As the officer who'd spotted the car was calling in to report his finding, a man had come out of a nearby house and started to enter the car. The officer had confronted him and now had him handcuffed and in the back seat of his cruiser. Another unit was on its way, probably already there, to assist him. The man matched McConnell's general description. He's denying he's McConnell, claiming he's a visiting professor from Oxford. The group in the basement couldn't conceal their smiles as David continued.

"We aren't positive yet, but it seems like too many coincidences not to be fairly certain it's him. The English accent, about to get in the same car McConnell used, the physical match. They're bringing him in. I've instructed all three officers to ride with him with their guns ready. I expect them here in the next ten to fifteen minutes."

"We'll be there!" Mike said. "Judy and I were just headed out when you called. That's fantastic news, prayers being answered."

"Remember, we're not certain yet," David cautioned. "I . . ."

"Hi David, it's me, Kath. I'll be coming in, too, with the others. I can ID him in a second. Congratulations!"

People were patting the backs of one another as Mike communicated to Steve and Larry and the others the news they'd just received. There were whoops of joy.

Upstairs, minutes later, there was still a shared feeling of euphoria. Judy was in the process of getting a change of clothes together. She'd thought she'd change now, but Mike suggested she not take the time.

"Steve, why don't you come with Judy? I'll go ahead with Kelly and Kath, and we'll see you there. There's no need for you to conceal yourself in the back seat, as a matter of fact, you could actually drive."

Judy overheard their conversation from her bedroom. "No, it's fine, I can drive. I'll just be a couple more minutes."

•

The drive to headquarters was a happy one, all four of them, with Larry driving, reveling in their good fortune.

"I wonder if Greg knows yet," Kelly said. "The timing's wonderful for him."

"That's for sure," Mike said. "The timing's right for everyone, for that matter. I have an urge to shout out the window at everyone the news he's been caught."

Larry laughed. "Me, too. But let's be one hundred percent certain before we get too crazy."

Following that admonition, Larry rolled down his window and stuck his head out. "Hallelujah!" he shouted, his laughter joining in with the others.

## Chapter 62

Steve took the hanger on which Judy's change of clothes hung and the shoes from her other hand. The back door of the car was already open and he put the hanger on the hook inside above the door and tossed the shoes onto the floor of the back seat. While he'd been doing that, Judy had climbed into the driver's seat and had already started the engine as Steve slid into the seat next to her.

"I'm still having difficulty digesting our good fortune," Judy said. "I'm embarrassed to say I feel kind of blah along with this true sense of joy."

"I identify with that," Steve said. "No need to apologize, just shows you're normal. We've been on a high the past couple days, hard to believe

386

it may be over."

Judy had backed out of the driveway and headed to the corner where she'd turned right, towards Seventh.

"I also forgot," she said, turning to Steve. "Everything we say is being monitored."

Steve smiled, acknowledging he'd also forgotten. "We're on our way!" he shouted out for the benefit of whoever was listening.

Judy was already beginning to slow down for the stop sign at the intersection at Seventh as a car pulled away from the curb a few yards in front of them. It stopped at the corner with its right-turn signal flashing as Judy pulled up behind the car. As the vehicle moved forward to turn onto Seventh, Judy glanced to her left and seeing the traffic still clear, started to follow.

"Watch out!" Steve said as the brake lights of the car in front suddenly came on. Surprised, Judy slammed on her brakes, a fraction of a second too late. Their car bumped into the vehicle in front of them.

Judy was shaking her head as Steve said, "There's no way you could have avoided that."

She realized her mind was preoccupied, but still the driver shouldn't have stopped so abruptly. Steve already had his hand on the handle of the door as the man in the car ahead jumped out of his car and came around to assess the damage. He was wearing a baseball cap and had a ponytail, dressed in blue jeans and a dark blue sweatshirt. He also had sunglasses on.

"I'll handle this," Steve said, getting out of the car. "I don't think there's been much damage."

As Steve started toward the man who was removing what looked like a pen and business card from his pocket, probably wanting to take down her name and phone number, Judy announced to those who were monitoring her, "You won't believe this. We, I mean I, just tail-ended a car. Nothing serious, the driver's surveying the damage now, doesn't appear to be much. Steve's talking with him now."

Judy had her gun on the seat next to her and debated whether she should take it with her as she climbed out to join Steve. She decided to leave it.

The driver of the other car was talking to Steve. "I know it was my fault as much as hers." Glancing up as Judy approached, he grinned as he took in her appearance. "Maybe it's not my unlucky day after all," he said.

There was a slight twang to his speech. He appeared to be in his late twenties or early thirties, tall, with a surprisingly round, chunky-cheeked face considering his almost slim build.

"I'm sorry, but you stopped . . . " Judy had begun to say as the man suddenly whirled around facing Steve, pointing the pen at him. He'd fired or launched a dart or needle at Steve, who'd stepped back in shock and surprise, clutching his chest.

Judy recoiled in alarm and turned, heading back to her car for her gun and to alert those monitoring them. Over her shoulder she saw Steve lunge forward. The man easily dodged him and was pointing the pen or another pen in Judy's direction. Steve was stumbling, falling to his knees on the pavement as Judy felt a prick on her left shoulder. Leaning into the car, she screamed, "Help! Steve and I have . . . "

A hand clamped over her mouth as she was shoved face-first onto the car seat, her head bouncing off the steering wheel. She was losing control of her muscles as she clawed at the hand over her mouth. The man had turned on her car's radio and adjusted the volume control to its highest level, the sound of the blaring music was deafening. The last thought Judy had before blacking out was remembering Elizabeth Edwards had probably been killed by a drug injection.

•

At headquarters, the officer who'd been monitoring Judy had heard a man's voice saying something about not being so unlucky after all, then Judy's cry for help, sounds of a commotion followed by loud music. Within seconds, the officer had informed all units, including the two teams in unmarked cars stationed along the route Judy and Steve were taking to headquarters. Within three minutes at the most, a police cruiser with its dome light flashing and one of the unmarked cars were parked next to Judy's empty car. Its door was open, with the radio blaring. Steve's body was face-down on the pavement in front of Judy's car. One of the officers kneeled down and tilted Steve's head to the side.

"He's alive, a strong pulse," he informed the other officers, one of whom was already on the phone calling in for an EMS unit. At the same time, another officer was on the phone with the officer who'd been monitoring Judy.

"Did she describe the car she'd rear-ended?"

"No. No description of its driver either, except we know it was a man."

The radio had been switched off. One of the officers was saying, "No reason to check for prints. We know who the hell he is."

•

Larry had just pulled up to the front entrance at headquarters to drop the others off before parking his car. As Kelly and Kath and Mike were exiting the car, David came charging out the door. Shaking his head, he quickly explained to the four what had just happened.

"Hopefully, Judy's still alive and he's just taken her hostage to use as a bargaining chip."

As they listened, all shared a common fear. McConnell might already be in the process of venting his anger and rage on Judy now.

"That means the man you apprehended wasn't him?" Larry asked David.

"I assume that's the case," David answered.

"They should have whoever it is here in another minute or two. Possibly he's teamed up with someone. We should know for sure soon. Come on inside; they'll be bringing him in through the back entrance."

•

An elderly woman who had witnessed the incident from the window of her house on the corner had come out to speak with the officers. She'd placed a 911 call immediately after seeing the man drive off, after he'd put Judy in the rear seat of his car. She'd described how the man had dragged Judy over the pavement, his hands under her armpits. One of Judy's shoes had slipped off in the process. After roughly lifting her and sliding her onto the back seat, he'd walked back and retrieved the shoe.

"He was very nonchalant about the whole thing," the woman told the officers. "He didn't seem hurried or nervous. After he'd tossed the shoe onto the back seat next to the woman, he slammed the door and climbed into the driver's seat and headed off. That way," she said, pointing. "He turned left onto Seventh. I wouldn't say he sped off, just driving normally. You're sure this man's going to be okay?" she asked, referring to Steve.

"We're quite certain he will be, but can you describe the car again for

389

us?" one of the officers asked.

"I'm sorry, I'm not really into cars," she replied. "As I told the opera-tor, it was blue, a dark blue. I didn't even notice if it was a Michigan plate. It was four-door, of course. Maybe a Buick or an Oldsmobile. Don't hold me to that though, I'm sorry I can't be more helpful."

She was asked to describe the man again, how he was dressed and his general appearance. She remembered more about Judy than she did about the man. They thanked her for all her input and said they might be contact-ing her again. In answer to her question, they'd told her they knew the identity of the woman and were also fairly certain who the man was.

"I hope she'll be all right," the woman said. "Just a lover's spat or something."

The officers questioned several other residents in the area, but learned nothing further. It appeared the woman had been the only witness to the incident.

Steve had been taken to University Hospital's Emergency Center, along with a dart-like object the officers had found on the pavement nearby. Hopefully, they could quickly analyze and determine the drug or poison used in the attack.

•

The man they'd apprehended was only half-way out of the police cruiser in which he'd arrived when Kath blurted out, "It's not Joe, defi-nitely no." None of them were surprised by her statement.

"We'll still question him," David said. "Try to determine if there's any connection to McConnell."

The others could tell by his tone of voice and expression, he already thought the answer would be negative.

•

A call for Kelly Travis came in on one of the 911 lines at nine-twenty a.m. The operator explained to the male caller that he was on an emer-gency line, and asked if she could give him Ms. Travis's direct number. He'd become belligerent, shouting, "I know what line I'm on, this is an emergency. Tell her it's the Candy Man calling."

The operator realized the implications of the call and motioned to another operator to start a trace as she tried to keep her voice as calm as possible, saying, "Hold on, I'll see if I can locate her."

She knew Kelly and several others were in Benton's office and dialed his extension. He'd immediately answered his phone and the operator quickly briefed him, saying she was putting the call through. David thought briefly about putting the call on speaker and then decided against it, handing the phone to Kelly as he said, "I think it's McConnell asking for you."

"Hello," Kelly said.

"This is going to be short and sweet." She recognized McConnell's voice. "I want the flyer published in today's edition of the *Ann Arbor News*. If it is, you'll be rid of me. I'll call and let you know where to find Miss Smartypants, alive and unharmed. If it doesn't appear, you can't say you weren't warned. Think it over, I'll call back in thirty minutes for your answer."

He'd hung up before Kelly could reply.

Kelly had been in David's office with Mike, Larry and Kath, discussing how best to handle the media briefing, in light of what had occurred. She quickly filled them in on what McConnell had said.

"He said he'd be calling again in thirty minutes, that's just a couple minutes prior to when the briefing is scheduled to begin."

"I say we don't give him an answer until we're able to talk with Judy, to make sure she's still alive, even then I don't trust him," Larry said.

"I guess the major question is whether or not we even want to consider his demand," David said. "And even if we decided to meet his demand, the *Ann Arbor News* would have to agree. And that's not a for-certain."

"I don't think his demand comes as a surprise to any of us," Mike said. "I've been giving thought as to what our answer would be, should be, if he made a demand of this nature. I don't think we should go along with it, try to persuade the *News* to buy into it. We'd become a party to destroying the reputations of those five people. Regardless of what explanations are provided later, the damage will have been done. Even if the five of them agreed in order to possibly save Judy's life, I wouldn't advocate it. We have to stall him, maybe buy twenty-four or forty-eight hours, tell him we're having problems convincing the publishers of the *Ann Arbor News* to agree. In the meantime, do everything possible to locate him and rescue Judy."

"That's your opinion Mike, even if the five of them were to give it their blessing?" Larry asked.

Mike nodded. "Yes it is, but as you indicated, it's just my opinion. I'm open to hear what the rest of you think, any arguments to the contrary."

"You won't hear them from me," Larry replied. "I share your opinion and I think it's important to say I think Judy would too, if she were here."

"I was just about to say the same thing," Kath said. "I say you shouldn't knuckle in to his demand for maybe a different reason, though. As much as I sympathize with those five people, the bottom line is you can't trust him. Meeting his demand could backfire, be the worst thing we could do in terms of keeping Judy from being injured or even killed."

"How about you, Kelly?" David asked. "What's your read on what we should do?"

"The same, but I think we have to bring Greg Collier, the *Ann Arbor News*, into the loop. Tell them of his demand and what our thoughts are. If we try to stall McConnell, telling him we're having difficulty convincing the *News* to publish the flyer, he might go straight to them with his demand. If they're in the dark, it could add to the problem."

"Good idea, Kelly," David said, reaching for the phone. "Greg's here for sure. I'll have someone round him up and bring him in."

## Chapter 63

Judy's eyes blinked open as the cold water from the showerhead blasted onto her face. She tried to turn her head to avoid the full impact. She was propped up in the bathtub, her hands cuffed behind her back, manacles also holding her ankles together. Her teeth were chattering as she shivered in the cold spray. Her head was throbbing as she saw the shower curtain open and McConnell's face appear. He was grinning, a hateful expression on his face.

"That should wake you up," he snarled. "Do I see your teeth chattering? What a shame!" He just stood there for a couple minutes, savoring her anguish, before reaching in and turning the water off.

"Pay attention now," he said, glaring down at her. "I'm going to be calling your friends back in a couple minutes. I think they might ask to talk to you." He smiled. "Wanting to know if you're still alive. I've asked them to publish my flyer, in today's paper, the *Ann Arbor News*. I've told them if it appears, they can have you back, alive and unharmed. You better start praying they meet my demand."

He held up the gun in his hand. "I'm just looking for an excuse to use this. Not to kill you, maybe a kneecap or two to begin with.

"I'm going to unlock the cuffs to allow you to change. I have a pair of boxer shorts and a shirt out here on the toilet seat you can wear. Remember, no tricks. I'm not a happy camper. I can't exaggerate how much you'll regret it if you don't do exactly as you're told."

He leaned down and unlocked the cuffs from one of her ankles and then roughly shoved her onto her side and unlocked the cuffs from one of her wrists.

"I'll be just outside the door. Keep it open. And get yourself cleaned up, you're an absolute mess."

•

Removing the pants had been a struggle, similar to getting out of a too-tight swimming suit. The dangling cuffs on one ankle didn't help. Judy's entire body ached and she was still shivering. As she was putting the boxer shorts on, McConnell called out, "Get a move on in there, and stop mooning me."

Judy had attempted to move off to the side, from the open door to the bathroom to avoid his leers. She realized she hadn't been successful, as she heard him laugh as she began to unbutton her blouse. She kept her back to the door as she removed the soaked blouse and bra. Toweling herself off, she reached for the man's dress shirt sitting on the toilet seat and slipped it on. She moved to the sink and viewed herself in the mirror as she buttoned the shirt. McConnell was right, she was a mess. Her wet hair was plastered to her head, make-up streaked over her entire face. She reached for a washcloth and the soap. Her eyes lit up as she eyed the Clarion Inn logo on the soap wrapper. So that's where we are, Judy thought, the former Holiday Inn West on Jackson Road. It made sense, she thought, certainly one of the easiest and quickest motels to get to after he'd taken her hostage.

•

McConnell's call came in at nine-fifty-three. The attempt to trace his earlier call was unsuccessful. They were able to verify, however, that he

393

was using a cellular phone, probably from the current car he was using.

"Is it all set?" he asked following Kelly's hello.

"We're still working on it," Kelly replied. "They won't be able to get it in today's edition, that's all ready to go to press. Chances are good though, it'll be published tomorrow."

"Damn it, that's not good enough. I said today and I meant today," he screamed into the receiver. "Don't play games with me. You can get it in today if you pull out all the stops and that's what I've asked you to do."

"You don't understand," Kelly said. "We're not the ones dragging our feet. The *News* has to get approval . . . "

"Shut up and listen," McConnell screamed again. "It's today or forget it. I've got other options, but you don't. 'Big Mouth's' fate is in your hands."

"Referencing Judy," Kelly said, attempting to keep her voice as calm as possible, "we need to talk with her before we give the *News* a final go-ahead."

"I thought you might. I'm going to hand her the phone now. Keep it brief."

"Hi, it's me," Judy said. To ask how she was, if she'd been injured, they'd decided would serve no purpose. With a gun pointed at her head, there could only be one answer.

"Hi, it's really great to hear your voice," Kelly said. "Can you tell me who's pictured in the photograph on your desk?" They needed to verify they weren't hearing Judy's voice on tape, with pre-recorded answers.

"That's easy," Judy replied. "Chip and Indy, my nephew and niece."

Kelly was taken by surprise and the others, including Greg, who had now joined them, observed her startled look. Before Kelly could respond, Judy said, "Could inside work, I . . . "

Judy had been cut off and it was apparent he'd yanked the phone out of her hand as his voice thundered, "Damn it, I'll handle the negotiations. An inside page is fine, providing it's not buried in the Food section or someplace else. I want to see it in a prominent position, mention of the fact it's inside and the page number appearing on the front page. Highlighted. I'll call you in half an hour."

Kelly looked at the others as she hung up the phone. "Do any of you recall the names of Judy's niece and nephew?"

No one answered as they exchanged glances.

"You're thinking it's not Chip and Indy?" David asked. "I saw your look of surprise.  Someone has to know," he said, reaching for the phone.

"I was impressed you thought to ask that question," Greg said.  "But you mean you don't even know the answer to it?"

"No," Kelly replied.  "I'm quite sure their names are Billy and Becky, Rebecca.  I'm just looking for verification."

"That means she's trying to tell us something," Kath said.

"Also with that other comment she made, out of the blue," Larry said. "Something about using an inside page for the flyer."

"Could inside work?" Mike said.  "Those were her exact words."

As David hung up the phone, he said, "Mary thinks the names are Billy and Beth.  She's going to be checking with some of the other women. But she definitely knows the names aren't Chip and Indy."

Kelly glanced over at the notes Mike was making on the yellow legal pad in front of him.  He'd written, 'Chip and Indy' followed by the initials 'C.A.I.'  He'd also written 'Could inside work' followed by the initials 'C.I.W.'  As Kelly watched he was drawing circles around the 'C' and the 'I' in each set of initials.

"I think Mike has it, the common thread, the initials C and I."

Kath's eyes bugged.  She broke out into a smile as she screamed out, "Campus Inn.  She's telling us she's at the Campus Inn."

Mike shook his head.  "How would he get Judy through the lobby?  It doesn't sound logical he'd use the Campus Inn.  Just a few blocks from us, where we almost apprehended him once before.  But I guess we've seen him do the unexpected enough not to rule it out."

"There's a Comfort Inn on the east side of town, on Carpenter Road," Larry said.  "That might be more logical.  He could have avoided going through town, made his way over to Stadium and skirted the city."

Banging both her fists on the table in front of her and breaking into a smile, Kelly said, "I think I have it, the Clarion.  They've taken over the former Holiday Inn West out on Jackson Road."

Heads were nodding as Mike said, "That makes the most sense of all. He could have turned west on Huron off Seventh and been there within minutes of having abducted Judy.  I'll get the Clarion on the phone now. See if anyone with a description anywhere close to McConnell's checked in today, possibly yesterday.  Good thinking, Kelly."

"I'm going to have to leave you and handle the media briefing," David said.  "I'm already a few minutes late.  Kelly may be right and I don't want to dampen your enthusiasm, but C.I. could stand for Chicago, Illinois.  The message could be they're on their way to Chicago, he may be calling from a car phone."

"They've been local calls though, David," Mike said. "I don't picture him leaving the area until he's able to verify first-hand whether the flyer's been published."

"You're probably right," David replied. "And he can't wander very far if that's his plan. I'll try to make this short, but I doubt if I'll be back in time for his next call. We shouldn't promise the flyer will be in today's paper. When he sees it's not, he's liable to vent his anger on Judy."

Kelly and Mike nodded in understanding as David left the room, followed by Greg and Larry.

•

"Sorry for the delay," David said, beginning the briefing, "but there's been a disastrous development. Judy Wilson, the detective who conducted yesterday morning's briefing, was kidnapped by McConnell earlier this morning."

Jaws dropped, and there was a visible, collective gasp from the audience of nearly thirty media people.

"He's already been in touch with us. I'm sorry I can't go into the details of those conversations, except to say Miss Wilson is still alive and we're fairly certain she hasn't been harmed. This will be a short briefing, but I'll quickly fill you in on the circumstances of her abduction and the events of last night, which preceded it."

•

About ten-fifteen, there was a knock on the door. Kath was the first to see Steve as he entered the room. She gasped in surprise. Mike's and Kelly's expressions also showed their surprise and delight to see him.

"Thank heavens you're all right!" Kelly said. "But you shouldn't be here, you should be home or still in the hospital."

Mike nodded in agreement.

"No way!" Steve replied. "I hear he's been in contact with you. I really goofed things up, didn't I?"

Over the course of the next couple minutes, Steve filled them in on the details of what he remembered.

"He must have had his cheeks padded, it's amazing how that altered his appearance. But those sunglasses should have alerted me to have had my gun out from the start."

Mike and Kelly brought him up to date on the earlier calls, the possible clues Judy had provided them as to where she was being held hostage. They also explained they were expecting another call any minute. Steve was agitated and angry, but he seemed to be alert, in full control physically and mentally, with no side effects from his ordeal.

•

The next call came in just before ten-thirty. Immediately after Kelly had said hello, he fired off the question, "Do you know where the flyer will be positioned?"

"Not for certain," Kelly replied. "There's a better than fifty-fifty chance it will make today's edition, with a hundred percent certainty for tomorrow. Quite frankly, they think they've made a major concession in agreeing to publish the flyer and see the day's delay in . . . "

"I thought I made myself clear," McConnell screamed. "I know this call's probably being recorded," he continued in a softer, menacing tone. "When you play it back for them, they might get a better understanding of the need for urgency."

Kelly could hear the sound of the phone being placed on a table or desk top.

In the motel room, Judy was sitting in a straight-backed chair, her ankles and wrists shackled, the latter behind her back. McConnell had the gun in his left hand. After laying the phone down, he reached out with his right hand and grabbed Judy's left breast, squeezing hard and viciously twisting her nipple. Judy lurched back in the chair. The pain was excruciating and tears welled in her eyes. But she was biting her lip, trying her best not to scream or call out.

Kelly could hear his voice ordering Judy to "Scream, damn it!" He'd grabbed her other breast. Tilting back, Judy toppled the chair backwards onto the floor. Kelly could hear the sounds of commotion and tried to picture what might be taking place.

McConnell's voice came on the line again. "The bitch is a little tongue-tied at the moment, but that's not going to last for long. Tell the *News* if I don't see the flyer published in today's edition, they're going to be receiving a little package in the mail tomorrow. Her tongue! Maybe a finger and ear as well. I'm serious."

He'd hung up. Kelly sat frozen in horror, the receiver still in her hand. Mike and Steve both had the palms of their hands on the table top, their faces flushed in anger.

"He's sick, sadistic," Steve said. "A real bastard. I'd love to get my hands on him."

"I'm going to call the Clarion again," Mike said. During his earlier call, Mike learned there had been a half a dozen men who'd checked in prior to eight o'clock this morning. There had been a shift change at eight, and the current clerk had been unable to provide any descriptions of the men. The man who'd been on duty during the earlier shift was thought to be still in the motel, working on a special function. The clerk had said he'd try to run him down and have him ready to talk to Mike when he called back in about fifteen minutes.

•

McConnell was standing, glaring down at Judy as she struggled to sit up. "That wasn't too bright. I think there's a tool kit in the car. There's bound to be a pair of pliers. I wonder if you'll be as brave when I start yanking out your fingernails or a toenail or two. I really don't give a damn whether you scream or not though, now. In fact, I should probably gag you." He glanced at his watch. "It's going to be at least a couple hours, possibly three before we're able to see if the flyer's been published. We might as well make good use of the time, don't you think?" he concluded, laughing.

Judy sat on the floor staring at him, trying to show no reaction to what he was saying. Inwardly, she was trembling in fear. In addition to her breasts, her whole body ached. Hopefully, someone had been able to decipher her clues.

McConnell went over to the phone and dialed the front desk. "Good morning," he cheerfully said. "I'm wondering if you could tell me what time the *Ann Arbor News* generally arrives." He listened for a moment and then said, "Thank you, I appreciate it."

He noticed Judy's stare and said, "Usually by two o'clock. Plenty of time for fun and games."

He picked up the chair next to Judy and righted it, using only his right hand, the gun still held in his left.

"But first, I have to use the bathroom. I want you to get up here on this chair and sit down again. Don't move as much as a muscle." He tilted the barrel of his revolver up and down as he spoke. "And keep quiet, understood?"

Judy nodded her head as she sat down in the chair again, after struggling to her feet.

"Do you think you could manage a 'yes, sir,' better yet, a 'yes, master'?"

Judy hesitated and then mumbled, "Yes, master." McConnell's face lit up in a smile. "That's better, that's a good start."

A shiver went through Judy's body as he headed into the bathroom.

•

Mike was on the phone with the young man at the Clarion who'd been at the registration desk early this morning. Two of the six men who'd checked in earlier were quickly eliminated. One had been a very dark African-American, the other an Asian of rather small stature. The descriptions of two of the remaining four men also seemed to eliminate them. One had a beard and was portrayed as rather stocky.

"I'd call him fat, if you promise not to quote me," the registration clerk had said. The other questionable one was described as extremely tall and thin. "He had to be at least six-foot-six inches tall and less than a hundred and fifty pounds," the man explained to Mike. While they couldn't be totally ruled out, they appeared to be unlikely candidates, Mike thought.

That left two, a John A. Wheelock from Chicago, and a Charles Campbell from Toronto. From their physical descriptions, either one could be McConnell, Mike concluded. Kelly, who'd been sitting next to Mike, saw his expression change to a smile, as he drew a couple stars on his legal pad next to Campbell's name. Glancing at Kelly, he wrote on the pad, 'He says the man has a marvelous English accent.'

Mike thanked the young man and told him that he, and perhaps a couple uniformed policemen as well, would be at the Clarion in less than twenty minutes.

"Wouldn't it be wonderful if it is him?" Kelly said.

Mike nodded. "Why don't you come with me? I'll arrange for a couple officers to meet us there. I'd like you to stay here Kath, see if you can be of help to David. Let's check with Steve and see if he's discovered anything of value at the Comfort Inn."

While Mike had been on the phone in the conference room, Steve had gone to his own office to call the Comfort Inn and perhaps the Campus Inn as well.

•

As David completed his remarks, a man towards the back of the room raised his hand with a question. David recognized him as the high-profile anchorman for Channel Four.

"Yes," David said, pointing to him.

"I'm really not wanting to be overly critical or antagonistic," the man began, "but truthfully, Chief Benton, can you recall a case where the police made so many mistakes?"

David's face flushed in anger. Control your emotions, he reminded himself as he began his reply.

"Last night, at one point we had approximately ten officers with their guns aimed at McConnell, all within fifty to sixty feet of him. I'm sure there are a number of people who think at that stage we should have acted as judge and jury, had everyone primed to shoot to kill, as we attempted to capture such an obviously guilty and dangerous fugitive. We chose to play by the rules. It would be a sad day if law enforcement personnel arbitrarily elected to suspend the rules at their whim.

"Does that mean we won't react differently if the same circumstances present themselves in the future? Of course not. We'd act sooner to try to disable him, not kill him. We'd have more than one officer authorized for the initial shot. We weren't prepared for the grenades. Hindsight is great, but even with hindsight, I'm not about to blame myself or my people for making too many mistakes. If Detective Wilson had told us the make, model, color and license plate number of the car she'd rear-ended, this briefing would probably be dealing with McConnell's arrest. Did she make a mistake? Yes. Did she also make a mistake in volunteering to risk injury or even her life in a plan to entrap him? Maybe so.

"All I ask is for you not to lose your perspective. The bad buy is McConnell. And we're going to need your help, the public's help and a break or two in order to bring him into custody."

David was pleased with his answer. He hoped it would serve to defuse some of the criticism. He wasn't so sure though, when the next question was asked.

"I realize you were acting under the assumption McConnell was already in custody when Detectives Wilson and Renz left her house to drive to police headquarters. But even so, in light of the one-man military assault hours before, wouldn't it have made sense to have a police cruiser bring her in?"

David took a deep breath before beginning his answer.

•

In the corridor outside the conference room, Kelly and Mike saw Steve headed toward them, a look of excitement on his face. He was still at least ten feet from them when he blurted out, "We may have hit paydirt! A man who checked into the Comfort Inn around seven-thirty this morning registered under the name of James McCumber. The physical characteristics, the woman I spoke with described, match McConnell's."

Seeming disappointed that Kelly and Mike weren't showing more enthusiasm in their reactions to his news, he asked, "You understand what I'm saying, don't you? The initials J.M. match McConnell's."

Kelly nodded. "We understand. It certainly warrants checking out, the timing, the description. But remember what David told us. How many instances did they come across last night of people with the initials J.M.? I think he said they found over fifty registered in motels and hotels in Washtenaw County."

Steve nodded, remembering David's statement. "By the way, I came up with zilch at the Campus Inn."

"Tell him about our possibilities at the Clarion," Kelly said to Mike. "We're headed there now," she said to Steve. "That's the main reason we aren't showing more excitement over your findings, we think we're on to something."

Mike explained to Steve about the man with the 'marvelous' English accent who'd checked in just before eight this morning.

"As in your case, Steve – the general description matches. There's also one other good possibility. Just those two though, virtually nil as far as all the others who checked in this morning. As Kelly said, we're headed there now, we've made arrangements for a couple officers to meet us. You might want to do the same at the Comfort Inn. Maybe Larry will join you."

401

"What name is the man with the English accent registered under?" Steve asked.

"Charles Campbell from Toronto," Mike answered. "And we're apt to find a true Scot, brogue and all, rather than McConnell masquerading as an English aristocrat. The other one's registered under the name of John A. Wheelock from Louisville, Kentucky. That's right, isn't it Kelly? Not the name, I'm sure about that. But was it Louisville?"

As Kelly nodded, Steve said, "Did you realize those are Judy's initials? J.A.W., Judith Ascot Wilson. Just a coincidence, maybe."

Kelly and Mike exchanged surprised glances; they hadn't picked up on that. Probably just that – a coincidence. On the other hand, using Judy's initials for the name of the person, in whom the room in which she'd be held hostage was registered, was something McConnell might do. He was still treating this entire escapade as if it was a game. Leaving a clue such as the initials, taking an added risk, daring them to figure it out, it all seemed to fit his pattern.

"Wheelock should probably go to the top of the list," Mike suggested. "You surprise me sometimes, Steve. How did you happen to know or remember Judy's middle name?"

Steve grinned as he replied, "You really don't want to know, but I guess I'll tell you anyway. Remember that period when the two of you, Judy and you, were vying to head up the division. You might not have been fully aware of it, but she was definitely trying to undermine you in any way she could. Because of her initials, J.A.W., I gave her the nickname of 'Jaws.' Anytime I ran across her trying to pull a fast one, I'd asked her what Jaws was up to now. David knows all about 'Jaws,' I told him."

Mike grinned back at Steve. "You're right, I guess I wasn't totally aware of what was going on then, except I know it became a little tense for a while between Judy and me. 'Jaws,' uh, thanks Steve."

The briefing had just ended and Kelly, Mike and Steve were able to corner David in his office, where he'd retreated after adjourning the session. They told him of their findings and of their plans to head to the Clarion and the Comfort Inn to check them out. Kelly also told David the gist of McConnell's last call, the threat to send parts of Judy's body to the *Ann Arbor News* if the flyer wasn't published in today's edition.

"He was trying to get her to scream to intimidate us to comply with his demand," Kelly said. "He may have hurt her."

"The only thing he succeeded in doing," Steve said, "at least in my case, was to convince me not to let up until that crazy S.O.B. is in custody."

"That's the problem, he's just crazy enough, maybe insane's the better word, so we can't ignore his threats," David said. "Let's hope, let's pray, one of those three men is him."

"Amen," Steve said. "Larry's going to be with me. We'll let you know if our lead pans out, David." Turning to Kelly and Mike, he said, "Don't take any undue risks."

•

McConnell had been in the bathroom for nearly fifteen minutes with the door ajar. Judy has heard the toilet flush a couple times during that period. She glanced at the clock on the table next to the bed. Just past eleven a.m.

The bathroom door suddenly opened and McConnell stood in the doorway, wearing a pair of boxer shorts, staring at her with a grin on his face.

"Miss me? Think I'd died in here, died and went to hell is probably what you were hoping, right?" He laughed as Judy tilted her head down towards the floor.

"You know, Miss Big Mouth, this may be your lucky day after all. I don't think I'm up for the fun and games I had in mind for the next hour or so. I'm sure you're disappointed, but my trots would interfere with the vigorous love-making I had planned for us."

Judy continued to stare at the floor, masking any reaction to what he was saying.

"Look at me when I'm talking to you," he said, raising his voice in anger. "Still tongue-tied? You were plenty chatty in bad-mouthing me, trying to humiliate me with your lies and insinuations, threatening to air tales about my childhood. You can't imagine the amount of restraint I'm showing in not . . . "

He appeared to take a deep breath as he paused for a moment. "You better keep praying the flyer's published in today's paper, that's the short of it. I promised if that was done you wouldn't be harmed. I intend to keep my word. What's the matter? You seem to have some doubts."

Judy was unsure of how she should be reacting. His mood changes were alarming, the least little thing could send him into orbit. What will his reaction be when he learns the flyer hasn't been published? She was almost certain it wouldn't be. She knew if she'd been involved in the deci-

403

sion she would have argued against it. Yes, he was right, she did have major doubts over whether she'd be released unharmed even if his demand was met. She nodded her head.

"Speak up, I didn't hear your answer," he said.

"Yes, I do," she replied.

"Yes, I do," he said, mimicking her and grinning. "Do you think we'll see the flyer in today's paper?"

Judy shook her head no. He cocked his hand to his ear to indicate he hadn't heard her.

"No, I don't," she said.

"For your sake, let's hope you're wrong. I said I was a man of my word. You heard my threat."

The evil look in his eyes prompted Judy to tilt her head towards the floor again. Could he sense her fear? Was her body trembling?

"I want you to stand up and slide your chair a couple feet to the right so I can keep a better eye on you while I'm shaving."

Judy raised her head as she rose from the chair, struggling to maintain her balance with her ankles cuffed and her hands similarly confined behind her back. She turned her back to the side of the chair and was able to grasp it and pull it over the carpet an inch or two at a time.

"That's good, now just sit back down and relax." He walked over to the sink and reached for the can of shaving cream on the counter. Observing her in the mirror as he spread the lather on his face, he winked.

## Chapter 64

As they pulled into a parking place not far from the Clarion Inn's front entrance, Mike commented, "That took less time than I thought it would."

They'd seemed to time every traffic light just right and the drive from headquarters had taken less than ten minutes. As they climbed out of Mike's car, they saw two uniformed officers accompanied by a young man come dashing out the door. One of the officers spotted Mike and yelled, "Campbell's just leaving, we think we can still intercept him." The three men turned to their right and raced into the parking lot. Mike and Kelly started in pursuit as a woman came out the door. Seeing them, she asked if they were also with the police. Noticing the gun in Mike's hand, Kelly

realized why the woman had been able to draw such a quick conclusion.

"Yes," Kelly answered as Mike nodded, halting in confusion, wondering if they should be following the two officers or stopping to talk to the woman.

"I'm the manager. They told me to be watching out for you. They're trying to catch up to one of our guests who just left the front desk a couple minutes ago. He's registered under the name of Campbell. He just made arrangements in case he had any calls for our switchboard operator to take a message or tell callers he'd be back by two p.m. He tipped that young man you just saw twenty dollars to instruct our operator and also gave him a second crisp, new twenty-dollar bill to give to her."

Quickly realizing what had prompted the officers to charge off in pursuit of the man, Mike raced off, as Kelly thanked the woman and headed after him.

•

As Mike rounded the corner of the building, he saw the officers less than a hundred yards ahead, their guns pointed at a man who had his hands on the hood of a dark blue car, with his legs fanned out. Mike accelerated his pace, his gun gripped firmly in his right hand. One of the officers looked up as Mike approached. Along with the other officer, he was in the process of reholstering his gun.

"False alarm, Mike."

Mike had noticed the Canadian plates on the car as he'd approached. A few steps closer and he could clearly see the man they had in custody was definitely not McConnell.

"I see," Mike said, responding to the officer.

"He exchanged money coming across the border early this morning," the officer explained to Mike. "That's where those crisp, new twenties came from."

Kelly had now joined them, as the other officer was apologizing to Mr. Campbell, telling him how sorry they were they'd mistaken him for an armed fugitive they were pursuing, a man who they had reason to believe was at the Clarion. Campbell appeared to still be flustered, just getting over the shock of the two officers confronting him with drawn guns as he'd started to drive out of the parking lot.

"That narrows it down to Wheelock," Kelly said to Mike. The two of them also apologized to Campbell and then briefed the two officers and the young man of their added reason, his initials, for suspecting Wheelock could be McConnell. Mike removed the sketch of McConnell from the inside pocket of his blazer and showed it to the young man.

"Does Wheelock look at all similar to the man pictured here?"

The boy shook his head. "I don't know, I've never seen him. Remember, I didn't come on duty until eight. He'd already checked in. You'll have to show the photo to Phil, he's the one you spoke with over the phone a little earlier, the one working the registration desk when Mr. Wheelock arrived."

"Sorry, I was aware of that," Mike apologized. Then, turning to the two officers and Kelly, he said, "We need to get back inside and round up that other young man and show him this sketch. Also, check to see if anyone else – room service for example – has seen him."

As Mike and the other four returned across the parking lot of the Clarion toward the entrance, the young man looked over at Mike and said, "I've never seen him, but I did talk to him over the phone."

Mike raised his eyebrows. "Wheelock? When was that?"

"Less than an hour ago, he called to ask what time the *Ann Arbor News* usually arrived."

Mike and Kelly halted in mid-stride and turned to exchange looks of surprise and delight. The two officers and the young man realized the broad smiles on Kelly's and Mike's faces had been prompted by this last statement.

"I think he's our man!" Mike exclaimed. "One coincidence too many, right Kelly?"

She nodded, her face still covered by a broad smile.

"What did you tell him?" Mike asked.

"I told him it was usually here by two o'clock. It actually gets here earlier, normally shortly after one."

One of the officers flashed a confused look at the young man, asking without words why he'd told Wheelock two p.m., when he should have said shortly after one p.m.

Reading his expression, the young man said, "I planned to give him a call when the papers arrived. That way he'd be pleased, rather than having to stand around waiting at one o'clock and if the paper's delayed being mad at me."

The officer smiled as he said, "And your call might have even prompted him to tip you too, right?"

The young man's face flushed as he sheepishly nodded.

•

Inside the manager's office, Phil, the boy on duty when Wheelock had checked in, verified the man in the sketch and Wheelock could be one and the same person.

"If you'd just shown me the sketch, I probably wouldn't have said or thought, hey, that's the man who checked in this morning. All I'm really saying is, yes it could be him."

Kelly nodded as she said, "We understand. Your description isn't the only factor in leading us to believe Wheelock is the man we're after, but thank you." Turning to the other young man, she asked, "Mr. Wheelock didn't ask you to notify him when the paper arrived?"

He shook his head. "No, that was my idea."

"I think we might be having you do that," Kelly said. "Right, Mike?"

"Perhaps so, we need to get a plan in place," Mike answered. "I'm

407

going to call David, get some added help." Turning to the manager, he asked, "Can you check to see if one of the rooms next door to Wheelock's is empty? We could use both, if both are free. Could you also check on whether or not one of the adjoining rooms would have a connecting door to Wheelock's room?"

"I'll do it right now," she replied. "I'll have those answers in just a minute." She headed out the door toward the front desk.

"Kelly, this is just a thought," Mike said. "Tell me what you think. I suggest we get you into a housekeeper's outfit just as quickly as possible, stationed in the hall a couple doors from Wheelock's room. Next to one of those service carts with the towels, soaps and so forth. You'd be armed, of course, and could confront him if he attempts to leave the room."

"Great idea!" Kelly replied. Looking at the two young men, she asked, "Can the two of you help me with that, or should we wait for her?"

"No, we can handle it. I'll dial Cindy, the lady in charge of house-keeping, and explain what we need," Phil said.

"Tell her time is critical," Mike said.

•

Mike was on the phone, elated over what he'd just learned after telling David their good news. Greg Collier had come into David's office minutes before Mike's call, with half a dozen copies of today's *Ann Arbor News*. On his own initiative, Greg had arranged to have a few "special" copies printed. In place of the regular page five, a blow-up of the flyer appeared, filling the entire page. On the front page, where a short article on the crash, earlier this morning, of a private plane at Ann Arbor's airport appeared in the regular edition, was a box, highlighted by a border, inform-ing readers of the page five, "Shocking Exposé" story.

"Greg thought an opportunity might surface to use them to confuse McConnell if he should make contact, alleging we hadn't complied with his demand. We could tell him initial copies of the paper didn't, but the presses were stopped and the remaining run did. But now, with this break you've had, we can make sure the first papers he sees are these. Kath and I will have them there in ten minutes. Better make it fifteen, I'm going to try and reach Frank and Billy and get them out to help you, too."

Mike had explained to David that one of the rooms, next to the room McConnell was thought to be in, was vacant. There was even an adjoining door. The two agreed the best plan would be to get some sensitive equipment in place so that every sound, any conversation, in McConnell's room could be monitored. With that information, an opportune moment might occur when they could confront him by surprise, charging into the room through the adjoining door.

Mike had also reviewed with David the need for unmarked cars and officers dressed in plain clothes. Three teams had already been dispatched. The two uniformed officers already present, had been cautioned not to leave the manager's office, to keep out of sight. One of the two had a very youthful appearance. After completing the call to David, Mike turned to him.

"We might have to call on you to impersonate Jeff, the young man working the front desk. McConnell's never seen him. In a little over an hour from now, we're going to have him call McConnell and tell him the *News* has arrived. Hopefully, that will bring him out into the hallway where we can surround him and take him into custody. There's the possibility though, he may ask to have the paper brought down to his room, not wanting to leave Judy alone. But if that happens, we're going to have Jeff tell him he's short-handed, his assistant still hasn't shown up for her shift and the bellman's away from his stand. Have Jeff explain it could be as long as an hour before he could get the paper to him. We think he'll be too anxious to want to wait that long before verifying the flyer's been published. We're hoping that will draw him out of the room, away from Judy. But we have to consider he may be content to wait. That's when the need to involve you would arise. You'll become Jeff. We'll have you make the delivery. You could use his clothes," Mike said, pointing out the office door toward Jeff who was behind the registration desk. "You're approximately the same size."

•

McConnell had taken his time, shaving, splashing on a generous amount of after-shave, spraying deodorant under his arms and brushing his teeth. Judy was amazed at how relaxed he appeared to be, humming to himself as he attended to his personal hygiene.

He came out of the bathroom and walked over to the bed. As he opened the small suitcase which was sitting there, he whistled a tune and turned, smiling at Judy. He'd removed what appeared to be a wig or a skull cap of some type. As he held it up so Judy could see it, he said, "A little surprise. I think you'll be amazed over how much this alters my appearance. You realize, don't you, that this is one of those win-win situations for me. If the flyer's published, I've accomplished what I set out to do. If not, I'm able to get my jollies at your expense. Either way it goes, whether I'm on my way out of here in a couple hours or taking delight in bouncing you off the walls, I'm excited. Quite frankly, I'd be a little disappointed not to have a go at you."

Judy cringed as she sat in the chair. For some time, she'd realized her only hope was in being found before he saw a paper, saw they hadn't acquiesced to his demand. Her accelerated heartbeat and dry throat were signs he was being successful in terrorizing her, she concluded, observing his evil smile.

"How about leveling with me, do all of you think I murdered Beth?"

Stall him as long as possible was the primary thought in Judy's mind as she answered, "To tell you the truth, we're almost evenly split."

"Really?" he asked in surprise. "How about you, what do you think?"

"Everyone knows I wanted to hear from you before making up my mind. Quite frankly, I was hoping that would take place after we had you in custody."

McConnell laughed. "I have to say I admire your spunk. If our positions were reversed, I'd have to say I'd probably be pissing in my pants."

He became serious for a moment, as if debating what he should be telling her. Then with anger in his voice, he said, "Dean Jameson is the son of a bitch responsible for her death. If it hadn't been for him, she'd still be alive today. Until he got to her, she seemed to be having as much fun and excitement as I was in setting up this caper, having a ball impersonating her sister.

"I still don't know how he actually did it – convinced her to try to talk me into backing out. Getting her to return all those photos and negatives. And she never did tell me what she'd done with, where she'd hidden, the money he gave her. Damn him! We'd have succeeded and she'd still be alive if he hadn't intervened."

Judy was attempting to mask her reactions, trying to appear to be sympathetic and understanding, nodding her head as he continued talking. It made sense, Beth must have tried to protect her sister. Must have put the onus on Jameson for her change of heart, as her reason for wanting to pull out.

"I still think there was a labeling error. I was being extra careful to

410

avoid an overdose. I had to use it to be sure she was being truthful with me."

As he rambled on, another thought came to Judy. His confession might place her in further jeopardy. Would he feel the need to silence her? Would he allow her to survive to tell others what he'd just told her? Of course, it would only be her word against his, as far as what he'd said.

"Things would have been different if he hadn't screwed everything up. Those other people probably wouldn't have been hurt. I didn't plan to. I was forced to."

He was working himself up, nearly shouting as he tried to position Jameson as the scapegoat for all the havoc for which he himself was responsible.

"Remember though, those who've been injured were professionals just like you. They knew the risks they were taking. They . . . "

"What about Tony McGuire?" Judy asked. She found it hard to believe she'd asked the question. The harm was already done, she reasoned. Obtaining a further confession from him wouldn't add to her risk or plight. Was McGuire's death a suicide prompted by McConnell, or had he actually shoved him out the window?

McConnell glared at her, his face flushed in anger. "You'd love to know, wouldn't you? You'd also love to know how I finally forced Beth to 'fess up. I think you'll soon find out the answer to that second question."

He was breathing heavily, his eyes were glazed. "I still think there's a chance they'll publish the flyer. You better hope they do. I think they believe – and rightly so – that I'll carry through with my threats."

He glared at her for a few more seconds. Judy was pleased she'd found the courage to stare him down, rather than looking down and avoiding his gaze as she'd done previously. He wheeled around, the wig in one hand, the gun in the other, and stormed into the bathroom.

•

Kelly had been in luck. In addition to finding an outfit and shoes in her size, she'd also been able to borrow a black wig from one of the other housekeepers. She was standing next to a service cart, two doors down the hall from McConnell's room, the door in front of the cart standing open as if she was in the process of cleaning the room. Her gun was lying in an easily accessible spot on the top of the cart. Mike was in the room to the

411

other side of McConnell's, a few yards from where Judy was positioned. Five minutes later, Kelly saw Frank and Billy coming down the hall with another officer, who was dressed in a coat and tie. Billy was carrying a large, black case. Frank's eyebrows arched as he recognized Kelly standing next to the cart. He smiled, nudging Billy. The three waved as they entered the room to join Mike.

There had already been one snag in their plans. Even though the rooms had a connecting door, it had to be unlocked from both sides. There was only a remote possibility that McConnell's side was unlocked. Mike probably already knew if that was the case. The connecting door would at least allow them to overhear more clearly what was happening in the next room. If it became necessary, they could always enter McConnell's room by way of the hallway door. They already had a key. Their success or lack of success in enticing McConnell out of the room, would determine if it would be needed.

•

Billy and Frank had quickly attached listening devices to the connecting door as well as the wall adjoining McConnell's room. Both were wearing headphones. Billy handed his to Mike, whispering, "I just heard the toilet flush." Mike strained to listen. There was no sound of voices. He hoped that Judy was still alive, he probably had her bound and gagged. There was also the possibility she'd been drugged. He thought he heard the sound of running water, perhaps in the bathroom sink. He handed the earphones back to Billy as he glanced at his watch, eleven-fifty. Nearly an hour before they planned to ring up McConnell and inform him the newspapers had been delivered. Any earlier would probably rouse his suspicions.

Their phone rang, startling them. Mike immediately picked up the receiver and answered in a hushed tone. David and Kath had arrived with the dummied up copies of the paper. They'd been accompanied by several other officers, two of whom had already headed for their room. Steve and Larry would be arriving in the next couple minutes, having to no one's surprise come up empty handed at the Comfort Inn. Mike explained to David that they could hear someone moving about in the bathroom in McConnell's room, but they still hadn't heard any conversation.

Across the room, Frank's face lit up and Billy was giving Mike a thumbs-up signal.

"They're picking up something now," Mike whispered to David. "I'll call you back in a minute or two."

•

"What do you think?" McConnell asked as he came out of the bathroom. He'd spent the past several minutes putting the skull cap and wig in place, applying make-up to hide the seam on his forehead. He'd also applied powder to his face to give it a pasty look. He appeared to be a man in his late fifties or early sixties.

"I'd have trouble recognizing you," Judy replied.

He walked over to the side of the bed and removed a camera from his suitcase.

•

Frank and Billy had heard both their voices, their respective comments. Billy handed his earphones to Mike as he whispered, "She's still alive," forming an O.K. sign with his index finger and thumb. Mike had been disappointed to find the connecting door locked. They'd have to use the hall door if it became necessary.

•

"I think it might be a wise idea to get a photograph of you now," McConnell said. "If you're right and the flyer's not in today's paper, they might have trouble recognizing you after I'm done with you."

He laughed as he aimed the camera at Judy. "How about a big smile?" he snarled. Don't panic, Judy said to herself as the camera flashed.

"Thirsty?" he asked, after replacing the camera in the suitcase. Judy nodded. "Thought you might be."

As he went into the bathroom and returned with a glass of water, he said, "You probably need to use the facilities, too, right?"

Judy nodded again; she'd contemplated making that request for the past hour or so. As she leaned forward as he raised the glass to her lips, Judy wondered momentarily why the attitude change. Why was he suddenly trying to be nice to her? Just as her lips were about to touch the rim

413

of the glass, McConnell yanked the glass away. With a look of hatred, he brought his arm forward, throwing the cold water into her face. Judy jolted back in the chair, blinking to get the water out of her eyes.

"I promised I wouldn't harm you if they complied with my request. I didn't promise to baby you." He glanced at his watch. "We still have a couple hours before we'll know if the flyer's been published."

He placed the barrel of the gun he was holding under Judy's chin and lifted her head up, glaring down at her. "I don't want any accidents, you better hope you can hold it." He laughed again.

•

Mike had heard everything and handed the headset back to Billy. He walked across the room and called David.

"I think we should up our timetable. Judy's alive and probably not seriously injured yet, but that could change any minute. He's putting her through hell, playing mental games with her. Barging in through the hall door is too great a risk in my judgment. Get Jeff set to make the call. I'll let you know when."

•

Standing in front of Judy, McConnell appeared to be contemplating his next course of action. He finally turned and walked over to the open suitcase on the bed. He reached inside, shuffling things around, finally pulling out a roll of wide adhesive tape. Reaching in again, he removed a pair of scissors.

"I think it's best to tape your mouth shut now." Seeing the look of fear in Judy's eyes, he laughed again. "It's nothing you've done, as a matter of fact you've behaved rather well. But when I asked you a couple minutes ago how I looked, I could read your mind. Remember the statement you made about a sick little boy playing dress-up games? That wasn't nice."

As he talked, he'd taken a large strip of the adhesive tape and wrapped it around Judy's head, over her mouth.

"There, that should work," he said, standing back. "We have plenty of time to wait and I thought I could have a little fun while we're waiting. There are a number of things I can do that won't leave a mark. You might say, just between you and me."

⚫

"Make the call! Now!" Mike said to David.

⚫

McConnell had just begun to unbutton Judy's shirt when the phone rang. It startled both of them. Glaring at her, he crossed over to the phone on the bedside table.

"Hello, Mr. Wheelock, this is Jeff at the front desk. I don't know what the special occasion is, but the *Ann Arbor News* just arrived. It's almost an hour earlier than usual. I know I told you earlier it usually didn't arrive 'til around two p.m. I was stretching the time a bit. It's actually usually here shortly after one. But it's even earlier today. I thought you'd like to know."

"Jeff, that's so nice of you to call. Thank you. Could you bring a copy down to my room? As quickly as possible? There's a large tip waiting for you."

"I'm sorry, Mr. Wheelock. We're shorthanded just now. The girl who works with me hasn't shown up yet and our only bellman just got sent on an errand. I'm sorry."

McConnell glanced down at the clock radio. He hadn't planned to see a paper for another hour and a half or so.

"How long do you think it would be before you could get it down here to me?"

"I'm not sure," Jeff replied. "It could easily be over an hour. I could go outside and get one and have it waiting for you here at the desk."

"Why don't you do that," McConnell replied. "I'll either be down to see you shortly or I'll get back to you. Thanks again. I'll mention you on my survey card."

## Chapter 65

"Excellent job, Jeff," David said, commending the young man. "Very professionally done. I don't think he suspects a thing."

The phone rang. It was Mike. "We heard most of the conversation,"

Mike said. "Your timing couldn't have been better. We think he was just about to begin torturing her. Depending on what happens now, we may need to take the risk and charge in through the hall door. We'll keep listening and keep you informed. We're ready for him if he leaves the room."

•

McConnell stood next to the phone, seemingly mulling over his options. "Hear that? The paper's arrived," he said to Judy. She noticed him smile to himself as he picked up the phone again. He dialed room service and placed an order for a sandwich and a couple beers.

"How long do you think you'll be?" he asked. When told less than half an hour, probably closer to twenty minutes, he said he had a special favor to request. "Could you stop at the front desk on your way? Jeff has a copy of the *Ann Arbor News* there for me. Could you please bring it along with the order? Thank you."

After hanging up, McConnell, still smiling to himself, glanced over at Judy. "You just better hope the flyer's in it," he said to her in a threatening voice. Then he laughed. "Saved by the bell. You should count your blessings." Humming to himself, he began to get dressed.

•

Steve and Larry had arrived. Mike took them over to the far side of the room to update them, speaking in a whisper. He then dialed David, who informed him he was already aware of McConnell's, Wheelock's, call to room service. "Yes," David said, "they were planning on having the youthful looking officer Mike had spoken to previously bring the order."

"We'll position ourselves against the corridor wall on both sides of his doorway," Mike said. "We'll make our move when he opens the door to take the tray."

"Sorry Mike, but I don't agree with you," David said. "Judy might be the one in the doorway taking the tray, with a gun at her head. I think there's less risk if we wait and let him see the paper, make the assumption we've complied with his demand. Hopefully, he'll be elated and want to get out of town as quickly as he can. Head for Chicago or wherever. Before you answer, let me assure you I don't trust him either. If it appears Judy's in danger, we can still use the key and hopefully take him by surprise."

"You're right, of course," Mike replied. "We didn't take the time to think it out the way you have. We'll sit tight and keep monitoring everything that takes place."

•

Kelly had waved to Steve and Larry as they entered the room next to McConnell's to join Mike. She wondered what was happening. She'd been standing next to the cleaning cart in the hallway for nearly an hour. Other than having heard the phone ring in McConnell's room a short time ago, there had been nothing to hear or observe. She saw Mike come out of the room next to McConnell's and head towards her. Maybe I'll learn something now, she thought.

In a whispered voice, Mike explained to her that Steve and Larry were keeping an eye on the door to McConnell's room and suggested that the two of them get out of the hallway so they wouldn't be seen or heard while he brought her up to date. They used the room that was supposedly in the process of being cleaned, its door standing open. He quickly gave her a complete update. Mike's anger surfaced as he told her of the conversations they'd overheard. He explained David's reasons for not intervening when the room service order was delivered along with the doctored copy of the *Ann Arbor News*.

"We've arranged to have Chris, the youthful looking officer we met when we first arrived, deliver the order. I'm going to send Steve over here to be with you. We'll have him hide just inside this room. David thinks – hopes – McConnell will pack up and leave as soon as he sees we've complied with his demand. We'll swing into action as soon as he exits the room. Remember, don't hesitate in using your gun – he won't."

"You think Judy's still okay then?" Kelly asked.

Mike nodded. "He may have abused her some, but yes, we know she's still alive. Hopefully, she hasn't been seriously injured. There's the possibility he may turn on Judy before he leaves. If we hear that happening, or have any reason to believe it is, we'll go in after him. You're aware we have a key. It's a shame we aren't able to use the connecting door to enhance the element of surprise. The corridor is being blocked off and we'll have officers stationed at both ends." Mike smiled and squeezed her shoulder. "Hopefully, this will go smoothly. If so, it'll be a first for this case, right?"

Kelly nodded, returning his smile.

•

McConnell was standing in front of the bathroom mirror, adjusting his tie. As a final touch, he put on a pair of wire-rimmed glasses. He could probably walk through headquarters and not be recognized, Judy thought. Turning to face her, he said, "My sandwich and beer should be arriving in ten minutes or so. I think I'll have you bring the tray in. I'll just have him leave it outside the door. I'll be there, behind the door, with the safety off, ready to fire." He held the gun up as he spoke. "Remember, no tricks, your ordeal may just about be over."

Or just beginning, Judy thought, anticipating his disappointment and rage when he found the flyer hadn't been published.

"I'm going to unlock your wrists now. You can also use the bathroom if you need to. Don't dawdle, he'll be here shortly and we both want to see the paper right away, don't we?"

With her ankles still cuffed, Judy made her way into the bathroom. Maybe she could barricade herself in here. She glanced to see if there was a lock on the door.

"Leave the door open," McConnell commanded. "Completely open."

•

As Mike walked past McConnell's door, after leaving Kelly, he noticed something sticking out from under the door. Bending down, he quickly saw it was a twenty-dollar bill. He walked back to Kelly and whispered in her ear.

"It looks as if he's going to ask to have the room service order left outside his door. He's slid some money under the door frame, a generous twenty-dollar tip."

Kelly nodded in understanding.

"I'll be sending Steve over in a minute or two," Mike said, holding up his left hand with his fingers crossed. Kelly nodded again and returned his smile.

•

Frank and Billy had been concerned when they hadn't heard anything for the past several minutes. They smiled and nodded their heads at Steve and Larry and the other officer when they finally heard McConnell's voice again. In whispered tones, they told the others what had been said.

"I still think we should rush him when he opens the door to get the tray," Steve said.

Larry shook his head. "Judy will probably be the one in the doorway. Too risky, he'll have his gun trained on her. Besides, his last remark indicates he'll be playing right into our hands, leaving as soon as he's verified the flyer's been published."

"What about Judy, though?" Steve asked.

"Maybe he plans on taking her along as a hostage," Larry replied. "We'll just have to see."

"He might assume she'd attract unneeded attention. Sounds as if he's disguised himself. Isn't that the way you were interpreting it?"

Larry nodded as Mike walked into the room. They briefed him on the latest comments McConnell had made. Mike nodded and smiled, before directing Steve to join Kelly.

"He'll probably come your way, rather than through the lobby," Mike said. "I've told Kelly not to hesitate to use her gun. But remember Steve, our goal is to arrest him, disarm him, without anyone, including him, being injured. That's without question, the best scenario we could hope for."

After Steve left, Larry turned to Mike and whispered. "I'm a little worried about Steve. He seems to be of a mind to take on McConnell with guns blazing. As you just told him, that's to be avoided if at all possible. I question whether he's listening."

"I hear what you're saying," Mike replied. "Do you think, perhaps, you should go down there with Kelly and I'll keep Steve here with me, where I can keep an eye on him, reason with him?"

Larry shrugged his shoulders. "I don't know, maybe. Steve's a veteran, he'll read our minds if we change our plans now. And we certainly don't want anyone second-guessing themselves, hesitating before shooting and ending up getting shot themselves. Let's leave it the way it is."

•

At exactly twelve-thirty-two, Chris came down the hallway, dressed in a bellman's uniform, with a tray in his hands.

They nodded to him as he passed their open door. They heard him knock, the same knock Frank and Billy were hearing on their earphones.

"Room service," Chris called out.

"Sorry, I'm on the phone," McConnell answered. "Could you please just leave the tray outside the door? You'll see a twenty-dollar bill under the door, that's for you to share with Jeff, the boy at the front desk. You've got a copy of the *Ann Arbor News* there with my order, right?"

"Yes, sir," Chris answered. "I'd be glad to wait a couple minutes."

"No, thanks anyway though," McConnell answered. "I could be tied up for a while. Thank Jeff again for me, too."

"Will do and thank you," Chris replied, putting the tray down. Mike stepped into the corridor and gave Chris an OK signal. They'd contemplated drugging the sandwich, and even the beer for that matter. They probably would have, if it had not been for Judy. They were fearful that as he began to realize he'd been drugged, he might fly into a rage, and vent his anger by killing or injuring Judy.

•

Judy had returned from the bathroom and McConnell approached her, saying, "I'll get this tape off now. Wouldn't want someone spotting you with it on, would we? I see you buttoned the shirt back up, good."

None too gently, he removed the tape as Judy grimaced. "I'm also going to unlock your ankle cuffs. It'll make it a little easier for you to kneel down to get the tray. One more reminder, this gun will be aimed at the back of your head. We're going to wait a couple more minutes to make sure that waiter has cleared the area, then I'll open the door."

A minute later he opened the door a foot or two and Judy stepped out, picking up the tray and bringing it back into the room. As she did, she noticed a housekeeper a short distance down the hallway standing next to her cleaning cart. She'd appeared to notice Judy. McConnell quickly closed the door and locked it again. He grabbed the newspaper from the tray.

"Just put the tray down over there on the table," he instructed Judy. "Sorry, but I think it's best for both of us if these go back on," he said, referring to the handcuffs.

After snapping them back in place, he had her sit down on the chair once again. He'd placed the newspaper on the bed and now picked it up again. Quickly scanning the front page, his face lit up in a grin.

"Yes!" he exclaimed. "I think your prayers have been answered," he said, looking up at Judy and then opening the paper. "Wonderful!" He turned the newspaper toward Judy so she could see the page on which the flyer appeared. She was surprised to see it, a mixed feeling of relief and disappointment. They wouldn't have complied if I wasn't being held hostage, she reasoned. His threats had been too chilling for them to ignore. She faked a smile, saddened that she was a party to the publication of the damaging charges. She shuddered, thinking of the five people whose reputations had now been blemished, perhaps destroyed, by these allegations. As her mind raced, McConnell had started to whistle as he walked over to the table and pulled the tab from one of the cans of beer, slowly pouring it into the tilted beer glass in his hand. He lifted the glass to his lips and savored several sips.

"I should have ordered champagne! Would you like me to get another glass from the bathroom? You should be celebrating, too. You don't know how lucky you are."

Judy shook her head.

"Where's your smile?" he asked.

She forced another smile.

"That's better. Too bad I'm already dressed. I think we could have come up with some other ways to celebrate, too." He reached for a half of the sandwich and took a large bite. "Are you . . . ?"

Anticipating his question of asking if she was hungry, Judy again shook her head.

"I didn't want to talk with my mouth full," he said a couple minutes later. "Sure you don't want the other half?"

She again tried to force a smile as she replied, "No, but thank you for offering."

He smiled. "You know, under different circumstances . . . "

As she cringed inside, Judy tried to conceal from him just how repulsive she thought he was as he continued talking.

"I mean, for an older woman . . . " Seeing her blank stare, he quickly corrected himself. "That's not meant as a slam, I actually enjoy a more experienced woman; they're more appreciative."

Judy was glaring at him.

"I'm trying to be nice to you. I should really be treating you to a knuckle sandwich. I was almost forgetting what a bitch you are. I'm al-

421

most sorry they complied. Who knows?" he said, laughing, "Maybe our paths will cross again some day."

Finishing his final bite of the sandwich, he walked over to the bed and opened the small suitcase. He'd packed earlier, including his toilet kit.

"I want you to lie down on the bed now, I'm going to put you to sleep again," he explained as he removed a syringe from the suitcase. "A smaller dosage than last time. You'll just be out for an hour or so. I'll remove the cuffs in a minute or two after you're asleep."

Judy was terrified. Is this the way it was going to end? she thought, put permanently to sleep so she couldn't tell anyone about what he'd told her? He noticed her expression of fear and said, "Either this or I'll have to bind and gag you. Not just the cuffs, really immobilize you. Trust me, this is a much better alternative," he said, holding up the syringe.

The thought crossed Judy's mind, if he was really going to kill her he would have probably delighted in physically abusing her first. Maybe, just maybe, he was keeping to his word. But mistakes happen, she thought, thinking of Elizabeth Edwards.

"I trust you," she said, trying to force a smile. Judy made her way to the bed and worked herself into a prone position on her side as he stood waiting, the gun in one hand, the syringe in the other.

"You'll be asleep in a minute or two," he said as he injected the needle into her arm.

•

The same thoughts that Judy was having were going through the minds of Larry and Mike. They'd considered confronting McConnell before he could administer the drug. But Mike reasoned and had confided to Larry in a whisper. "I think if he really wanted to murder her, he wouldn't forego the pleasure of torturing her first. Our worry has to be that he won't give her an overdose by mistake."

"She survived that dosage earlier this morning," Larry said. "And he says he's not going to give her as much this time. I think we have to wait, pray we're right."

Billy began whispering to them. "He's just injected her, telling her to just relax, she'll be under in a minute or two."

422

# Chapter 66

McConnell slipped his gun into the pocket of his blazer. Even though Judy was probably unconscious by now, he'd wait a couple more minutes to be certain. Smiling, he reached down into the suitcase and grabbed a handful of Hershey's Kisses(tm). He tossed them onto the bed next to her. A few seconds later, he walked to the end of the bed and grabbed the big toe of one of her feet and tugged on it. There was no reaction. Satisfied, he unlocked both pairs of cuffs and tossed them into his suitcase. He glanced around the room to make certain he had everything, then closed the suitcase and walked over and unlocked the door. Slowly opening it, he stuck his head out. There was no one in the hall to his right and he turned his head to the left. A housekeeper was taking a handful of towels from a cart a couple rooms away. The door to the room she was working in was open. He couldn't be sure if she'd noticed him or not. He eased the door shut, as quietly as possible. I'll just wait a minute until she's back in that room, he thought.

•

Kelly had caught a glimpse of McConnell as he peered out the door of his room. She was stunned to see his appearance, a bald-headed, elderly man wearing wire-rimmed eyeglasses. He'd closed the door again, waiting for me to be out of the hallway, Kelly surmised as she walked into the open doorway. She whispered to Steve, who had his gun ready in his hand. Kelly realized her's was still on the cart. She darted out, eyeing the door to McConnell's room as she grabbed for her gun. Repositioning herself flat against the wall next to Steve, she dislodged the safety.

•

Mike and Larry and the other three men had heard McConnell as he'd opened the door. The door to their room was closed, but Larry had the handle turned so it could be instantly opened. They listened for McConnell's door to close behind him. When it did, very silently, Larry waited only a second or two before pulling their door open. Mike and the other officer sprang into the corridor in a crouch, with their guns drawn, surprised McConnell wasn't there. Realizing he must have checked out the hallway

423

and then decided not to venture out, Mike and the other officer retreated back into the room. As they were doing so, they saw Kelly reach for her gun on the cleaning cart and duck back in the open door behind her.

Within less than a minute, Kelly and Steve heard McConnell's door open again and then a slight click as it closed. He was suddenly there, just outside their door, hurriedly walking past the cart.

"Freeze!" Kelly and Mike screamed out in unison.

His head turned in surprise and his eyes bugged as he saw Kelly and Steve with their guns drawn. He seemed to sense the presence of others behind him as well. Reaching his hand into his pocket, he took off running down the hall.

"Halt or I'll shoot!" Kelly's voice and at least two others yelled. As she and Steve started after him, Kelly pointed her gun and fired. The bullet appeared to strike McConnell in his left shoulder, spinning him around to face them with his gun drawn. Steve shoved into Kelly, sending her reeling to the floor with him landing on top of her, firing shots in the direction of McConnell.

"He's down!" Larry shouted.

"Keep him covered!" Mike warned. Kelly and Steve were scrambling to their feet. McConnell was sprawled on his back. Larry raised his foot and stomped on McConnell's hand, dislodging his gun. Larry kicked it off to the side. One side of McConnell's blazer was flung open and a large blood stain was already forming on his shirt. Steve had fallen to his knees next to McConnell.

"Call an ambulance," Mike said to the other officer.

McConnell's eyes were open, a smile on his face. He was attempting to say something.

"I won . . . I . . . "

Steve grabbed the top of McConnell's head with both hands and tore the skull covering off, ripping it in the process. Steve was screaming, his face inches away from McConnell's. "You sick, dumb son of a bitch!"

Mike and Larry began to wrestle with Steve, trying to get him off of McConnell. Steve was still screaming. "You got the only copy with the flyer in it. You were outfoxed in your own damn game!"

"Calm down!" Larry said, as Mike and he continued to restrain Steve.

"He's dying, Steve!" Mike said.

McConnell suddenly appeared to have understood what Steve had screamed. The smile was melting away. In its place, a confused expression. He blinked his eyes, struggling to talk.

"Only . . . only copy?" he mumbled, a questioning look in his eyes.

Mike nodded as Larry led Steve off to the side. Mike knelt down next to McConnell. He felt Kelly's hand on his shoulder and glanced up at her.

"Are you okay?" he asked.

She nodded as a gurgling sound came from McConnell's throat as he struggled to speak. "I – I – should of guessed," he stammered. Blood was trickling from the corner of his mouth. His expression seemed to freeze as his eyes closed. Mike felt for his pulse.

"He's still alive, I don't know for how long."


## Chapter 67

Kath had joined Kelly and Mike, waiting for Judy to wake up. They'd calculated she'd be showing signs of consciousness in the next fifteen or twenty minutes. Members of one of the EMS units had thoroughly examined her and found a strong pulse. They'd also found the syringe McConnell had used in his small suitcase. If the label was correct, it was a drug the EMS personnel were familiar with and they believed Judy would have no complications or lingering side effects.

"You'll be amazed at how quickly she'll recover," one of the EMS people had said. "Similar to waking from a sound sleep, invigorated and full of energy."

Rather than taking Judy to the hospital, they'd recommended she just be kept where she was until the effects of the drug wore off. It seemed to make sense.

•

David had returned to his office and was now making numerous calls – Broadstreet, Masterson, Singleton, Hernandes, Jameson and Robinson – and probably some additional ones as well. Kath had already called her mother and brother and Kelly had talked to her parents and left a message on Rick's answering machine.

The local radio and television stations had already interrupted regular programming to announce or flash on the screen the fact McConnell had been shot in the process of being apprehended and was in critical condition

425

at University Hospital. He was not expected to live. Complete details would be provided during regularly scheduled newscasts. David had already announced plans for a five p.m. news conference. Newscasters had used various lead-ins for the announcement, ranging from the dramatic, "The curtain fell this afternoon on the drama which has terrorized the city of Ann Arbor for the past two weeks," to the abrupt, "A possibly deadly conclusion to Ann Arbor's murder investigation."

Kelly thought Channel Seven summed it up best with its statement, "The game ended this afternoon in Ann Arbor for the man who set out to discredit the image of the University of Michigan and destroy the reputations of several high-profile campus personalities in the process. His evil scheme died as the man, who became known as 'The Candy Man,' was critically injured in a shoot-out with police officers."

Steve had been sent home. Mike had provided Kelly with some additional insight which helped to explain his behavior. His wife had a recent dream in which Steve had been shot and killed in the line of duty. When she'd heard last night from one of the other officer's wives that several officers had been injured and hospitalized, she was sure one was Steve and that he was probably dead, her nightmare come true. She'd experienced a couple terrifying hours before finally discovering Steve was alive and well. Then the whole nightmare had begun again when McConnell had confronted Steve this morning. His wife had picked him up from University Hospital this morning. Before dropping him off at headquarters, Steve promised her he would definitely give up police work as soon as the current case was wrapped up.

•

Judy was stirring on the bed. After a few moments, her eyes fluttered open. She saw the faces of Kelly, Kath and Mike staring down at her.

"Did you catch him?" were the first words out of her mouth.

"Yes. He's at U Hospital. Not expected to live," Mike replied. "How do you feel? Are you all right?" he asked.

Judy nodded and started to sit up and Kelly leaned down to assist her as she swung her legs to the side of the bed.

"Tell me the details. Did we shoot him or was it of his own doing, an attempted suicide?"

"Steve and I shot him outside in the hallway as he was trying to flee,"

Kelly said. "He'd taken his gun out, aimed at us after I'd wounded him in the shoulder. Steve fired several shots in self-defense. They all seemed to find their target."

"None of our people were injured?" Judy asked. "Everyone's okay?"

Mike shook his head. "Everyone's fine. Kelly's second-guessing herself, though, thinking she may have reacted too quickly in shooting him."

"I wasn't there, but you did the right thing, Kelly," Kath said. "He's an evil man, he deserves to die. He was on a suicide mission, it was bound to end like this. We should be happy that more people weren't injured or killed in his crazy game. He was still up to his tricks right to the end," she said, pointing to the Hershey's Kisses(tm) scattered on the bed.

"I've told Kelly if he would have gotten a shot off, possibly hit some-one, a half dozen of us, other than Steve, would have probably emptied our guns at him. He would have been dead for sure, not that I'm giving him much of a chance for survival. His wounds appeared pretty serious."

"I hear what you're all saying," Kelly said. "It's just that I really didn't give him the chance to surrender."

"Nonsense, Kelly. Don't second-guess yourself," Judy said. "If any-one has any blame in this affair, other than McConnell I mean, it's me. I'm sorry you felt you had to accede to his demand to have the flyer published. If I hadn't . . ."

"But they didn't," Kath said, breaking into a smile. "We didn't tell you yet that Greg Collier arranged for only half a dozen copies of the paper with the flyer appearing inside."

"Really!" Judy exclaimed, clearly relieved. "So we ended up being able to trick him. It wasn't published?"

All three nodded, smiles on their faces.

"And that was you I saw in the hall," Judy said, looking at the house-keeping outfit Kelly still wore.

Kelly nodded. "I've left this on thinking you might be able to squeeze into my warm up, at least for long enough to get you home and into some-thing more comfortable."

"Why thanks, Kelly," Judy said. "I'll change now. Did I hear some-one say something about a five o'clock briefing? Am I expected? Are all of you planning on being there?"

The phone rang as Judy was asking her questions. It was David, call-ing to check on Judy's condition.

"Just a minute, David, I'll put her on. She can tell you directly," Mike said.

•

Kelly and Mike conversed with Kath while Judy was on the phone with David. Kath thought she'd be flying home for the weekend.

"I think I can be of help to my mother and brother," she said. "And after that, who knows. Maybe I'll be transferring to Michigan State, begin a career in law enforcement," she added with a twinkle in her eyes.

And then for the third or fourth time in the past hour, she thanked the two of them for allowing her to be involved in the whole process of tracking down the man who murdered her sister.

"I guess anyone's death is a tragedy, I know Beth's was. Can't say I'll be shedding any tears for Joe, though, if he doesn't survive, sick though he may have been."

Judy was just hanging up from talking with David. She was laughing. "You'll appreciate this," she told them. "Larry was going through McConnell's suitcase and found a small box addressed to the publisher of the *Ann Arbor News*. Inside was a note, saying it was his last warning, that he was expecting them to carry through on their promise to publish the flyer in Wednesday's, tomorrow's paper. There was a piece of candy enclosed, a sucker in the shape of a thumb. A company called Amurol manufactures it, a division of Wrigley, according to Larry. The sucker is in a pliable plastic, thumb-shaped container. A child can use it as a mold to make additional thumb suckers, freeze 'em in the refrigerator. His message, I guess, was that my thumb would arrive in a like package if the flyer wasn't published."

Kath flinched. "Gruesome!" she said. "It must mean he really didn't expect the flyer to appear in today's paper. That must have come as a surprise to him."

"Maybe," Mike said, "the more likely scenario, I think, is that he was planning ahead, covering all the bases. I bet if we knew of all his fall-back plans, there would be a few surprises."

"Speaking of surprises," Judy said, "David's asked me to handle this afternoon's briefing, if I feel up to it. He thinks if I'm involved personally in telling the entire story, our strategy to provoke McConnell into exposing himself, Collier's actually, the ordeal he put me through, his threats and demands, everything, will defuse any criticism of the department's tactics and the . . . end result."

"The question is, do you really think you are up to it?" Mike asked.

"I think so, I think I can handle it."

"We know you can," Kelly said. "I think David's right, too, coming from you rather than a third party, will carry extra meaning."

"He wants me back to norm, though, as far as what I wear," Judy said, a grin on her face.

"He's speaking for himself," Mike joked. "I kind of liked the new Judy. We'll drive you home so you can change."

•

Kelly and Mike were standing at the rear of the room during the news conference. She jumped slightly, as she felt Mike's hand clasp hers, and turned toward him. He was smiling as he whispered, "Would you be available for dinner tomorrow night?"

"Are you asking for a date?" she whispered back, feeling his hand squeezing hers.

He nodded. "I know I could be charged with sexual harassment," he whispered, "but the reward is worth the risk."

"Think so?" Kelly asked, smiling. "My answer's yes, I'd love to have dinner with you."

She gave his hand a squeeze, before pulling her's away and joining in the applause for Greg Collier. Judy had referred to him and the role he'd played in the case several times in the course of her remarks. She'd smiled and suggested the media might wish to recognize "one of their own," whose suggestions and input helped bring an end to this nightmare.

"One other individual who's also won our respect and admiration," Judy continued, "is the attractive, intelligent young woman you met when she spoke to you early on in our investigation, Kath Edwards, the sister of Elizabeth Edwards. She's worked diligently with us to ensure the murderer of her sister was brought to justice. Her input was invaluable in our planning sessions, as the person who knew McConnell the best, the one who was best able to predict his actions and reactions. She literally risked her life and limbs these past few days. During the period when it appeared that McConnell was able to anticipate our every move, I'm sorry to say I questioned whether she might be feeding him information. I've never ever been involved in a case, or heard of a case, where the relative of a victim

429

played such a vital role. I realize you have mixed thoughts and feelings at this juncture," Judy said, turning her head and speaking directly to Kath, who was standing next to Larry Martino, along the wall on Judy's right, "but I just want to express the appreciation of the entire department for all you contributed. You're an amazing young lady! Thank you!"

For the second time in the past couple minutes, the room erupted in applause. There were tears welling up in Kath's eyes. She nodded her head at Judy, acknowledging her comments and then gestured with her hand to those who were clapping, mouthing a thank you.

"I'm about finished," Judy said, smiling. "And then I'll open this up for your questions. I assume you'll have several. But first, there are two other people present who I personally want to recognize. They don't need your applause, but I need to express my heartfelt thanks to them.

"They've been involved in this case from day one. Directing the investigation, the pursuit of McConnell. They were, they are, a hell of a team. They helped to keep us focused, our spirits up, during this . . . roller coaster ride. It was a team effort, but Kelly Travis and Michael Cummings were invaluable. I'm indebted to them for saving me from serious injury, perhaps even saving my life. I'm proud to be associated with them."

Judy waved to Kelly and Mike. "Thank you! And now if you have questions, we . . . "

Kath's face was beaming. She began to clap her hands. Judy waved her hands, indicating that wasn't necessary, that wasn't the purpose for her comments. But it was too late. Larry and David had also started to enthusiastically applaud and others quickly followed. Kelly's and Mike's faces were growing red in embarrassment as they turned and looked at each other. A sweet ending, to McConnell's deadly game.